Hammond
Innes

Hammond Innes

Wreckers
Must Breathe

The
Mary Deare

CHANCELLOR

PRESS

Wreckers Must Breathe first published in Great Britain
in 1940 by William Collins Sons & Co. Ltd
The Mary Deare first published in Great Britain
in 1956 by William Collins Sons & Co. Ltd

This edition first published in Great Britain in 1983 by
Chancellor Press
59 Grosvenor Street
London, W.1.

ISBN: 0 907486 33 9

Printed and Bound in Great Britain by Collins, Glasgow

Hammond Innes

Contents

Wreckers Must Breathe

The Mary Deare

Hammond Innes

Wreckers Must Breathe

PART ONE

THE DISAPPEARANCE OF WALTER CRAIG

I

INTERRUPTED HOLIDAY

CORNWALL is a wrecker's coast. But when I left for my holiday I
thought of the wrecker as a picturesque ruffian of several centuries
ago who lured ships to their destruction with false beacons and
waded out into the angry seas to knife the crew and unload the
cargo as the vessel broke up. I did not think of Cornwall as being
still a wrecker's coast, and I knew nothing of the modern wreckers
I was to find havened beneath the shadow of those grim cliffs. I
had intended going to the Lakes, but fate decreed that the
gathering storm of the Polish crisis should keep my companion at
his desk in the newsroom and that I should pick on the Lizard for
my holiday.

I stayed at Church Cove, where white, thatched cottages,
massed with flowers, straggled down a valley to the dark cleft of
the cove with the round capstan house on its shingle beach rotting
because no boats came. The Kerrises' cottage, where I stayed, was
at the upper end of the village and backed on to a farm.

The cottage was really two cottages thrown into one to make a
guest house. Kerris, who had done the knocking together himself,
was very proud of the result. Before I had been there half an hour
he was taking me over the place, showing me with his toothless
mouth agrin all the pieces he had obtained from the *Clan Malcolm*
which had been wrecked that winter. He had relaid the floors
throughout the cottage during the winter and as far as I could
gather the work had all been done with wood from the *Clan
Malcolm*. There were brass doorsteps, chairs and ship's lamps, all
from the same luckless ship. He was a great wrecker, was Kerris.
When I expressed my amazement at the amount of stuff he had
collected from that one ship, he shook his head with a rueful
smile. 'Ar, she were a grand wreck,' he said. 'We'll never see the
like o' her again, sir – never. She came ashore this side of the
Lizard. Caught on the rocks, she was, and broke her back. She
was no use for salvage purposes, so Lloyd's told the Cadgwith

people that if they liked to go out and salvage what they could and put it up for auction in the village they might collect a percentage of the proceeds.' He shook his head again. 'Ar, she were a grand wreck, sir. If we had one like that every winter, we'd not have to work.'

I spent five days there in a pleasant haze of bathing, lazing, pubs and Cornish cream. Then Thursday dawned, and with it the shock of a newspaper placard at the Lizard – Soviet-German Non-Agression Pact. I stopped the car and stared at it unbelievingly. Groups of holidaymakers stood about outside the newsagents' reading the papers and talking in low tones. Europe, Hitler, the whole world-fear of Nazism seemed suddenly to have enveloped the place like a sea mist. I jumped out of the car and bought a copy of my own paper, the *Daily Recorder*. It was true enough, and, what was more, Britain was calling up reserves and there were reports of mobilization in France.

I tossed the paper into the back of the car and drove on to Gunwalloe Church Cove, the other side of Mullion. What was the use of spoiling a holiday by getting upset about the international situation? Wasn't this what I had expected – the usual autumn crisis? But I had not expected a Soviet-German Non-Aggresion Pact and I knew that it might well throw all calculations out of gear. The fear of a war on two fronts removed, the German High Command might well decide to make a lightning thrust against Poland and then, if necessary, fight it out with the democracies on the Western Front.

I thought it all out as I drove across the Goonhilly Downs with the warm heavy scent of sun after rain in my nostrils, and by the time I had convinced myself that the pact was not as serious as it had at first seemed, it was twelve o'clock, and I was at Gunwalloe Church Cove. Two day ago there had been at least three hundred cars in the park. I counted a bare fifty. The beach seemed empty. Yet it was a glorious day. I had a bathe and then strolled along the beach. A tubby little man in grey flannels with a panama stuck squarely on his head nodded to me. 'Things look pretty bad this morning, don't they?' he said.

'Not too good,' I replied. 'But it's a fine day.'

'Aye,' he said, 'that's raight, it is. And we'd best make the most of 'em. Two men in our hotel have been called oop. Wired for last night.'

Five minutes' conversation with this gentleman left me with a feeling of utter depression. I had lunch and tried to settle down to read, but my mind would not concentrate and I was conscious all the time of the emptiness of the beach. I had my third bathe of the day and went home to tea to find the cottage empty of visitors. The two couples had gone; one of the men was in the emergency reserve of officers and the other had received a telegram from his office.

And yet, as I had driven back, I had seen the harvest being gathered in and had passed cows being driven to the farms to be milked. It had only touched Cornwall through the visitors. It had not touched the real Cornwall. The everlasting struggle of man to extract from the soil and sea a winter's living went on just as before. That was reality. While that other life of diplomacy, propaganda, machines and herded populations tense and fearful with the sense of impending catastrophe was artificial, a complicated nightmare conjured by civilization. I sat for a while over my tea, wrapped in the horror of it. Before my mind's eye swept fragmentary pictures of the last war. I had been at school, but it had not passed me by entirely. I remembered the cadet corps, the boys who left never to return, the dark nights in London and the searchlights flickering like pencils across the sky; the troop trains and the hospital trains; Summerdown Camp, Eastbourne. And then I remembered the books and the plays that had followed – Sheriff's *Journey's End*, Remarque's *All Quiet*, now banned in Germany, and Henri Barbusse's *Under Fire*. It could not happen again. But I knew it could. A new generation and the horror is lost in the glory that is cried to the rooftops by a ruthless propaganda machine, and from the rooftops echoes back to a nation steeped in Wagnerian idolatry.

The radio interrupted my thought and the bland voice of the announcer gave me the weather forecasts. I waited, fascinated, yet wanting to get away from the damned thing and enjoy my holiday. More incidents on the Polish frontier. Berlin report of ten German soldiers shot on their own side of the frontier. Polish customs officials seized in Danzig. Mobilization in France. More British reservists called up. I got up and went out into the quiet of the evening. The announcer's voice followed me down the street. I made for the cove and then struck away to the left towards Cadgwith.

I reached the top of the cliffs and paused for a moment to look down at the calm leaden sea that heaved gently against the rock-bound coast. The cry of the gulls was balm to the turmoil of my thoughts. That high screaming cry had always been synonymous with holidays to me, for from my earliest childhood I had always spent them on the rocky coastlands. There was peace here and quiet. I looked back at the little group of cottages huddling down the valley to the cove. It was satisfying to think that whatever happened this coast and the cottages would remain to bring peace of mind to those who lived on and to other generations. Two gannets swung effortlessly down the coast, their black wing-tips showing clearly in the slanting rays of the sun. The air was still and breathless. Not a ripple stirred the burnished surface of the sea and the white streaks of the currents setting from the Lizard were plainly visible. Every now and then a little patch of dark troubled water showed as a shoal of mackerel or pilchards broke the surface in their evening play.

I went on with the ache of a great beauty and a great peace in my heart. The other world that was mirrored like a monstrous nightmare in the pages of the newspapers seemed even more unreal. Being a dramatic critic, I think I had become infected with a characteristic which I have often noticed in actors – I was unable to apprehend reality. Probably because their brains and senses are so accustomed to reacting to stimuli which are imaginatively but not factually true, actors envisage the situation more vividly than the next man, but once envisaged, it is done with. They have difficulty in accepting it as actual, irrevocable. There is an instinctive feeling that at the appointed hour the curtain will come down and one can go home to supper. I think I suffered now from this limitation – or if you like this blessed ability. However grim the drama, I felt there must still be an alternative world outside it. Thus I alternated between moods of blank despair and moods of refreshing, almost gay normality.

Twenty minutes' walking brought me to the Devil's Frying Pan. I skirted that huge circular inlet with its archway of grass-grown rock to the sea and, passing through a farmyard, obtained my first glimpse of Cadgwith. They say it is the only real fishing village left in Cornwall. Certainly the little fleet of blue boats drawn up side by side on the beach and the wheeling screaming gulls dominate the huddle of white thatched cottages. The noise of the gulls is incessant and the boats and the smell of fish testify to the industry of the villagers. And yet the place looked sleepy.

I went down the steep road to the village itself. There were cars drawn up by the shingle. One, backed close against the lifeboat, had a string of mackerel tied to its bonnet. Opposite the cars, on an old spar which did service as a bench, fishermen were sitting, smoking. I went on to the pub. The place was dark and thick with tobacco smoke and there was the airless warmth that men love who lead an open-air life. On the wall was a painting of the village. It was by a local artist, I discovered later, but it missed something. It took me some time to realize what it was. The village dominated the boats. If I had been painting the village, I should have done it so that it reeked of fish.

I ordered a bitter and sat down next to a big man in a fisherman's jersey. He had a small beard and this increased the Slav effect of his high cheekbones and small nose. A heated discussion was in progress. I caught the word spongecakes several times. An old fisherman was thumping the table angrily, but I could make no sense of what the whole room was arguing about. I asked the man with the beard. 'Oh, they've bet him five bob he can't eat a dozen spongecakes straight off. You know, the old game – it looks easy, but after you've had about four your mouth gets so dry you can barely swallow.'

'I tell you it's easy,' the old man roared, and the whole room laughed knowingly.

At that moment a young fellow in dungarees came in. His plimsoles were sopping wet and his hair curled with salt water. He went straight over to two lads seated at a table in the corner drinking from pint glass tankards. 'What luck?' they asked.

For answer he tossed a telegram on to the table. 'I'm afraid you'll have to count me out tomorrow. I've got to join my ship at Devonport. I'm leaving right away.'

Their conversation was drowned in a sudden flood of talk. 'It's been the same hall of the bloody day,' the old man who had wanted to eat the spongecakes said. 'The visitors hare going back and some of hour lads have been called up for the naval reserve.'

'Did ye see the fleet going down the Channel?' somebody asked.

'They've been going down the whole ruddy day,' said a young round-faced man. 'I seen 'em from my boat. They bin going down all day, 'aven't they, Mr Morgan?' he asked the coastguard, who was sitting smoking quietly with his back against the bar and his white-rimmed hat on the back of his head.

He nodded. 'That's right, Jim – all day.'

'Did ye see how many there was, Joe?'

'Ar, I didn't count,' replied the coastguard, his voice quiet but firm.

War had invaded the snug friendliness of the bar. The older men began to talk of the last one. The man next to me said, 'I counted upwards of fifty. That'll fix Italy all right.'

I felt somehow annoyed that talk of war had obtruded even into the warm seclusion of this pub. 'To hell with the war,' I said. 'I'm trying to enjoy a holiday.'

'What's wrong with a war?' he demanded with a twinkle in his grey eyes. 'A war would see us nicely through the winter. It's either that or steamboating.'

I looked at him. Behind the twinkle in his eyes was a certain seriousness.

'Yes,' I said, 'it must hit you pretty bad coming two years in succession and right on the holiday season.'

'Well, it wasn't so bad last year – it came later.' There was a trace of a brogue in his voice, but otherwise it was devoid of any local accent. 'Even then,' he said, finishing his beer, 'I had to do six voyages. It'll be worse this year. You can't make enough out of fishing nowadays to carry you through the winter. And the Government doesn't give any help, sir – though they want us badly enough when it comes to war.'

'Can't you do any fishing in the winter?' I asked.

He shrugged his shoulders. 'We go out when we can, but mostly the sea is pretty big outside. And then we've got all our gear to make. We're running two hundred pots a boat here, as well as nets. And there's not so much fish as there used to be. They change their grounds. Something to do with the Gulf Stream, I suppose. I tell you, sir, this is a dying industry. There's only three thousand of us left on these coasts now.'

I said, 'Yes, I know. Down at Mullion, for instance, all the young men are going off to work in the towns.'

'Ar, but you won't find that here. We're not afraid of work. The young 'uns, they're not afraid of work either. Now, in the summer, we're out at five with the pots. And then when I come in, I'm taking parties out for the rest of the day. Sometimes I take out three parties a day. That's pretty long hours.'

I nodded and ordered two beers. He took out a pouch and rolled a cigarette. 'Have one?' he asked. We lit up and sat drinking in silence for a while. It gave me an opportunity of studying him. He was a man of tremendous physique. He was over six feet with broad shoulders and a deep chest. The beard completed the picture. With his Slav features and shock of dark brown hair he looked a real buccaneer.

His eyes met mine. 'You're thinking that all I need is the gold earrings,' he said unexpectedly.

I felt extremely awkward until I saw the twinkle in his eyes. Then I suddenly laughed. 'Well, as a matter of fact,' I said, 'that's just what I was thinking.'

'Well, you must remember that some of the Armada was

wrecked on those coasts. There's Spanish blood in most of us. There's Irish too. When the fishing industry was at its height down here girls would come from Ireland to do the packing.' He turned to the bar and tossed a florin on to it. 'Two halves of six,' he ordered.

'No, I'm paying for this,' I said.

'You're not,' he replied. 'It's already ordered.'

'Think of the winter,' I said. 'I'm on holiday. It doesn't matter to me what I spend.'

He grinned. 'You're drinking with me,' he said. 'We're an independent lot of folk down here. We don't sponge on visitors if we like them. Our independence is all we've got. We each have our own boat. And though you can come out mackerel fishing with us and we'll take your money for it, we'll not take you out if we don't like you.'

'Anyway,' I said glancing at my watch, 'I ought to be starting back. I shall be late for my supper as it is. I walked over from Church Cove.'

'Church Cove,' he said, as he placed a stein of beer in front of me. 'I'll run you back in the boat.'

'That's very kind of you. But it won't take me long to walk it and you certainly don't want another trip in your boat when you've been out in it all day.'

'I would. It's a lovely evening. I'd like a quiet run along the coast. The boat's out at her moorings. It won't take me ten minutes.'

I thanked him again and drank my beer. 'Why did you call this a half of six?' I asked. 'What beer is it?'

'It's Devenish's. There are three grades – fourpence, sixpence, and eightpence a pint. If you come here in the autumn you'd only be offered four.'

I nodded. 'Do you like steamboating?'

'Oh, it's not so bad. It would be all right if I could take Cadgwith along with me. I hate leaving this place. I did six voyages to the West Indies last winter. You can always pick up a berth at Falmouth. This time I think I'll try a tanker on the Aden route. If there's a war, of course, we'll be needed for the minesweepers or on coastal patrol.'

I offered him another beer, but he refused and we left the pub. It was not until we were walking down the village street in the pale evening light that I fully realized the size of the man. He was like a great bear with his rolling gait and shaggy head, and the similarity was even more marked when he had put on his big sea boots, for they gave him an ungainly shambling walk.

I enjoyed the short run back to Church Cove. For one thing, it gave me my first glimpse of the coast from the sea. For another, I got to know my friend better, and the more I knew of him the more I liked him – and the more I was intrigued. In that short run we covered a multitude of subjects – international situation, bird life on Spitzbergen, stocks and shares, Bloomsbury, Cadgwith. My impression of him was of a rolling stone that always and inevitably returned homesick to Cadgwith. But though he had obviously gathered no moss – he lived in a little hut on the slopes above Cadgwith – he had certainly gathered a wide knowledge of life, and that knowledge showed in his eyes, which were shrewd and constantly twinkling with the humour that bubbled beneath the stolid exterior of the man. His nature was Irish and his features Slav, and the mixture was something new to me.

Once I expressed surprise, for he told me that War Loan had risen $\frac{7}{8}$ to $89\frac{3}{8}$ on the previous day and suggested that, since the Stock Exchange was apparently taking quite an optimistic view of the situation, war did not seem likely.

I could not help it. I said, 'What do you know of stocks and shares?'

He grinned at my surprise. 'I could tell you the prices of quite a number of the leaders,' he said. 'I always read the City page of the paper.'

'Well, it's the first time I ever heard of a fisherman reading the City page of a paper,' I said. 'Whatever do you read it for?'

'I'm in a capitalist country, running a luxury business. Stock and share prices are the barometer of my summer earnings. When prices were going up in 1935 and 1936, I did pretty well. Since then there's been a slump and I have to go steamboating in the winter.' He looked at me with that twinkle in his eyes. 'I read a lot of things you probably wouldn't expect a fisherman to read. There's a free library over to Lizard Town. You can even get plays there. I used to be very fond of plays when I was in London.'

I explained that plays were my life and asked him what he had done in London. 'I was in a shipping office for a time,' he said. 'But I soon got bored with that and turned to stevedoring. I was with the River Police for a time. You know, you meet people down here, quite important people, on holiday. And they say you're wasting your time in Cadgwith. It's not difficult to get the offer of a job in London or to pull strings when you're there. But London is no life for a man. After a few months, Cadgwith calls to me again, and I come back.'

That I suppose was why he spoke so well. Talking to me, his voice had no trace of the sluggish Cornwall accent. Yet I had noticed that the local accent came readily enough to his lips when he spoke to the villagers.

Interspersed with our conversation, he pointed out interesting parts of the coastline as we went along. He showed me the seaward entrance to the Devil's Frying Pan with its magnificent arch of rock. He also pointed out Dollar Ogo to me. The cave did not look particularly impressive from the outside, but he told me that students from the 'varsity had come down and explored it for five hundred yards. 'They had to swim most of the way,' he said, 'pushing biscuit tins with lighted candles in front of them.'

'How far can you get up it by boat?' I asked. I was thinking that it would give me such an excellent opportunity of examining the various rock formations. Geology was one of my hobbies. But his reply was, 'Not very far.'

When we arrived at Church Cove, I said, 'I must come out mackerel fishing with you some time.'

'Any time you like, sir,' he said as he carried me pick-a-back ashore. 'Any of the boys will tell you where I am.'

'Who shall I ask for?' I enquired.

'Ask for Big Logan,' he replied, as he shoved the boat off and scrambled on board. 'That's what they all call me.'

'After the Logan Rock?' I asked with a grin.

He looked at me quite seriously and nodded. 'Quite right, sir,' he said. 'After the Logan Rock.'

That was the last I saw of Big Logan for a whole week. When I got back to the cottage I found a letter waiting for me. It was from my editor. He was not recalling me, but he wanted me to do a series of articles on how the international situation was affecting the country.

Kerris came in to see me after supper. He had seen that the letter was from my paper and he wanted to know whether I was leaving or not. I explained the position and said that I might be away a night or two, it depended how far afield I found it necessary to go for material, 'By the way,' I said, 'do you know Big Logan of Cadgwith?'

'Surely,' he said, 'Why?'

'He brought me back here from Cadgwith this evening by boat. Nice fellow, isn't he?'

'Ar, very nice fellow to speak to,' was his reply. 'To speak to, mind you.' He looked at me for a moment and the temptation to gossip was too much for him. 'But no good,' he said, shaking his head. 'Not worth that plate. Comes of a good family, too – his mother was a lady at one of the big houses over to Helford.'

'And his father?' I asked.

'One of the fishermen at Cadgwith.'

And then I understood why it was that he had been named Logan. It explained so much of his complex character. 'He was born at a house near the Logan Rock, wasn't he?' I asked.

'Ar, it was at the farm up there.' He shook his head. 'But he's no good,' he said. 'He's proved that. He married a Birmingham girl who was here on holiday. She had money and she built a house over to Flushing in Gillan. She were a lovely garl. But he didn't know when he was well off. He played around with the local garls and she's divorced him now and gone back to Birmingham. Now he lives alone in a little shack in Cadgwith.' He shook his head again. 'He's no good is Big Logan,' he said as he went out of the room.

I smiled to myself at that. Generations of wreckers in Kerris, I felt, spoke that condemnation of Big Logan. I felt sure that it wasn't because he had fooled around with the local girls that he thought Big Logan no good, but because, having got on to a good thing, Big Logan had let it go as Kerris never could have done. Big Logan's parentage explained so much.

That evening I settled down by the light of the oil lamp and wrote the first of my articles. The other two, however, were not so easily written and required a good deal of travelling, including an excursion into Devon, where I spent a night at Post Bridge in the midst of Dartmoor. Cornwall was much more affected by the crisis than Devon, for in general it was the departure of the visitors that brought it home to the country districts at that time. Not until later were the farmers inundated with schemes for growing more food. It is true that in the towns and even in the villages men were being called up, but this hardly touched Dartmoor and the more agricultural areas of Devon. In South Devon and in South Cornwall, however, I found the atmosphere very tense around the big towns. I had a look at Falmouth, Devonport and Plymouth, and in none of these ports was a warship to be seen. 'Most of them left last Thursday,' I was told. It was this departure of the fleet that brought it home to them. That and the appearance of sand-bags, tin helmets and gas masks.

Back at the Lizard again I found things much the same. There were fewer visitors and the villagers spoke of cancelled bookings. But visitors still came and gradually everything was slipping back towards normality. Most of the tourists I spoke to were trying desperately hard to ignore the news and enjoy their holidays. 'God knows when we'll get another,' was their justification. But they read the newspapers just the same and still hoped against hope.

Then on Thursday, 31 August, came the news that the children were to be evacuated and I had to re-write my final article, for Cornwall was a reception area and this brought the crisis right home to even the remoter farms and villages. On Friday I spent the day lazing and bathing, determined to forget the war scare. But when I got back I was just in time to see the first bus-load of Midlands children arrive with their teachers at Lizard Town. They looked tired, but happy. I stopped and spoke to them. They thought it a grand adventure. I found one little boy with a gas mask that seemed larger than himself who had never been outside Birmingham streets. There were many who had never seen the sea. I went home to be met by Kerris in a state of some excitement. 'Have you heard the news, Mr Craig?' he asked. 'Germany has marched into Poland. It came through on the news midday. And we've got three little boys billeted on us. Fair bastards they be. Still, mustn't grumble. Government pays us eight-and-sixpence each for them.'

My stomach felt suddenly hollow within me. So it was war after all. Somehow, I had always felt that Hitler must climb down if we called his bluff. 'Well, at least the tension is over,' I said dully. 'We know the worst.'

When I had finished my tea I went out for a walk, taking the path along the cliffs towards Cadgwith. The peace of the coast closed in around me, but it was a bitter balm. The fact that this would remain, whatever happened to my generation, no longer afforded me the satisfaction it had done a week earlier. Rather, I hated it for its aloofness and felt that it had no right to be so serene and beautiful when all Europe was to be subjected to the torture of war. I found myself even longing for the appeasement of the previous September. But it was the cry of emotion rather than reason. I knew that it could not be this time. We were not simply tied to Poland by a treaty. We were faced with the forces of oppression and brute force and we had to tread them under-foot before they ran riot over all Europe and had outgrown the strength of democracy.

I found myself suddenly looking down upon Cadgwith without any knowledge of the walk there. It was just the same as before, the boats drawn up on the beach, the gulls wheeling and screaming, the little white cottages and the smell of fish. That men were dying in a desperate fight for freedom against a mechanized army that had no thought but those instilled into its soldiers by a vast propaganda machine, left this little fishing village untouched. And the probability was that it never would be touched. I shrugged my shoulders. War or no war, there was no reason why I should not get an evening's fishing. I went down into the village and found Big Logan operating the donkey engine that hauled the boats up. While the wire hawser was being hitched on to the next boat I had time to arrange for two hours fishing on the following day at six in the evening. I went to the pub where I heard that five destroyers had been seen going down the Channel. The rumour was that they were going to pick up the *Bremen* now two days out from New York after the hold-up by the American authorities. And I spoke to a man who said that the coastguard had seen a submarine about six miles off the coast moving westward. 'That will be a bloody U-boat,' my informant told me.

Like all the other people still on holiday, I tried hard to treat the following day as a normal one. Only when actually in the water, however, did I forget the atmosphere of tension that gripped me. On the beach, I felt moody and depressed. I could not settle down to enjoy the sunshine and the temptation to go back to the cottage to listen to the news bulletins which were broadcast with disturbing frequency was too much for me. Automatically I listened to broadcast after broadcast that were no more than a repetition of the previous ones, in most cases not even worded differently. There was nothing new – no ultimatum, no outbreak of hostilities on the Western Front; only the rapid progress of German troops into Poland. By the time I left for Cadgwith I was heartily sick of the news.

With a pair of lines over the side of the boat and the gentle chug-chug of the engine, I was at last able to forget that the country was living under the threat of war. And soon my whole mind was occupied with the task of landing mackerel. Big Logan stood facing me at the tiller, whistling softly through his teeth. He hardly spoke a word, except when I hauled a line in and he looked astern for the darting strip of silver that would tell him there was a mackerel on it.

We went as far as Dinas Head. As we headed back the wind began to freshen from the sou'west and little scuds of cloud appeared, flying low across the sky. By seven-thirty the light was beginning to go. 'Looks like a bad night,' I said.

'Ar, it's going to rain all right.' He rolled himself a cigarette and put the boat in towards the cliffs. 'We might have a try for pollock,' he said.

The sea was getting up and away on the starboard bow I could see the waves swirling white round a submerged rock. 'You want to know this coast pretty well,' I said.

'You're right there. It's a wicked bit of coast this – submerged rocks everywhere. And they're not rounded like they are over to Land's End, but all jagged. See the Gav Rocks over to Kennack here?' He pointed across the bows to the jagged reef, now half-submerged, that curved out across Kennack Sands. 'A Dutch barge went aground there – oh, it must have been four winters back. In three days there was nothing of her left except an iron stern post that's there to this day, wedged among the rocks.'

'Have you had any wrecks recently?' I asked. 'There was the *Clan Malcolm*, I know – but since then?'

'Not just round here. There was one over to St Ives.' He lit his cigarette. 'Now the *Clan Malcolm*, she was a lovely wreck – a real Cornishman's wreck.' He shook his head over it. 'If we had a wreck like that every year we wouldn't need to worry about the winter.' He put the tiller down and edged the boat along the shore. We were very close in now and the sea was making it difficult for me to stand. 'You might get at pollock here,' he said, taking over my other line.

But, though we circled for more than ten minutes around the spot, all I got was a snide – a cross between a baby swordfish and an eel that made the bottom of the boat abominably slimy and got thoroughly tied up in the line. At length Big Logan headed the boat out to sea again. 'You ought to get a few mackerel on the way back,' he said. At that time I had caught just on forty. The sea was getting very jumpy, and every now and then I had to sit down on the thwart for fear of losing my balance. The movement of the boat did not seem to worry Logan. With feet spread slightly apart his great hulk seemed to tread the planks and almost to steady the boat.

We were level with Caerleon Cove and about half a mile out when I got my next bite. I felt one sharp tug and then the line went quiet. I pulled it in. It was a mackerel all right. They always seemed to lie quiet after they had been hooked. I left Logan to deal with it and went over to the other line. As soon as I felt it I knew it was shoal mackerel for there was one on this line too. I began to pull it in. Suddenly there was a flash of broken water in the trough of a wave. I caught sight of it out of the corner of my eye. Something solid went streaking through the water beside the boat. The sea swirled and eddied, and before I had time to see what it was the line went tight in my hand and I was whipped overboard.

Instead of bobbing to the surface immediately, I seemed to be sucked down into the sea. I was seized with a sudden panic. My breath escaped in a rush of bubbles and with my lungs suddenly emptied, I found myself as near to drowning as I have ever been. I fought my way upwards with a horrible feeling of constriction across the chest. And when I thought I could not restrain my lungs from functioning normally any longer, I came to the surface and trod water, gasping for breath.

Almost immediately Big Logan hailed me from the boat, which had now circled and was making towards me. A moment later he had hauled me on board and I lay panting on the bottom of the boat. A fish flapped unhappily on the boards beside my head. I rolled over and found myself face to face with the mackerel that I had left Big Logan to deal with. It's plight was so similar to what mine had been an instant ago that I scooped it up in my hand and threw it back into the sea. Then I sat up and looked at Big Logan. 'What was it?' I asked.

He shook his head and tugged at his beard. 'I'd just got the mackerel off your line,' he said, 'and had dropped the weight back into the water, when suddenly the whole boat was rocking like hell and you were overboard. I looked up just in time to see your feet disappearing over the side. The line was tight in your hand, I could see that. Something pretty big must have got hold of it. It not only jerked you overboard so violently that your feet did not even touch the gun'l, but it snapped the line as clean as though it had been cut with a knife.'

The boat was now headed back towards Cadgwith, and I scrambled to my feet.

'How are you feeling?' he asked.

'Unpleasantly wet, but otherwise all right.' But I was a bit shaken and had to sit on the thwart. 'Does this sort of thing often happen?' I asked him. I glanced up and surprised a rather puzzled look on his face.

'Never known it to happen afore, sir,' he replied.

'What was it?' I persisted. 'An outsize in pollock, a tunny fish, a shark – or what?'

'Well, it might have been a tunny or a shark,' he said, a trifle doubtfully I thought. 'You had a mackerel on that line, didn't you?'

I nodded. 'And I saw something break the surface of the water just beside the boat,' I said. 'It was in the trough of a wave and moving fast in the direction of the mackerel. Would it have been the fin of a shark, do you think? Do you get sharks round this coast?'

'Sometimes. You get 'em on most coasts.' He shook his head. 'It must have been a pretty big one,' he murmured. 'You should have seen the state of the sea after you'd taken your header. It was as though a whale had submerged.'

He rolled a cigarette for me and we fell silent, smoking thoughtfully. I was beginning to feel pretty cold by the time we reached Cadgwith. As soon as we had landed he took me straight up to the pub, where I was introduced to the landlord, given a pair of old trousers and a jersey, and my wet clothes hung up to dry. I ordered a hot rum and lemon. Big Logan and the landlord joined me with whiskies and then fell to an interminable discussion of the whole business. I had already decided it was a shark and I was not interested. Sitting in front of the warm kitchen range I soon began to feel sleepy.

Big Logan had to shake me awake in order to tell me that he would take me back to Church Cove by boat. I could hear the wind howling in the chimney and I shook my head. 'I'll walk,' I said.

'Your clothes aren't dry yet and you're tired,' he said. 'Much better let me run you back. There's still a little light left and the sea isn't too bad yet.'

But I shook my head. 'Honestly, I'd like the walk,' I told him. 'It'll warm me up. That is, if you don't mind my hanging on to these clothes until tomorrow?' I asked the landlord.

'That's all right,' he said. 'You're welcome. And if you'll come over tomorrow we'll have your own clothes dry for you by then.'

I thanked him and got to my feet. I tried to pay Big Logan for the fishing trip, but he said he didn't accept money for nearly drowning people. And when I tried to insist, he thrust the pound note back into the pocket of my jacket, which I had put on, wet though it was, because it contained my wallet and my keys. He even offered to accompany me along the cliffs, but by this time I was feeling sufficiently wide awake and buoyed up by the drink to insist that I should enjoy the walk.

As he came out of the pub with me, he called to two fellows in the bar to come and help him in with his boat. The evening light was still sufficient for me to be able to see it bobbing about at its moorings. The wind was rising still and already the waves were beginning to sound noisily on the shingle beach as they tumbled into the inlet. I climbed the roadway to the cliffs and met the full force of the growing gale. I was more than ever glad then that I had not accepted Logan's offer to run me back to Church Cove.

The heat of exertion made the jersey and the rough serge trousers most uncomfortable. I had nothing on underneath them and my skin was sensitive to the rough material. Moreover, my shoes, which were still wet, squelched at every step. I found the farmyard, and climbing the stone stile, reached the path that skirted the Devil's Frying Pan. The flashing of the Lizard light was plainly visible along the coast. There was still a slight glow in the sky ahead, but despite this I found it very difficult to see the path and every now and then I was reduced literally to feeling my way along for fear I should strike out towards the edge of the cliffs.

I passed the big white house on the headland and in a little while came to a part-wooden bungalow that did service as a café. Half of a window still showed light through orange curtains, but the other half was already blacked out with brown paper. I suddenly remembered that for more than three hours I had forgotten all about the crisis. The rum seemed to recede all at once from my brain and leave me wretchedly depressed. I climbed another stone stile and followed the path inland as it circled a long indent. I followed it automatically, for my mind was entirely wrapped in a mental picture of the Western Front. And I suddenly felt that, having come so near to death that night, a merciful God should have finished the job rather than spare me to rot in a stinking trench.

I was possessed of the cowardice that is the heritage of an imaginative mind. It is anticipation and not the pain itself that breeds fear. I singled myself out for a horrible death as I trod that cliff path. In fact, from the way in which I regarded my death as inevitable one would have thought that it was for that sole purpose that Hitler had regimented Germany for six years. And when I almost stumbled into a man standing, a vague blur, on the path in front of me, I recoiled involuntarily with a little cry.

'I am sorry. I am afraid I frightened you,' he said.

'Oh, no,' I said. 'You startled me a bit, that's all. I was thinking about something else.'

'I was hoping you could direct me to a cottage called Carillon that lies back from the cliffs somewhere near here.'

'Carillon?' I murmured. Suddenly I remembered where I had seen the name. 'Is it above Church Cove?' I asked.

'That is right,' he said. His speech was so precise and impersonal that I felt he must be a BBC announcer on holiday.

'If you care to come with me,' I said, 'I think I can find it for you. It lies just back from this path about half a mile further on.'

He thanked me and fell into place behind me. As I went past him I found that the rather stiff looking waterproof he wore was soaked practically to the waist.

'You're wet,' I said.

There was a moment's pause, and then he said, 'Yes, I have been out in a boat and had some trouble getting ashore. The sea is getting quite rough.'

'Funny!' I said. 'I've just got wet through too.' And I told him about my little adventure.

Somehow I got the impression that he was rather impressed by what had happened. 'And what do you think it was?' he asked, when I had finished.

I told him I thought it must have been a shark. He had drawn level with me as the path widened, and I saw him nod. 'They are to be seen about these western coasts. It went for the mackerel.' He then referred to the crisis and asked me whether there were any fresh developments. Then he asked if I had seen anything of the fleet. I told him it had passed down the Channel a week ago and that not a single naval vessel had been seen off the coast since then, except for five destroyers and one submarine of unknown nationality.

He sighed. 'I am afraid it will be war,' he said.

I nodded. 'Oh, well,' I said, 'it's no more than one expected. But it's a bit of a shock when it comes.' I sensed that he too was depressed. 'Will you be called up?' I asked.

'I expect so.'

'What branch?'

'Navy.'

'It's better than most,' I consoled him. 'Better than the trenches.'

'Maybe,' he said, but he did not sound very enthusiastic.

For a time we walked in silence. Then to take our minds off morbid thoughts I began to talk of the coast, the submerged rocks and the wrecks. 'The fisherman I was out with today told me of a Dutch barge that was completely broken up on the Gav Rocks at Kennack in three days,' I said.

'Yes, I have been here before,' he said. 'It is a bad coast.'

I nodded. 'It is,' I agreed. 'And they say that quite a lot of the submerged rocks aren't even charted and are only known by the local fisherman.'

'I know,' was his reply. 'There is a great reef out off Cadgwith that is not properly charted. It is the worst bit of coast I think I have ever seen.'

'Of course, these fishermen know it all,' I said. 'They know just where to find a sand bottom among the rocks. I suppose the knowledge of the rock formations on the bed of the sea is handed down from father to son and grows with the knowledge gained by each new generation.' We had reached the top of a headland and a path branched off to the right, skirting a field. 'You go up there,' I said. 'The cottage is on the right.'

He thanked me and we parted, his slim erect figure merging into the gloom. I went on down into Church Cove.

2

SUSPICION

'WILL listeners please stand by for an important announcement which will be made at nine-fifteen.' It was early Sunday morning and even the announcer's voice sounded strained and unfamiliar. I sat in the Kerrises' kitchen, smoking cigarettes and waiting. So we heard of the final two-hour ultimatum delivered by Sir Neville Henderson. Later came the news that the Prime Minister would broadcast at eleven-fifteen. Rather than hang about waiting for what I knew to be inevitable, I got the car out and drove over to Cadgwith with the clothes the landlord had lent me.

When I returned to the car, with my own clothes dried and neatly done up in brown paper, I met Big Logan coming up from the beach. 'You don't mean to say you've been out with the boats this morning?' I said. There was quite a sea running, though the wind had dropped and it was a fine morning.

He laughed. 'War or no war we've still got to earn our living,' he said. 'I hope you're none the worse for your bathe last night?'

'Not a bit,' I replied, as I threw the bundle of clothes into the back of the car. 'Funny thing was,' I added, shutting the door, 'I met a fellow on my way back to Church Cove who had also got pretty wet landing from a boat.'

'Landing from a boat?' He looked puzzled. 'Where did he land?' he asked.

I shrugged my shoulders. 'I don't know. Somewhere round

here, I suppose. I met him on the path just past that little café on the cliff.'

'No boat came in here. We were the last in.'

'Well, he probably landed somewhere along the coast,' I suggested.

'Why should he do that? Nobody would think of landing anywhere between here and Church Cove with the sea as jumpy as it was last night – unless of course he had to. How wet was he?'

'I should say he had been up to his waist in water. Anyway, what does it matter?' I demanded. I was a trifle annoyed at his persistence.

He hesitated. His feet were placed slightly apart and his hands rested on the leather belt around his waist. At length he said, 'Well, I've been thinking. That business last night – how do we know it was a fish?'

'What else could it have been?' I asked impatiently.

He looked at me, and once again I was impressed by the shrewdness of his small eyes. 'It might have been a submarine,' he said.

I stared at him. 'A submarine?' Then I suddenly laughed. 'But why should a submarine jump half out of the water and pounce upon a poor inoffensive mackerel? Submarines don't have to feed. Anyway, it would be dangerous to come so close in without surfacing.'

'Did it jump half out of the water?' he asked, and I saw that he was perfectly serious. 'Are you certain it was after the mackerel?'

'Perhaps jumping half out of the water is an exaggeration,' I admitted, 'but at least I saw a fin or something streak through the water in the trough of a wave.'

'Or something,' he said. 'Mightn't it have been a periscope?'

I thought about this for a moment. 'I suppose it might,' I agreed. 'But why should it take my line?'

'The line might have got caught up in the submarine.'

'But it's absurd,' I said.

'You didn't see the water after you'd taken that header. It boiled as though a bloody whale had gone down. The disturbance was too much for a shark. Anyway, that's what I think.'

'But, whatever would it be doing so close in?' I asked.

'That's what's been puzzling me,' he said. 'But you mentioning that fellow you met having got so wet has given me an idea. They might have wanted to land someone.'

I thought this over for a moment. It was not altogether fantastic. And yet it seemed incredible. Looking back, I think that what seemed so incredible to me was not the presence of the submarine, but the fact that I had become involved in its presence. I am not accustomed to being caught up in violent adventures. My job is to comment on drama, not take part in it, and I felt somehow a little sceptical of my being knocked overboard by a submarine.

'Did the fellow you met say anything to you?' Big Logan asked.

'Yes, he asked me the way to a cottage called Carillon, which stands back from the cliffs above Church Cove.' It was then that I remembered his perfect English, and suddenly it seemed to me that it was almost too perfect. Word for word, as far as I could remember it, I repeated my conversion with the man.

The conversation seemed harmless enough. But Big Logan was plainly excited. 'How did he know there was a hidden reef off Cadgwith?' he demanded.

'He'd been down here before,' I pointed out. 'It may have been you yourself who told him. He probably went out fishing.'

'Then can you tell me how he knew it wasn't properly charted?'

I couldn't, but at the same time I was by no means convinced that this made the man a spy. Nevertheless, I was glad Big Logan had not realized that in conversation with this stranger I had given him important information concerning the movement of the fleet. Anyway, I consoled myself, if he were a spy he would have the information soon enough.

'I suggest we go along and have a word with Joe,' Logan said. 'He knows everybody around these parts. He'll be able to tell us about the people who own this cottage.'

I followed him back into the pub. We found the landlord in the bar. He had been going over his stock and he had the radio on. He put his fingers to his lips as we went in. Two of his visitors were sitting listening.

'This morning the British Ambassador in Berlin handed the German Government a final note stating that unless we heard from them by eleven o'clock that they are prepared at once to withdraw their troops from Poland a state of war would exist between us. I have to tell you that no such undertaking has been received and that consequently this country is at war with Germany.'

The voice was Chamberlain's. The fact of war came as no great shock to me. It had been a certainty for the past twenty-four hours. Yet my stomach turned over within me at the actuality of it.

The Premier's speech was followed by announcements, commencing with details of the sounding of air raid sirens. The two visitors got up and left the bar, one saying that he was going to telephone his brother. When they had gone, Big Logan turned to the landlord. 'Do you know who lives at Carillon now, Joe? It must be over two years since Mrs Bloy died.'

'Nearer three,' replied the landlord. 'Old man of the name of Cutner has owned it ever since. Retired bank manager, I think. What do you want to know for?'

Big Logan hesitated, and then said, 'Oh, nothing – this gentleman wanted to know, that's all.' He caught me looking at him in some surprise and glanced hurriedly away. 'Know whether he has many visitors?'

'How should I know?' The landlord was looking at him curiously.

'No, of course you wouldn't. I was only – ' He stopped short. The three of us glanced round the room uneasily, aware of a sudden change. I think we all realized what it was at the same moment, for we turned and stared at the radio set at the far end of the bar. The current was still on and we could hear it crackling, but the air had gone dead. At the same moment the visitor who had gone out to phone his brother came in with an anxious look on his face to say that the local exchange could get no answer from London.

He and I were the only ones who leaped immediately to the obvious conclusion. I thought of Bloomsbury with its old houses. They would be absolute death traps. And the trees and the Georgian houses in Mecklenburg Square – should I see those again as I had known them? 'If it is a raid,' I said, 'it's quick work.'

'Perhaps it's only a test,' he said.

'Or just a coincidence,' I murmured. 'The BBC is working under emergency conditions and London is probably inundated with calls.'

'Yes, that's probably it.' His voice did not carry much conviction. Later, of course, we heard that an air raid warning had been sounded, but the possibility of both radio and telephone systems having broken down at the same time enabled us to continue our conversation while the visitor went back to the phone to try again.

Big Logan steered off the subject of the owner of Carillon without any explanation as to why he had been interested in the man. We had a drink on the house and, after discussing the war for a while, we left the pub.

Outside, Big Logan said, 'We'd best go up and have a talk with Ted Morgan.' Morgan was one of the coastguards and it was plain that my companion was not feeling too sure of himself. He had not told the landlord about his suspicions, and had thus prevented the story from circulating throughout the village. Clearly he now wanted confirmation of the conclusion he had arrived at. The coastguard was the sort of father of all wisdom in the village.

But when I was introduced to him in the Board of Trade hut on the cliffs, I doubted whether he was as shrewd as Big Logan. In their relations with the Government, however, the fishermen of the village always turned to Morgan, since he understood the regulations and knew all about the forms they had to fill in. The habit had stuck.

Big Logan told him the whole story. With his feet thrust slightly apart and his thumbs in his leather waistbelt, he seemed to fill the whole hut, his head wagging up and down as he spoke. By comparison, the little Welshman, seated at the desk before the telescope, seemed very small indeed. When Logan had finished I sensed that Morgan was sceptical. He put his head on one side like a bird and drummed with his fingers on the desk. 'It is possible, of course,' he conceded, and he darted a glance at the big fisherman. 'It is possible. I saw what I think was a U-boat about six miles off the coast only yesterday.' He leaned forward in his chair. 'But where would he have landed?'

'What about the Devil's Frying Pan?' suggested Logan.

'Yes, indeed – but it was very choppy last night. The boat would have been stove in.'

'They have collapsible boats,' replied Logan. 'They're made of rubber.'

'Well, supposing it was possible to land a man safely from a submarine at the Frying Pan, why should the Germans want to? Surely they would have all their spies in the country by now?'

It was a very reasonable point. Logan shrugged his great shoulders. 'I'm not responsible for their actions,' he said. 'Maybe this man Cutner is a spy and one of the officers of the U-boat was sent ashore to collect important information from him.'

The coastguard considered this for a moment whilst he explored his small discoloured teeth with a toothpick. At length he shook his head and said, 'You know, there are sharks on this coast.'

'Good God Almighty!' exclaimed Big Logan with sudden exasperation. 'Do you think I don't know a bloody shark when I see one? This wasn't a shark. The displacement of water was too great. It was either a submarine or a whale. And if you think you've ever seen a whale from this little perch of yours, you'd better put in for your discharge right now.'

This outburst apparently left the little coastguard unmoved. He continued to drum with his fingers on his desk and to pick his teeth with the toothpick. In the end he turned to me and said, 'What do you think about it, Mr Craig?'

His question put me in an awkward situation. I was not at all convinced that Logan was right. It seemed much too fantastic. On the other hand, I did not want to offend him. I said, 'I think the matter ought to be investigated.'

The coastguard then turned to Logan. 'What would you like me to do about it? Get on to the police?'

'What the hell's the good of the police?' demanded Logan. 'Either get on to the Admiralty, or phone Scotland Yard and tell them to pass the information on to M.I.5.' It was only then that I realized that he must be old enough to have been through the last war. Generally the inhabitants of English country districts call it the secret service. 'If you don't feel like doing either of these,' he continued, 'I suggest we settle the matter locally.'

'How?'

'Well, figure it out this way,' he said. 'You're probably right when you say a spy wouldn't be landed by submarine – certainly not on this part of the coast. If he is a German, then he'll have been landed to collect information. And if he's been landed to collect information, he's still got to get it back to the submarine. Our job is to see that he doesn't.'

'He may have rejoined his boat already,' I said.

'What – last night?' Big Logan shook his head. 'The sea was rising fast. By the time he'd reached the cottage and got back to the shore again it would have been absolutely impossible to get a boat in anywhere along the cliffs there. It would have been pretty bad landing at Cadgwith even. What I suggest is, we lie in wait for him on the cliffs above the Frying Pan tonight. If he doesn't come – well then, we can consider what's best to be done.'

The coastguard considered this. Then he said, 'All right, Big Logan. You and Mr Craig here wait for him on the cliffs. I'll take two of the boys and keep watch by the head there.' He nodded through the window to the opposite headland that guarded the entrance to Cadgwith from the south west. 'I suppose we can take your boat?'

Big Logan nodded. 'Surely. And take that old service revolver of yours, Ted – you may need it.'

The coastguard pulled open a drawer and, routing among a pile of government forms and other papers, produced a revolver. He turned it over reflectively in his hand as though it brought back old memories. Then he shook his head. 'It's early for spy scares. Still, it won't do any harm to take it along.'

So it was that at nine-thirty that evening Big Logan and I met on the path above the Devil's Frying Pan. By that time I had heard the news of the sinking of the *Athenia* and was suffering from that indefinable desire to express my horror in action. This, I think, is the most deadly moral effect of war. As I had walked along the path from Church Cove my mind had evolved all sorts of wild schemes by which I could bring about the destruction of the submarine. It wasn't until I had settled down to the long vigil on the cliff-top that I gave a thought for the men in the boat itself. Then all the horror of the *Thetis* disaster flooded back into my mind. Journalism and the theatre foster the growth of an imagination. And in war an imagination is a definite handicap. I could not help – despite the sinking of the *Athenia* – a sudden feeling of deep sympathy for men of the German submarine service scattered about the high seas, cooped up in their steel shells, facing a horrible and almost inevitable death.

But after all, there was no question of destroying the submarine. Somehow I felt thankful that Big Logan had not felt sure enough of himself to insist upon the Admiralty being notified. I could picture the torpedo boat waiting under the shelter of the headland and then dashing out, as the U-boat submerged, to drop depth charges that would blow her back to the surface and destroy her utterly. But there was only Big Logan's boat waiting, with no bigger armaments than the coastguard's revolver, and the two of us sitting on top of the cliffs. Anyway, there probably was no U-boat.

That belief grew as the hours slipped monotonously by. We could neither smoke nor talk. We sat on a great rock on the westward side of the Frying Pan, watching the sea until everything merged into the blackness of a tunnel. There were no stars, no moon – the night was like a pit. I had brought some chocolate. We ate that, spinning it out as long as possible, for it gave us something to do. At length I began to feel drowsy. It was then nearly two. I was cold and stiff. For a time I felt angry with Big Logan for assuming that I would accompany him on this damfool errand. The belief that he did not know a shark when he saw one had grown to a certainty by the time I fell asleep.

It seemed but a second later that I was being shaken out of my sleep. I opened my mouth to speak, but a rough hand closed over it and Big Logan's voice whispered in my ear, 'Keep quiet and watch the sea.'

I felt suddenly tense. The night was as black as ever and, as I stared out into it, I felt that I might just as well be blind. Then suddenly a light showed out there on the water. I saw its reflection for an instant in the sea. Then it was gone, and the night was as dark as ever, so that I felt it must have been my imagination.

Big Logan did not move. I sensed the rigidity of his body. His head, only a few feet away from my own, was just visible. It was tilted slightly to one side as he listened, his eyes fixed on the spot where I supposed the water must flow into the Frying Pan.

At length he rose. And I scrambled to my feet too, though I had heard nothing. He took my arm and together we moved with great care back on to the path. There we waited, huddled against the wall of the big white house that lay back from the Frying Pan. 'The boat has arrived,' he whispered in my car. 'It's down in the Frying Pan now. And I saw the flash of your friend's torch away along the cliff as he signalled the submarine.'

It seemed hours before we heard the sound of footsteps on the path. Actually I suppose it was only a few minutes. They drew nearer. I felt Logan tense for the spring. Then they ceased. Almost at the same time there was the flash of a torch reddened by a screening hand. And in that flash the slim waterproof-clad figure stood out quite clearly. He had left the path and had reached almost the exact spot where we had been sitting. He was descending the steep shoulder of the Frying Pan towards the archway.

For all his bulk, Logan moved swiftly. He was down the slope, a vague blur in the darkness, almost before I had crossed the path. As I scrambled down the shoulder I saw him pounce. It was so dark that it was difficult to distinguish what happened, but I think the man turned just before the attack. My one fear had been that he would have a revolver. But if he had, he got no chance to use it. Logan had the advantage of the slope and his own huge bulk. They went down together, and when I reached them Logan had his man pinioned to the ground, his hand across his mouth. 'Search him,' he said.

I ran my hands over his body and felt the outline of an automatic in the pocket of his waterproof. I was on the point of removing it when the whole scene was suddenly illuminated by a torch. I looked up and was almost blinded by its light. I have a vivid mental picture of Big Logan's bearded head in silhouette against that dazzling light. The light came steadily nearer. A tall man in uniform was standing over us. His arms rose and fell, and as it fell in front of the torch I saw that his hand grasped a big service revolver by the barrel. There was a sickening thud, and Big Logan slumped forward. The man in the waterproof thrust

37

Logan's body away from him and scrambled to his feet. Something cold and hard was pressed against my head. I knew what it was and I thought my last hour had come. The man had not switched off his torch and I could see Big Logan's head hanging loosely over a rock and blood was trickling down from his scalp into his beard. I thought the blow had killed him.

'Wir werden sie beide mitnehmen.' It was the man in the water-proof speaking. I was never so thankful for a knowledge of German. Their decision to take us along was presumably due to a desire to leave no evidence of the fact that they had landed and to safeguard, as far as possible, the owner of Carillon.

The man in the waterproof turned to me. 'You must regard yourself as our prisoner,' he said in his precise English. 'You will walk two paces in front. Any attempt to escape or to attract attention and you will be shot.' He motioned me forward with his automatic, and then he and the other German each took hold of one of Logan's arms. The torch was switched off and in the sudden darkness I could hardly see where I was going. I could hear Logan's feet dragging along the ground behind me as I went down the slope to the bottom of the Frying Pan. The Germans frequently had to pause in order to adjust Logan's wieght between them and the sound of their breathing became louder.

It grew darker than ever as we descended and I almost stumbled into the arms of a man waiting at the water's edge. He challenged us in German. 'Schon gut, Karl,' answered the man in the water-proof. 'Sehen Sie, dass die Leute ins Boot kommen.'

'Zu Befehl, Herr Kapitaenleutnant.'

So Logan had been right. It was the commander of the U-boat that had been landed. I began to wonder what it was that he had come ashore for. It must have been something of considerable importance for him to run that risk at the outbreak of war. We ought to have realized that one of the boat's crew might come up to meet him. Our only hope now lay in the coastguard, waiting off the headland – or had they already dealt with him? Was that what had put them on their guard?

The boat was dragged in closer. It was a collapsible affair with two oars, and by the time Logan's inert body had been placed in it, there seemed no prospect of it holding four more men. However, it did, though it sat very low in the water as a result. The commander sat facing me with his automatic ready, while the other two men took an oar each.

Silently we slid beneath the great archway that had originally formed the entrance to the cave before it had collapsed to make the Frying Pan. It was lighter as soon as we got out into the open sea and it was possible to distinguish the dim outline of the cliffs towering above us. Soon, however, even this landmark merged and was lost in the night. It seemed impossible to believe that we should find the submarine in the dark until, turning my head, I saw the merest pinprick of a light showing straight over our bows.

I looked back at the commander. He was watching me, the automatic gripped in his hand, its barrel pointed at me. Big Logan lay inert between us. There was no sign of the coastguard's boat. Then I began to think of the information that the U-boat commander had presumably obtained. What was it – movements of merchant ships, fleet dispositions, transport sailings? It might mean the loss of hundreds of lives if he were allowed to reach the submarine with it. I shifted my position. The boat rocked dangerously. 'Still!' Though the commander spoke English, his voice was not English. There was something cold about it, and I sat rigid, the automatic thrust a few inches nearer.

But it was my life and possibly Big Logan's against the lives of many others. On me lay the responsibility for action. I hesitated. Then suddenly I made up my mind. I would jump on the side of the boat. It was bound to capsize. Then anything might happen. I tensed my muscles for the spring.

And at that moment I heard the roar of a powerful engine. A searchlight suddenly stretched out a white pencil of light across the water. It swept round in a short arc and came to rest on the rubber boat, blinding us completely. The drone of the engines grew louder and then came the rattle of machine gun fire. Little spouts of water flew up all round us. One of the men at the oars slumped into the bottom of the boat, almost capsizing it.

The searchlight bore rapidly down on us. The boat's intention was obvious. It was going to ram us. Close behind us came a sudden ear-splitting explosion. A huge spout of water flew up white in the searchlight. Another flung spray right over the advancing boat. It veered away and I saw the grey lines of a British torpedo boat flash past our stern, the water swirling up from its bows. Before I had time to do anything the steel bows of a submarine nosed alongside.

The Commander jumped out on to the deck, which was half awash. In an instant I found myself hauled out of the boat and bundled towards the conning tower. I passed the for'ard gun just as it fired again and my ears went completely deaf. As I was thrust down the conning tower hatch I saw the torpedo boat swing in a great arc. Its searchlight suddenly went out and everything was black. The commander dropped down beside me, shouting a string of orders so fast that I could not understand them. Immediately the submarine's engines came to life and she began to swing sharply to port. I knew then that the commander was afraid of being torpedoed and I felt a sudden emptiness inside me.

Logan's great body, still unconscious, was thrust down the hatch almost on top of me. We were pushed out of the way and the crew scrambled down, two carrying the man who had been hit. The hatch closed with a bang. The sound of the engines immediately seemed like a great throbbing pulse. It was very warm and there was a strong smell of oil. We were bundled into two bunks out of the way. Every man was at his action station.

The boat seemed to shudder as she gathered way. A bell sounded, and a few seconds later the floor took a decided tilt. We were diving. It was a crash dive and the roar of the electric motors took the place of the diesels. We were no sooner on an even keel than I sensed rather than actually felt the boat turning. I had read enough about submarine experiences in the Great War to know what the commander was trying to avoid. The muscles of my face contracted in anticipation and my hands were clenched so tight that the nails bit into the palms.

A second later it came – a terrific crash. The U-boat bucked as though it had hit a rock and there was the sound of breaking crockery. The lights went out and, with the fuses blown, the motors stopped. There was a sudden deathly stillness. And in that stillness it was just possible to hear the drone of the torpedo boat's propellers on the surface of the sea above us. The emergency lighting came on. The shock of the depth charge had rolled Logan out of his bunk into the gangway. He picked himself up, fully conscious now. Then he saw me and said, 'My head feels bloody. There are sort of explosions going on inside it. It feels as though it will burst.'

I was about to enlighten him when a second depth charge exploded. It was not so near as the other, but even so the U-boat rocked violently for the trim was bad. The bows seemed to dip and then there was an ominous jar for'ard. Logan took one look round the place and understood. He was like a drunkard that has suddenly sobered up by danger. His eyes cleared and he was instantly alert.

The commander shouted some order. Two seamen dashed down the gangway, pushing Logan to one side. They were followed by the man who had knocked Logan out. He was the first-lieutenant. For a moment everything seemed pandemonium.

Orders were shouted and men rushed aft. Then there was quiet. Water was flooding in from the control room. The crew were on the hand gear for everything to save noise. The only sound was a gramophone playing 'Deutschland, Deutschland über Alles.' For the second time that night I found myself thinking of the *Thetis* disaster, but there was little comfort in Professor Haldane's assurance at the enquiry that the men would not have suffered greatly.

The regulating tank had been flooded and the submarine was now on an even keel. I found I had scrambled out of my bunk. The Number One came back along the gangway shouting, 'Die Kammer achtern ist unter Wasser, und Wasser dringt in den Maschinenraum.'

'Do you understand what he said?' asked Logan.

'He said the stern compartment is flooded and water is coming into the engine room,' I told him.

Then there was a report of water coming in for'ard. But by this time the leak in the control room had been stopped. Two more depth charges boomed in the distance. The commander came out of the control room and was met by the engineer officer. He reported engine room leak stopped, but port motor damaged. One of the watchkeepers who was down with 'flu walked dazedly past along the gangway in his pyjamas. 'What's happened?' he asked.

'Plenty – your temperature is a hundred and two,' came the answer. 'Report to your bunk.' Then to the engineer officer, the commander said, 'What about the starboard motor?'

'Propeller shaft fractured.'

'Well, see if you can get the port motor working.'

The commander then had a long talk with his second. Part of it I could not catch. But the gist of the second's remarks gave me some idea of what had happened following the first depth charge. The explosion had apparently blown open the engine-room hatch allowing a huge volume of water to enter. Then the pressure of water from outside had sealed the hatch completely. Moreover, it appeared that the boat was now far too heavy and bobbing about between fifty and sixty feet. 'We'll have to empty the bilges,' the commander decided suddenly, 'even if the oil does give our position away.'

The second gave the order, and soon even a layman like myself could realize that the boat was lighter and more manageable. Then the second and the commander bent over a chart. I could just see them from where I was seated on my bunk. I think the commander must have sensed me watching him, for he looked up and his gaze swung from me to Logan. Then he strode down the gangway. He was still dressed in civilian clothes and wearing his stiff military-looking waterproof though the interior of the submarine was getting extremely hot. He stopped opposite Logan. 'You are a fisherman, are you not?' he asked.

Logan looked up and nodded.

'Well, I do not expect you want to die any more than we do,' the commander said. 'I should be glad if you would help us. We are lying at about fifty feet. The motors are out of action and that torpedo boat of yours is somewhere up above waiting for us. We dare not surface. But we do not know the drift so close to the shore. If we stay down we may pile ourselves up on the rocks. I calculate that at the moment we are less than a quarter of a mile off the entrance to Cadgwith.'

Big Logan stroked his beard and looked across at me. I felt a sudden excitement. It was almost exultation. I think he sensed it, for he turned to the commander, grinning all over his face. 'You're given me a crack on the head and dragged me on board this blasted tin fish of yours,' he said, 'and now you want me to get you out of the mess you've got yourself into.'

'Pardon me, but it was you who got us into this mess – or rather your friend here. We did not arrange for a British torpedo boat to be waiting for us.'

'Torpedo boat, was it?' Big Logan suddenly clicked his fingers. 'Well, I'm damned,' he said. 'So Ted Morgan took my word for it after all. And he wanted me to believe it was a shark.' He poked a large forefinger into the U-boat commander's ribs. 'It wasn't this gentleman – ' he indicated me – 'that gave you away. It was your bloody submarine coming up right under my boat when he and I were out after mackerel last night. A shark! Well, I'm damned!' And suddenly he began to laugh. He laughed until the tears ran down his cheeks. The crew gathered round, staring at him. I think they thought he had gone off his head with fright.

At length, weak with laughter, he said, 'And here you are, like a lot of stuck pigs, just because you interfered with this gentleman's fishing.' I thought he was going off into another paroxysm of laughter. But suddenly he sobered up. 'Know what I'll do?' he said. 'I'll make a bargain with you – the papers you got from your friend at Carillon for information about the currents.'

I thought the commander would strike him. He was a young man and Logan had made him furious. He was a nice looking lad, very slim and erect, but he had the Prussian features and the Prussian lack of any sense of humour. The joke was on him and he could not see it. 'You are a prisoner,' he said. His voice was cold and precise. 'You will do as you are told.'

'I'll see you on the Gav Rocks first,' was Big Logan's reply. And he began to bellow with laughter again.

The commander's hand came up instantly and smacked Logan first on one cheek and then on the other. Logan's answer was instantaneous. He laid the commander out with one blow of his huge fist.

The second immediately drew his revolver. I read Logan's death sentence in his eyes and at the same time one of the crew seized me from behind. But as the second raised the gun it was struck out of his hand by another officer who had appeared behind him. It was the navigating officer. 'Don't be a fool,' he said in German. 'He's our only chance of getting out of this alive.'

Then he turned to Logan and said in broken English, 'Eet ees the lifes of you and dese other gentleman who ees at stake, as well as our own. Will you not help us? The torpedo boat, she will wait all night for us. Eef we could drift half a mile down the coast without wrecking ourselfs we could surface. Then we should be all right.'

Logan's reply was, 'I've told this officer' – he indicated the inert figure of the commander – 'what my terms for helping you are. I've lived by the sea all my life and I'm not afraid to die by it, even if it is in a glorified sardine tin.'

'And that goes for me too,' I said. It was a heroic little gesture for my stomach felt queasy at the thought of death by suffocation. I suppose most people with any imagination possess a mild form of claustrophobia, but I must say that Logan's phrase about a glorified sardine tin struck home.

The navigating officer, whom I guessed to be a far more human individual and consequently a much better reader of character, immediately took Logan at his word and set reviving the commander. This took several minutes, for Logan's whole weight had been behind the punch.

The man eventually staggered to his feet, but he was so dazed by the blow that it was several minutes before the navigating officer could make him understand the position. When he did he blazed up in a fury. 'You have the audacity to try to make terms with me,' he cried turning on Logan. But he kept his distance this time. 'You came aboard this ship as a prisoner, you behave like a lunatic, strike the commander and then expect to barter information which you possess on fantastic terms.' He gave an order to the crew. Three of them closed in on Logan. Logan remained calm

and impassive, but his little grey eyes roamed the narrow gangway, guaging distances and possibilities. It looked like a real scrap.

The navigating officer, however, continued to talk in low tones
with the commander. The two men were of completely contrasting
types. The navigating officer was small in height and rather stocky,
with a round ruddy face that spoke of years at sea. The commander, on the other hand, was a typical Nazi – excitable, over-
bearing and cold-blooded. However, the navigating officer
apparently got his way, for the commander turned to Logan and
said, 'If you help us, we will land you and your companion on
shore as soon as it is safe to do so.'

I pictured the surface of the sea, the towering cliffs, Cadgwith
and the green fields beyond. What a relief it would be to get out of
this little nightmare world of machinery that reeked of oil and was
so hot and stuffy. A word or two from Logan and we were safe. He
glanced at me. Something stubborn and perverse seemed to rise
up within me. I shook my head. He nodded and smiled. 'We want
the papers,' he said.

The commander swung round on him. 'Well, you won't get
them – understand that.'

'Then neither will your superiors,' Logan answered quietly.

When the fury of a man's emotions gets the better of him and he
is at the same time baffled, it is not a pretty sight. I wondered how
long his nerves would hold out against the incessant tension of
service in U-boats. The strain had been too great for a number of
submarine commanders in the last war.

At last he mastered himself sufficiently to say, 'Very well, we'll
stay down for half an hour.'

'And send youself and your crew to certain death?' asked
Logan. He looked at me. 'That serves our purpose just as well, eh?'

I had to agree with him, though I felt like being sick.

The commander tried to bluster for a moment. 'You are
bluffing,' he shouted angrily.

Logan shrugged his shoulders. 'You'd best call my bluff, if you
think so.'

The man's uneasiness, however, got the better of him. He stood
watching Logan for some seconds and then he said, 'All right. I'll
get you the papers.' He turned and strode down the gangway to
the officers' quarters.

I looked at Logan, wondering what good it would do to get hold
of the papers since the man might very well have a copy or have
memorized them. 'Why don't you keep silent and let them run on
the rocks?' I asked in a whisper.

'Because,' he replied, 'the drift of the current here is seaward. They're as safe as houses, if they only knew it. If we can't get an undertaking from them to wireless the information through to Fort Blockhouse, then we'll have to try and scare them into surfacing and hope that the torpedo boat will still be around.'

The prospect seemed pretty grim.

It was some time before the commander returned. He held in his hand a single sheet of paper. This he handed to the navigating officer, who passed it on to Logan. 'Now step up here and explain the drift on the chart,' the commander said.

Logan glanced at the sheet of paper and then held it out so that I could also read it. I cannot remember all the details of it. But it gave the position, longitude and latitude, of a rendezvous for three separate squadrons of British ships – one from Gibraltar, one from the Atlantic and one from Portsmouth. Logan explained to me that the rendezvous was about thirty miles south of the Shambles Light – that is off Portland. Those coming from Gibraltar and the Atlantic were largely capital ships. Those coming from Portsmouth were mainly destroyers and mine-sweepers.

Logan placed his big forefinger on the list of those coming from the Atlantic. 'They're short of destroyers,' he said. 'Until they meet up with the Portsmouth boats those four battleships will be sufficiently screened. What a chance for the U-boats!'

There were certainly not nearly so many destroyers and torpedo boats with this squadron as with that coming up from Gibraltar. My eyes travelled on down the paper. The rendezvous was for Monday, 18 September at 13.30 hours. The object of the gathering was to sweep up the Channel, pass through the Downs and carry out a raid on the Kiel Canal. Blockships were to be waiting in the Downs and these were to be sunk in the canal if it proved possible to silence the shore batteries. Raids by Bomber Command of the R.A.F. were to accompany the attack and three fighter squadrons would co-operate in preventing enemy aircraft from harassing the raiding fleet.

As I grasped the magnitude and daring of the plan, I could not help being amazed at the ability of the German secret service to obtain information of such a vitally secret nature. 'Have they got a chance of sinking those four battleships?' I asked.

'Quite a good chance, I should say,' Logan replied. 'And if there are enough U-boats in this vicinity they might have a shot at the main gathering.'

Our conversation was interrupted by the commander. 'Stop

that whispering,' he ordered, 'and let us have the information we require.'

Logan strode down the gangway towards the control room. 'Certainly,' he said, 'if you'll transmit a message to Fort Blockhouse, Portsmouth.'

The commander's eyes narrowed. 'You have the information I obtained. Keep your side of the bargain.'

'You know my purpose in requiring this information before directing you to safety,' Logan answered. 'My intention was to prevent its use by the enemies of my country. If you have a copy of this or if you have memorized – '

'I have neither copied it nor memorized it,' the other cut in.

'In that case there is no objection to your sending my message to the Admiralty.'

The commander moved forward. There was something stealthy, almost cat-like in the way he moved. 'I will not be called a liar in my own ship – certainly not by a verflucht Britisher. You have the insolence to demand that this ship's radio be used to transmit messages to the British Naval authorities. I'll see you in hell first.'

'Then, you won't have long to wait,' was Logan's reply.

The navigating officer, who had been following the conversation intently, said, 'Eet will be your lifes as well as ours.'

'If these ships meet as arranged,' Logan replied, tapping the paper in his hand, 'it may mean the loss of hundreds of lives. It's our lives against theirs. We prefer that it should be two and not several hundred British lives that are lost. So it's Davy Jones for you if you don't give me a solemn pledge to radio my warning to the authorities as soon as I have got you out of this mess and you have a chance to dry off your aerials.'

'As you wish,' said the commander. There was something of a sneer in his voice. I think he thought we might crack up under the strain, for after he had barked out an order in German he stood watching us. The hiss of the compressed air entering the tanks of the submarine, forcing the water out, was incredibly loud. It seemed to fill my ears.

'Now do you still withhold the information we need? If you do, I am going to surface and take a chance with this torpedo boat of yours.' And when neither of us answered, the commander shrugged his shoulders. 'Gun crews stand by!' he ordered in German. Then he disappeared up into the conning tower.

The next few minutes were some of the most unpleasant I have ever experienced. It was not difficult to sense the tension in the submarine. The atmosphere was by now getting very heavy and I was sweating like a pig with the heat of the place. The hiss of the compressed air gradually lessened. The second officer adjusted the trim. The submarine had risen on an even keel and was now, I presumed, lying at periscope depth while the commander watched the torpedo boat and chose his time. I wondered whether the port diesel had been affected or not. If it had, then we were for it.

The commander's voice suddenly called out, 'Blow all tanks! Surface!' The compressed air hissed in the tanks and the boat shot up so quickly that I could hear the sea water flooding back from the deck. 'Geschuetzmannschaften auf Bereitschaft!' The gun crews swarmed like monkeys into the conning tower. The hatch slammed back and feet sounded over our heads. Then the one diesel engine began to throb and the ship shuddered as the bows bit into the waves.

The gun crews would be at their stations now. I could hear the swirl of the water overhead and I presumed we were travelling with decks awash in order to keep the boat steady. The U-boat's surface speed of 18 knots was reduced, Big Logan reckoned, to about 9 or 10 as a result of the damage to the starboard propeller shaft. The speed of the torpedo, on the other hand, was well over 40 knots. We had not long to wait. A bell sounded in the engine room. The pulsing of the single engine grew more and more frenzied. The whole ship seemed to be shaking and rattling. The din was incredible. Then suddenly there was a sharp detonation and we were almost thrown off our feet. For a moment I though we had been hit by a torpedo. But I had barely recovered my balance when the explosion was repeated and I realized that it was the after gun being fired. So the torpedo boat had spotted us and we were in action!

To analyse my hopes during the minutes that followed is quite impossible. I was torn between the desire for self-preservation and what I sensed to be my duty. The two were completely ir-reconcilable. I have, however, a vivid recollection of growing horror at the idea of being imprisoned and suffocated in that infernal U-boat, and towards the end of the action I must admit that that was my dominating thought. I must have been in a pitiable state of funk by the end for I remember nothing about it except that I babbled incoherent nonsense whilst Logan shook me till my teeth rattled in order to prevent me from going completely off my head.

It was a most unpleasant experience, and as an exhibition it must have been disgusting. Strangely enough, it did not make it impossible for me afterwards to go in a submarine again. In fact, those twenty minutes seemed to sweat all terror of death by suffocation out of me. Logan, on the other hand, preserved that same calm throughout the engagement, though he informed me afterwards that he had never actually been in a submarine before. All his experience of submarine warfare in the last war had been gained on minesweepers and coastal patrols, and later on 'Q' ships.

I do not remember much about that engagement. All that remains vivid in my mind is the throb of the engines, which seemed to pulse right through me, the draught from the open conning tower hatch, the incessant gunfire and my own terror. I remember that a few minutes from the outset the after gun crew ceased firing. But they remained at their stations and some ten minutes later the for'ard gun opened fire and at the same time the commander ordered an eight point turn to starboard – eight points represent a right-angle. I think it was this order that really finished me, for I was pretty certain that it meant a torpedo had been launched at us.

Later, I learned from listening to the conversation of the officers and men that we had surfaced about half a mile out off Caerleon Cove, which lies just east of Cadgwith. The torpedo boat was still off Cadgwith, but within a few seconds her searchlight had picked up the U-boat. The torpedo boat had immediately extinguished her searchlight. The commander, explaining the action to the navigating officer later, said that the drone of the torpedo boat's engines was plainly audible from the conning tower even above the sound of the U-boat's own engine. The order had been given for the U-boat's searchlight to be switched on and as soon as it had picked out the attacking craft the after gun crew had opened fire.

The U-boat was then travelling almost due east with the torpedo boat dead astern. Shortly afterwards the gun crew scored what looked like a direct hit and the torpedo boat swerved off its course and was lost to sight. The U-boat then made a turn of sixteen points and doubled back in the hope of shaking off the torpedo boat if it were still in action.

What actually happened I have pieced together from a talk I had some months later with the coastguard who was on board the torpedo boat. After getting out of range of the U-boat's searchlight, the boat had hove-to and listened for the sound of the submarine's engine. As they had expected, the U-boat's searchlight was extinguished and it began to double back. By this time the clouds had thinned and a rather pale young moon had appeared. As the U-boat approached they got under way with their engines just ticking over and moved up between the shore and the U-boat, endeavouring to merge their craft into the background of the cliffs. This proved so successful that they had actually manœuvred into position and fired their torpedo before they were sighted. In actual fact, it was the torpedo, and not the torpedo boat, that the U-boat commander first sighted, for the wake of the torpedo showed like a streak of silver in the moonlight. It was then that the order for an eight point turn was made. At the same time our own searchlight picked out the torpedo boat and the for'ard gun opened fire. As the submarine swung on to her new course the after gun crew took up the fire. The torpedo apparently almost scraped the U-boat's side.

The gun crew had the range almost immediately this time and their third shot hit the sea just behind the torpedo boat, seriously damaging the engines and injuring one man. At the same time our port look-out reported a ship on the port bow. All he had seen was the white bow wave. But through his glasses the commander picked out the shape of a destroyer coming at full tilt to the scene of action.

Down in the bowels of the U-boat we heard orders being shouted and then the clatter of sea boots on the deck plates above our heads. The men came tumbling down through the conning tower, the hatch cover slammed to and in a few seconds I was experiencing my second crash dive of the evening.

This time, however, we were far enough out for the commander to have complete confidence in the charts. There was apparently a sand bottom and the dive was straightened out, the boat trimmed and we settled slowly on to the bed of the sea. For nearly an hour we could hear the ugly boom of depth charges in the distance. None came very near us, however, and we settled down to a long vigil.

I think it was this long vigil that really cured me of my terror. Time dulls the senses and in the end I settled down to a game of cards. That we were allowed, as prisoners, to indulge in a game of cards by a commander who obviously could not regard us in too friendly a light may seem surprising. I think my own exhibition of terror was the cause. Fear is catching, and fear in a submarine at a time of emergency is to be avoided at all costs.

That game of poker must constitute something of a record. It started at three o'clock in the morning and it went on, subject to various interruptions, until nearly midnight the following night. We sat or reclined on the bunks and for a table we had a packing

49

case from the store chamber. The light, which was directly above us, threw the interior of the bunks into complete darkness, so that it was impossible to see anyone's features, and even when they leaned forward to put their cards down it only shone on the tops of their heads. The contrast between Logan's head and those of the Germans who played with us remains very vivid in my mind. His hair stood up like a great mop, which together with his beard, gave him a very wild look. The Germans, on the other hand, had close-cropped heads and even those whose overalls were blackened with oil still managed to look quite smart.

The navigation officer played with us most of the time, acting as interpreter. At Logan's suggestion I pretended that I did not understand a word of German, a pretence which was to stand us in good stead later. Different members of the crew joined us at various times. They gave us the benefit of the tourist rate of exchange for our money. Nobody seemed to feel like sleep until well into the next day.

I began to feel drowsy, however, quite soon after breakfast, which was an excellent meal of pressed ham and hard boiled eggs. For a time I played more or less automatically. Big Logan, on the other hand, seemed to remain quite fresh. Despite the language bar, he seemed to get on the best of terms with those he played with, laughing and joking, so that it was difficult to realize that we were in imminent danger of our lives. In fact, the atmosphere became so friendly that, with the sound of Big Logan's voice booming in my ears, I found it difficult to believe in my drowsy state that I was not back in the pub at Cadgwith.

By midday the air was beginning to get pretty bad and most of us lay down and tried to sleep. Throughout the whole time we were submerged the engineers were working on the port electric motor. Twice it was started up, but each time there was an awful clanking sound. By lunch-time they had given it up, and in the afternoon they also turned in.

The only man who did not seem to sleep at all was the commander. I did not like him. He was the personification of the effects of Nazism upon the youth of Germany. He was cold-blooded, brutal and very ready to sneer. But he was efficient. He could not have been more than about twenty-five, yet his men had complete confidence in him. His coolness when actually in action had the quality of a machine, and I could not help thinking that if the German army were officered by a sufficiency of young men of his calibre it must be a very powerful machine.

But like so many Germans, especially those of Prussian stock, he lacked any understanding of the importance of psychology. He formed his opinion of men and expected them to act thereafter according to a formula. As far as the men under his command were concerned this seemed to work out well – he knew how each one would react in given circumstances. But like so many Germans he had no understanding of the English. Whether we are a much more complex race than the Germans I do not know – perhaps we are. At any rate, I had several verbal clashes with him, for when I told him I was a journalist he began to question me about the reasons Britain had entered into the war. He simply could not understand that we had entered purely and simply because we hated the precepts of Nazism and refused to live indefinitely under the threat of aggression. He spoke sneeringly of imperialistic aims and honestly believed that the whole thing had been engineered by Churchill and Eden.

As regards myself, too, he revealed himself as having not the slightest understanding of the complex psychological reactions that go on in the mind of a man accustomed to living an entirely individualistic life. Because I had been terrified when the action with the torpedo boat had been in progress, he thought I was a coward. And the more he implied that I was a coward, the more determined he made me to prove, as opportunity offered, that I was not a coward.

We remained on the bottom until shortly after midnight. By the time the order was given to blow the tanks, the atmosphere was so thick that it was really painful to breathe. Certainly by then I was cured of any fear of being cooped up in an air-tight vessel. Haldane is perfectly right. You gradually reach a condition in which your senses become so dulled that the prospect of death is by no means unpleasant.

We stopped at periscope depth. The commander reported all clear and at long last we rose to the surface. The conning tower hatch was thrown back and a sudden waft of cool air entered the submarine. I never realized till then how lovely it was to actually feel yourself breathing good life-giving air. Each man was allowed a few minutes out on the conning tower platform and I don't think I have ever enjoyed a few minutes fresh sea air so much. The submarine was travelling at about 8 knots with her decks awash and the water creaming up white over the bows. It was a fine sight to see the vague outline of her slipping steadily through the long Atlantic swell. The night was cloudy, but there was a faint luminosity from the moon.

'We're travelling due west,' Logan whispered.

'How do you know?' I asked.

'The moon, for one thing,' he said.

'What are they going west for?' I asked. 'Surely with a fractured propeller shaft and one of the motors out of action they'll have to return to Germany for repairs?'

'They wouldn't stand much chance of getting through the Straits now that they can't travel under water. Maybe they're going to try and get round the north of Scotland. Or perhaps they have a base in Spain or somewhere like that.'

Our guards, who kept very close to us in case we attempted to jump into the sea, indicated that our spell of fresh air was over. With the boat rolling heavily, I found the descent of the conning tower ladder something of a feat. We went back to the bunks that had been allotted to us, and for the first time since we had come on board I really slept. I think it was the drone of the engine that did it. The incessant rhythmic throbbing lulled my senses.

When I woke up the engine had stopped. There was considerable activity for'ard. I leant out over the edge of my bunk and peered into the one below where Logan lay. 'What happened?' I asked.

'I don't know,' he replied. And then in a whisper, he added, 'I reckon we're not far off the North Cornish coast.'

'How do you know?' I asked.

For answer he moved his arm so that I could see he held in the palm of his hand a big silver watch that he always carried in his trouser pocket. It was turned face downward and the flap at the back was open revealing a luminous compass. 'It's now just after four,' he said. 'We moved off from Cadgwith shortly after midnight. Then for nearly two hours our course was practically due west. At two-twenty we bore away to the north – presumably rounding Land's End. By three-fifteen our course was practically north nor'east. We hove-to about five minutes ago.'

'What's the idea, do you think?' I asked. 'Perhaps the commander is passing on the information he received to another boat?'

Logan did not reply, but turned his watch the right way up. The flap at the back closed with a snap. I looked up to find that our guard had risen from his seat on a bunk a little way down the gangway and was watching us warily. The conning tower hatch was still open. If we could rush the guard, get hold of his revolver and reach the controls of the tanks we might be able to submerge the U-boat. Death would come quickly with the conning tower hatch open. But even as I pondered the idea, trying to remember all the controls I had seen being used, there came the sound of feet on the deck plates above our heads and the members of the crew who had been up above began to tumble in through the conning tower hatch. The commander was last down and the hatch closed with a bang. I cursed myself for not having thought of the scheme sooner.

The order was given to submerge and the inrush of water into the tanks was plainly audible. There was a grating noise for'ard that I did not quite understand and the U-boat slowly submerged. Then there was silence. The commander, who had now left the conning tower, picked up an earphone that hung from a hook in the control room and began speaking into it. His voice was subdued, but I caught the words 'motors' and 'fixed.' Almost immediately the grating sound was resumed.

'We're facing sou'east,' Logan whispered.

'Then if you've worked out our bearings right,' I said, 'we are facing in to the coast.'

He nodded.

Twice the submarine seemed to bump the bed of the sea. I became convinced that we were moving forward, though the motors were silent. There was suddenly a horrible grating sound against the hull just behind our bunks, then another bump and the movement of the boat ceased. The tanks were then blown and we rose slightly.

The commander put down the earphone and moved out into the gangway. 'All right, boys,' he said, 'we've arrived.'

The burst of cheering that followed this announcement was almost deafening in that enclosed space. The men came hurrying from their stations, pushing past our guard in a sort of mad race for the conning tower. In a few seconds, it seemed, the boat was empty. Our guard motioned us forward with his revolver. We scrambled out of our bunks and went along the gangway and up through the conning tower.

I cannot describe my amazement as I came out on to the bridge of the U-boat. I had presumed that we had been brought alongside a ship. Several ideas had occurred to me. I knew that supply ships were essential if repeated and hazardous returns to bases were to be avoided and I thought it possible that the Germans had produced some sort of vessel with a false bottom into which the submarine rose. That, I felt, would account for the fact that we had had to submerge first. What in fact I found was something much more sensational.

3

THE GESTAPO

The U-boat was lying in a colossal cave. From end to end this cave was nearly a hundred yards long. The width, however, was only about forty or fifty feet. The roof, which was arched like a huge tunnel and about forty feet high, was strengthened by huge steel girders. The whole place was lit by brilliant arc lights and echoed to the hum of giant machinery. I know it must sound fantastic. I was myself utterly astonished when I saw it. The U-boat commander realized this, as he stood beside me on the bridge, and there was a sort of smug satisfaction in the way he said, 'The world has yet to understand – and the English in particular – that Germany does not go to war unprepared. Already we are sweeping your shipping from the high seas. Your papers will be reassuring your people that Germany cannot do this for long as her submarines will have to return to Germany for munitions and supplies. This is the answer. It is a complete naval submarine base. We even have our own foundry.'

As he spoke my eyes took in the whole scene. The crew of the U-boat, some sixty men in all, were crowding the deck for'ard. Right at the bows three men were working to cast off a big cylindrical buoy to which the submarine was moored. The buoy itself was attached to a big chain which ran round a powerful-looking donkey-engine and dropped back into the water. I gathered that it was by this chain that the submarine had been dragged through the underwater entrance and guided to the surface.

'You'd be in an awkward fix if the British secret service discovered your hide-out,' I said. 'With only that one exit you'd be caught like rats in a trap.'

He laughed. 'Strange to say, that thought had already occurred to us.' He took a step towards me. 'And don't think you're going to be the little hero that takes word to the authorities. Or you either,' he added, swinging round on Logan. 'You'll earn your keep with hard work and you'll not leave here alive till Germany has won the war.'

'Then it looks as though we're doomed to die here,' said Logan with a twinkle in his eyes.

The muscles on the back of the commander's neck tightened. I waited for the inevitable. But he thought better of it and went down from the bridge on to the deck.

'I'm afraid you're getting the wrong side of him,' I said.

Logan shrugged his shoulders. 'What's it matter,' he said. 'He's not in charge of this place, and as soon as his ship is repaired he'll put to sea again.'

'Well, at least try and keep on the right side of the man who is in charge,' I said. 'Somehow we've got to get out of here.'

At that moment the cave echoed to the fussy chug-chug of a small boat which appeared from one of the archways leading off the main cave. In several of these archways I could see the dark grey sterns of submarines. The buoy had by now been cast off. A hawser was paid off to the boat, which did service as a diminutive tug. As soon as the hawser had been made fast the boat took the submarine in tow.

At the far end, the cave suddenly widened out into a big semi-circle. Radiating from this semi-circle were no less than seven caves. Each of these was wide enough to take one submarine and leave a reasonably broad dockside. Each cave was numbered. U 34 which was our boat, was taken into No 5 berth. A number of the men had small boat hooks with which they fended the submarine off the rough-hewn rock sides of the dock. As the conning tower passed the entrance I saw the top of a metre guage sticking up out of the water, while folded back against the sides of the dock were strong gates. The tide was apparently at the high. When the tide was low, the water could then be drained out of each basin and the gates closed to constitute a dry dock. The ingenuity of the whole place was incredible.

As soon as the submarine had been moored, we were led along the dockside and up a slope to a gallery that ran along the ends of the docks. We turned right, past docks 6 and 7 and up a long sloping ramp that curved to the left. This brought us to the first of two upper galleries. Here were sleeping quarters for hundreds of men, with rest rooms, which included billiard tables and equipment for all sorts of other games. There were also kitchens and lavatories, and the whole place was air-conditioned and kept free from the damp, that was so noticeable in the galleries at dock level, by means of double doors. The walls, floors and ceilings of these galleries were all cemented so that, though here and there trickles of moisture were to be seen, they were in general remarkably dry.

The crew of the submarine were each allotted a little cubicle which contained a camp bed. Logan and I were handed over to the watch. This was in reality a guard. We were taken to the upper level galleries and into the guard-room where we were introduced to a little man in civilian clothes who smoked endless cigarettes. He had a square head, a rather heavy jowl and little blue eyes placed too close together. He was quite pleasant to us, but I did not like him. Later, I discovered that he was a member of the Gestapo. Apparently even in the submarine service the Nazis do not trust their men, for there were four agents at this base, and I learned later that in each submarine there was always one man in the pay of the Gestapo. The four men at the base, though they were ostensibly there to deal with any prisoners like ourselves that were brought in, divided the day into eight-hour watches, and were in fact the watchdogs of the base, wielding practically unlimited power. I was to observe this power later to our disadvantage.

A few routine questions were put to us, and then we were marched down to the dock-level gallery. We turned off this opposite No. 6 dock into what I believe miners would call a cross-cut. Here several small caves had been hollowed out of the rock and fitted with steel grills across the entrance. We were both put into one of these. I had more immediate needs than sleep, but as I turned to explain the matter, the grill clanged to, the key grated in the lock and the guard marched off.

The only furniture in the cells was two camp beds with three blankets at the foot of each. I wondered how long the blankets had been there, for the rock floor sparkled with water and the place was chill with damp. The naked electric light bulb in the gallery outside remained on and though it was manifestly absurd that there could be any movement of air, a sort of chill draught rose from the docks where the U-boats lay. The sloping tunnel leading down to No. 6 dock was just visible from the corner of the cell.

I got little sleep that night. I suppose it was past five by the time we were under out blankets. But the unfamiliarity of the place combined with the chill and glare of the light to keep me awake. When at last I did get off to sleep it was to be woken up almost immediately by the clatter of electric welders and the roar and bustle of what sounded like a huge steelworks, for every sound was magnified a hundredfold by the caves and galleries. Sounds mingled so extraordinarily that, except for the welders, I could not identify a single noise. Every sound was made hollow and reverberating by the echo, so that it was as though it were being amplified by an old-fashioned loudspeaker with the tone control set to pick out the drums.

I looked at my watch. It was nine-thirty. Logan, his feet sticking out over the bottom of the bed, was sound asleep. Above the general roar I could just hear the snoring intake of his breath. I lay half awake for some time in that uncomfortable state of reluctance to get up that is induced by an insufficiency of bed-clothes. I felt chilled to the bone, yet I had not the strength of will to climb out from beneath my inadequate covering.

At ten o'clock sharp a guard of three men appeared – a petty officer and two ratings. They were equipped with side arms and revolvers. We were marched to the washrooms. But though we were allowed to wash, we were not given any razors, and even after a thorough clean-up I could hardly recognize my own features in the glass. My rather long face was rounded by the beginnings of quite a healthy-looking beard. My eyes were sunken and red-rimmed. In fact, I looked a proper ruffian. I said so to Logan. 'That's nothing,' he replied with a bitter laugh. 'You wait till these bastards have been at you for a week. If the naval authorities here had control of the prisoners it wouldn't be so bad. But you're in the hands of the Gestapo. We're going to have a helluva time.'

He was right, of course – I knew that. But I felt he might have been a little more optimistic. As soon as we had completed our toilet, we were marched off to the guard-room, where we were introduced to another Gestapo agent who was presumably on the day turn. He was a little man with a large head and a sharp face. I liked him no better than the first. He picked up a green-coloured form from his desk, glanced through it and then led us down a narrow gallery that led off the guard-room and into the office of the commandant of the base. This was Commodore Thepe. He was a short thick-set man with greying hair and a fine head. He impressed me quite favourably and I recalled Big Logan's words in the washroom.

The Gestapo man conferred with the commodore for a time in low tones while we stood between our guards at the door. At length the commodore ordered us to approach his desk. 'You know the Cornish coast – is that so?' he asked Logan. He had a quiet precise way of speaking, but his English was not as good as that of the U-boat commander.

Logan nodded, but said nothing.

'We are in possession of charts detailing all coastal information,' he went on. 'We have not, on the contrary, the fullest information about the rock formation and currents close in to the shore. This we require and you can give it to us, yes?'

Logan shook his head slowly. He had a puzzled look, rather like a dog that has been refused a bone. 'I don't know,' he said.

'You don't know? Why?' The commodore glanced at the form before him and then at Logan. 'You are a fisherman, yes?'

Logan was still looking puzzled. 'Yes,' he said hesitantly. 'I believe so – I don't know.' I glanced at him, wondering what had come over him. I thought at first he was playing some deep game. But he had his hand to his head and he was rubbing his eyes as though he had just been woken from a deep sleep.

The commodore looked at him closely. 'You are a prisoner. You understand that?'

Logan nodded. 'Yes, your honour.'

'As a prisoner you must answer questions.' The commodore spoke kindly as though to a child.

'Yes.'

'Then come over here.' The commodore led him over to a glass-topped cabinet in the corner. Beneath the glass was a chart. He slid this out and replaced it with one of the west Cornish coast from the files which filled the cabinet. 'Here is Cadgwith,' said the commodore, indicating a point on the map with his finger. 'Now are all the submerged rocks charted?'

Logan did not answer, but just stood staring at the chart in a dazed kind of way.

'Are they or are they not?' demanded the commodore, getting impatient.

'They may be,' murmured Logan, lapsing into the slurred syllables of the Cornish dialect.

'Answer the Commodore's question,' ordered the Gestapo man, coming up behind Logan. He had a sharp penetrating voice and spoke English fluently.

Logan looked round furtively, like a trapped beast. 'I can't,' he said. And for a moment I thought he was going to burst into tears, his face was so puckered.

'Explain yourself,' snapped the Gestapo man.

'I – I just can't. That's all. I don't remember.' And Logan suddenly turned and went blindly towards the door like a child in a panic. His breath was coming in great sobs as he passed me and I could see the tears running down into his beard. To see a grown man crying is always rather pitiful. But to see Logan crying was so unexpected that it shocked me profoundly.

The guards turned him back and for a moment he staggered round in a circle. Then he stood still, his face buried in his hands. His sobs gradually lessened.

I saw that both the commodore and the Gestapo agent were puzzled. Well they might be. I was puzzled enough myself. They talked together for a moment in low tones, and then the commodore turned to Logan and said, 'Come here.'

Logan approached the desk at which the commodore had resumed his seat. When he had reached it the commodore said not unkindly, 'I fear you have had an uncomfortable time on the submarine. I am sorry. But this information I require urgently. Either you take hold of yourself or else we shall be forced to make you talk. Is that chart correct for your area?'

Logan's great fist descended with a crash on the desk. 'Don't keep asking me questions,' he roared, and his voice was almost unrecognizable it was so high-pitched and hysterical. 'Can't you see I don't remember. I don't remember anything. My mind is blank. It's horrible.'

I don't think I have ever seen two men more surprised than those Germans. Until that moment I think they had regarded Logan as either a half-wit or a prisoner bent on playing them up.

Logan looked at them with what can only be described as compassion. There was something extraordinarily animal-like about him. 'I'm sorry,' he said. 'I have frightened you. I didn't mean to. It was just – just that I didn't remember anything. I was afraid.' His hands fluttering uncertainly, were surprisingly expressive.

The commodore glanced at me then. 'What is the matter with your friend?' he asked.

I had to admit that I did not know. 'He seemed all right in the submarine,' I said. 'But last night he became rather morose.' Then suddenly I remembered. 'When we were captured,' I said, 'he was clubbed with the butt of a revolver. That may be the trouble. Later, in the submarine, he got a bit excited.'

The commodore pondered this information for a moment. Then he ordered one of the guard to go and fetch the U-boat commander and the doctor.

The doctor was the first to arrive. He examined Logan's head and reported that, though the scalp was cut and rather swollen, there were no signs of any fracture. Whether or not Logan was suffering from concussion he would not say. He thought it unlikely, but pointed out that it was impossible to be sure.

The U-boat commander, when he arrived, testified to the fact that Logan had had a severe blow from the butt end of a revolver and to the fact that, though he had seemed to have all his wits about him when in the submarine, he had at the same time behaved as though he were a little unbalanced. He explained how Logan had roared with laughter when he had been asked for information that would have saved the U-boat from disaster, but he made no mention of that part of the episode in which he had been knocked down.

In the end, we were returned to our cell. As we went out I heard the commodore giving instructions to the doctor to keep an eye on Logan. As soon as we were alone I said, 'Look here, Logan, are you playing them up or are you really ill?'

He looked at me apathetically.

'Is this some deep game you're playing?' I persisted.

'Would you call it a game if your mind were a complete blank and you were fighting all the time to remember things?' he asked.

Even then I could not believe that he had really lost his memory. 'You seemed all right this morning,' I said.

'Maybe,' he said, as he lay down on his bed. 'It wasn't until they began questioning me that I realized what had happened.'

But it was not until I had seen him refuse his lunch, his tea and his supper that I really began to regard the matter as serious. Throughout the day he lay on his bed, mostly with his head buried in his arms. Sometimes he groaned as though the effort of trying to remember something were too great. Once or twice he suddenly started to beat the pillow in a frenzy of frustration.

When he refused his supper I asked the guard to leave it with me. Bit by bit I coaxed him to eat it. It was like getting a sick child to eat. When the guard came in for the tray I asked if he could fetch the doctor. He understood the word 'doctor.' By that time I was really worried.

About half an hour later the doctor arrived. Logan was lying face downwards on the bed. But he was not asleep. I explained that I was worried because he had refused his food and seemed so abjectly unhappy. Fortunately the doctor understood English, though he could not speak it very well, so that I was still able to keep up my pretence of not being able to speak German. When I had explained, he told me not to worry. He pointed out that it was quite natural for a man who had lost his memory to be unhappy. 'Would you not veel onhappy?' He spoke very broken English and often had to pause for a word. 'He ees among strangers – a preesoner. He fears what will 'appen to 'im. And 'e cannot remember what 'e was before. He can remember nothing. Eet ees very sad. You must 'elp 'im. Tell 'im about 'is home, 'is village – perhaps 'e remember later, yes?'

He gave me two sleeping tablets to give Logan in some cocoa he would have sent down. I thanked him. He was a kindly man. As he left he pulled a packet of cigarettes from the pocket of his mess jacket. 'These may 'elp,' he said. The packet was nearly full.

Later two steaming cups of very excellent-smelling cocoa arrived. As the man who had brought it placed it on the floor between our beds the guard outside sprang to attention. A tall slim rather elegant man appeared at the entrance to our cell. He was quite obviously a member of the Prussian officer class, the type that would have worn a monocle in the days of the Kaiser. 'What's this?' he barked in German, indicating the cups of cocoa.

The man who had brought them explained that the doctor had ordered them to be sent down to the prisoners. He dismissed the man and turned his attention to us. 'Stand up!' He spoke a thick guttural English. I got to my feet. But Logan remained lying full length on the bed. 'Stand up, do you hear!' he thundered. Then, as Logan made no move, he drew the bayonet of the guard standing beside him and stepping deliberately on to the tray containing the cups of cocoa, dug the point of the bayonet sharply into Logan's buttocks. I saw the pleasure that act gave him mirrored in his little grey eyes.

Logan jumped to his feet with a cry. I feared for a moment that he would strike the man, and I could see by the look on the other man's face that he was hoping he would. Then as Logan stood sullenly in front of him, he said, 'So you have lost your memory?' There was no attempt to veil the sneer.

Logan said nothing. He looked very unhappy.

'Well, we'll soon get it back for you,' the other continued. 'Tomorrow you'll go to work – both of you. We'll soon sweat this insolence out of you.'

I said, 'The man is ill.'

He swung round on me. 'Speak when you're spoken to.' He turned to the man who had accompanied him. It was the little Gestapo agent who had taken us in to see the commodore that morning. 'Put them to work on the hull of U 39 tomorrow,' he said in German. As he moved to go, he turned to me and said, 'I should advise you to see that your friend finds his memory.'

I said nothing, but my eyes fell to the two cups of cocoa now lying on their sides, the cocoa still steaming as it mingled with the water on the floor. I knew it was no use asking for more. The grill clanged to.

'Who was he?' asked Logan dully.

'Senior agent for the Gestapo at the base, I should imagine,' I said.

'What is the Gestapo?' he asked.

I was puzzled. 'You understood what the Gestapo was earlier today,' I said. But there is no accounting for the effect of loss of memory upon a man's brain. 'Never mind,' I said. 'The doctor has given me two sleeping tablets for you. They'll help you to remember things. Don't worry about the Gestapo.' I got him to lie down again and then I collected a sufficiency of water in the least broken of the two cups from a little trickle that ran down the wall at the head of my bed. I crushed the tablets into this and gave it to him. He drank it without question like a child. 'The doctor gave us something else, too,' I said, and showed him the packet of cigarettes. I gave him one and he smiled happily. Then I found that we had no matches. Our clothes had been taken from us together with all the possessions in their pockets, and we had been issued with a pair of coarse dungarees each.

I went to the grill and attracted the attention of the guard. I indicated by signs that I wanted a match. There were two men on guard and they both shook their heads. 'Verboten,' said one. I nodded, but pointed to my companion. 'He is ill,' I said. 'It would help him.' They did not speak English, but they seemed to understand, for after glancing hurriedly up and down the gallery one of them passed me a box of Swedish matches with the drawing of a sailing ship on it through the bars.

I lit our cigarettes. As I passed the matches back to the guard I asked who the officer was. He understood the word 'officer.' 'Herr Fulke?' he asked. 'Er ist in der Geheimen Staatspolizei.' Having said this he turned away. He did not wish to talk. I went back and got into bed. I smoked my cigarette slowly and with great relish and watched a tiny fresh-water shrimp slip slowly down the wall in a little rivulet of water. The guard was changed at nine. By that time Logan was fast asleep. I tucked the bedclothes round him and went back to my own bed, drawing the blankets right over my head in order to keep out the light. It was a long time before I could get to sleep. I was not accustomed to sleeping in my clothes and I found the rough blankets very irritating to the skin of my neck. They had a peculiar stuffy smell similar to British army blankets and took me back to my schooldays and camp.

And as I lay there listening to the sounds of footsteps and voices from the galleries above, made hollow by the echo and barely distinguishable above the incessant hum of the dynamos, I felt more miserable than I think I had ever felt before. I had that lost feeling that one has as a new boy in a big school. Had Logan been all right, I think I should have been able to keep my spirits up.

But in his present state he only contributed to my dejection. It was not only a question of loss of memory. It seemed to me that his brain had been rendered defective. He had become so childlike that I felt responsible for him, and I was fearful of what the Gestapo might do to him if they were not quickly convinced that he was really ill. I was under no delusion as to the sympathy he might expect from these men. I had spoken to too many who had suffered agonies in German concentration camps to be in any doubt as to what we might expect. The only consolation was that neither of us looked in the least like Jews.

The next day we were woken at six and set to work on the hull of U 39, which stood up, stained and dirty, like a stranded fish in the empty dock. I gathered from the conversation of the men working with us that she had docked the night before our own boat after a cruise on the north Atlantic trade routes. This accounted for the fact that her hull was coated thick with sea grass. Our job was to scrape it clean.

Our guard had been changed at three in the morning. It was changed again at nine. The petty officer of this guard was a real slave driver. To give him his due he had probably received instructions to see that we worked at full pressure all the time, but by the way he watched us and yelled at us as soon as we slowed down I knew he enjoyed the job.

Logan seemed to like the work. Perhaps it took his thoughts off the blankness of his mind. At any rate he went steadily forward with the work, never flagging and doing about ten square feet to my four. My muscles were soft with years of sedentary work and I quickly tired. By eleven the guard was making use of a bayonet to keep me at it. But the stab of the point in my buttocks was as nothing to the ache in my arms and back. We were allowed a twenty minutes break for lunch at twelve. Then we had to set to again. The sweat streamed off me and my arms got so tired that I could hardly raise them and at the same time hold the scraper in my shaking fingers.

Sheer dogged determination, induced I think more by a desire not to make myself conspicuous rather than by fear, kept me going. But about two hours after lunch I blacked out. Fortunately I was only standing on the lower rungs of the ladder and the fall did not injure me. I came to with an unpleasant sensation of pain in my ribs. I looked up. The hull of the U-boat bulged over me, whilst very far away, it seemed, the petty officer was telling me to get up and at the same time kicking me in the ribs.

Then Logan's huge body came into my line of sight. He

stepped down off his ladder and with quiet deliberation knocked the petty officer flying with a terrific punch to the jaw. Then, before the guard had time to do anything, he had climbed back on to his ladder and resumed his work.

I scrambled painfully to my feet. The guard was looking bewildered. Quite a number of men had witnessed the affair and they were making humorous comments to the guard. 'Why don't you call the police?' asked one, and there was a howl of laughter. There was no doubt that Logan had made something of a hit with the men. From their tone I gathered that the petty officer was not popular.

As the petty officer remained quite motionless where the force of Logan's blow had flung him, one of the guards at length announced that he was going for the doctor. Logan continued with his work as if nothing had happened. It was not that he was trying to pretend that he had nothing to do with the business. He seemed completely oblivious to the fact that he had knocked a German petty officer cold. A crowd had gathered on the dockside above us. Everyone seemed to be talking at once and the sound merged into a low roar that almost drowned the roar of machinery. Men were attracted from other docks, and I could see that the crowd was growing every minute because the ones in front had to strain backwards in order to avoid being pushed over the edge of the dock. Some of them had jumped on to the submarine itself in order to see what was happening.

Nobody seemed to think of going to the assistance of the petty officer, so I went over to where he lay crumpled up against the side of the dock in a pool of water. His clothes were already wet through. I felt his heart, fearful that Logan might have killed him. But it was beating faintly and there seemed nothing the matter with him except for the punch on the jaw he had received. In falling against the side of the dock his head seemed to have been protected by his upflung arm.

I made him as comfortable as I could, and by that time the guard had returned with the doctor. The electric arc lights glinted on his pince-nez as he climbed down the steel ladder into the dock.

His examination of the man was brief. 'He's all right,' he said in German, and ordered two men to take him to his bunk. As the petty officer was hauled up to the top of the dock, the doctor turned to me. 'Vat 'appened?' he demanded. I told him. He nodded. 'Your friend vill be in troble,' he said.

A sudden hush fell over the men on the dockside. I looked up.

The Gestapo man – Fulke – had arrived. Like shadows the men seemed to melt away. He descended to the bottom of the dock. 'I hear that man – ' he indicated Logan – 'has knocked down an officer of the guard. Is that right?' He spoke in German, and there was a kind of eagerness in his eyes that it was impossible to mistake. The man was a sadist.

'That is true,' the doctor replied. 'But he did it because – '

'The reason does not interest me,' snapped Fulke. He turned to the guard. 'Take that man to the guardroom. Strap him to the triangle. I'll teach prisoners to knock down officers of the Fuehrer's navy. Get Lodermann. He is to use the steel-cored whip. I will be along in a few minutes. And take this man with you.' He nodded in my direction. 'It will doubtless be instructive for him to see how we maintain discipline.'

The guard saluted and turned away, at the same time indicating that I was to follow him. They took Big Logan from his work and marched him along the dock gallery and up the ramp to the guard-room. I went with them, a horrible empty sickness in the pit of my stomach. Behind me, as I left the dock, I heard the doctor saying, 'You're not going to have that man flogged with a steel-cored whip, surely? He's not well, mentally? Anyway, his action was not unjustified.' There followed a sharp altercation between the two, but I was by then too far away to hear what was said. In that moment I was thankful to know that there was one man in the place with some human understanding.

But I knew it was useless to expect that he would be able to prevent the flogging. The Gestapo's commands were law, and I was convinced that his man Fulke wanted to see Logan flogged. I had heard tales from refugees of floggings in concentration camps with this same steel-cored whip. It cut a man's back to ribbons and he seldom survived the full number of strokes to which he was sentenced. Something seemed to cry out with agony inside me. As I watched them strip Big Logan and tie him to the heavy iron triangle in the guard-room, I think I went through almost as much mental agony as Logan would go through physical agony later. I felt entirely responsible for what had happened, and it was pitiful to see Logan's docility. He did not seem to understand what was happening. Stripped, his terrific physique was even more evident. I felt that if he cared to let himself go, he could have killed every member of the guard with his bare hands, and I longed to call out to him to do so. But what was the use?

A big powerful seaman had taken the steel-cored whip from an oblong box. He had removed his coat and rolled up his sleeves.

65

The bristles on the back of his thick neck gleamed in the electric light. He adjusted the position of the triangle so that the whip, which was short and knotted, would not catch the walls. The guard had been augmented to six men. The little Gestapo man whom we had first met had taken control. There was a deathly stillness in the room as the man with the whip made his dispositions. The clock on the wall ticked monotonously on as we waited for Fulke.

At length he arrived. 'Close the door!' he ordered. Then he crossed the room and took up a position on the other side of the triangle. His narrow face shone with sweat and his eyes had a glassy stare. 'Why did you strike an officer of the guard?' he asked in English.

Logan made no reply. It was as though he had not heard.

Fulke's hand shot out and he slapped Logan across the face. He did it with the back of his hand, so that a gold ring set with diamonds which he wore on his right hand scored Logan's cheek. 'Answer me, you dog!' he shouted.

Logan's face remained completely vacant.

'Geben Sie ihm eins mit der Peitsche, das wird ihn aufwecken,' he ordered.

The seaman measured his distance. Involuntarily I closed my eyes. The steel-cored thongs sang through the air and cracked down with a thud. Three red lines immediately showed on Logan's brown back. They broadened and merged together into trickles of blood that ran down his hairy buttocks.

'Now will you answer me? Why did you hit the officer of the guard?'

Still Logan made no reply. In sickening anticipation I waited for the order to give the next stroke. But at that moment the door of the guard-room opened and the commodore came in, accompanied by the doctor.

'Who gave the order for this man to be flogged?' demanded the commodore. There was an ominous ring in his voice that no one could mistake. A sudden feeling of excitement gripped me.

'I did,' replied Fulke, stepping forward to meet the other. 'Do you challenge it?' There was a veiled sneer in the way he put the question. He seemed very sure of his ground.

The commodore's only answer was to order the guard to release Logan from the triangle. Fulke advanced a step. For a moment I thought he was going to hit the commodore. A vein on his temple was throbbing violently. 'He has struck the officer of his guard,' he said. 'He is to be flogged. Order and discipline are

66

to be preserved in this base. Heil Hitler!' He raised his right hand.

The commodore seemed quite unmoved by this display. He did not answer the Nazi salute. 'I am in command here.' He spoke quietly but firmly. Then to the guard, 'Take that man down.'

'My instructions are that this man be flogged,' Fulke almost shrieked.

The commodore ignored him. 'Take that man down,' he thundered, as the guard hesitated. At that the men jumped to it. In an instant Logan had been released from the triangle.

'You exceed yourself, Herr Commodore.' Fulke was almost beside himself with rage. 'That man is to be flogged. If you persist in your attitude my next report will be most unfavourable. You know what that means?'

The commodore turned and faced Fulke. He was completely unruffled. 'You forget, Herr Fulke – we are now at war,' he said. 'For three months you have bounced around this base, over-riding my orders, undermining the morale of my men by your schoolboy ideas of discipline. This is the submarine service, not a Jewish concentration camp. For three months I have borne with you because you had the power to hinder my work. Now we are at war. We have work to do – men's work. No reports, except my own will leave this base.'

'You will regret your attitude, Herr Commodore,' snarled Fulke.

'I think not.'

'I'll have you removed from your post. I'll have you discharged the service. You will be sent to a concentration camp. I will see to it that – '

'You will not have the opportunity. In any case, Herr Fulke, you must realize that men with long experience in the services are indispensable in wartime. On the other hand, the Gestapo is not indispensable. For instance, I cannot think of one useful thing that you can do. Doubtless we can teach you to cook. You will report on board U 24 which leaves for the Canary Islands tomorrow. You will replace their cook, who is ill.'

Fulke's hand went to his revolver. The commodore did not hesitate. His fist shot out and laid the Gestapo agent out with a lovely right to the jaw. I do not know how old the commodore was – at least fifty I should have said – but there was plenty of force behind that punch. His hand was raw after it, where the skin had split at the knuckles. 'Guard! Arrest that man!' he ordered. The two nearest men jumped forward. He turned to the other Gestapo agent. 'You are under arrest, Herr Strasser. Disarm him!'

When both men were disarmed, he turned to his orderly. 'Fetch Commander Brisek here! You'll find him in the mess.'

The orderly disappeared. The commodore rubbed his knuckles gently. There was the beginning of a smile on his ruddy face. 'I don't know when I've enjoyed myself so much,' I heard him whisper to the doctor. Aloud he said to the doctor, 'You'll look after the prisoner?' He indicated Logan. 'Have them both transferred to quarters on the other side of this gallery.' He stroked his chin gently, and there was a twinkle in his eye. 'I think we might put Fulke and his friends in the wet cells that he insisted on having constructed. I wonder how they'll take to the U-boat service – do you think they'll be frightened?'

'I have an idea they will,' replied the doctor with no attempt to conceal his smile. 'What I know of psychology prompts me to the view that Fulke at any rate will be very frightened.'

The commodore nodded. 'I will give Varndt instructions to stand no nonsense.'

The door swung open and a naval officer entered followed by the orderly.

'Ah, Heinrich, I have a little commission for you which I think you will enjoy. I have placed these men' – he indicated the two Gestapo agents – 'under protective arrest. Take a guard and arrest the other two.'

'Very good, Herr Commodore.' Commander Brisek marched out with three men of the guard.

The commodore turned and went out of the room, followed by his orderly. The doctor went over to Logan and took him by the arm. As he led him towards the door, he nodded to me. I followed him. He took us to a small but comfortable little cell on the other side of the gallery, almost directly opposite the door of the guard room. He sent a man for his bag and in a very short while he was easing the pain of the cuts on Logan's back. Almost immediately afterwards our evening meal was brought to us. It was six o'clock.

When the doctor had finished and had left us, I said to Logan, 'Well, thank God for that! I didn't think it would end as comfortably as this. How are you feeling?'

'My back is bloody painful,' he said.

'I'm sorry,' I said. 'But you're lucky to get away with nothing worse.' I felt this was ungracious so I said, 'Many thanks for doing what you did. I owe it to you that my ribs are still intact. But it was a dangerous thing to do.'

'Ar,' he said, 'but it was a real pleasure.'

I looked at him closely. His eyes were shut and he was grinning happily. There was something very Irish and a little unbalanced about him. I said, 'Well, for God's sake leave me to get out of my own scrapes. If you knock any more officers out you'll be for it.'

'Is that why they were going to whip me?'

'Of course. What did you think?'

'I don't know,' he said. 'I thought it might be their idea of fun.' He turned over so that he was facing the wall. 'Good-night,' he said.

I stared at him. He just did not seem to grasp things. The old alertness was gone. He seemed dull and slow-witted. I put the light out and climbed into my bed. 'Good-night,' I said.

The warmth of the cell and the darkness were wonderfully comforting after the wet cells in the dock gallery. But even so I found it difficult to get to sleep. My brain was too full of thoughts to be still. The fantastic events of the last few hours ran through and through my mind. I had keyed myself up to see Logan whipped to death before my eyes for something that he had done for me. Miraculously he had been saved from that and now he did not seem to realize what had happened. It was pitiful. But gradually the relief of the changed circumstances – no cold damp cell – no Gestapo – lulled me into a state of coma. I kept on seeing Fulke's face, shiny with sweat, as he realized what the commodore's words meant, the loose twist of his normally set lips, his sudden dive for the revolver. In how many sections of the German war machine were service men suddenly throwing off the yoke of the Gestapo? I had seen the relish in the commodore's eyes as he had hit Fulke. Then his words to the doctor – 'I don't know when I have enjoyed myself so much.' If the services felt like this towards the watchdogs of the Nazi Party, how did the German people feel? Was there hope in this for a short war, or merely food for thought? Questions, questions, questions – but no answers.

4

U-BOAT BASE

It was breakfast at seven next morning and then we were set to work on the hull of U 39 again. Logan worked stripped to the waist because his clothes rubbed against the wounds on his back. But though he moved rather stiffly, he worked with the same methodical speed that he had done on the previous day. My own muscles soon lost their stiffness, and I found the work required less effort.

So morning ran into evening and evening into morning again with only the routine of the place to distinguish night from day. We worked a ten-hour day, from seven-thirty in the morning until six in the evening with a half-hour break for lunch. Hull scraping only occurred when a submarine came in from a lengthy cruise. If it were a rush job a whole party of ratings was put on to it with us and it only took a few hours. Otherwise, we had the work to ourselves and it took nearly two days. When there was no hull scraping, we worked in the canteen, washing up, peeling potatoes. Sometimes, when a submarine was due to go out we had to help carry provisions from the store-rooms and load them on to the submarine. Every morning, whatever else we had to do, we cleaned out the latrines, which were of the bucket type.

Now that we were no longer under the control of the Gestapo we had less supervision. So long as we did our job and kept to the times laid down for us, chief of which were to rise at seven in the morning and return to our cell at seven in the evening, there was little fear of trouble. But we remained under a guard. The officer of the day was responsible for us. He was in charge of fatigue parties. Fatigue parties were provided as required by the sub-marines in the base, so many men being detailed from each boat. No man went on fatigue more than once until every other rating from his own boat had also done his turn. The whole point of the base, so far as the crews of the U-boats were concerned, was to provide the maximum relaxation – a thing that was very difficult to achieve in view of the cramped quarters which were really very little different from quarters in a U-boat. The main trouble, of course, was that the men never saw the light of day in the base. It was all underground, and, with the constant sound of machinery and the queer echoes, the place was apt to get on men's nerves.

These fatigue parties worked on more or less the same basis as we did, though they were free to do what they liked when they came off duty at six. Like ourselves, however, they had to hold themselves ready for duty when a submarine was coming into the base or leaving it. This meant that the fatigue parties were often called out in the middle of the night as it was only during the hours of darkness that the boats could get in or out of the base.

Thus it was that I was present when U 24 left the base. This gave me great joy for it enabled me to watch Fulke's arrival in charge of two guards. Until then I do not think I had ever seen real panic in a man's eyes. He was struggling like a madman and I was certain he would prove quite useless as a cook and be an infernal nuisance to every one on board. The crew lined up to watch him come on board and there were broad grins on their faces. It was plain that the men of the German submarine service had no use for the Gestapo. It is not altogether surprising. Fulke demanded complete and absolute obedience to every petty and arbitrary rule he made. This may be all right in the army and possibly in the big ship navy, but it does not work in submarines.

The submarine service is probably much the same in all countries. It differs from every other branch of the services because of its danger. It is not a question of tradition or the honour of the service. To be of the service is in itself to be a hero. And a hero is above discipline. Throughout the service stress is laid on efficiency – nothing else. It is a question of existence. Each man has in his hands the fate of the whole ship. In these circumstances discipline is automatic. But when they return to base, especially a base like this, the crews want to relax, not to be pestered by petty disciplinary regulations.

And so Fulke was given a warm welcome by the crew of U 24. I don't know what the man had originally been. Some thought he was one of the Munich Putsch crowd. I doubt it. But at any rate, he had apparently been with the Party since 1933 and had wielded for a sufficient length of time the power of life and death to have become completely callous to his victims' feelings. And now he was scared. I heard one man on the dockside say that he had been in the submarine that had brought Fulke to the base. 'He looked pretty scared then,' he said. 'And he'd been drinking heavily before he came on board. He's a coward – no doubt of that.' And he spat. Then in a whisper he added, 'I wouldn't wonder if most of the Gestapo aren't afraid as soon as they get the wrong end of the lash.'

Perhaps they did Fulke an injustice. Perhaps he had second sight. At any rate, U 24 was sunk by a seaplane in the Bay of Biscay two days later.

Before U 24 went out the commodore walked down with her commander, Varndt. Whatever time of the night a submarine left he always accompanied the commander to his boat. It was a ritual. I saw Varndt's face as he went on board. It was set, but cheerful. Before descending the conning tower, he saluted, then waved his hand. They were all the same, these U-boat commanders – their men, too, for that matter. Most of them were young. They knew what they faced. The chances of death at that time were only two-to-one against every time they went out. The odds were short enough. They had responsibilities thrust upon them at which much older men would have blenched in peace-time. Yet they accepted these responsibilities and the danger without question, and with set faces and sublime cheerfulness went out to almost certain death.

Before I had been in the base more than a few days my admiration for the German submarine service was immense. And I was filled with a great sense of depression. These men were mostly young. They faced death and accepted their responsibilities without question. They were the pick of Germany's seamen. And they were being thrown away to fulfil the destinies of a man whose boundless ambition spelt ruin for his country, himself and half the civilized world. More, they were given orders the execution of which brought universal opprobrium upon them and their Service. In the first days of the war, it was in fact for German youth that my soul cried out against that fanatic, who had diagnosed his country's and the world's disease correctly, yet attempted a cure that had been tried before and had been found only to increase the suffering of the masses.

As far as Logan and I were concerned life was not unpleasant. We worked hard, it is true, and the air was not too good despite a system of ventilation. But in the evenings, when we retired to our own quarters, there were German magazines to read. There was a plentiful supply of these available and I would surreptitiously read stories to Logan. He enjoyed this, but though I talked to him endlessly of Cadgwith and South Cornwall, his mind seemed quite blank. He had loved the place. It had been, I think, his only permanent love. Yet he showed no interest in it and never at any time asked me to tell him about it or describe it to him in greater detail. Much of his time he spent fashioning pieces of wood into models of boats with an ordinary table knife. I suppose it was some sort of subconscious manifestation of the life he could no longer remember. No one seemed to object. In fact the doctor encouraged it. He said he thought it might help him to remember. Sometimes Logan would spend hours carving his name on the wooden legs of his camp-bed as though he were afraid of forgetting that, too.

As time went on, we were allowed to mix more and more freely with the men. They took to Logan very quickly. They made fun of him, but he did not seem to mind. His great bulk and terrific strength seemed to fascinate them. And as it became quite obvious that he was not only rather simple, but also quite harmless, they

would take him into the mess of an evening and stand him drinks
and put him through his tricks. His tricks were largely a matter of
strength. He could lift two average size sailors up on to the bar by
the seat of their pants. This, and the fact that a very few drinks
now seemed to go to his head and make him fuddled and rather
amusing, made him popular. Big Logan had become something of
a buffoon, and I found the spectacle somehow rather revolting.

Meanwhile, I learned my way about the base. Generally
speaking, we had the freedom of the three galleries, but not the
docks nor the repair and munition depots. There were grave
penalties for entering these other than when ordered to do so.
Nevertheless, in the course of my duties I eventually penetrated to
even the most remote sections of the base, and gradually I was
able to build up a plan of the place in my mind's eye. When I had
a complete picture of it clear in my mind, I made a rough plan,
and this, with a few comments added later, I have reproduced.

I have always credited the Germans with a greater eye for
detail than any other race. But it was not until I had a working
knowledge of that U-boat base that I fully understood what the
thoroughness of the German mind meant. It was incredible. Later
I was to learn that it had taken two years to build and had cost the
equivalent of about £5,000,000. Moreover, all equipment, or the
raw materials to manufacture the equipment on the spot, had
been brought into the base by a submersible barge. I have already
explained the dock sections, the long cave into which the submarines rose, the heavy haulage gear and the seven docks
radiating off from the slightly wider section of the main cave.

I should perhaps explain the haulage gear more thoroughly,
though here again I did not discover the details of its working
until later. First, no U-boat was allowed to enter the base in any
circumstances during the hours of daylight or in moonlight. The
haulage gear itself ran out through the underwater mouth of the
cave and round a pylon fixed to the bed of the sea about a
hundred yards or so off the shore. In suitable conditions, a glass
ball of a type used by fishermen for their nets was floated up from
the pylon. This ball was coated with mildly phosphorescent paint,
and was attached to the pylon by ordinary rope. This in turn was
connected electrically with the shore. Any sharp tug on the glass
ball – the buoyancy of the ball was not sufficient – started a
buzzer in the haulage gear control room. A submarine commander
desiring to enter the base had to give in morse by tugs on the ball
the number of his boat and his own name. If any unauthorized
person attempted to haul it up it was immediately released.

When a U-boat had given the correct signal, a small buoy was released in which there was a telephone. Communication was thus possible between the base and the incoming submarine. When required the main buoy was released, the submarine was coupled to it by a grappling hook at the bows and the U-boat then submerged. Care was necessary to submerge in the correct position, namely at right angles to the shore, or two points south of due west. The reason for this was that the submarine had to come to rest on an iron cradle which ran on a line laid from the cliffs out along the seabed. This, I understand, was the most difficult of all the tasks that confronted the German engineers. The sea-bed was mostly rock and rails were the only means of preventing the submarine being injured while being hauled into the base.

The base itself had three galleries. The first was at dock level. The wet cells were situated on this level. This gallery ran in a semi-circle round the ends of the submarine docks. Opposite each dock was a tunnel leading down into relatively large caves. These were the store-rooms. They were guarded by steel doors. At each end the gallery cut sharply back from the docks into really big caves strengthened by girders. In the cave near the ramp leading to the upper galleries were the dynamos run by diesel engines, and farther back a complete foundry with electric furnaces. And still farther in were the workshops where there were lathes and machine tools capable of producing every component of a submarine. The big cave at the other end of the curved gallery was a gigantic fuel and munition store. The fuel was in great tanks that resembled the tanks on petrol trucks. There were also stocks of copper, steel ingots, lead, zinc, manganese and other vital materials.

The upper two galleries ran straight, one on top of the other. These were the men's quarters. At a pinch there was accommodation for nearly seven hundred men. The personnel of the base itself numbered over a hundred, while most of the U-boats using the base were of the deep-sea type and had a crew of sixty or more.

These galleries were all cemented to avoid damp and leading off them were big food store-rooms.

The time required to complete the construction of this colossal undertaking and the huge quantities of material which would have had to be brought in through the under-sea entrance made me convinced that Logan's belief that we were on the north coast of Cornwall was incorrect. True, he had appeared to be all right when following the submarine's course with his compass, but in a mental case appearances were, I knew, often deceptive, and I was by no means sure that at that time his mental faculties were quite sound. My own belief was that the direction of the submarine's change of course had been southerly and not northerly, and that, in fact, the base was somewhere on the north Spanish coast.

Though I did not at that time know precisely how long it had taken to build the base. I knew that it must have been a considerable time. This tied up with the fact that the Spanish civil war began in July, 1936. Germany came into it from the start, and one of the reasons she did this was to obtain air and submarine bases in that country. The more I thought about it the more convinced I became that Logan had not been in a fit mental state to plot a course at the time U 34 was making for the base. And yet he was quite capable of thinking things out for himself. He could do a job of work as well and as thoroughly as any one. It was mainly in his conversation, or rather his lack of it, that he revealed his mental state. He very seldom spoke, and even when asked a direct question would as often as not reply with a non-committal, 'Ar!' I had two conversations with the doctor about him, and found him frankly puzzled. On each occasion, he stressed that he was not a mental specialist. 'I do not onderstand vat ees the matter vith him,' he said on the second occasion.

This depressed me and so did the atmosphere of the base, for as the days passed there was an almost imperceptible change in the spirit of the men. The reason for this was the score boards. At the end of each of the big canteens were large blackboards. On the left hand side were the numbers of all U-boats operating from the base. In all there were seventeen, their numbers ranging from 15 to 62. As and when opportunity offered the boats radioed their sinkings in code to the base. Such communication was often delayed owing to the necessity of surfacing and drying off the aerials before communication could be established. However, experience showed that in general boats reported at least every other day, and there was a standing order that they should endeavour to do this, if possible, in order that the commodore should be able to replace as early as possible boats stationed on particular trade routes which were believed lost.

Information regarding sinkings was chalked up on the boards opposite the number of the submarine responsible. Wherever possible the tonnage as well as the name of the ship was given. One of the first to be marked up was the *Athenia*. This was marked up the day before our arrival at the base. I did not see the boards

until after we had been at the base three days. But from the conversation of the men I gathered that they were very jubilant about
it. They were not so jubilant, however, when those who understood English and listened in to American broadcasts realized the
heavy loss of life and the tone of the American press. Moreover, the
attitude of the German High Command towards this sinking was
not encouraging. The base was notified of their attitude through
the English broadcasts. The base had no wireless transmitter and
there was no attempt to keep in direct wireless contact with
Germany. Moreover, the base had no separate wavelength for
receiving instructions from Germany. Instructions were given to
the base by way of an ingenious code worked into the broadcasts
in English. It was only by accident that I learned this – my
unrevealed knowledge of German was the cause. All communications to the base were included in announcements about
U-boats. How the code worked I do not know, but the idea of it
was clever, for no one would look for coded instructions in
German propaganda broadcasts.

Whenever the wireless-room orderly entered the canteen to
chalk up sinkings there was great excitement among the men at the
base, for quite heavy bets were constantly being made either on
the basis of the submarines with the greatest tonnage of sinkings or
on the basis of the number sunk. But by the end of the first week
four boats had not reported a sinking for three days. After ten
days, there were seven boats that had not reported for three days
or more. Moreover, four days after our arrival at the base, U 47
had come in with her after deck ripped open as a result of being
rammed. She was leaking badly and had eight men killed. Three
days later, on the Sunday that was, U 21 docked with her bridge
twisted to ribbons and her for'ard gun and both AA guns wrecked
– total killed, twelve, nine wounded. Including our own boat, U
34, there were three boats in for heavy repairs.

That was the reason for the change of atmosphere. I do not
believe that the German naval authorities had reckoned with
losses on this scale. Every man in the service knew that the losses
in modern warfare would be heavy. But seven in two weeks and
three badly damaged out of a total of seventeen, was something
that brought death very near to every U-boat man. On 14
September the boards were taken down. Every man in the base
knew what that meant. Losses were, in the official view, becoming
so heavy that they were likely to affect the morale of the men.

It was only then, I think, that I really understood how it was
possible for the commodore of the base to take such drastic action

against the Gestapo as Commodore Thepe had done. It could never have happened in Kiel or even at a base in the South Atlantic. What had made it possible here was the cramped quarters. The commodore had been thrown into too close contact with Fulke for over three months. Moreover, as in the removed-from-the-world atmosphere of a school, the commodore had come to regard the base as his whole world. Germany and the Gestapo were no longer real to him.

Throughout the day following the removal of the score boards the whole base radiated an atmosphere of tension. And just before U 41 went out, shortly after midnight, I thought the men would refuse to go. They came down to the dock looking haggard and dejected, and some of them seemed definitely mutinous. Once fear gets hold of a man there is no buoyancy in him. But the commander was a tough little bow-legged man, and he came down as cheery as I've ever seen a man who was going to his death. He came down with the commodore full of jokes about what he'd do when he met the British Atlantic fleet. The crew went aboard all grins. A week later U 41 was rammed and sunk by a British destroyer convoying a fleet of tankers from the Gulf of Mexico.

U 41 was the last boat to leave the base for some time. Thereafter, boats were laid up as they came in and the crews told to take a rest. By that I knew some big operation was pending and I remembered the paper that the commander of U 34 had given Logan. The date for the meeting of those units of the British fleet was 18 September. It was now 14 September. We had three days in which to do something.

This sounds rather as though I had only just remembered this aspect of the affair. That is not strictly true. It had loomed in the back of my mind as something which had to be faced sooner or later. I had certainly not forgotten about it. After all, it was the cause of our presence at the base. But the many little everyday problems of life as a prisoner and the life itself combined to drive it into the background. Only when I saw the U-boats being held back at the base and heard the vague rumours circulating of a big action pending, did I realize that the responsibility for endeavouring to prevent the loss of many British lives rested entirely on my shoulders.

It was up to me to think out some scheme whereby the U-boats could be prevented from leaving the base. And that brought me face to face with another problem – the sacrifice of my own life. I don't suppose I am any more of a coward than the average person.

After all, I had been willing to sacrifice my life when on board the U-boat. But it is one thing to accept the line of action decided upon by someone else and quite another to settle down in cold blood deliberately to plot one's own death. But this is what I had to do. I could not imagine any possibility that might achieve my purpose that would not mean my own death and Logan's.

I don't believe I slept at all that night. Interminable hours I lay there in the dark, thinking. I heard the guard changed at three. I was feeling tired but determined to think out a scheme. I wanted to talk the matter over with Logan, but he was snoring peacefully and anyway I was convinced that he would be quite incapable, in his present state, of assisting in the evolution of a workable scheme, and also I feared he might not be discreet. At the same time, I was certain I could count on his help – he did everything I told him like a child.

Not unnaturally my thoughts centred around high explosive, of which there was a big store in the base, if only one could get at it. There seemed, on the face of it, two possible schemes. One was the complete destruction of the base by detonating the munitions store. The other was the blocking of the entrance by means of some sort of explosive charge. Of the two I favoured the latter. It at least gave us a chance of escape, slender though it was. At the same time the submarines were left intact. At the back of my mind I think I had a vague picture of myself presenting the First Lord with half a dozen submarines as my contribution to Britain's war effort. It was the sort of grandiose fantastic vision that revolves in one's brain when one is on the verge of sleep.

I suppose I must have then slept, for the next thing I remember is being woken up by the guard. 'Fatigue!' We tumbled out of bed. I glanced at my watch. It was five o'clock. When we got down to the docks we found that it was the submersible barge that was coming in. It was the first time I had seen it. In appearance it looked like a small tramp steamer – the sort of coastal barges that you see carrying oil fuel up the Thames. She plied between Dublin and Lisbon, calling at the base on each journey and always arriving empty at these two ports. Her papers were faked, I suppose.

We were back in our cell again just before six. As I lay in bed I could hear the rattle of cups in the guard-room. They were always served with coffee at six. I lay awake, thinking. A depth charge would, of course, be the most satisfactory method of blocking the entrance to the base. But there were no depth charges available and anyway I didn't know how to handle them. Another idea was to fire the after torpedo of U 21 which was lying in No. 4 dock. This dock was the centre one of the seven and the submarine's stern would be facing straight down the main cave so that the torpedo would strike that part of the cave which was directly above the under-sea exit. Even if the fall was only slight, it would take a diver some time to clear it away for the cradle to run out smoothly on its rails. The rails themselves might even get bent and have to be relaid.

The only snag was that I knew nothing about torpedoes and felt certain that they were highly complicated. Moreover, the dock gates would have to be open and the submarine floating. At present she was sitting high and dry in a dock that had been emptied of water. There remained only the guns. The after six inch gun of U 21 was in working order. But I was not quite sure what impression a six inch shell would make on the rock. In addition, of course, I had not the faintest idea how it worked or how I could get hold of the ammunition. And then there was the question of my own guard.

The key grated in the lock of our door and a petty officer poked his head in. 'Aufstehen!' he said. I dressed myself quite automatically, ate my breakfast and started my daily chores with my mind full of the wildest and most fantastic schemes for getting control of the after gun of U 21. I now considered this the only practical means of achieving my aim of blocking the exit. It was now Friday, 15 September. The rendezvous was for 1.30 p.m. on Monday, 18 September. That meant that the U-boats would leave the base on Sunday night. Between now and Sunday evening I had got to find out how the gun worked and think out all the details of the plan. It was a horrible responsibility, and, because my mind was elsewhere, I was reprimanded several times for slacking.

Throughout the whole of the morning we did service as stevedores, unloading the store barge and piling cases of provisions on trolleys which were then dragged off to the various store-rooms of the base. Some went to the store-room opposite each dock to provision submarines. Others went to the stores in the upper galleries and were for consumption in the base. There were in all about fifty men working on the barge or busy storing the cargo in the various store-rooms.

After lunch, however, I had a bit of luck. We were taken to No. 4 dock where men were working with a mobile automatic drill. We were given shovels and a barrow with which to remove the debris. What was happening was that it had been found necessary to remove the for'ard gun of the U-boat *en bloc* from the deck so that the deck-plates, which had been buckled, could be renewed while the gun itself was repaired on the dockside by the workshop engineers. When we arrived, the gun had been unbolted from its mounting, but in order to sling it on to the dockside it was necessary to erect a derrick. One leg of the derrick could be braced against the opposite side of the dock, but it had been found necessary to drill holes to steady the two shorter legs on the dock itself.

The first little pocket took about ten minutes to drill. The granite was extremely hard and splinters kept on flying from the point of the drill. But the other one proved quite simple owing to a fault in the rock and to the appearance of a much softer strata. This, as soon as I began to shovel up the broken chunks, I found to be limestone. It was an interesting discovery for any one who studied geological formations. I looked at the stone closely. It was carboniferous limestone of the type that predominates in North Cornwall from Tintagel to Hartland Point. My immediate interest was in the fact that a fault of carboniferous limestone should occur in rock that was, as far as I had been able to see, entirely igneous. Igneous rock is the oldest of the pre-cambrian group, whereas limestone belongs to the palæozoic group, which occurred much later in the evolution of the world. It suggested that there must have been some movement of the granite formation long after it had been thrown up.

And then another thought occurred to me. Here was a fault of carboniferous limestone, a rock that covers practically the entire north of Cornwall. And the fault was in igneous rock which, though comparatively rare, certainly occurs in the mining districts of Cornwall. Perhaps Logan had been right after all. On the other hand, the north-west corner of Spain has much the same rock formations, with limestone and igneous rock in close proximity. Brittany also has a similar formation. I decided in the end that I was no further forward at all and having, as a matter of interest, traced the fault right back to the main gallery and into the store gallery opposite, widening all the way, I transferred my attention to the gun. Our two guards seemed quite content, after watching over our removal of the debris, to stay and see the gun manœuvred on to the dockside.

It was swung across by lengthening the long leg of the derrick, and as it was lowered on the ratchet chain it descended slowly on to the dockside only a few feet from me. I had ample opportunity to examine the weapon. But though I could understand the breech mechanism and guess at the handgear for sighting it, I did not see how the thing was fired and I certainly could not imagine how I was to get hold of the necessary shells. The magazine, I knew, was somewhere beneath the gun, but how the lift worked I did not know.

I suddenly remembered that Logan had been on a 'Q' ship in the last war. 'Do you know how these things work?' I asked.

He looked at me quickly. Then he frowned. 'I feel I should,' he said slowly. 'But I don't know.' He shook his head from side to side. He did not seem really interested.

It was up to me to learn for myself. I watched them dismantle the barrel, saw the breech opened and shut and the firing position altered by the handgear, but still I did not see how it was fired. However, if I did not discover the workings of the gun, at least I learned something from the conversation of the men who were working on it. The U 47, which had got so badly damaged by being rammed, had been patched up and was leaving for Germany by way of the Irish Sea and the Hebrides that night. This was only an operating base capable of keeping submarines supplied and effecting light repairs. U 47 had apparently taken such a beating that the engineers considered that nothing short of a general overhaul and refit would make her properly seaworthy. So, patched as well as the base could do it, she was to make a bid for Kiel and the old Germania yard. Apparently she made it, for she was later, I heard, sunk in the South Atlantic. This left only four boats in the base. Among them was our own boat, U 34, now ready for sea again. Two more boats were apparently expected in that night. That made a submarine fleet of six boats, provided the U 21 were ready in time. It was not a pleasant prospect. If they got out it might mean the end of all four of the capital ships in the Atlantic squadron and possibly the loss of some of the Mediterranean squadron at the rendezvous.

At that moment there was a sudden shout of 'Wache!' Our two guards looked uncertainly at each other. The men at work on the gun paused and listened. The sound of heavy boots on rock echoed down the galleries. Men were running. More men joined them. Doors slammed. The call was repeated – 'Wache!' Then through the galleries rang the clamour of a bell. 'The emergency alarm!' exclaimed one of the engineers at the gun. And another said, 'Yes, that means action stations.' At that they all went running down the dockside and into the gallery at the end. One of our guards began to follow them. The other hesitated and shouted something, indicating us. Then the one who had been so anxious about us remained whilst the other dashed off to see what had happened.

It was the chance of a lifetime. I looked at Logan, but he seemed quite unconscious of anything unusual. Our guard was watching the gallery at the end of the dock rather than us and his senses were centred on the medley of sounds coming from the upper galleries in an effort to discover what had happened. I heard the ring of rifle butts against rock and rapid shouts of command. The tramp of feet began to resound through the base. I glanced at the guard. He was still watching the end of the dock. Slowly I began to edge away towards the gangway that led on to the submarine. I had almost made it when he caught sight of my movement out of the corner of his eyes and in the same instant his revolver was covering me. 'Ruhe!'

Was it just luck that Logan was now directly behind him? For one wild moment I thought that Logan was going to lay him out. Then the sound of feet marching in the gallery that ran past the end of our dock drew my eyes. A double file of ratings came marching on to the dock. Others marched on to the farther docks. The guard relaxed. The chance was gone.

The ratings were fully armed and under the command of their officers. They were the crew of U 21. Apparently as soon as the alarm sounds each man has to report with arms outside his quarters. They are then marched to the dock in which their submarine lies and there await instruction. Ten men in each submarine are attached to the base guard as emergency watch. These report to the guard-room immediately on the sounding of the alarm. It is their job to defend the base until the last U-boat has got clear. When all the boats are away, and that may be several hours because of the necessity of waiting for the tide to flood the docks, they have to destroy the base and any submarine that has not been in a fit condition to escape. Then, and then only, are they allowed to surrender. The chances of being alive after the destruction of several hundred tons of high explosive and a large quantity of fuel oil are, of course, not very great.

I could not help wondering at that time why it was necessary in an underground base of this type to have emergency regulations for its defence. Clearly, nothing could attack the base from the sea except by shelling the cliffs above the underwater entrance. It is possible that naval vessels might locate and sink submarines as they left the base, but the U-boats were attached to the buoy on the haulage gear by an automatic coupling that could be released without surfacing. The tricky surface work was only necessary on entering the base. In any case, there was a look-out, the entrance to which led off the cliff side of the upper gallery just near our own cell. This look-out made it possible for U-boat commanders to be notified of any craft in the vicinity when ready to go out.

Presumably, therefore, they feared an attack from the land. And if there were a way of getting into the base from the landward side, then there must be a way of getting out. The thought sent a thrill of hope through me. This sudden sense of exultation was followed almost immediately by a mood of complete and utter despair. What chance was there of discovering this bolt-hole of theirs, let alone escaping through it?

I was brought back to a sense of the immediate happenings by the arrival of our other guard. 'We are to take them to their cell,' he said. He was flushed with running and his words came in short gasps.

'What's happened?' demanded the one who had stayed with us.

'I don't know – nothing yet. The emergency alarm went in the guard-room a few minutes ago. Eight men were sent out to reconnoitre. Come on! We're to put these men in their cell and report to the guard-room. The emergency guard has been called out and every one is standing by.'

We were told to march. By this time the dockside was empty. The crew of U 21 had gone to their stations. The tide was at the high and I could hear the gurgle of water as the dock was flooded. The commander and his Number One were standing on the bridge. The boat was not ready for sea, yet they were prepared to take her out and risk it if necessary rather than leave her to be destroyed. It was the gesture of a proud service. As we marched down the gallery and climbed the ramp to the next level our two guards continued their conversation:

First Guard: 'Are we being attacked?'

Second Guard: 'I don't know.'

First Guard: 'Well, what are they doing about it? Who sounded the warning?'

Second Guard: 'They don't know yet. But they've sent out a reconnoitring party.'

First Guard: 'Maybe it's a false alarm.'

Second Guard: 'Maybe.'

First Guard: 'Suppose we're being attacked – what do we do?'

Second Guard: 'Who do you think I am – Commodore Thepe? I don't know.'

First Guard: 'Well, I do. We blow up the exit galleries and

then we're caught like rats in a trap. We're marines. We don't belong to the submarine service. But the only chance we'll have of getting out of this base will be by submarine – and the hell of a bloody chance that will be!'

As far as I was concerned the conversation ended there, for we were bundled into our cell and the key turned in the lock. I heard the clatter of the guards' boots as they went into the guard-room opposite. And then an unearthly stillness descended on the place. I had never heard it so silent. All the machinery, even the dynamos, had been stopped. I felt a sense of frustration. Something exciting was happening. Something that might vitally affect our lives. Yet here we were cooped up in a cell with no means of knowing what was taking place. It was complete anti-climax.

I glanced at Logan, who was sitting placidly on his bed. He was listening, too. He sensed I was watching him and he looked up at me. 'What's happening?' he asked. I said I didn't know. I began pacing the cell, but it was so small that I eventually sat down on my bed again. We sat there, listening to the silence, while quarter of an hour slipped by.

I began to imagine things. Somewhere at the back of the base were underground workings. Perhaps even now the guard was fighting an enemy whilst the U-boats slipped out of the base. It did not matter that it was daylight for the exit. How long would it be before they were all clear? Five boats and the barge – that might take between three and four hours. Then what? Would they destroy the base? The silence and my own enforced inactivity began to get on my nerves.

Then suddenly there were voices, the clang of a door and silence again. Ten more minutes passed, and then the sound of the guard-room door being opened and the scuffle of service boots running down the gallery. Within a few minutes came the murmur of many voices and the clatter of boots. Then the gentle soothing hum of the dynamos was resumed. Life at the base was normal again.

'I wonder what all that was about,' I said. I felt almost exhausted by my own curiosity. 'Perhaps it was a false alarm,' I suggested. 'Or just a test.'

Logan made no reply, but I could see him listening intently. I began to talk to him again and then stopped, realizing that it was pointless. I sat on my bed and waited, watching the minutes tick slowly by on my wrist-watch, which I had been allowed to keep. Shortly after four-thirty the grill opened and I just caught a glimpse of the nose and eyes of a man looking in at us before it clanged to again. Then there was the sound of boots on the rock outside and the door of the cell to the right of ours opened and then closed. I could hear the faint murmur of voices, but the rock walls were too thick to distinguish what language was being spoken. The cell door beyond closed with a bang and the grate of a key in the lock. Then the guard-room door slammed to and there was silence again.

Another quarter of an hour passed. Logan was getting more and more restive. Once he tried to pace up and down the cell as I had done, but it was too small for him and he resumed his seat on the bed. I was beginning now to think in terms of mutiny. After all it was not impossible. The men were by no means happy. I remembered the departure of U 41. The commander had only just saved the situation then. The only thing against the possibility of mutiny was the fact that the morale had been better during the past few days – in fact, ever since the word had gone round that something big was pending. It is inactivity more than fear that undermines morale, and now that they had something big to look forward to, I could not quite see a mutiny.

I had just arrived at this conclusion when there came a dull explosion that seemed to shake the very rock out of which the cell was hewn. It was followed almost immediately by a second. And then silence again. Both of us had automatically jumped to our feet. Were they scrapping the U-boats? The thought flashed through my mind. But I knew that it was out of the question. If they had blown up two of the boats the explosions would have been terrific, and they certainly hadn't exploded the munitions store. These explosions were muffled and far away. Perhaps the entrance to the base was being shelled from the sea.

The door of the guard-room opened, footsteps sounded and then the door of the cell to the left of us was opened. There was the murmur of voices. Then the door of the cell was closed and locked, and the footsteps returned once more to the guard-room. Silence again. The tension was making me over-wrought. I forced myself to sit down on the bed again, and I tried desperately to control my excitement. But I could not keep my hands still.

Logan had taken up his stand by the door. I looked up at him. He was standing quite still, his huge body leaning against the door. But for once his face seemed alive and I realized that he was listening. I strained my senses. I could hear nothing. Logan went over to his bed and set his ear to the wall. I did likewise, but I could hear nothing. I went back to my own bed. I found myself wondering how much more of this tension would break Logan's brain completely and transform him into a raving lunatic.

I picked up a magazine and began to read a story. But I could not concentrate. I kept on catching sight of Logan listening at the wall. At length I put the magazine down. 'Can you hear anything?' I asked.

'No, can you?'

As a conversation piece it was not brilliant. I gave it up and for the next five minutes my mind chased the story about the man who asked a lunatic who had his ear to the ground that same question. Someone knocked on the door. I looked up. Logan was standing there, beating a tattoo with his fist on it. Footsteps sounded in the gallery outside. He ceased. But as soon as the guard-room door had shut again, he resumed his knocking.

'Look, suppose I read you a story?' I suggested. I picked up the magazine again.

He did not reply, but stretched out his hand and picked up the spoon from his plate which was still lying on the bed. With this he began to strike the iron bars of the grill. It was getting on my nerves. 'Come and sit down,' I said.

He turned and looked at me, and he was grinning broadly. 'What is the name of your paper?' he asked.

'The *Daily Recorder*,' I said. 'Why?'

But he had begun tapping again, this time much slower. Then he stopped and listened with his head tilted slightly on one side like a dog's. I was getting a little nervous. It would be more than two hours before our evening meal was brought to us and that would probably be my first chance of getting hold of the doctor.

Then suddenly Logan turned to me. 'Here's a pencil,' he said. He drew the half-chewed stub of one out of the pocket of his dungarees and tossed it over to me. 'Put this down on something.' He began tapping again with his spoon. Then he stopped and listened. 'I,' he said, '-c-a-m-e break h-e-r-e break – ' He was spelling the words out letter by letter very slowly, sometimes with quite long intervals between each letter. 'W-i-t-h break t-p-l-e-e break.' He tapped with his spoon on the iron grill again. And then went on, 'C-a-n-c-e-l break t-h-r-e-e break m-i-n-e-r-s.'

AT this stage it is necessary to digress in order to recount the experiences of Maureen Weston, the novelist, which had such an important bearing on later events. She very kindly offered to allow me to lift *en bloc* the story as she told it in her book *Groundbait for death*. I should like to take this opportunity of thanking her for her kindness. I have, however, refrained from taking advantage of her offer because I feel that the bare facts as she gives them in her communications to Charles Patterson, news editor of the *Daily Recorder*, together with various other communications which complete the picture, are more suitable to a straight forward narrative of this type. I should state that I am also indebted to the authorities at Scotland Yard for their kind assistance in supplying me with copies of a number of official communications.

PART TWO

THE DISAPPEARANCE OF MAUREEN WESTON

Wire from the news editor of the Daily Recorder to Maureen Weston, Sea Breezes, St Mawes, dispatched from Fleet Street at 12.15 p.m. on September 4:

Note story in *Telegraph* seven two stop Can you cover disappearance Walter Craig query Still a member Recorder staff stop Full details obtainable Cadgwith – Patterson.

The following story appeared under a D head in the Telegraph of September 4, page seven, column two:

U-BOAT ATTEMPTS LANDING

BELIEVED SUNK BY TORPEDO BOAT

From Our Own Correspondent

Somewhere on the Coast of England – Sept. 3: A daring attempt was made this evening to effect a landing from a German U-boat. It is believed that the intention was to land a spy in this country. Thanks to the British Secret Service, however, the U-boat's intention was known beforehand and the naval authorities at Falmouth notified.

As a result, a British torpedo boat was waiting for the U-boat. As soon as the U-boat surfaced it put off a boat. The torpedo boat attempted to ram this and at the same time opened fire on the U-boat.

The submarine replied and a smart engagement followed. The boat was not rammed and its crew escaped on to the submarine again. The torpedo boat then fired a torpedo at the U-boat, but failed to register a hit. The U-boat then submerged. The torpedo boat immediately dashed to the spot and dropped depth charges. The first of these brought a quantity of oil to the surface and this encourages the belief that the U-boat was destroyed.

Two men, who were watching for the U-boat from the shore are reported to be missing. One was a local fisherman named Logan and the other, Walter Craig, the well-known dramatic critic.

Wire from Maureen Weston to Charles Patterson of the Daily Recorder dispatched from St Mawes at 2.55 p.m. on September 4:

Busy on new book stop Walter untype involved scrape – Maureen.

Wire from Charles Patterson of the Daily Recorder to Maureen Weston dispatched from Fleet Street at 4.5 p.m. on September 4:

Damn book stop Yard asking questions stop Convinced story stop Cannot spare any one investigate from this end stop Relying on you stop Writing hotel Cadgwith stop Suggest five pound daily retainer expenses plus space – Patterson.

Wire from Maureen Weston to Charles Patterson of the Daily Recorder dispatched from St Mawes at 6.20 p.m. on Spetember 4:
Okay stop God help if wild-goose chase – Maureen.

Letter from Charles Patterson of the Daily Recorder to Maureen Weston at the hotel Cadgwith, dated September 4:

DEAR MAUREEN,
Officers from Scotland Yard questioned me about Walter Craig yesterday morning. There is apparently not the slightest doubt that he and this man Logan have disappeared.

In some respects the story in the *Telegraph* is not quite accurate. For one thing the U-boat was not landing any one, but taking off a man who had been landed the previous night. I gathered from the detectives that Craig met this man shortly after he had been landed and that later he became suspicious. The coastguard is mixed up in it somewhere. It was he who warned the naval authorities at Falmouth. I believe Craig and this fellow Logan lay in wait for the German above the cliffs. The police seem to think that both were captured and taken on board the submarine. There is some doubt as to whether it was destroyed.

The question is – why did the submarine land this German? Who did he contact on shore, and why? It must have been something urgent for them to have taken that risk.

I am sorry to have dragged you out of your book. I tried to get you on the phone in order to explain the situation, but every business in London has moved out to the West Country and it is quite impossible to get a call through. At the moment I dare not spare any one from this end, for though we are running a smaller paper and half the staff is hanging about doing nothing, at any moment a rush of war news may come through. At the same time local men are no good for a job of this sort.

What I am hoping for is a first-class spy story. Good hunting, and very many thanks for helping me out.

Yours sincerely,
CHARLES PATTERSON.

Transcript of a code wire from Detective-inspector Fuller to Superintendent McGlade at Scotland Yard and dispatched from Cadgwith at 4.15 p.m. on September 5. The wire was decoded and sent by special messenger to M.I.5:

Enquiries about disappearances being made by Maureen Weston stop Description height about five-two black hair parted left waved brown eyes slim nails painted young attractive stop Arrived hotel about seven last night in green Hillman ten number FGY 537 stop Has contacted Morgan and now walking over cliffs inspect Carillon stop Keeping contact pending instructions – Fuller.

Transcript of a code wire from Superintendent McGlade to Detective-inspector Fuller at the police station at Lizard Town and sent on by hand to Mr Fuller's lodgings at Mrs Forster Williams', arriving shortly after 7 p.m. on September 5:

Maureen Weston was a reporter on *Daily Recorder* until year ago when retired to St Mawes to write stop Now acting for *Recorder* again stop Editor concerned as to whereabouts of Walter Craig stop Have no power to prevent her conducting own enquiries stop Suggest you help and facilitate disinterest – McGlade.

Typescript of a phone call by Charles Patterson of the Daily Recorder from Maureen Weston just before 5 p.m. on September 6 and taken down in shorthand by his secretary:

I have been shown the spot where the submarine's boat landed. I have talked to the coastguard and have walked over to Carillon, the cottage inquired for by the man landed from the submarine. But I am no further forward.

However, this much I have got. It gives the background. Walter Craig went out after mackerel with a man known locally as Big Logan and came back soaking wet. Big Logan, by the way, is a bit of a character – apparently he is very large and bearded, about forty, tough and fond of the girls. Well, apparently Walter had got pulled into the sea by what he thought was a shark which went for a mackerel he had just hooked. Logan thinks this over and decides it isn't a shark but a submarine. Then, when Walter comes down on the Sunday and begins talking of a fellow he met on the cliffs going home the previous night who had just come in by boat, Logan gets properly suspicious, for his boat was apparently the last one in at Cadgwith. The man Walter met asked the way to a cottage called Carillon on the cliffs above Church Cove.

Logan asks the landlord at the local who the owner of Carillon is. That is as far as they go with the landlord. After that they trot off to the coastguard. I could not get much out of Morgan even though he is Welsh. He is in bed suffering from shock and feeling rather sorry for himself. Apparently the U-boat came very near to sinking the torpedo boat. He says that he is not allowed to say anything about it – not even to get his picture in the papers.

A Mr Fuller introduced himself to me this morning. He seemed to know all about me and why I was in Cadgwith. I began to get suspicious. And when he told me he was from Scotland Yard I was quite certain I had found the master spy. However, it turns out that he is from the Yard and he helps quite a bit. Here's the low down.

It was arranged that Walter and Logan should wait on the cliffs whilst the coastguard and two other fishermen lay in wait just around the headland in Logan's boat. It appears, however, that the coastguard, on thinking the matter over, decided to notify Falmouth, and the naval authorities dispatched a torpedo boat to intercept the submarine. The action was much as the *Telegraph* account describes it. The U-boat is believed damaged, but it is by no means certain that it was destroyed. Fuller told me that the police had found marks on the slopes above the place where the landing was made which indicate a struggle. Their theory is that both Walter and Logan were taken prisoner. Incidentally, the boat made the submarine. It was a collapsible rubber boat and was picked up farther down the coast the next day. On it was painted the letters U 34.

The owner of Carillon was arrested that night. His name is George Cutner. He had been at Carillon just over two years. I gather that he paid frequent visits to London and other places. Nobody down here seems to know much about him. To them he was a foreigner and regarded much as the summer visitors. Any one is a foreigner down here who was not born in the district. He was very fond of fishing, though he seldom went out in a boat. He was often with a rod at a picked spot called the Bass Rock at the extremity of one of the headlands. There was nothing in the least unusual about his appearance. He was about fifty-five, short and rather bald – in fact, much like the retired bank manager he was meant to be. There is a police guard on the cottage and I cannot find out where the man has been removed to. Moreover, friend Fuller seemed to expect me to be satisfied with what he had told me and clear out, so perhaps I had better. I shall take up the search with the agents from whom Cutner purchased Carillon.

I don't know whether you will be able to get a story out of this. However, I will hope to get something really hot in due course. Incidentally, this is the last time I try and get you on the phone. I waited two and a half hours for this call. I'll wire in future.

Cutting from the front page of the September 7 issue of the Daily Recorder:

RECORDER MAN EXPOSES

GERMAN SPY

AND BECOMES FIRST BRITISH

WAR CAPTIVE

NOW PRISONER ON BOARD DAMAGED U-BOAT

Walter Craig, the *Recorder's* theatre critic, is the man responsible for the exposure of the first German spy to be captured since the outbreak of war. His action has cost him his freedom and possibly his life. He is now a captive on board a German U-boat, which is known to have been damaged and may well have been destroyed.

The spy was posing as a retired bank manager at a little coastal village. For reasons of national importance names and localities cannot be given. His capture was the result of a remarkable piece of deductive work on the part of Walter Craig.

Here is the story as told by one of his colleagues who went down to the place where he had disappeared in an endeavour to discover whether he was alive or dead.

Every detail of Maureen Weston's story that could be got past the Censor was included in this splash. The story was taken up by the evening papers and caused something of a sensation in the Street.

A cutting from the Daily Recorder of Friday, September 8. It appeared in the form of a box on the front page and was based on nothing more hopeful than a wire dispatched from Penzance at 4.45 p.m. the previous day and reading:

Agents not very helpful but looking around – Maureen.
The box read as follows:

RECORDER SPY HUNT

Following Walter Craig's brilliant exposure of the first German spy to be captured since the beginning of the war, the *Daily Recorder* has sent one of its star reporters to take the hunt where Walter Craig was forced to lay it down.

The *Daily Recorder* is convinced that Walter Craig's brilliant work opens the way to the exposure of a whole network of German espionage in England. This must not be regarded by readers as being in the nature of a spy scare. It is nothing of the sort. But it would be foolish to imagine that Germany, which has been preparing for this war for over five years, will not have perfected an intelligence system of the greatest efficiency in this country. This will have been facilitated by the influx of refugees into this country since Nazism first began to spread terror in Europe.

This does not mean that you should regard all your neighbours, especially those with foreign names, with suspicion. But you would be wise to remember not to discuss in public the little pieces of information, military and civil, that you glean in the course of your business or through conversation with friends. Remember – Walls have ears. In the meantime the *Daily Recorder* is investigating this menace.

Wire from Maureen Weston to Charles Patterson of the Daily Recorder dispatched from Falmouth at 4.45 p.m. on September 8:

Cutner imprisoned here stop Local force succumbed but Cutner unhelpful stop Declares visitor was commander U-boat and he gave him envelope contents unknown stop Insists he was purely an intermediary stop Discussion with estate agents at Penzance unhelpful – Maureen.

Letter from Maureen Weston at the hotel, Cadgwith, dated September 10 and received by Charles Patterson of the Daily Recorder on the morning of Monday, September 11:

DEAR CHARLIE,

It's not for the recipient of a £5 daily retainer to doubt a news editor's wisdom in continuing it, but I must admit that you don't seem to be getting your money's worth. Needless to say, I'm doing my best, but it doesn't seem to be leading any place. Either I'm no good as an investigator or else Cutner was just what he said he was – an intermediary. The only objection to this theory is that his identity was rather elaborately faked – at least that my opinion.

I stayed the Friday night at Falmouth and on the Saturday morning received an answer to a wire I had sent to the local paper at Gloucester the previous night. Gloucester was where Cutner was supposed to have been a bank manager and I had asked for full details as to appearance, interests, visits abroad if any and present whereabouts. The description given in the reply tallied with Cutner in every detail. Interests were given as golf and bridge – golf handicap was four! He was a widower and, following his retirement in June, 1936, he had embarked on an extensive tour of Europe. Present whereabouts was given as Carillon, Church Cove, near Lizard Town, Cornwall.

I then presented myself once more at the local police station. But the law had become unpleasantly official overnight. Exit your glamorous investigator, baffled, to meet friend Fuller on the doorstep. He did not seem in the least surprised to see me and frankly admitted that he was responsible for the attitude of the local force. So I weighed in with a few questions: What were the countries visited by Cutner in his European tour? Was Germany one of then? Did he play golf? If so what was the handicap and had they found out whether he really could play? And so on.

When I had finished, Fuller said, 'So you've got that far, have you, Miss Weston.' I said, 'What do you mean – that far?' He said, 'Never mind.' We then discussed the weather and left it at that. He was not inclined to be helpful.

Deductions, my dear Watson – lucky I write detective stories, isn't it? – are as follows, Cutner vanished in Germany. His passport, clothes, and in fact, his whole personality were taken over lock, stock, and barrel by the gentleman now in prison. This gentleman returned, and, with Cutner's background to fall back on if questioned, purchased Carillon from the executors of the deceased Mrs Bloy. This all sounds rather like an excerpt from one of my books, but I am quite convinced that if only I could get this man Cutner on to a golf course I could prove it. The average German isn't very interested in golf and I doubt whether the man would know one end of a club from another.

However, the net result of this was to send me posthaste back to Cadgwith in an attempt to pick up the threads from that end. But nothing doing. The man had few visitors and no one seems to know anything about them. The police have withdrawn from the cottage and last night I went over it. Not a smell. The police will almost certainly have removed anything they thought might be interesting. But I doubt whether Cutner was the man to leave anything about. When I saw him in the cell at Falmouth he struck me as a secretive little man. He looked like a bank manager. His whole appearance shrieked figures, routine and a methodical mind. I doubt whether he ever had an affair in his life. Incredible the sort of people who will go in for intelligence work! There's not an ounce of romance or adventure about him. If he is a master spy, he's a damned dull one. But there you are, that's just the sort of man you want for a spy.

The point I am leading up to is this. I am no further forward on this business than when I started. I don't mean I've discovered nothing. But I have not discovered anything that would lead me to a big spy network or even to suggest that such a network existed. From your point of view I'm a washout, and after this letter I'm quite expecting you to wire me to get back to my book. The only trouble is I've got interested in this business. The way I look at it is this. Presuming my deduction to be right, why did the German Intelligence go to such pains to plant at Cadgwith a man who was to be no more than an intermediary? It doesn't make sense. Any one would have done for the job of intermediary.

Now I have a proposition to put forward. I continue this investigation and the *Recorder* pays me expenses. I'll chuck it as soon as I realize I'm getting no further. And if I chuck it you'll only be out of pocket to the extent of my expenses. If, on the other hand, I get on to something that is really worth while you can pay me my daily retainer for the period and for whatever you are able to print. Let me know what you think.

Yours,
MAUREEN WESTON.

Wire from Charles Patterson of the Daily Recorder to Maureen Weston at the hotel, Cadgwith, dispatched from Fleet Street at 11.10 a.m. on September 11:

Okay go ahead stop Good luck – Patterson.

Letter from Maureen Weston at the Red Lion Hotel, Redruth, dated September 12 and received by Charles Patterson of the Daily Recorder on the morning of Wednesday, September 13:

DEAR CHARLIE,

Believe we may be getting somewhere, but God knows where. Am leaving here early tomorrow for St Just near Land's End. It's a long shot and can't for the life of me think why I am feeling suddenly optimistic.

My last letter, if I remember rightly, was written on Sunday evening at the hotel in Cadgwith. On Monday morning I ran over to Penzance and had another talk to the agents who sold Carillon to Cutner. I don't know whether it was a sort of hunch or just that, having drawn blank at Church Cove, I turned in desperation to the agents as the one possible link between Cutner and the others.

The agents were Messrs Gribble, Tolworth and Fickle – incredible, isn't it? Previously I had only spoken with the chief clerk. This time I demanded to see the senior partner. This was Mr Fickle, the other two being dead! He was a pompous little Scotsman and vera vera careful. The police had apparently been at him and he was beginning to fear for his reputation. When I told him that I represented the *Recorder*, I feared he was going to throw me out. However, we played the old game and I said it would look as though he were concealing something if he was not prepared to discuss the matter openly with a representative of the press. In the end he told me everything I wanted to know, and it wasn't much at that.

Cutner had purchased the cottage on February 2, 1937. He paid for it with a cheque on the branch at Gloucester where he had been manager – ergo, if my reasoning is correct, this makes him a passable forger as well. He had looked at a number of cottages before choosing Carillon. Several of these were inland, but Fickle seems to have been left with the impression that what Cutner was really interested in was one on the coast. An interesting point is that he offered him one at Sennen Cove, which was in every way ideal and much more suited to his stated requirements than Carillon, but he turned it down without even bothering to go and look at it. For some reason it had to be in South Cornwall. In all, Cutner spent the better part of a week in Penzance, motoring out daily in various directions to have a look at properties. An entry in the register at the Wheatsheaf Hotel, Penzance, where I stayed the night, shows that he was there from January 27 to February 1, 1937. He instructed his purchase agreement to be sent to his hotel at Torquay. He was resident at that hotel from December 4, 1936, to January 26, 1937, and again from February 2 to February 28, 1937, when he took up his residence at Carillon.

All this is getting nowhere, you'll say. Quite right, but it shows that I'm being thorough. Now here we come to the little sequence of coincidence which is sending me scuttling down to St Just. The hall porter at the Wheatsheaf remembers Mr Cutner. And the reason he remembers him is that he tipped him with a dud ten shilling note. I know what you're going to say. That dud ten shilling note shows, Miss Weston, that your reasoning is all wrong. Cutner was not ingeniously smuggled into this country by Germany. He is just a petty criminal passing dud notes and ready to take on anything, even a little espionage work, to keep himself in funds. But wait a minute. This man paid his bill by cheque, and it was honoured. He paid in two cheques at his Torquay hotel and both were honoured. As far as I can find out this was the one and only dud note that he passed. My conclusion is that it was just one of those things. But it has served my purpose, for to this day the hall porter remembers all about Mr George Cutner. He remembers that he wore brown boots with a dark grey suit and that he kept a big gold watch, which he would frequently consult, in his waistcoat pocket. And that during his stay at the hotel he had a visitor. This visitor was a man of the name of Robertson – short and thick-set, with rimless glasses, heavy cheeks and a way of puffing as he moved as though he were perpetually short of breath.

Using the office of Gribble, Tolworth and Fickle as a poste restante I wired this description to Cutner's Torquay hotel and to Detective-inspector Fuller at the Falmouth police station. The reply from the Torquay hotel was not long delayed. It read – 'Man answering description visited Cutner several times stop Name Jones.' I waited at the estate agents for some time, hoping for a reply from Fuller. In the end I gave it up and went along to see the editor of the local paper. Here I drew blank. No one in the office knew any one of the name of either Jones or Robertson who answered to the description. In fact, no one knew any one at all who answered to that description.

So back to the hotel and further talks with the porter. A genuine ten shilling note changes hands – this will be included in expenses – and from the depths of the remote past this worthy individual, who has needless to say the acquisitive nature of the Cornish wrecker well developed, conjures the memory of a telephone call from said Mr Robertson to Cutner when the latter was out. Later Mr Robertson rings through again and as Cutner is still out leaves a message. The message is to the effect that Cutner is to meet him in Redruth that evening. When the porter asks where and at what time, this Robertson says, 'Seven o'clock. He knows where.'

So then I get the car out and start for Redruth. And as the estate agents is on the way I stop off to see whether Fuller has answered my wire. I should have been warned by the sleek black roadster that is drawn up at the curb. Detective-inspector Fuller is waiting for me inside with a whole heap of questions. How did I get to know about this man? Who had seen him? Where did I get my description from?

'So you recognize the description, do you?' I asked.

And he said, 'Like hell I do. I've been trying to trace this man ever since Cutner was arrested.'

'Well, isn't that a coincidence,' I said, 'I'm trying to trace him too.'

And then we start the questions all over again. But I get the answer to my wire. This fellow Robertson had visited Carillon several times. So I say good-afternoon and thank him for being so kind as to come all the way over to Penzance in order to reply to my wire. He thinks I think I've made rather a hit and that makes him very embarrassed. Even so he sticks to the point and keeps on with the questions. We both get rather hot under the collar and in the end he takes himself off to go the round of the hotels and through the whole gamut of investigation that I've just been through, while I go on to Redruth.

And here everything tumbles right into my lap. The editor of the local paper listens to my description and says, 'Sounds like Tubby Wilson. Started up the old Wheal Garth mine and packed up about a year back.' Then he gets down two bound volumes of the paper and after about ten minutes search produces a photograph of a fat little man standing with feet apart, his thumbs in his waistcoat pockets and a broad grin on his moon-like face. The man has a battered trilby on the back of his head and I can see a faint mark on his waistcoat that looks like a watch chain. The photograph appeared in the issue of March 2, 1937 – that is shortly after he had had these meetings with Cutner. And the reason the photograph is in the paper is that he has just floated a small private company called Cornish Coastal Wilson Mines Ltd. Then in the issue of March 16 of that year appears the announcement of the purchase of the Wheal Garth tin mine near St Just.

Eighteen months later the mine closed down. But it evidently had good backing for there was no question of bankruptcy – all the creditors were paid in full and the mine is still the property of this now very nebulous company. Well, that's the low down on Tubby Wilson. By the time you get this letter I shall be on my way to have a look at his mine and talk to people in the neighbourhood of St Just who worked there – that is if friend Tubby is the man I think he is. I obtained two back numbers of the issue in which his photograph appeared. One cutting I have sent to my friend, the hotel porter, with a request to wire me in the morning if he recognizes it as Robertson. The other I am keeping myself for identification purposes. In the meantime I am trying to ferret out Tubby's antecedents and history. The editor of the local paper, a jovial old boy who regards me as something of an *enfante terrible*, is taking me to the local mineowners' club tonight. I threatened to go on my own, but apparently he didn't think that would be quite, quite. In the meantime, could you have someone go along to Bush House and look up Tubby's ancestors? If you have any luck wire me at the St Just post office.

I suggest you keep these interminable reports and publish them under the title of 'Letters of a Special Investigator to her Employer.'

Yours,
SHERLOCK WESTON.

Wire from Maureen Weston to Charles Patterson of the Daily Recorder dispatched from Hayle at 10.5 a.m. on September 13:

Porter corroborates identity stop John Desmond Wilson known in Redruth prior flotation stop Something of rolling stone been prospecting various goldfields also tin Malay stop Writing arrival Saint Just – Maureen.

Wire from Charles Patterson of the Daily Recorder to Maureen Weston at the Post Office, St Just, dispatched from Fleet Street at 11.15 a.m. on September 13:

Born Düsseldorf ninety four naturalized British twenty two stop Keep going – Patterson.

Letter from Maureen Weston, c/o Mrs Davies, Cap View, Pendeen, Cornwall, dated September 13 and received by Charles Patterson of the Daily Recorder on the afternoon of September 14:

DEAR CHARLIE,

I'm feeling a little scared. Your special investigator is going down the mine tomorrow morning, and she's not the least bit keen. This is the most God-awful place. I've never seen these Cornish mining villages before – they're even worse than the Welsh. They're so drab and the coastal scenery is so colourful. Today, for instance, as I pottered around the cliffs looking at the mines, the sea was a brilliant turquoise blue with a white edge where it creamed against the cliffs. It reminded me of the Mediterranean, except that the coast here is much more ragged and deadly looking than anything I have seen before. From this I came back to Pendeen to make inquiries as to who had worked in Wheal Garth, and by comparison this little huddle of grey stone cottages is unbelievably squalid.

However, I have been quite lucky. I am installed in a little cottage half-way between Pendeen and Trewellard and clear of the depressing atmosphere of a mining village. But there is no opportunity to forget that I am in the mining district of Cornwall. There is open ground on the other side of the road and it is dotted with grass-grown slag heaps, piles of stones which were once miners' houses and ruined chimneys that acted as flues for the ventilation shafts of the mines. This is what I look out on from my bedroom window. And, believe me, when it rained this evening it looked a scene of utter desolation. It is getting dark now and I'm writing this by the light of an oil lamp. A sea mist has come up and the lighthouse at Pendeen Watch is moaning dismally. However, when it's fine it is possible to see right across to the cliffs, and I can just see the top of Cape Cornwall, which I gather is why the cottage is called Cap View. I feed in the kitchen with the family – mother, father, daughter aged seven, and an evacuee, male, aged five. And from the window there you look up the slope of the moors to the huge pyramid heaps of the china clay pits.

So much for the local colour. Now to the result of my labours. First thing I did on arrival was to locate the mine. Refer to your collection of Ward, Lock, and in the West Cornwall volume you will find it given as lying between mines Botallack and Levant, both now defunct. I have had quite an interesting prowl round. There is the remains of what looks like a miniature railway running for the better part of half a mile along the very edge of the cliffs. There is just the cutting left and an occasional wooden sleeper. In fact, but for the wooden sleepers, I should have said it was a water duct, for it is a definite cutting all the way. Maybe what I think are sleepers are old slats of wood that formed the framework for the wooden trough in which the water ran. Whatever it is, I think it once belonged to Wheal Garth. What I take to be the main shaft of the mine is about a hundred yards in from the cliff edge. There's a high stone wall round it that looks fairly recent. I climbed over and had a look down, lying flat on my stomach. There's a sheer drop of about a hundred feet to a lot of old pit props, and there's the sound of water dripping – most unpleasant! The cliffs here are simply pitted with these shafts. Each has its stone wall, but that is the only protection. Others have been filled, some have fallen in, and the scars of diggings and the mounds of old slag heaps are everywhere.

Your acquisitive little Maureen was seen making for the local with several small-sized boulders clasped to her bosom. Some of the stones on the slag heaps are beautifully coloured, but actually what I had got were several pieces of greenish rock flecked with gold. Optimism outran intelligence and I pictured myself opening up Wheal Garth as a gold mine.

At the pub I find a most admirable and intelligent landlord. Note the style of Pepys! I order a gin and lime, dump my little pieces of rock on the bar and ask if the bright stuff is gold. Whereupon my drink is delivered to me with a huge guffaw and a smell of stale beer. 'Aye, that's raight foonny!' he says. He hails from the North in case you hadn't noticed my spelling. 'That's moondic, that is. Arsenic deposit. Ee, we allus gets a laff oot o' t' visitors wi' moondic. They arl think it's gold.' He produced a piece of rock from the back of the bar that shone like solid gold only the look of it was rather more metallic. This was a lovely example of mundic. Then he showed me a piece of what they call mother tin from a new lode that had just been struck at Geevor. The whole village, incidentally, now seems to live on Geevor. It's the only mine for miles around that is still working.

I know what you're muttering to yourself – when is this so-and-so woman coming to the point? Well, here it is. The landlord recognized the picture of Tubby. As soon as he sees it, he says, 'Ee, 'a knaw 'im raight enoof. That's Toobby Wilson, that is.' Then over a pint of mild and bitter he gives me the low down on the mine.

Wheal Garth is what they call a wet mine, or rather it was in the old days. Its hey-day appears to have been about 1927-28. Tin was around £240 a ton at the time and they were working on a three-foot wide seam of mother tin. Profits of Wheal Garth for 1928 were something like £200,000. This was on a capital of some £60,000, the mine having been bought for a song in 1925. That's the way with these Cornish mines, derelict one year and then some small speculating prospector strikes a seam and a fortune is made. Apparently this seam ran out under the sea. That was why it was a wet mine. It resulted in very bad silicosis. In the words of the landlord, 'Nae boogger laiked t' place.'

Then in November, 1928, the undersea workings collapsed and a whole shift – thirty-two men – were trapped and killed. It was, I understand, one of the worst disasters in the history of Cornish mining. An inquiry was held and it was found that a huge underwater cavern, which ran into the face of the cliff immediately above the galleries leading into the undersea workings, extended much deeper than had been thought. Thus, instead of having, as they thought, some twenty feet of solid rock above the underwater galleries, there had only been some three feet. The cave was known of course to the engineers and divers sent down when the galleries were first cut in 1916. But the sand that filled the bottom of the cave had proved deceptive. Frankly I doubt whether the engineers took full precautions. Owners are notoriously free with the lives of miners, and 1916 was a year in which every effort was being made by the Cornish mines to meet the demands of the war machine. There might be a story in that for you later – How Cornwall is Feeding the Tinplate Industry. As far as I can gather no effort was made by the company that took over in 1925 to check the safety of these galleries. They were in fact safe enough at the time. It was only when they came to widen them in order to lay a small railway and so increase the output of the mine that they collapsed.

You are probably wondering at my preoccupation with the mine rather than with Tubby Wilson. I must admit that when I last wrote you my idea in coming down here was simply to check up on the man and see if I could find out whether any other suspicious persons had contacted him at the mine. What decided me to pay close attention to the mine itself was the talk I heard at the mineowners' club in Redruth last night. Apparently Tubby Wilson and his activities at Wheal Garth had always been something of an enigma to some members. The point to remember is that these boys have been in the business for years. They know how to run a mine. They know what to look for and what to go out for without involving themselves in terrific costs. When Noye, the local editor, collected a few of his particular cronies – big men in the tin business, as he told me – round the bar and explained that I worked for the *Recorder* and wanted information about Wilson, they were only too ready to discuss the business. When Tubby

Wilson floated his company and opened up Wheal Garth, the price of tin was falling sharply. And they naturally thought that what he was going to do was drive another shaft and run fresh galleries out to pick up the undersea lode beyond the spot where the old workings had ceased, so by-passing the danger area. The only thing was, they thought his capital insufficient for the job. They told him this, but he throws a wide guy act and says he's got other ideas. Well, these other ideas are apparently to go for the shore end of the lode. Now this is a bum idea and they tell him so. The lode was discovered only about twenty feet from the sea and some thirty feet below sea level. The shoreward end was worked out before ever they started on the undersea section. Moreover, prospecting work was carried out over a wide area at the shoreward end in a fruitless effort to discover the continuation of a lode. The boys at the club told him he'd be throwing his money away if he started looking for that end of the lode. His reply was that he had an idea. Well, his idea was to sink a new shaft about a hundred yards back from the cliffs dead in a line with the cave, then he throws new galleries out until he meets the cave which apparently extends some two hundred yards inland. Then he begins to cast about in a big semi-circle with broad adits running off every few yards into the cave. Then he casts inland in two great drives at each end of his main gallery. Then he runs adits off opposite the ones he has run into the cave. Then he tries a higher level. Then a higher level still. Then he goes bust and the mine closes down.

The boys I spoke to thought he must have spent in all four times the nominal capital of the company. He employed forty men on the job and an engineer who came down from London and didn't know a thing about Cornish tin mining. They think he was nuts. What do you think?

Anyway, that's why I'm fussing over the mine. I'm also interested in this engineer from London – long lean fellow with horn-rimmed spectacles, thinning hair and what is thought to have been the makings of a Scotch accent. The name is Jesse Maclean. See what you can get?

It was the landlord who put me on to Alf Davies. Davies is a Welshman, whatever, and was foreman of the Wheal Garth under Maclean. I thanked him and asked whether it would be possible to have a look over the mine. He said it was closed, but that Alf Davies would be able to tell me all about it.

Davies is a proper little Welsh miner, short and broad, a bundle of muscle and vitality, with false teeth and a sour glum-looking face beaten brown by the wind. But for all his glumness, he's got a sense of humour and smiles sometimes. When I asked him after tea this afternoon whether he could take me down Wheal Garth he said, 'Indeed and I'd like to, but look you the mine is closed.' I said there must surely be some way in and offered him a fiver for his trouble – please note for expenses! I saw him hesitate, for he is on the dole now, and then he said, 'Well, if you're so anxious that it's worth that much to you to go down a lousy mine like Wheal Garth I can't stop you. But there's no dependence on the old workings whatever and it's rough going, by damn it is.' I said I didn't mind, so it's all fixed up. In due course I'll let you know what happens. I must admit I haven't the faintest idea what I'm expecting to find. It's just that I'm curious.

Yours,
MAUREEN.

Transcript of code wire from Detective-inspector Fuller to Super-intendent McGlade at Scotland Yard, dispatched from Penzance at 3.15 p.m. on September 13:

All information John Desmond Wilson mine owner and gold prospector please stop Formed Cornish Coastal Wilson Mines Ltd April thirty seven – Fuller.

Transcript of a code wire from Superintendent McGlade to Detective-inspector Fuller at police station, Penzance, dispatched at 5.55 p.m. on September 13:

Wilson born Düsseldorf ninety four naturalized British twenty two stop No police record stop *Daily Recorder* made similar inquiries today stop Intelligence officer meeting you in morning – McGlade.

Letter from Maureen Weston posted at Penzance on the evening of September 14 and received by Charles Patterson of the Daily Recorder on the Friday afternoon:

DEAR CHARLIE,

Further to my report of September 13, I have examined the mine and quite frankly the experience was not a pleasant one. For one thing, you've no idea how eerie the place was. It reeked of water and the air was pretty stale. For another, my guide seemed to become rather uneasy when we reached the lower levels. I know that must sound silly – it does to me now I am sitting writing about it in the cosy warmth of my little bedroom. But, believe me, it is unpleasant enough going down a discarded Cornish tin mine without your guide getting scared. Perhaps 'scared' isn't quite the right word. 'Puzzled' might be better – and yet he was more than just puzzled. He was quite confident when we started. After all, it was his mine, so to speak. But there are all sorts of funny noises in those empty galleries. The drip of water echoes and is magnified. There are strange creaking sounds where old props are taking a strain, queer glimpses of pale light where old shafts come down, the sound of falling stones, the weird echo of one's own footsteps going up one gallery and coming back at one down another, and at the lower levels a faint roar as of water falling. I didn't worry much about all these weird sounds until I sensed that Alf was uneasy. Then these sounds became so magnified in my imagination that at times I could have sworn we were being followed and at other times that the roof of the gallery was coming down.

This probably reads rather like the hysterical blathering of a woman who has been thoroughly frightened by her first experience of going down a mine, so I had better begin at the beginning. To start with, I'll go over my conversation with Alf Davies on the previous night in greater detail. When I asked him whether he could take me over the mine and he hesitated at the suggestion of a fiver, he told me one or two things. First, that so far as he knew the mine had not been entered since it had closed down in 1937. Second, that the new main shaft had been blocked at the bottom. Third, that the only possible means of getting into the mine was the way they had got into it when they opened it up in 1937. Fourth, that this entrance meant going through the old workings which were not particularly safe, and that to get into them necessitated climbing down an old half-ruined shaft with the aid of a rope. I must admit the prospect was not exactly encouraging, but I had made up my mind to have a look at the mine, so I put the best face I could on it and said I adored climbing down unsafe shafts on the end of a rope.

Well, we left at eight-thirty this morning equipped with a coil of rope, a pair of electric torches and a packet of sandwiches apiece. Fortunately I had had the sense to bring a pair of old corduroy trousers with me on this assignment of yours so that I looked reasonably business-like. We walked for about a quarter of a mile through the waste of old mine workings opposite the cottage and then went through a gate and crossed a field. Thence through another gate on to the sort of heath that runs to the cliff edge. There were no mine chimneys here, but grass mounds and barrows pointed to old workings, and here and there were the small circular walls that marked a shaft. We struck away to the left along the wall that circled the field, pushing our way through a tangle of briars. We then came to a vague fork in the path and bore right, away from the wall. The ground here was covered with briar and heather – or heath, I never know which.

I don't think I've ever seen such a frighteningly desolate spot. The ground about us was pock-marked with old workings, all overgrown and ruined. Some of the shafts had only pieces of rotting timber across them with a few lumps of rock thrown carelessly on top. One or two we passed were practically unprotected, with ferns growing out of the sides and very wet. Alf told me that the cattle quite often fall down these shafts. 'Quite a good place for a murder,' I said, wondering whether to make this the setting for my next book. But Alf – I'd told him what I did for a living – said, 'Yes, indeed, it is creepy enough, but you would not get away with it.' Apparently as soon as a carcase that has fallen down a shaft begins to rot the birds gather over it in clouds. That was the moment he chose to introduce me to the entrance to the old workings of Wheal Garth and I had an immediate vision of ravens and gulls and choughs wheeling in a monotonous screaming symphony of black and white over our decaying bodies.

A more evil looking spot than the entrance to those workings I cannot imagine. Out of a tangle of briars rose an old lichen-covered wall that was rapidly disintegrating. It was circular, like all the rest, and about twelve feet in diameter. And when I looked over, it was to peer down into a black wet pit surrounded by ferns and water-weed. 'Do I have to go down that?' I asked. At that he grinned. 'Indeed and ye don't have to, miss, it's your own party.'

I smiled a little weakly. He was right – I didn't have to. Quite frankly I nearly walked out on him. However, I asked him whether he thought it was all right, and he said, 'Yes, indeed, why not?' And he seemed so confident about it and so matter-of-fact that I said nothing when he began looking around for a suitable rock to which he could secure the rope.

By the way, I think I owe you an apology for writing you such long screeds when from your point of view there is very little news in them. But I am regarding these daily reports to you as a sort of diary, and whatever material you don't use I shall probably incorporate in a book.

Well, he secured the rope to a good-sized rock, clambered over the wall and dropped the other end of it down the shaft. He then asked me whether I thought I was capable of climbing down the rope or if it would be better for him to lower me down. When I discovered that if he lowered me it would necessitate my going down first and waiting at the bottom alone, I decided to risk the climb. The depth of the shaft was apparently only a matter of thirty or forty feet. As he lowered his legs into the shaft he looked up at me and said, 'Don't ye mind about anything else but the rope.' I asked him what he meant and he grinned and quoted, 'Fra' ghoulies and ghosties and long-leggety beasties. I'm not saying there mayn't be a bat or two down here,' he explained. 'Just you remember to hang on to the rope.' Then he caught hold of the rope and disappeared. It was a good start.

I could hear his feet scrabbling against the uneven stone sides of the shaft, and several times stones clattered down into the depths, making a hollow unreal sound. Then the rope went slack and his voice came up the shaft, deep and cavernous. I climbed over the wall and sat down with my legs dangling over the edge of the shaft. And there I remained for what seemed an age. I suppose it was, in fact, only a few seconds, but I thought I should be rooted there for ever. There were large ferns in the shaft and the stone sides were all slimy with water. And there were little noises that I could not recognize.

The feeling I had sitting on top of that shaft was horribly primitive. It's funny. I wouldn't have minded going down a new shaft. In fact, I shouldn't have hesitated. We're quite accustomed to going underground. We do it every day in London. But when the shaft leading underground is shorn of its civilized trappings you suddenly realize that when you descend you will be going *under ground*.

Then Alf's voice came floating up to me again, and I knew it was very little different from the first bathe of the season and that the sooner I got on with it the better. So, before I could change my mind and start panicking again, I had swung my legs over, gripped the rope with my feet and was lowering away. Strange as it may seem, it wasn't as unpleasant as I had expected, chiefly, I imagine, because my whole attention was concentrated on the task of keeping hold of the rope. I thought my arms would never stand it. I couldn't come down gripping the rope with my feet because it swung close to the wall and was apt to rub my nose against the slimy water-weed. I had to let my arms take the strain and brace my feet against the many crevices that I found in the side. There were quite a number of cobwebs and I'm sure that I should have hated it if I'd had a torch. But as soon as I had got about ten feet down it was quite impossible to see a thing except the glaring white circle of daylight at the top, and this gradually diminished in size. Once, I did encounter a bat, but by that time I was too concerned about whether or not I should ever last out till the bottom to worry about it. It fluttered about for a few moments and then settled again. I think it was dark enough for it to see me and avoid me. What I should have done if it had flown in my face I don't know.

Just as I thought my arms would be wrenched from their sockets, I felt Alf's hand grip me and I stepped down on to the level floor of the shaft. 'Ye ought to come to Wales and do some real climbing,' he said. It was a compliment which I felt I had deserved. I moved my feet and immediately there was a dry rattle. I flashed my torch and stared a little uncomfortably at the skeleton of what I presumed had once been a cow.

Alf switched his torch on and disappeared along a wet stale-smelling tunnel that gradually sloped at a steeper and steeper angle. I followed him. It was rather like exploring a long cave. There was little to show that the walls had been cut by human hands. They were rough and not hewn to any definite shape. Here and there were slight falls that had to be negotiated, sometimes with considerable difficulty, and the floor was irregular and strewn with stones that made it treacherous. In places it was like the bed of a stream. Alf told me that he believed these particular workings dated back more than two centuries. I could well believe it. But the thought that they had stood for that long comforted me. In one part, however, there had been a particular bad fall and for a time we thought we should not be able to get through. But by removing one or two rocks we were able to crawl under it on our hands and knees. Alf spent some time examining this fall, and when I asked him what he was up to, he said he was just wondering what had caused it.

After about half an hour's very uncomfortable travelling, mostly down a sharp incline, we suddenly struck the level and the roof rose so that we could walk upright. We had reached the more recent workings. My back ached abominably. However, from then onwards the going was much less difficult.

Now this is what I want to impress upon you. The unpleasant part was over. We had left the old workings. The workings we were in now were quite safe – that is as mines go down this part of the world. Yet we hadn't progressed more than a hundred yards into these new workings before I began to feel uneasy. That sounds daft, I know. But the fact remains that throughout our scramble through the old workings it had seemed rather fun – an adventure. Now I didn't like it.

The reason, I am convinced, was Alf. He was the guide and he had been so assured coming through the old workings that I had complete confidence in him. It was his mine and I felt he ought to know his way about it like his own house. But my reliance on him made me very susceptible to his mood, and I was not slow in sensing what I think was a certain bewilderment – the sort of feeling one has if one is not sure of the way out. Its effect on me was to produce an immediate sense of uneasiness. I became jittery and all the unfamiliar little sounds about me – the drip of water, the rattle of stones and the echo of our movements – became magnified in the stillness.

I didn't get as frightened as all that at once. It was cumulative. It started when we came to a point in the more recent workings where the water that ran down from the old workings, and it was deep enough now to be over our ankles in places, was diverted from what I believe is known as a winze. This is a sharp slope going down from one level to the next, and a little wall of stones had been erected across it and cemented together so that the water continued along the level on which we stood. Alf examined this artificial barrier for a moment in the light of his torch. He even bent down and felt the cement with his hand. Then we splashed on along the level and heard the sound of falling water. It was a faint splashy sound, and suddenly we came to the end of the level.

At this point the gallery was wide enough for us to walk abreast and I got rather an unpleasant shock when in the light of the torch I saw that the floor level simply vanished. We could hear the splash of water on rock many feet below. There was no ceiling either. In fact the level ran out into an old shaft that was blocked at the top.

I don't know why the discovery that the level just ended in a sheer drop should have upset me so much. I think there must always be something very unpleasant about finding a sheer drop underground. Probably it is the immediate and involuntary feeling that if one had no torch and stumbled on it in the dark one would now be lying at the bottom where the water was splashing. I felt rather foolish really, because quite automatically I had clutched at Alf's arm – and as a one-time Fleet Street woman I pride myself on being tougher than most females. I mean, damn it, one knows quite well that mine shafts are put down and levels cut at various depths.

We retraced our steps and went down the winze into the next level. At the bottom we turned left until we came to what Alf described as a cross-cut. We took this and at the end turned right. By this time I was feeling an uncomfortable desire to cling on to his arm. With all these bewildering turns and the memory of that drop into the old shaft, I was terrified of being separated from him. I remembered all sorts of ghoulish stories about the catacombs of Rome, and pictured myself wandering alone in the place till I either died of starvation or killed myself by falling down a shaft in the dark. It was from this point, I think, that I began to get really frightened of the dark. It seemed to press in on us from every side as though endeavouring to muffle our torches. The air was warm and stale and damp, and the echo of our footsteps had an unpleasant habit of coming back at us down the disused galleries long after we had moved.

Quite often now Alf would pause and listen, with his head cocked on one side. I asked him once whether he was listening for ghosts, thinking of the miners who had been trapped. But he didn't smile. His round craggy face was set and taciturn. Every time we paused we could hear that faint roar, as of an underground waterfall, and the echo of footsteps came whispering back at us. It was then I began to feel that we were being followed. I no longer felt sure it was the echo of our own footsteps. Again I remembered the men who had lost their lives in that disaster ten years ago. We were nearing that section of the mine and I began to see in every shadow the ghost of a dead miner. Once I cried out at my own shadow cast against a wall of rock ahead of me. I tell you, I was really frightened.

By this time we had descended another winze and Alf announced in a whisper that we had reached the lowest level in this section of the mine. And a second later down the gallery behind came the whisper – 'the lowest level in this section of the mine' – with the sibilants all magnified. It was uncanny. There was a good deal of timber in this section, not all of it sound. Much of it was green and beginning to rot. Once I stumbled on a piece of rock and clutched at a prop to save myself from falling. The outer surface of the wood crumbled in my hand, all wet and sloppy.

Then we came to the bricked up foot of the new shaft. We bore away to the left along a gallery in which the timber was still grey and sound. The gallery sloped downwards and curved away to the right. Sections of rail still lay along the floor and the roar of distant water was much louder. The sound was peculiar and distorted, more like a hum, as though a rushing cataract were pouring through a narrow gorge. Remembering the disaster, I felt that at any moment we might be overwhelmed by a wall of water, though Alf assured me we were still well above sea level. My nerves were completely gone.

At length the gallery flattened out and branched into three. Alf hesitated, and then took the right-hand branch. The sound of water became even louder. The gallery here was very well built. It was about seven feet wide and the same high, and in places it was cemented to keep out the water. Then suddenly we rounded a bend and came face to face with the most ghastly-looking fall. The whole of the roof had simply caved in and the gallery was blocked by great chunks or rock that looked as though they might have been part of Stonehenge. It suddenly made me realize that it is possible to get trapped in even the soundest-seeming galleries.

Alf played his torch over the debris and at length we turned back and retraced our steps to where the main gallery had branched. We took the next branch, and before we had gone more than forty feet we came up against another huge fall. I began to have a feeling that the whole place must be unsafe. All I wanted to do was to get out of it before it caved in on top of us.

Alf spent even longer examining this fall. But at length he led me back and down the next branch. It was the same thing. Thirty feet or so down the gallery we were stopped by a fall. I guessed then that there must be a serious fault in the whole rock formation at this point. I said as much to Alf, but he only grunted and continued to poke about amongst the debris. Then he began to examine the walls.

At last I could stand it no longer. 'I'm getting out of this,' I said.

He nodded. 'All right, miss,' he said. But he made no move. He simply stood there with his head on one side, listening. Involuntarily I began to listen too. I could hear the hum of the water somewhere beyond the falls and occasionally there was the creak of a pit prop.

I suddenly clutched his arm. 'I can't stand this,' I said. 'What are you listening for? What's the matter with the place?' He seemed a little put out by my questions. 'You're uneasy, aren't you?' I went on. 'I've felt it ever since we left the old workings. For God's sake tell me what it is. Have we lost our way, is somebody following us – what? I don't mind so long as you tell me what it is.'

Then he told me. 'Somebody has been in this mine since it was closed down,' he said. He told me not to be alarmed. Then he said, 'Remember that fall we had to scramble through in the old workings?' I nodded. 'That was what first made me uneasy,' he went on. Then he explained that he thought the fall unnatural. 'Do you suppose it would have been done to discourage people from entering the mine?' he asked. Then he pointed out that the watercourse had been diverted. Normally it would have run through these workings and out beyond into the cave. And what about these falls, he asked. He took my hand and showed me clean-cut flakes on the walls and marks as though the rock had been blackened. 'These falls are not natural,' he said. He spoke fast and excited in his musical Welsh voice. 'The rock has been blasted. Those marks are the marks of dynamite. Someone has blocked off the new workings.' He swung round on me. 'Why is that?' he asked. 'Indeed, and can you tell me why you wanted to come down this mine?'

I explained that I had reason to be suspicious of the last owner. He looked at me with his head on one side. 'Mr Wilson was not a good man,' he said. 'But I did not think him dishonest.'

He took my arm and led me back up the gallery. 'Tomorrow we will come down with two friends of mine. I believe we may be able to find a way through this fall.'

And that is how things stand at the moment. We got out of the mine shortly after one. I felt pretty near exhausted and very dirty. Since then I have had a wash, a meal and a rest. I don't know what to think. I had a hunch that the mine would be worth looking at. Now I've been down it and am informed that someone has tampered with it since it was closed – in fact, that someone has deliberately produced four falls of rock. But we were able to get through the first fall – the one in the old workings. Was that design or inefficiency? Was I mistaken when I had that unpleasant feeling that we were being followed? And the three big falls – what was on the other side? What is that faint roar of water? Alf says it doesn't sound like water. Is somebody drilling? The whole thing is so fantastic. Do you remember Conan Doyle's *Tales of Horror and Mystery*? Well, I feel as though I'm writing the diary in one of his tales of horror that will be found after I am dead and from which others will draw the wildest conjectures. Suppose there is an underground race and they are coming to the surface to conquer us? Stupid! But when you are deep in the bowels of the earth anything seems possible. Quite frankly I'm not looking forward to tomorrow.

Your scared investigator,
MAUREEN.

P.S. Since writing this I have heard rather a peculiar thing. I went down to the local as Alf's guest. They're a tough crowd at Pendeen, but very friendly. I met Alf's pals who are coming on tomorrow's expedition. One's tall and the other's short, and they both look very tough indeed. They're out of work, like Alf. Both worked in Wheal Garth under Maclean. What I wanted to tell you, however, is a curious little story that is drifting around. They are very superstitious in this neighbourhood and apparently there has been talk recently of the miners who were killed in that disaster lying uneasy. They say that the white skull of a dead miner can be seen on dark nights floating in the sea just off Wheal Garth right over the spot where they were trapped.

Now the talk was going on about this when an old boy in the corner of the pub gives tongue and says that his son that keeps a bar over to St Ives told him a fisherman coming back late the other night picked up a glass net float that was bobbing up and down in the water and shining like a little full moon. It was apparently covered with phosphorous. 'That's what you see,' the old man said. 'That flawt were drifting and a phawsphorescent fish rubbed itself against it. The skull of a dead miner!' He laughed.

I thought about this as Alf and I were walking home. 'What do you think?' I asked. He shrugged his shoulders. 'Miners are superstitious folk,' he said. It was a dark night. 'I've got a pair of binoculars in the car,' I said. 'Would you care to walk with me as far as the cliffs?' He agreed, so we fetched the glasses and walked over to the cliffs. Well, it was there all right. At first I could see absolutely nothing. It was so dark that, looking through the glasses, it was as though I had covered the lenses with my hands. And then suddenly I saw a faint little point of light bobbing about like a will-o'-the-wisp. Alf saw it too. It was so faint that it was barely visible. But it was there all right.

Now what do you make of that? I hear there's a boat to be hired at Cape Cornwall. Tomorrow night, if I get back from the mine in time, I'm going out to have a look at the skull of that miner if I can get someone to come with me. Alf was very silent as we walked back. I don't know whether he, too, is superstitious, or if he was just trying to reason things out. I must admit that I don't feel too happy myself. It's easy to be matter-of-fact in a newspaper office and pour verbal ridicule upon country super-stitions. But down here there seems a bit more to it. After all, there are thirty odd men lying dead under the bed of the sea there. I think I'm going to have nightmares tonight. Now I must go out and post this endless screed. I'll report developments tomorrow. I wonder how long it will take us to get through one of those falls? – M.W.

Wire from Charles Patterson of the Daily Recorder to Maureen Weston at Cap View, Pendeen, dispatched from Fleet Street at 3.25 p.m. on Friday, September 15:

Jesse Maclean British now directing mining work of national importance for Supply Ministry stop No police record nothing against him – Patterson.

Wire from Charles Patterson of the Daily Recorder to Maureen Weston at Cap View, Pendeen, dispatched from Fleet Street at 6.10 p.m. on Friday, September 15:

Letter received grand work stop Wire results days operations – Patterson.

Wire from Charles Patterson of the Daily Recorder to Maureen Weston at Cap View, Pendeen, dispatched from Fleet Street at 10.5 a.m. on Saturday, September 16:

Report at once results yesterdays activities – Patterson.

Wire from Charles Patterson of the Daily Recorder to Davies at Cap View, Pendeen, dispatched from Fleet Street at 12.35 p.m. on Saturday, September 16 and carrying with it a reply-paid form:

Please inform whereabouts of Maureen Weston residing with you – Patterson.

Pre-paid wire from Mrs Alf Davies to Charles Patterson of the Daily Recorder dispatched from Pendeen at 2.40 p.m. on Saturday, September 16:

Miss Weston and my husband visited Wheal Garth mine yesterday and have not returned stop Search party organized – Davies.

Transcript of a code wire from Detective-inspector Fuller to Superintendent McGlade at Scotland Yard dispatched from Pendeen at 2.50 p.m. on Saturday, September 16:

Maureen Weston and three local miners missing stop Went down

Wheal Garth mine yesterday following visit previous day stop **Am** convinced she had discovered something stop Mine reported to be unsafe stop Two falls heard late yesterday afternoon stop Locals fear they are trapped stop Rescue parties have opened up new shaft and are working desperately to clear falls stop Advise detention of Jesse Arthur Maclean late engineer to mine for questioning stop Description tall lean dark hair thinning glasses Scotch stop Also locate and detain Wilson – Fuller.

Record of a phone call put through by Superintendent McGlade of Scotland Yard to Chief-inspector Saviour of Durham at 3.45 p.m. on Saturday, September 16:

I want you to detain Jesse Arthur Maclean, engineer in charge of the mining work at the munitions dump at Dutton. You can do it under the Emergency Powers (Defence) Act – I've nothing against him so far.

Note from Superintendent McGlade to Colonel Blank at M.I.5. and dispatched by a special messenger at 5.30 p.m. on Saturday, September 16:

For your information I enclose copies of a number of letters and telegrams sent from a Miss Maureen Weston to Charles Patterson, news editor of the *Daily Recorder*. They may be of interest to you. You will remember she was investigating the disappearance of Walter Craig in the Cadgwith U-boat incident for her paper. I am detaining the man Maclean mentioned in her letters who is now working on a munitions dump and am endeavouring to discover the whereabouts of Tubby Wilson.

This file of communications received by Patterson from Miss Weston was handed to me this afternoon by Patterson himself after he had learned that the girl had not returned from an expedition into the Wheal Garth mine.

I should be glad to hear what you think of them.

Yours.
McGLADE.

Memorandum from the Naval Intelligence Department of the Admiralty to Colonel Blank of M.I.5 dispatched by special messenger at 8.45 p.m. on Saturday September 16:

Here are details of reports of U-boats in the vicinity of the Cornish coast received since the outbreak of war from coastal patrols of the Navy and the Fleet Air Arm:

September 4,51.12 north 51.48 west. September 6,49.54 north 5.5 west. September 9, 49.51 north 3.36 west. September 10, 49. 11 north 2.24 west. September 10, 51.8 north 5.21 west. September 13, 52.3 north 5.48 west. September 14, 50. 17 north 5.54 west. September 15, 49.45 north 6.35 west. September 15, 50.25 north 5.31 west.

In most cases depth charges or bombs were released, but only in two cases has the destruction of the U-boat been definitely achieved. Hope this is what you wanted – F.E.

Communiques dispatched from the War Office and the Admiralty shortly after 9.30 p.m. on Saturday, September 16, as a result of phone calls from M.I.5:

From the War Office to officer commanding H.M. Forces encamped at Trereen, Cornwall:

Dispatch immediately two companies of infantry to Pendeen. One company is to mount guard on all exits of the Wheal Garth mine. If one company proves insufficient further troops must be dispatched. The second company is to enter the mine. Contact Detective-inspector Fuller of Scotland Yard who will be awaiting your arrival at the inn. He will provide guides to the mine and will inform you of the position.

From the Admiralty to commanders of destroyers EH 4 and EH 5 stationed at Newlyn:

Proceed immediately to 50 degrees 23 minutes north 5 degrees 43 minutes west and patrol West Cornish coast from Botallack Head to Pendeen Watch.

PART THREE

THE WHEAL GARTH CLOSES DOWN

I

PLANS

WITH a sudden thrill of excitement I realized what Logan was doing. He was carrying on a conversation in morse. But was it a conversation? Was he making it up? I looked at what I had written down. It read: 'I came here with three miners. Progress into new workings blocked by falls. Had removed part of lightest fall and found way through when met by armed Germans. What is this place?'

I looked up at Logan. His face was intent on the movements of the spoon against the iron bars of the grill. Heavy tap, pause, four light taps, pause, tap tap, pause, tap tap tap, long pause, short short, pause, short short short, long pause, short short short, short short long – and so it went on. I did not understand morse, but I presumed he was replying to the question.

I looked down again at what I had written. It made sense. It suggested that this was part of a mine. That tied up with the idea of the base being either in Cornwall or in Spain. It certainly did not read like the imaginings of a man who was mentally sick. I got up and went over to the door. Logan had finished tapping. Faintly I heard a metallic click, then two more, louder and close together. Then short short short short, pause, dash dash dash. There was no doubt about it. Someone was morsing from the next cell. 'Who is it?' I asked Logan.

'That's just what he's asked us,' he replied. 'One of the first things he said when we established contact was that he repre- sented the *Daily Recorder*. Evidently they sent someone out to look for you.' He resumed his tapping with the spoon. I waited. So Logan remembered his morse, did he?

He stopped tapping and listened. Then he took my pencil and wrote down slowly in block letters – IS CRAIG REALLY THERE THIS IS MAUREEN WESTON. 'Good God, it's a woman!' said Logan. Then he wrote: PATTERSON SENT ME TO INVESTIGATE YOUR DISAPPEARANCE.

I was amazed. 'Ask her how she found us,' I said.

The spoon went tap-tap again and presently Logan began writing the reply: 'Worked back from the spy at Carillon. This led me to phoney mine owner. And this is the mine. It lies four miles north of Saint Just.'

'So you were right,' I said. 'This base is in Cornwall. Ask her whether any one knows where she is.'

Back came the reply: 'Please repeat slower. I am working the code from a diary.'

Logan wielded the spoon again with longer pauses between each letter. Then came the reply: 'Yes. But the Germans have blown up galleries in old workings so that it will look as though we have been trapped by a fall. Have you any plans?'

Heavy, light, pause, heavy heavy heavy went the tapping of Logan's spoon. It was so short that I knew what that must be. Then we were interrupted by the opening of the guard-room door. Shortly afterwards our evening meal was brought to us.

When we were alone again I said: 'You know, we've only got till Sunday evening at the latest?'

He nodded with his mouth full of potato stew and contrived to grin at the same time.

I looked at him closely. 'Do you remember who the owner of Carillon was?' I asked.

'Ar, his name was Cutner – is that right?'

'Your memory is not so bad after all,' I said. 'I suppose it's all come back to you?'

'That's right.' He nodded and grinned, and there was that twinkle in his eyes that I had not seen since Cadgwith.

I was still not altogether convinced. It seemed incredible that the man could have put an act over on me so completely. After all, I had been his constant companion for nearly two weeks. Anyway, I failed to see the necessity of it. I tried him with another question. 'Can you tell me the name of the coastguard at Cadgwith?' I asked, and there was a trace of anxiety in my voice, for I was desperately anxious for someone to share with me the responsibility of immobilizing the base.

'Let me see,' he hesitated, his Slav features puckered with amusement. 'It wouldn't be Ted Morgan, now, would it?'

I felt a sudden great relief. 'Thank God for that,' I breathed. 'But why the devil didn't you tell me you were only shamming?'

'I would have,' he said, 'but I figured it out that I'd have a better chance of putting it across if you thought I was going balmy too. Anyway, I'm no actor. I knew the only thing was to make myself believe I was balmy. I tell you, at times I was afraid I really was.'

I gave a short laugh. 'That's what most actors have discovered,' I said. 'But what was the idea?'

'I wanted to avoid giving them the information they were after. And also I thought it might help.'

'Well, it doesn't seem to have,' I said.

'Hasn't it?' He beckoned me across to his bed. 'Here's the result of my carving,' he said. He bent down and tilted the bed up so that he could get hold of the leg nearest the wall and farthest from the door. With the help of his knife he began to prise very carefully at one of the letters of his name which he had cut on the inside of the leg, low down. And in a second the whole section with his name had come away, and in a hollow cut below it was a key fitted snugly into the wood.

He put the section back and tapped it carefully into position. It fitted perfectly and very tightly. Unless any one were looking for it, it was unlikely to be discovered. 'What key is it?' I asked.

'The key to this cell.'

'But how did you get hold of it?'

He returned to his stew. 'There are four cells along here,' he said, 'and the locks are all the same. Remember those ratings that were put in the other cells to cool off after a brawl last Monday? The guards used the same key for all the cells. And I noticed another thing. The guards were sometimes careless. They left the keys in the cell doors instead of returning them to the guard-room. So I started my craze for modelling and hollowed out my little hiding-place. Because I was supposed to be daft I got away with it. And two days after I had finished it I had the chance of lifting a key from the lock of the neighbouring cell. It was missed about two hours later. You remember we were searched on Wednesday night and the whole cell turned upside down by the guard? But by then it was safely tucked away.'

'I wonder they haven't put bolts on the door,' I said.

'Probably the guard didn't report the loss.'

I sat down on my bed again and considered the matter. It was certainly a step forward. We had the means of getting out of our cell at any time of the night. But having got out, what then? The various stores were all locked and we hadn't the key to any of these. That meant we could not get at either the fuel or the munitions. And the guards went the rounds every hour. Moreover, the arrival of Maureen Weston and her three miners complicated matters in that any plan to destroy the whole base meant the loss of their lives as well as ours.

The same thought seemed to have crossed Big Logan's mind, for he said: 'What's this Maureen Weston like?'

I cast my mind back to the time when she had been on the staff of the *Recorder*. 'She's small and dark and very attractive,' I said. 'She has Irish blood in her and as women go she's pretty tough.' I suddenly remembered that big men like small women. 'She's just your type if you're feeling repressed.'

He grinned. 'Sounds interesting,' he said. 'But just at the moment I was thinking out some way of destroying her and every one else in this base.'

'So was I,' I said. 'But how are we going to do it?'

'We should be able to deal with the guard. There are only two who actually do the rounds. All we have to do is to get the keys off them, go into the munitions store and blow the place up.'

'It sounds easy, put like that,' I said. 'But suppose we aren't able to deal with the guards silently and they rouse the base?'

'We'll have to take the chance. Even if they were able to give the alarm we'd still have plenty of time.'

'True,' I nodded, 'but, on the other hand, we can't afford to take chances. Can't we manage it without attacking the guards? What I've been thinking about is those six-inch guns on the submarines. You know how to handle them, don't you? The after gun on U 21 is in working order and the boat lies with its stern facing straight down the main cave. One shot with that could surely be sufficient to block the underwater entrance. That would stop the submarines leaving without destroying them.'

He shook his head. 'We must destroy the submarines,' he said. 'They might blast their way out through the cliff. And the only way to destroy the boats is to blow the place up. Your scheme would only work if we could get out of the place ourselves and warn the naval authorities.'

'Listen!' I said. The relief of being able to discuss the position with someone instead of just lying and racking my brains had made me somewhat excited. 'Maureen has brought three miners with her. If we could release them and, after firing the gun, get into the landward exit with picks and so on, we might be able to get through the falls they have made this afternoon.'

At that he laughed. 'Do you know what a bad fall of rock in a Cornish tin mine is like?' he demanded. 'There's maybe a hundred feet of roof brought down along our exit gallery. And the blockage will be caused by huge chunks of granite. And you suggest three miners get through it with picks!'

'Well, there are mobile drills in the base,' I said, a trifle put out.
At that he stopped grinning and said: 'So there are.' He sat
silent for a moment, stroking his beard. 'The trouble is they'd
guess where we had gone. As soon as they had searched the base,
they'd be after us, and we shouldn't have a dog's chance.'

'I'm not so sure,' I said. 'In the first place they would probably
be too worried about other things to come after us for some time,
and by then we could have partially blocked the exit gallery
behind us. For another, we could lay for the guards and if successful, arm ourselves at the expense of the base. What I mean is that,
though I think it rather risky to be dependent upon a successful
attack on the guards for our means of destroying the base, I think
we might deal with the guards as well as man the gun. If we
succeeded with the guards we should have about ten minutes,
maybe quarter of an hour, in which to ransack the base for the
equipment and weapons we required. If we didn't succeed, then
we'd be no worse off. With the gun loaded and sighted, it would
only be a matter of an instant to fire.'

Logan snapped his fingers. 'Sure and I believe you've got it,' he
said. 'The next thing to do is to get in touch with this Weston girl
again and find out what part of the base she came out into.'

At that moment we were interrupted by the arrival of the guard
to collect our empty stew cans. 'You'd better get some sleep,' he
said in German, pointing to our beds and laying his hands against
his cheek to indicate what he meant. 'Two submarines are
coming in tonight.' He held up two fingers in front of my face and
said: 'Boats.'

I thanked him and he departed smiling. He was one of the
nicest of our guards, a large fellow with a frank open face and a
ridiculous little moustache. I passed the information on to Logan.
'Thank God, they're both coming in tonight,' I said. 'That leaves
tomorrow night free. Unless of course U 47 doesn't leave tonight,
as planned.'

He got up and went over to the door. In his hand he held the
knife he had used to hollow out the leg of his bed. But there
seemed much more activity than usual in the gallery. In fact, it
was not until nearly ten o'clock that he was able to establish
contact with Maureen Weston. Movement in the gallery outside
remained remarkably active, and as a result he was not able to
keep up a sustained conversation. What he learned was very
damping to our spirits. The mine gallery by which she and her
companions had reached the base entered it by way of a recess in
the guard-room. Moreover, the mine gallery was practically

blocked about two hundred feet from the base.

This meant that the possibility of getting anything like a mobile drill through was small and in any case the chances of ever having the opportunity of entering the mine by way of the guard-room seemed somewhat remote. I understood now the cause of the activity in the gallery outside and the continual movement of men in and out of the guard-room opposite. It was from the guard-room that they were prepared to meet an attack. Probably they had machine-guns ready mounted in the mine galleries in case miners cleared the falls.

But this activity did not explain the faint but persistent clatter of electric welders and the muffled roar of machinery. Usually at this time of night the base was comparatively quiet, save for the hum of the dynamos and the murmur of voices. But for the fact that my watch said it was ten-twenty I should have said it was daytime. It could mean only one thing. 'They're rushing the repairs to U 21,' I said.

Logan nodded. 'I'm afraid they are,' he agreed. 'Which means that they're going to send the boats out tomorrow night and not Sunday.'

'Maybe they'll get some away tonight.'

'Hell! I wish I hadn't left it so late.'

'Why did you?' I asked. 'For the same reason that I did?'

'What was that?'

'Oh, just that I put it off until I couldn't put it off any longer.'

'Perhaps,' he said. 'Also I wanted to get the maximum number of boats in the base. Your friend Maureen doesn't seem to have helped us much.'

'Except in so far as her disappearance may make people suspicious about this mine. Patterson is no fool.'

'But why should they suspect that there is something wrong with the mine? The girl goes down with three miners to look over it and doesn't appear again. Two deep rumbling sounds are heard – an explosion or a fall? A search party is organized. They find the workings blocked by a big fall. Every one is then satisfied as to the reason why she and her companions never got back.'

'That depends on Patterson,' I said. 'Ask her how often she was reporting to Patterson and how much she has told him about the mine.'

But to get a message through now took some time owing to the activity outside. In all I think it was nearly half an hour before we got the full reply. It came through bit by bit as opportunity offered. It read: 'Patterson has no idea mine is submarine base.

All he knows is that I was suspicious of it and that on the first occasion I went down I found falls that should not have been there and that looked unnatural.'

'And that's that,' said Logan, returning to his bed.

'Patterson is no fool,' I reiterated. 'And he's got the sharpest nose for news of any man I know. I think he'll move heaven and earth to get the mine opened up.'

'Ar, that may be so, but who is going to do the opening up? To clear a big fall of rock takes time and costs a deal of money. Who is going to pay for it – not the paper, I know.'

'Well, it's our only hope,' I said, 'if they send the boats out tomorrow night.'

At that moment the key grated in the lock and one of the guards came in. The first of the two U-boats was coming in and we were marched down to the docks.

We had a wait of more than fifteen minutes in the cold damp atmosphere of No. 3 dock with the constant chugging of the donkey engine echoing from the main cave. In the course of this time I gained several pieces of interesting information. All work had been suspended on U 47 and she would not be ready to go out until Sunday night at the earliest. The whole engineering effort of the base was bing concentrated on U 21 and the word had apparently gone out that she must be ready for active service by tomorrow afternoon – that was Saturday. This confirmed my belief that the whole fleet would go out on the Saturday and not the Sunday night. There was a rumour that the boat coming in now was the one that had sunk the *Athenia*. And there was also talk that the second boat was already waiting to come in. That meant that in a few hours' time there would be no less than six of Germany's largest ocean-going U-boats in the base, as well as the store barge.

I passed on the information to Logan. But I did not hear his comment for there was a sudden swirl of water in the dock and a large wave slid quietly along it overflowing on to the dockside and thoroughly wetting our feet. There was much seething of water in the main cave, then the slam of metal against metal, followed by prolonged cheers. The first of the two U-boats had arrived.

The diminutive diesel-engined tug fussed noisily about the main cave and in a few minutes the bows of the U-boat appeared opposite No. 3 dock. A rope was tossed on to the dockside and we passed it from hand to hand. As soon as it was fully manned the order was given to heave and we dug our heels into the uneven rock floor and strained at the rope. Slowly the boat slid into the dock, the ratings that lined her decks fending her off from the sides with boat-hooks.

You seldom realize how wide a submarine is below the surface until you see one manœuvred into a confined space. Empty, the dock presented quite a wide surface of water, oily and glinting in the electric light. But the U-boat filled it from side to side, and her conning tower almost touched the roof of the cave. I could not help feeling then how entirely insulated this base was from the outside world. It was, in fact, a world of its own. And after a fortnight there it seemed to me quite possible that no other world existed, that my memories of green fields, of huddles of white cottages among the Cornish cliffs, of Piccadilly, of factories and ships were all a dream, and that this was the only reality. And now here was this U-boat come from that other world with probably Kiel as its last port of call.

As soon as the boat had been made fast the crew were assembled and marched off to their quarters. Normally we should have then been taken back to our cells. But on this occasion we were taken to the next dock, No. 4, where the U 21 lay. Men were required to assist in moving the for'ard six-inch gun from the electric trolley on which it had been taken to the foundry, back on to the deck of the submarine. Repairs to the gun had been completed.

There was ten minutes' back-breaking work as it was lifted on pulleys attached to the steel derrick and swung, largely by brute force, into position. It was while this was happening that a slight accident occurred which had a wholly disproportionate influence on what happened later. The commander of U 21 had come down to welcome the Number One of the boat that had just come in, U 27, who was apparently a particular friend. And having seen him to his quarters, he came down to see how the engineers were getting on with his own boat. He was smoking a cigarette. This was strictly against regulations, but no one seemed inclined to point that out to him. There came a moment in the hoisting of the gun when every man was required to strain his utmost to keep the mountings from swinging against the side of the submarine. The commander did not hesitate, but threw his weight in with the rest. It reminded me of a scrum down. We were all pushing against each other with our heads down until at last the mounting was clear of the deck and was allowed to swing slowly inwards.

We were just straightening our aching backs and getting our breath back when suddenly somebody said: 'There's something burning.' The acrid smell of smouldering rags seemed all around us. Then something flared up by one of the legs of the derrick. For a split second every one stood motionless and my mind recorded a vivid impression as though I were looking at a still from a film. Then one of the engineers dived at the flames and began stamping them out with his feet. What had happened was that the commander had thrown the stub of his cigarette away before helping with the gun, and it had set fire to a mass of oil-sodden rags. Probably they were impregnated with petrol as well. Before the engineer could muffle them the flames had caught at his overalls and the oil in them was burning.

The U-boat commander ripped off his jacket and flung it round the man's burning legs. For a second every one seemed to forget about the fire itself, which was now flaring noisily and causing some to move back on account of the heat of it. Moreover, the dockside itself, impregnated with oil, was alight in places. Having settled the engineer's trousers, the commander flung his jacket on to the flames and stamped them under with his feet.

By this time we were all coughing with the smoke, which was very heavy now that the flames themselves were muffled. As he stamped with his feet the commander kept coughing. I could see the sweat gathering in beads on his forehead. Then suddenly his knees seemed to sag under him and he collapsed. One man pulled him clear of the smouldering pile of rags, while two others finished the job of extinguishing the fire.

The doctor was sent for, but it was some time before the commander came round and every one who had been standing near the fire seemed to be feeling queer. One man actually fainted, but recovered as soon as he had been laid out a little farther down the dock. I myself found difficulty in breathing and my head reeled as though I were a little drunk. Logan, too, complained of feeling peculiar.

Then the order was given to get over to No. 1 dock as the second submarine was coming in. It was shouted by the officer in charge of the fatigue from the end of the dock. Some men obeyed, but the majority were too busy getting their breath back or arguing as to the cause of the trouble. The order was repeated. But instead of obeying it Logan swung himself on to U 21 and joined the engineers in their struggle to lower the gun into its correct position. I followed him. We had lost touch with our guards. The gun was eased into its mountings. The operation took about three minutes and gave us ample opportunity to look around. But the result was most discouraging. Even ready-use ammunition was stowed below deck and it was quite impossible to get at the armoured ammunition truck.

Our guard then re-established contact with us. As we climbed down on to the dockside I saw that the commander was now on his feet again, looking very white and his clothes in a filthy state. He still seemed a bit short of breath. The doctor said something about asphyxiation, but I couldn't hear the whole sentence. We were marched down to No. 1 dock. The fatigue party had already manned the hawser and I could see the dark pointed bows of the submarine nosing into the dock. As we took our place, Logan said: 'What was the matter with him?'

'Asphyxiation of some sort,' I said.

'Yes, but why did we all suffer from it? What caused it?'

I said I didn't know, but presumed it was something to do with the burning waste. Our conversation was interrupted by the order to heave. As soon as the submarine had been made fast, the fatigue party was dismissed and we were taken back to our cell. When the door was closed Logan said: 'This is a helluva mess. Your idea of manning the after gun of U 21 is quite hopeless.'

'You mean we can't get hold of the ammunition?' I said.

'Not only that. There's the guard. It wasn't until I saw the one on the bridge that I remembered they mount two guards on every submarine in the base day and night. The other was in the bows.'

I nodded. I was feeling very despondent. When I had discovered that Logan was as alive as I was to the situation, I had for some reason felt that success was assured. His great bulk gave one confidence where it was a question of action.

Not only were the guns out of the question, but we had only twenty-four hours in which to carry out any plan. And throughout that time the base would be a hive of activity. It was, as Logan put it – a hell of a mess. Failure would mean the loss of hundreds of British lives. Moreover, it would mean a severe blow to British prestige, and might as a result seriously affect the course of the war, for neutral opinion was a vital factor in the initial stages. I had a sudden picture of those four great ships of the Atlantic squadron wallowing up the Channel, of periscopes cutting the water inside the screening destroyers, of sudden explosions and the sterns of those proud ships lifting as they sank. It was not to be thought of. Something had to be done.

'Well?' Logan said.

I began removing my wet shoes and socks. 'Looks as though we make a desperate attack on the guard,' I said.

'When?' he asked. 'Tonight?' His tone was sarcastic. He had taken off his dungarees and was climbing into bed. 'I'm going to sleep on it,' he announced.

'But, good God, man,' I said, 'this is the last full night we've got in which to do something.'

'And the base full of men repairing things. Did you see No. 3 dock after we had berthed that last submarine? The stores department were already at work replenishing the supplies. They'll be at it all night – food, water, munitions. U 21 has got to be finished by tomorrow afternoon. You told me so yourself. And every other boat in the base will have to be ready for sea by then. We'll have to wait. If we left this cell now every one we met would wonder what we were up to. But if we left it in the daytime – say, when we were having tea – no one would pay any attention to us. They'd just think we were on fatigue. They're used to seeing us around the base in the daytime.'

'I see your point,' I said, and put the light out and climbed into bed. He was right, of course, but at the same time it made it a rather last-minute job. The truth was that now zero-hour had been definitely fixed my whole soul revolted against it. It is extraordinary how powerful the will to live is in the average human being. If it had been a question of immediate action, I could have faced it. Subconsciously, I suppose, I had keyed myself to expect action that night. I had felt that it was tonight or never as soon as I knew for certain that the boats were going out the following night. And I honestly believe that if it had been a question of instantaneous action, I would have walked out of that cell and blown the whole place up quite calmly. But to plan such and action sixteen hours in advance somehow revolted me.

Sleep was out of the question. I simply lay in the darkness and thought and thought till plans went round in my head without meaning. And as I became more and more mentally tired, my plans gained in phantasy until they had no relation to reality whatsoever. Schemes for blasting a way out through the cliff by firing a six-inch gun like a machine-gun, for escaping through the main entrance in diving suits, for constructing all sorts of Heath Robinson contrivances to blow the base up without killing myself rattled round my brain. I even remembered the strata of limestone I had discovered and thought of drilling through that to the main shaft of the mine or burning piles of oil-impregnate cotton waste in order to asphyxiate Fulke.

And then for some reason I was awake. It did not take me long to discover the reason. My subconscious schemes were still clear in my head and I realized that my mind had connected the limestone strata and the burning waste and I was back in my school-days listening to a rather portly man with a mortarboard and horn-rimmed spectacles initiating myself and about fifteen others into the mysteries of chemistry.

I leant over and shook Big Logan. Instantly it seemed he was wide awake. I heard him sit up in his bed. 'What is it?' he asked.

'Listen!' I said, I was excited. 'Do you know what happens to limestone when it's heated? It gives off carbon dioxide and leaves calcium oxide, which is quick lime. If I remember rightly the equation is – $CaCo_3 = CaO + CO_2$.'

'How does that help?' he asked.

'Well, don't you see? Carbon dioxide is poisonous when it replaces air – lack of oxygen causes suffocation. That's what happened to the commander of U 21 tonight. There's a strata of limestone running down No. 4 dock and across into the storage cave opposite, and it broadens out to a width of about five feet at the entrance to the store. That burning waste was lying on this strata of limestone and was giving off CO_2. The commander passed out through lack of oxygen and we were all affected slightly. Now, suppose we could get a really big fire going on the limestone.'

'And then ask the commander of the base to hold a scouts' jamboree round it,' suggested Logan.

'I'm serious,' I said.

'I know you are,' he said. 'You've been lying awake thinking up all sorts of impossible schemes to avoid being killed yourself.'

It was a direct accusation of cowardice and I resented it, largely because I knew it to be true. 'I was only trying to think out a scheme that had a chance,' I said. 'I'm not afraid of dying.'

'Well, I am, if it's unnecessary,' he replied.

'Then think up something better,' I said, and turned over.

He did not reply, and when I had recovered from my resentment at his attitude, I began to consider the scheme in detail. Certainly the bald outline I had given did not sound particularly convincing. Several questions immediately leapt to my mind. First, how were we to make the necessary fire without it being put out before it had got to work on the limestone? Second, how were we to immunize ourselves? Third, what about Maureen and her companions? And fourth, was the ventilation system so good that it would be impossible to get sufficient CO_2 into the base to render every one unconscious?

I began to consider these questions one by one. The first, of course, depended upon circumstances. It was a matter for action when the opportunity offered. Tanks of oil and petrol were often being trundled round the base when a submarine was being refuelled. I had a box of matches in the pocket of my dungarees. A drum would have to be broached and some of its contents poured over the limestone strata. The flames would then have to be fed. A mixture of oil and petrol would be best. Then we should want picks and shovels to break up the limestone and build it round the flames. Moreover, the flames must not be allowed to spread – there was a good deal of oil on the docksides and in the dock gallery. What we really ought to do was to build a little circle of broken limestone and pour petrol and oil into the centre. Then there was the question of our own immunization. I began to see the reason for Logan's sarcasm.

At that moment Logan turned over towards me and said: 'What exactly is the effect of carbon dioxide? Does it kill a person?'

'It's not exactly poisonous, like coal gas,' I said. 'It just uses up the oxygen in the atmosphere. You saw the effects this evening. A man gets dizzy and then passes out. Put him in the fresh air and he comes round again. But I believe it can be lethal if it goes on long enough.'

Then he began asking all the questions that I had been asking myself. And the more we discussed it the more elaborate and impossible the whole thing seemed. To immunize ourselves we needed an oxygen cylinder. How were we to get hold of one? True, there were plenty in the base, but would one be around just when we wanted it? Then there was the question of the four other prisoners. Logan said: 'They would have to take their chance. In a locked cell they might not come off too badly and you say we can revive them with oxygen.' As to the air conditioning, Logan pointed out that fresh air was brought in through a hole drilled in the cliff above the underwater entrance and the stale air was driven out through the look-out hole, the entrance to which led off the upper galleries. 'That means the carbon dioxide would circulate through the entire base,' he said.

But though this seemed to help, I must admit I had by then come to the conclusion that the scheme was unworkable. And after we had talked it over for some time, I said: 'For heaven's sake try to think out some scheme by which we can get at the munitions store and blow the place up.' I was by then tired and discouraged. We discussed various plans for dealing with our guards at a time when the munitions store was open, getting into it and using one of the many mines stored there to explode the place. But Logan kept reverting to my own scheme and asking questions. I suppose my brain must have been tired out, for my answers became more and more vague, and the next thing I remember is being shaken by the guard and told to get up. I looked at my watch. It was seven o'clock and my breakfast of porridge, bread and jam and tea was lying on the floor beside me.

2

ACTION

LOGAN was already seated on his bed, eating his porridge. As the door closed behind the guard, I said: 'Well, have you decided on any plan of action?'

He shook his head and continued eating. 'We'll have to take advantage of any opportunities that offer,' he said. He made no mention of my own scheme, and frankly, when I came to consider it with the prospect of putting it into action within the next few hours, it did not seem practicable. There were so many snags. I felt nervous and depressed. We had no plan, and yet we had to do something within the next twelve hours.

When he had finished his porridge, Logan knelt down on the floor and removed the key from its hiding-place. 'What do you want that for?' I asked, as he slipped it inside one of his socks and began putting on his shoes, which were still wet from the previous night.

'We may need it,' he said.

Even then, though I knew he had no plan, he gave me confidence. It wasn't just a question of his strength. There was something solid about the man, and I thanked God that his brain was all right and that I had not got to carry out some desperate plan on my own. At that moment I wished that my experience on the *Daily Recorder* had been as a reporter and not as dramatic critic. I could think of one or two men in the news-room who would have revelled in a situation like this, men who had lived on their wits and knocked about the world all their lives. I had never had to use my wits as a means of livelihood in that sense. How much Big Logan had had to use his wits, as opposed to brute force, I did not know, but his swift adaptation to circumstances on the cliffs above the Devil's Frying Pan and later in the U-boat was encouraging.

Almost before we had finished breakfast, the guard was back again. But instead of beginning the morning's work in the latrines and kitchens, we were taken straight down to the docks and set to work carrying stores from the store-rooms to U 54, which was the boat that had come into No. 1 dock the previous night. This seemed promising, for No. 1 dock was the nearest to the munitions store. And I felt a distinct zero-hour feeling within me.

We obtained the stores from No. 1 store-room, directly opposite the dock. That meant crossing the main gallery and entering an electrically-lit tunnel, protected by sheet metal doors, that led to the store itself. These doors now stood open and the key was in the lock. It would take only a matter of a second to close the doors and lock them. That would look after the provisioning officer of U 54 and the four men who were working under him in the store. The trouble was that, though our own two guards did not present much difficulty since they had become accustomed to us and regarded us as quite harmless – it must be remembered that Logan was still a mental defective to all who knew him in the base – there were the customary two guards on the U-boat itself, one standing on the bridge and the other near the bows, as well as several men lifting the stores from the deck, where we placed them, and passing them into the submarine through an after-hatch. Even supposing we were able to deal with all these, there was still the problem of the guards to the munitions store. I had never been into this store. Only certain men were allowed in. But I had been as far as the entrance. A huge steel bulkhead had been built across the entrance in an effort to protect the base from any mishap. The door through this bulkhead was only just wide enough to take a munitions trolley. The guards were stationed one on either side of the tunnel that led off the main dock gallery just beyond No. 1 dock.

The prospect seemed hopeless. But at least we were near the munitions dump, and I was keyed up ready for a desperate attempt. But Logan made no move, even when we were joined by three more men, dressed in dungarees like ourselves. They were under a guard of two ratings and a petty officer, and were presumably Maureen Weston's miners. The guard complicated the position, for, unlike our own guards, they were watchful of the new-comers. But the miners did represent an addition to our force, especially as they looked to me about the toughest trio I had ever set eyes on. One, who seemed to be their leader, was short and bow-legged, and had a Welsh accent. The other two were undoubtedly Cornish. Whether Logan thought that their use-fulness was cancelled out by the guard they had brought, I do not know, but when I asked him in a whisper if he was going to make a move, he replied: 'Not yet.'

Once we had to go to the foundry, which was right at the other end of the dock gallery, to collect the conning tower hatch, which had been fitted with a new rubber jointing ring. The activity along the whole gallery and in most of the docks was terrific, especially in docks 3 and 4. When we passed No. 4, fresh water was being run into U 21 from a mobile tank and torpedoes were being hoisted aboard from a munitions truck. Riveting had ceased, but engineers were still at work on one of the AA guns. The boat that had come into No. 3 dock the night before was being provisioned and fuelled.

Listening to the talk of the men, I found there were only two topics of conversation – the coming action and the rumour of a woman in the base. No statement had been issued about the previous day's alarm, but it seemed to be generally known that certain prisoners had arrived in the base, including a woman. Doubtless the emergency guards had passed on the information to their friends. What interested me was the effect that the unseen presence of a woman in this monastic place had on different men. Those who had been stationed on the Atlantic trade routes and at the base long before war broke out had not seen a woman now for some months. Some became sentimental and talked of their sweethearts and wives. But the majority seemed to take it as a great joke and already obscene stories, based on Maureen's presence in the base, were going the rounds. It seemed strange that I should see this stock theatrical situation actually happening in real life, especially against such a novel background.

But though a girl's presence in the base was something of a sensation, the coming action was the main topic of conversation. I realized then how similar must be the feelings of these men to my own at that moment. Zero-hour for them was somewhere about midnight. At present they were safe enough, if somewhat bored. But tonight they were leaving the safety of the base for the unknown. The chances of ever returning were not great, they knew that. And like me, probably their best chance of remaining alive rested in failure.

About eleven o'clock, when we had completed the piling of the necessary stores on the after deck of U 54, Logan and I were marched off to our usual job of emptying the latrines. Death has its compensations! When we had finished we were marched back to the docks, and joined the three new prisoners at carrying stores to U 21. The dockside seemed littered with stores of various kinds. There were cases of margarine and jam, tins of biscuits, cardboard cases full of tinned foods and packets of coffee, sugar, salt, and all sorts of other foodstuffs. The three miners had carried all this from No. 4 store and were piling it on the dockside, opposite the after-hatch. Mines were being loaded into the after-mine-laying compartments and a huge tank of oil had been brought on to the dock on a trolley. There was also a smaller tank of petrol. But refuelling operations had not yet begun.

We stood about for a time, and then several of the crew, together with the cook, arrived. The after-hatch was opened and they descended into the bowels of the submarine. We then brought a small gangway and laid it from the dockside to the submarine. Our job was to carry the stores from the dock to the submarine and lower them through the after-hatch on a rope.

It was now nearly twelve – first lunch. There were two lunch times – twelve and twelve-thirty. This made it easier for the kitchen staff when there were a large number in the base, as there were now, and at the same time enabled any rush work to be carried on without any complete stoppage for the midday meal.

We had not been carrying on this work long when, just as I was lowering a case of margarine down the hatch, I saw Logan time his arrival at a pile of cases at the same moment as the little leader of the miners arrived with the next load. I could not be sure, but I felt convinced that Logan said something to the man. I did not get an opportunity to speak to Logan for some time, but I noticed that the miners, instead of putting the cases down anyhow, were piling them on top of one another, so that they made a sort of wall of cases across the dockside.

Convinced that something was afoot, I gradually speeded up my work so that, instead of alternating with Logan, I was bringing my cases up just behind him. At last I managed it so that I put my case down on the deck of the submarine at the same time as he put his down. I had just opened my mouth to question him when he whispered: 'Stand by.'

A few minutes later orders were suddenly shouted from the main gallery. I glanced at my watch. It was midday. I looked down the length of the submarine. Men in their white uniforms were passing along the gallery in the direction of the ramp leading to the upper galleries. The docks were much quieter now and there was far less movement of men up and down the gallery at the end of the dock.

I took a quick look round at the disposition of the guards as I walked off the submarine. Our own two guards were standing chatting beside the pile of cases. One was actually leaning on them. The U-boat guard was now reduced to one and he was standing on the deck for'ard of the conning tower. The other guard was on duty inside the submarine as base personnel were now storing munitions. A munitions trolley loaded with shells was standing on the dockside. Another gangway had been thrown from the dockside to the deck of the submarine and these shells were being carried in through the for'ard hatch. At the moment the trolley, with upwards of twenty shells on it, was standing deserted on the dockside, the personnel having gone to first lunch. There remained only the miners' guard of a petty officer and two ratings.

I was now following close behind Logan and feeling uncomfortably self-conscious. Our guards were deep in conversation, with their backs half-turned to us. As we approached the pile of cases, one of them looked round. I could not believe he would not notice the air of expectation about me. We each took hold of a case of canned goods. The guard turned to answer a question the other had put. Logan carefully replaced his case. Then he straightened up. Until then I don't think I had realized how enormous his hands were. He stretched them out and took each of the guards by the throat. His body seemed to brace itself and the muscles of his arms swelled as he forced those two men silently to the ground behind the barrier of packing cases. They seemed to lose consciousness without even a kick.

'Get into his uniform,' he said, pointing to the smaller of the two men.

I did not hesitate. The die was cast now. We could not go back. And strangely enough, now that I had something to do, I did not feel in the least nervous.

Logan glanced over the boxes and then picked up a case and took it on to the deck of the submarine. Feverishly I worked at the uniform of the guard, afraid that at any moment he might become conscious again or that the miners' guard would reappear. By the time Logan was back I had got the uniform off the man. One by one he banged their heads sharply against the rock floor. I thought he had smashed their skulls, but he must have seen my look of horror, for he said: 'It's all right. Only making certain that they stay out.'

It was a matter of seconds for me to slip into the man's uniform. Logan glanced once more round the store boxes. Then he dragged the man whose uniform I had borrowed to one side and covered him with cases. Then he said: 'Step out on to the deck and call to the petty officer of the guard. His name is Kammel. Just call his name and beckon to him.'

I did as he told me. I stepped out from behind the cases. 'Herr Kammel!' I called. 'Here!' And I nodded to him with my head. He came at once and I stepped back behind the cases. Logan told me to kneel down and pretend to be examining the unconscious guard. I knelt down and supported the man's head with my arm.

The footsteps of the petty officer rang sharply on the rock as he approached. I never saw the blow, but I heard it. It was a low dull thud and was accompanied by the sound of splintering bone. I felt slightly sick as I looked up and saw Big Logan holding the man by the scruff of his neck like a puppy as he lowered his unconscious body beside the other. The man's mouth was hanging open. The jaw had obviously been broken.

There remained the two ratings. And then there was the guard still standing serenely on the deck of the submarine just in front of the conning tower. Looking over the cases, I could just see part of his uniform and his right hand. The three miners had just appeared out of the store at the end of the dock and were being escorted towards us by their guard. 'What do we do now?' I asked Logan.

'Get the guard,' he said, and bending down he removed the petty officer's revolver from its holster. 'When they come up to the cases, you be bending down over the petty officer and tell them to get hold of his legs and shoulders. Make your voice sound as though it were urgent. I'll do the rest.' He pushed the unconscious guard, who had acted as decoy for the petty officer, under the cases with his mate, and then waited, the revolver behind his back.

I bent down and lifted the petty officer's head. I waited until I heard the sound of cases being stacked and then I called out in German to the two ratings. 'The petty officer has fainted,' I said. 'Come and help me lift him.' I heard their boots on the rock behind me. I did not dare look up. It was a nasty moment. I was dressed as a rating and consequently could not give them an order.

'What's the matter with him?' asked one. He spoke with a soft Bavarian accent.

'I don't know,' I said. 'You take his feet.'

Out of the tail of my eye I saw him take hold of the petty officer's feet. But the other man remained standing, obviously expecting me to take hold of the arms. 'You take his arms,' I said, and began to unbutton the petty officer's tunic and loosen his collar.

There was a moment's hesitation, and then the man bent down and slipped his hands beneath the officer's armpits. I remember noticing that his nails were unpleasantly bitten. 'Ready?' I said. And at the same moment came the sickening thud of metal on bone. As the man holding the petty officer's feet collapsed, I straightened up and covered the other with my revolver. He was too surprised to cry out. He looked from the fallen man to me with his mouth agape, and in that second strong hands gripped him by the throat. I looked round as the man slid unconscious to the floor. The little bow-legged miner was standing over him. I got to my feet. It had all happened in a flash. When I looked over the barricade of cases, I could see no one on the dockside. The guard on the U-boat was still standing just for'ard of the conning tower.

'Get into these uniforms as quick as you can,' Logan told the three miners. 'And if any of them come round, you know what to do.' Then he nodded to me and lifted one of the cases. I followed him up the gangway, my revolver swinging from its lanyard. He lowered the case through the hatch. Then we moved quickly for'ard, the grey curved bulk of the conning tower between us and the last remaining guard.

We stopped at the after gun. 'Get him round here,' Logan whispered. 'Pretend you've discovered something wrong with the gun. Keep your face turned away from the light.'

I nodded. 'Wache!' I called. Then I repeated it. 'Wache!' There was the sound of boots on hollow steel and the ring of a rifle. Unlike our own guards, who were armed with revolvers, the ratings that provided the U-boat guards were equipped with rifles and had bayonets fixed. I pointed to the telescopic sights at the side of the gun. 'Someone seems to have broken this,' I said.

It was simple. He peered at the sight. The next second I had caught hold of him as he fell. He never made a sound as Logan hit him. We laid him out on the deck. 'Quick!' said Logan. He ran to the ladder leading to the bridge. I followed him. At the top he paused. Someone was passing along the gallery at the end of the dock. I glanced back. Our miners were now struggling into the uniforms. I looked up at Logan. He seemed very different from the friendly Cornish fisherman I had known – and very different indeed from the friendly half-wit the base had known. His face had an intent purposeful look and that huge bulk that had been a harmless spectacle to the German ratings now seemed most sinister. It seemed to me scarcely credible that the man should have dealt so silently and so swiftly with no less than four armed guards.

Logan waited until the man had passed the end of the gallery and then, in a flash, he was on the bridge, had tumbled down the conning tower hatch. I followed him. We passed the control room and moved silently forward. Both of us had our revolvers ready. Then Logan hesitated and nodded to me to go forward. We had reached a bulkhead. Beyond it I could see our last guard. He was leaning against a rack of rifles, humming to himself. I went in, my hand on my revolver. At the sound of my footsteps, he sprang to attention, thinking I was an officer. The butt of his rifle rang on the steel floor plates. 'Give me that rifle,' I said in German. And I stepped forward and grabbed hold of it. His first instinct was to obey the order, and before he had realized that Big Logan was covering him with a revolver, the weapon was in my hands.

'March him aft,' Logan said.

I gave the order and we went clattering down the gangway past the control room and the ward-room and into the storage chamber. Here three men and an officer were busy dealing with the cases that we had lowered through the hatch. They turned as we entered. They were unarmed and could do nothing.

'Tell them that I'll shoot the first man that utters a sound,' Logan said.

I told them.

'Now get up through that hatch and have all our late guards dropped down here,' Logan said to me.

I ran up that little ladder and out on to the deck again. As soon as I had signalled to the three men on the dockside to bring the bodies on board I ran for'ard and got hold of the guard we had knocked out by the after gun. When we had lowered the bodies we closed the hatch. Almost immediately the men inside were attempting to force it open. I sent two of the miners to bring the heaviest articles they could find on the dockside with which to pin it down. The largest of them, whose uniform incidentally was much too small for him, stood with me on the hatch and held it down. In a few seconds the other two returned, struggling with a small portable forge, which is part of the equipment of every submarine. It had been left against the wall of the dock and weighed several hundredweight. It was a most effective weight and we placed it on the hatch. Then the miner I had detailed to mount guard went for'ard.

By this time I was beginning to get anxious about Logan, who had not yet reappeared. I felt at any moment men might come on to the dock. Moreover, there was the possibility that the men in the store-room at the end of the dock might get curious as to why the prisoners were no longer collecting the cases. I hurried for'ard to the conning tower. As I climbed the ladder to the bridge, Logan's head appeared in the hatch. He carried a light machine-gun and several magazines. 'Get that trolley alongside the gun,' he said.

'Are they the right shells?' I asked.

'I don't know,' was his reply. 'We'll have to see.'

I signalled to the men aft and jumped on to the dockside. I walked down to where the munitions trolley stood. The little bow-legged miner seemed intelligent, for he appeared to understand what I was up to, and he and his companion, the big man who had helped me hold the hatch down, brought the gangway along. The iron wheels of the trolley clattered noisily as I dragged it along the dock.

Suddenly there was a shout from behind me and I spun round, my hand moving automatically to my revolver. A man was standing in the doorway of the store-room. 'What have you done with those damned prisoners?' he shouted. Someone passing along the gallery stopped to see what the trouble was.

I thought we were for it. 'The lieutenant wants them to clear this pile of cases off the dock before they bring any more,' I shouted back to him in German. 'And he wants these shells got off the dock.'

The man hesitated, and then shrugged his shoulders. 'Well, hurry up,' he grumbled. 'It's nearly lunchtime.' He went back into the store-room and the man who had paused in the gallery continued on his way. I thanked God for my knowledge of German and dragged the trolley level with the gun.

By this time the two miners had placed the gangway in position and we each took a shell up on to the deck of the submarine. Big Logan was already bending over the gun. As I climbed up on the deck, I saw the muzzle of it slowly falling as Logan sighted it on the far end of the main cave. As I reached him he flung the breech open. I slipped the shell in. It fitted perfectly. He closed the breech and straightened his back. 'There we are,' he said. 'Everything ship-shape and ready to fire. All you have to do now is pull that lanyard.' He pointed to the trigger lanyard. 'Then you fling open the breech – so. The used shell falls out, in with the next and fire.'

The two miners put their shells down beneath the gun.

'Do you know how to fire a machine-gun?' Logan asked them.

'We were both in the last war,' replied the little bow-legged one, whom I later discovered to be Alf Davies, one-time foreman at the Wheal Garth.

'All right.' Logan turned to me. 'Will you take charge?' he

said. 'There are rifles, hand-grenades and any other weapons you fancy in the submarine where we found that guard. Get what you want. Fire the gun only when there is no chance of holding the dock any longer. But it must be fired. I'm going to collect that girl.'

I said: 'Don't be a fool, Logan. You haven't a hope.'

'I've got the key,' he said. 'I'm still daft, remember. I think I'll get away with it.'

'Anyway, what's the good of bringing her down here?' I demanded. 'It's certain death.'

'That's where you're wrong,' he said. 'There's just a chance. I found three engineers in the engine-room and I've shut them in. All we've got to do is flood the dock and float the submarine out stern first. The tide is only about an hour on the turn. If we hurry we'll just be able to do it. Once out in the main cave we submerge and get out through the undersea entrance under our own power.'

'Good God, what a chance!' I exclaimed, thinking of the masses of complicated machinery with which the boat was filled. 'There isn't a hope.'

'Maybe not, but can you suggest anything else?' he asked. 'The mine is blocked, remember.'

I couldn't, and he jumped on to the dockside. I watched him walk down it, apparently quite calm, and disappear into the gallery. I told Alf Davies to man the gun and took the big miner up on to the bridge and down through the conning tower hatch. Well, I thought to myself, I suppose we're lucky to have any sort of a chance at all. After all, I had been expecting to try to blow myself and every one else into the next world. But I must say I did not relish the idea of trying to manœuvre the submarine out through the underwater mouth of the cave under her own power with only three men on board who knew anything about the works, and unwilling men at that. Our only hope was that they were not all the heroic type.

I led the way for'ard to the magazine room. It was the hand-grenades I was after. I had the germ of an idea at the back of my mind. At that moment I don't think it was conscious. But it was sufficiently strong to direct me towards the grenades. We took up four each in our pockets, two rifles and a box of ammunition between us. We brought our haul out and laid it on the deck beside the gun. Then I looked at my watch. It was one-twenty-five. Another five minutes and first lunch would be over. Surely Logan ought to be back by now? But he had to get up to the top gallery. If the guard-room door were open he might have to bide his time.

At that moment there was a shout from the end of the dock. 'Wache! Send those bastards down here to collect these cases.'

I poked my head round the conning tower. The same man was standing in the tunnel leading down to the store-room. 'They'll come as soon as they've packed the stuff away up here,' I replied.

Then my heart sank. An officer had appeared, and I recognized him as the commander of U 21. He stopped and spoke to the man in the entrance to the store. The fellow pointed to the pile of cases on the deck and shrugged his shoulders. The commander nodded and came striding down the dockside. 'Get behind that gun,' I said. I dragged the rifles and the machine-gun out of sight. Then the two miners and myself crouched down, waiting.

The commander paused by the gangway. He looked up at the man mounting guard just for'ard of the conning tower, who had not moved a muscle, and then back at the gangway. I could just see his face between the mountings of the gun. He was puzzled by the position of the gangway. At length he stepped aboard and went aft. I picked up a rifle which I had loaded. I pushed forward the safety catch with my thumb. We were for it now. He would see the forge lying over the hatch. I left my hiding-place and moved quickly after him, my rifle ready. He bent over the forge. Then he began to shift it. I was about fifty feet from him. I put one knee to the deck and raised the rifle to my shoulder. 'You're covered,' I said in German. 'Put your hands behind your back and keep still.'

He swung round, and without a second's hesitation his hand went to his revolver. The choice was his. I pulled the trigger. The explosion in that confined space seemed deafening. His hand suddenly checked as it touched his holster, then his knees began to sag. I did not wait to see if he were dead. But as I raced for'ard I heard him slump to the deck. 'Man that gun,' I ordered.

Davies took his place beside the gun as I ran up. 'Hand-grenades,' I panted to the other miner. 'You look after No. 3 dock. I'll look after No. 5. We've got to block the gallery both sides.' He dived for the grenades, and despite his bulk had jumped on to the dock in a flash.

I picked up three grenades and followed him. I had dropped my rifle, but my revolver was still hanging round my neck by its lanyard. As we raced along the dock several men came running down the gallery. Two went past in the direction of No. 5 dock. But three more paused and came running to meet us. Fortunately they were ratings and therefore not armed. I fired, and though I had not aimed at any of them, they broke and ran. I was not accustomed to a revolver and I found the kick unexpectedly powerful.

Men had by now appeared in the entrance to the store-room. But they, too, were unarmed and drew back into the tunnel. We had almost reached the end of the dock now and I had drawn level with my miner. And at that moment I saw that one of the guards from No. 3 dock had appeared. But he held his rifle uncertainly, put out by our uniforms. 'Get back!' I yelled in German. 'Guard your own dock. It's mutiny.'

He did as I had ordered. But when we came to the gallery itself we found that he and two other guards were now standing across the gallery leading to No. 3 dock with their rifles at the ready. 'Okay,' I said to my companions. 'Out with the pins and let 'em have it.' I left him to look after the three guards whilst I took the gallery between our own and No. 5 dock. I could see men coming from the other docks and out of the store-rooms farther along the gallery. I think we both tossed our grenades into the gallery at about the same time, for we were both running together with bullets singing past our ears and shrieking as they ricocheted off the walls.

Then came a terrific roar. And then another. The ground shook under our feet and a blast of hot air sent us both sprawling. My face hit the rocky surface of the dockside only half-protected by my upflung arm and I felt the blood warm in my nose. There was a horrible splitting noise as the rock began to crack. We clambered to our feet and staggered forward. And at the same moment there was a splitting and a rumbling behind us. I turned to see the whole roof of the gallery between our dock and No. 3 collapse. One moment I could see the white uniforms of the guards as they turned to run, and the next instant there was just a tumbled heap of rocks half-invisible in a cloud of dust.

My companion stumbled to his feet. There was a nasty cut across his left eye. The dust was beginning to clear now and I could see that the gallery leading to No. 3 dock was completely blocked. But I could not see what had happened to the right, between our own dock and No. 5, except that a whole lot of debris had spilled on to the floor of the gallery where it passed the end of our dock.

I ran back down the dock, a hand-grenade ready in my hand. The force of the explosion had broken most of the electric-light bulbs. But in the half-dark I was just able to see the white uniform of an officer, as he appeared up the tunnel from the store-room. The beam of a torch almost blinded me. 'What's happened?' he asked, mistaking me for one of the base guards. Then I suppose he saw the grenade in my hand, for he said: 'What are you up to?'

I had no alternative. I pulled the pin out, threw it into the tunnel in which he stood and ducked sideways. The bullet from his revolver sang past my head. A second later there was a flash and a great rumbling explosion. By one of those freak chances his torch remained alight and as it fell, it showed up for an instant the tunnel. The whole roof seemed to crumble. For an instant it actually hung suspended with small pieces of rock pouring from it. Then it came rumbling down and the whole scene went black.

I pulled the emergency torch that the guards always carried from my pocket and switched it on. The place was an absolute ruin. The whole of the end of the dock was just a pile of split and broken rock. Most of it was limestone, and it was then that I consciously realized why I had wanted the grenades. I had the limestone and there on the dock, behind me, was the oil storage tank and the smaller petrol tank. There was no chance of any one attacking us from this end for some time. I knew we had nothing to fear from the direction of No. 3 dock. Probably in all there were not more than twenty or thirty men working on docks 1, 2 and 3, including those in the munitions and fuel stores. They were trapped there, and the only means they had of rejoining the main body of the base was by swimming across the open ends of the docks. The danger would come from the direction of No. 5 dock. If only I had been able to block the ramp leading from the upper galleries! But I hadn't, and the whole personnel of the base would now be streaming into docks 5, 6 and 7. I listened. Between the intermittent sound of crumbling rock I could hear shouts and the murmur of voices coming from the open end of the dock. I clambered over the debris of rock and examined the fall between our own and No. 5 dock in the light of my torch. Where the gallery had been was solid rock from floor to ceiling. I reckoned that it would take them several hours to clear it sufficiently to attack us from this side, even using mobile drills to break down the large pieces of rock.

Having satisfied myself that we could not be taken in the rear, I scrambled back over the debris and rejoined the big miner. In an endeavour to wipe the blood from his eyes he had smeared his whole face with it. 'Come on!' I said, 'we've got to move the machine-gun up to the stern of the submarine.' My orders were entirely automatic. I had been over the whole thing so many times in my own mind that I knew exactly what to do. But I had lost all sense of reality. I had involuntarily slipped into the war mentality. When I had thrown the grenade at the stores officer he had been just a target, not a human being. It was the first time I had killed a man.

We ran back to the gangway and rejoined Davies and the other miner. They were both standing by the gun. Davies I told to remain with the gun. Briefly I explained the necessity of its being fired before we were overwhelmed. Then I and the big miner, whose name was Kevan, picked up the light machine-gun and carried it aft. The third miner, Trevors, followed with the magazines, a rifle and several grenades.

We rigged the gun up in the stern of the U-boat and stacked round it several cases of canned goods to act as a barricade. Then Trevors, who had been a machine-gunner in the last war, got down and fired a burst to make certain that the gun was in working order. It was. The clatter of it seemed to fill the cave. What is more, he hit his mark, which had been the top of the haulage gear buoy floating in the main cave. The bullets made a hollow sound as they struck the huge round cylinder and then ricocheted off to finish with a dull thwack against the sides of the cave.

As soon as I was certain that he could handle the gun satis-factorily, I took Kevan and ran back along the submarine to the conning tower. My aim was to get sufficient arms to ensure that we should be able to hold the end of the dock long enough for me to carry out my plan. It was the only chance – flimsy though it was – of our re-establishing contact with Logan and Maureen and of getting out of the base. There was no chance now of slipping out on the high tide and attempting to run the submarine through the undersea exit on her engines. As soon as we were out in the main cave we should be under the fire of the other submarines in the base and, before we had a chance to submerge, we should be sunk. True, that would probably achieve our object of blocking the undersea exit. But the plan I had in mind would achieve that and at the same time give us all a chance of escape.

Altogether we made four trips to the magazine of the submarine. The first thing we brought up was another light machine-gun, four magazines and some more hand-grenades. These we carried aft. Before going back for further arms, I made Trevors experi-ment with the changing of the magazines. It didn't take him long to find out how they worked and after seeing him fire a test burst from his gun, we returned to the submarine. Thereafter we

brought up another light machine-gun, which we placed beside
Davies at his post by the gun, four automatic rifles together with
the necessary magazines and a further supply of grenades.

As we came up with the last load the soft chug-chug of the little
diesel-engined tug could be heard. We raced aft, and at the same
moment Trevors opened fire with his machine-gun. We had
covered about half the distance when I saw a small dark object
hurtle through the air. It dropped into the water just abaft the
stern of U 21, and almost immediately a big column of water was
thrown up and was followed by a muffled roar.

We flung ourselves down behind the packing cases and Kevan
took over the spare machine-gun. I picked up an automatic rifle.
The deck was very wet and Trevors was soaked. It was clear what
they had tried to do. If they could cause a heavy fall of rock at the
entrance to the dock they could trap us completely. Their difficulty
was that they could not hit the entrance to the dock without
exposing themselves to our fire. Nevertheless, the underwater
explosion of the grenade they had thrown had apparently
damaged the flood gates of the dock, for I could hear the water
gurgling below us as it entered the dock. As far as I could tell the
tide was about an hour beyond the high.

The engine of the tug sounded very close now. The boat was in
fact off the entrance to No. 5 dock and was only protected by the
buttress of rock that separated the two docks. The tug's engines
seemed suddenly to rev up. Trevors reached for a grenade. He
had the pin out the instant the boat's nose showed beyond the
buttress. I knelt on one knee and raised my automatic rifle,
sighting it over the top of our protecting pile of packing cases. The
boat, with its propeller threshing the water into a foam at its stern,
seemed to shoot out from the cover of the buttress.

I sighted my rifle and pulled the trigger. It was like holding a
pneumatic drill to one's shoulder as it pumped out a steady stream
of bullets. I heard the clatter of Kevan's machine-gun at my side
and sensed rather than saw Trevor's arm swing as he threw the
grenade. The man at the wheel of the boat collapsed under our
fire and another in the bows stopped dead in the act of throwing a
grenade and crumpled up in the bottom of the boat. Almost
immediately there was a terrific explosion and the boat seemed to
split in half. It sank instantly, leaving a mass of wreckage, oil and
three dead bodies on the surface of the water.

It was not a pleasant sight. Kevan said: 'Good for you, Steve.'
But Trevors shook his head. 'Mine fell short,' he said. 'It was one
of you two shooting that fellow in the bows that done it. He had

the pin out when you hit him and the grenade exploded right in the bottom of the boat.'

At that moment we came under machine-gun fire from dock No. 7 But the shooting was wild, the reason being that the last explosion had put the remaining lights in our dock out. Shortly afterwards, however, they rigged up a searchlight. We then moved farther back into the dock. It was the only thing to do. They might risk casualties, but we daren't. We built a second barricade of packing cases, this time in a complete semi-circle across the deck, for we were being worried by the ricochet of bullets from the side of the cave. The trouble was that because the seven docks branched off fan-shape from the main cave, it was possible for the Germans operating from No. 7 to cover the mouth of our own dock.

I called up Davies to the shelter of our new barricade and we held a council of war. Then I explained my plan. 'It may work or it may not,' I said. 'We'll just have to risk it. Unless any of you have any other ideas?' But none of them had. We were trapped and it was only a matter of time before we would be overwhelmed. We were four against at least six hundred, and if we surrendered we should be shot. 'We can't hold this dock a minute if they float a submarine out before the tide falls,' I said. 'One shot from a six-inch gun at the mouth of this dock will trap us if it doesn't kill us. If they miss the tide, however, we may be able to hold out for as long as ten hours.'

'Whatever happens,' I went on, 'we've got to block the entrance to this base.' I then told them of the plan to attack a squadron of British capital ships which it was known would be for a time insufficiently screened by destroyers. I said: 'I suggest we proceed straight away with the demolition of the underwater entrance.'

To this they agreed. Even if they missed the tide I was afraid that under cover of fire from No. 7 dock they might try to block the entrance of our dock with grenades thrown from the collapsible rubber boats that the U-boats carried. I explained this and Trevors volunteered to go aft again and extinguish the light of the search-light with machine-gun fire. But I said: 'Wait until we've fired this gun.'

3

SURPRISE

I LEFT Davies to operate the gun and climbed up to the bridge of
U 21. I switched on the U-boat's searchlight and swung it round,
so that its brilliant beam was shining straight aft and illuminating
the whole of the main cave. Towards the seaward end the roof
sloped down until it disappeared below the level of the water,
which showed black and oily in the bright light.

'Is it sighted correctly?' I asked.

'All correct,' replied Davies.

I braced myself against the rail of the bridge. 'Fire!' I said.

I saw Davies pull the trigger lanyard. Instantly there was a
terrific explosion. I was practically thrown off my feet and I
heard the hull plates of the U-boat grate most horribly on the rock
of the empty dock. Almost simultaneously there was a blinding
flash in the roof of the main cave, just where it disappeared below
the water, and an explosion that seemed, in that confined space,
to numb my whole body. A great wind of hot air struck my face
and, in the light of the searchlight, I saw the whole far end of the
cave collapse in a deep rumbling roar.

As a sight it was terrific. I had not fully realized the explosive
power of a six-inch shell. The dock in which the U 21 lay was at
least a hundred and fifty yards from the spot where the shell struck.
Yet I could feel the whole of the rock round me tremble and
vibrate, and quite large pieces of rock fell from the roof of our
dock, making a hollow sound as they struck the submarine's deck.
At least thirty yards of the main cave had collapsed. Huge masses
of rock fell into the water, and as they fell a great wave rose in the
basin. I yelled out to the others to hold tight. I don't think they
heard, but they saw it coming – a great wall of water that surged
down the main cave and swept up into the dock. It must have been
a good ten feet high, for it swept into the empty dock almost at
deck height. The submarine reared up on it like a horse as it
suddenly floated. I had fallen flat on the bridge of the conning
tower, and as the submarine lifted, I heard the rail strike the roof
just above my head and the searchlight went out. Then the bows
jarred violently against the end of the dock.

At any moment I expected to be crushed to death. But after bucking up and down for a moment, grating sickeningly against the sides of the dock, the submarine settled down again, this time afloat. Through my singing ears I heard the water running out through the damaged flood gates of the dock. I scrambled to my feet. The place was as dark as pitch and I could hear shouts and cries. 'Are you all right, Mr Craig?' someone called out from the direction of the gun.

'Yes,' I replied. 'Are you?' And without waiting for his reply I hurried down the conning tower ladder. I paused at the bottom in order to accustom my eyes to the dark. There was a faint luminosity at the end of the dock. Presumably not all the lights of the base had been extinguished by the explosion. Around me everything was black with darkness, but where the dock ran out into the main cave there was a half-circle of indefinite light. Against this I could just make out the dark bulk of the gun and figures moving about it.

I suddenly remembered my torch. I pulled it out of my pocket and switched it on. The faces of the there miners looked white as they faced the light. But they seemed all right. Fortunately the water had not swept over the deck, so that, though they were all soaked with the water that had slopped up between the submarine and the dock walls, the machine-gun, rifles and ammunition were still beside the gun.

Armed with automatic rifles we went aft. The forge was still in position over the after hatch, but the water had swept right over the stern of the submarine and our barricades of packing cases had been swept away. The deck seemed strewn with tins and lumps of rock, and the dockside, which was still awash, was dotted with packing cases.

One of the machine-guns had fetched up against the deck stanchions. We retrieved this. The other was missing. The magazines were where we had left them and we were able to retrieve one of the automatic rifles from the dockside. Hastily we rebuilt our barricade of packing cases. This was not an easy task as both gangways had been smashed to pieces and most of the cases had to be passed up from the dockside and dragged up the sloping sides of the submarine by rope.

However, ten minutes' work saw our barricade complete again. All the grenades appeared to have rolled overboard, so I paid another visit to the magazine of the submarine. It was whilst I was getting the grenades from their racks that I noticed the crew's escape apparatus. It was much the same as the Davis equipment used in British submarines and they were stacked in a large rack of their own. I picked up one of them. It had a face mask and a large air bag which strapped round the waist. A small cylinder of oxygen completed the equipment. It was in fact just what I required.

I hurried on deck with the grenades to find the main cave brilliantly lit. The submarine in No. 6 dock had switched on its searchlight. Then I understood the reason for the cries and shouts. On the black oily surface of the water that was still slopping about in the main cave bobbed three collapsible rubber boats, two of them floating upside down.

'They were just going to launch an attack when we fired that gun,' I said, nodding in the direction of the boats, as I put the grenades down on the deck behind the packing cases.

Kevan said: 'Ar, we'll be able to hawld this place faw sawm tame naw.'

'How do you mean?' I asked.

'They'll nawt be able to get the bawts awt naw. Dawn't ye feel us grainding on the bottom of the dawck?'

He was right. I had been too busy to notice it. Though the water had flooded the dock, the tide had receded sufficiently for the hull of the submarine to be just touching the bottom.

'Thank God for that!' I said. They had lost their chance. Our worst danger had been postponed. We had ten hours' grace so far as attack from another submarine went. Then and there I decided that, if the worst came to the worst and my own scheme failed, we would try to get our own boat out before the others and go down fighting rather than face a firing squad. It seemed easy to face death now that we were in action. I wondered what had happened to Logan.

Having completed our barricade, I left Davies and Trevors to hold the end of the dock and took Kevan down on to the dockside. The water had receded now. By the wall we found picks and shovels that had been used the previous day for erecting the derrick. We took these to the end of the dock, where the gallery had been blocked, and set to work to clear a space in the midst of the debris. We kept our automatic rifles handy in case the open end of the dock should be attacked.

Mostly we did the work with our hands, advancing steadily into the debris and piling the rocks behind us. It was a gigantic task and I was thankful that the work I had had to do in the fortnight I had been at the base had hardened my muscles. Even so, I found that Kevan, despite the fact that he had been unemployed for a considerable time, worked just about twice as fast as I was able to.

Half an hour passed and the basin I was trying to hollow out in the debris was beginning to take shape. We worked in silence and without pause. The constant stooping to throw out great lumps of limestone soon made my back ache abominably. We had climbed high on to the pile of fallen rock and were tossing the broken lumps out behind us so that the rim of the basin behind gradually rose. It was slow and hard work. Not only did my back and arms ache, but we were both constantly coughing with the rock dust.

At the end of half an hour, as though by common consent, we straightened our backs, and took a breather. I looked at my watch. It was just past three. I was standing now behind a huge circular rampart of rock. The roof, all jagged and looking very unsafe, was about ten feet above my head. On three sides of us the broken limestone was piled right to the roof. Only in the direction of the docks did the rock fall away, and here we were piling it up in order to make a kind of rock tank. This rampart had grown by now practically as tall as ourselves. I looked over it and along to the open end of the dock. The searchlight was still flooding the main cave and the light from it glistened on the wet walls of the dock and threw the conning tower of the submarine into black silhouette. The great dark shape of the boat seemed to fill the whole cave, and at the far end I could see our barricade of packing cases. I could see no sign of Davies and Trevors, however, for they lay in the shadow cast by the cases.

As I bent to resume my work, I saw Kevan standing tense at my side, listening. There was the sound of slipping rock, and then voices. It came from behind the fall that blocked the gallery between ourselves and No. 5 dock. Then came the unmistakable ring of metal on stone. 'They're trying to clear the fall,' said Kevan.

'How long will it take?' I asked.

He looked at the fall. The whole gallery had been blocked. 'Depends on the depth,' he said. 'I reckon it'll take them all of a good hour.'

'Good!' I said. 'By then we'll have finished this. Then we'll wait for them to come through. The draught will help.'

We resumed our work. But about ten minutes later the whole place suddenly resounded to the clatter of machine-gun fire. It came from the open end of the dock. In an instant we were over the rampart of stone we had been piling up, had collected our automatic rifles and were running as hard as we could along the dockside.

There was a muffled explosion and a column of water shot up just abaft the stern of the submarine. We clambered on to the deck of the submarine and as I ran down it, I saw a figure half-rise from behind the barricade of packing cases and an instant later there was a loud roar and lumps of rock fell from the roof of the main cave into the water. At the same instant the searchlight was switched off.

We threw ourselves down behind the packing cases, our rifles ready. 'What's happened?' I panted.

'They had rigged up a raft,' replied Davies. 'There were several of them protected by packing cases. They had automatic rifles and one of them was flinging grenades. But Trevors got them with one of his grenades. Blew the whole raft apart.'

'Good work!' I said. 'Do you think you could hold them off for another half-hour, Trevors?' I asked.

There was no reply.

I put out my hand to where he lay behind his machine-gun. My hand touched his face. It was resting against one of the packing cases and it was warm and sticky. I screened my torch with my hands and switched it on. His muscular little body was crumpled up beside his gun, the back of his head resting on the protruding corner of a packing case. His blue unshaven jaw hung open, and his jacket was sodden with blood. A bullet had caught him in the throat.

I felt a sudden sickening sensation inside me. One out of four. There were only three of us now. Trevors had stood up in order to make sure of his aim. At the sacrifice of his own life he had demolished the raft. But there would be another raft and another. I said: 'We've got to get on with that job quickly. Can you finish off that basin, Kevan? It wants to be at least three feet deeper. I'll stay here with Davies and hold the fort.'

I heard him scramble to his feet. 'Give me a shout,' I said, 'when it's complete.' I gave him my torch and saw his big figure outlined against its light hurry back down the deck of the submarine.

Then Davies and I and the dead Trevors settled down to wait for the next attack. The searchlight had been switched on again and in its light I saw a German rating dive into the oily waters of the main cave and rescue a man who was injured and drowning. He was the sole survivor of the crew of the raft. Swimming steadily on his back and holding the injured man's head between his hands, the German disappeared into the neighbouring dock. Then the searchlight was switched off again. Three pools of light marked the entrances to docks 5, 6 and 7. Then one by one these were extinguished. To the left of our own dock everything was in complete darkness. To the right, however, docks 1, 2 and 3 still showed a faint glow of light.

Suddenly a voice shouted in German: 'Put those lights out over there.' The order was repeated several times. Then one by one the lights of these three docks were switched off. We were plunged into total darkness. It seemed to press down on us like a curtain. We could see nothing, not even the cases in front of us.

'They are going to try attacking in the dark,' whispered Davies.

'We'll just have to listen for them,' I said.

'Why wait for Kevan to deepen the basin?' he asked. 'Why not get on with your scheme right away?'

'It's no use doing it by halves,' I said. 'Once we get it going there's no possibility of feeding the fire.'

So we lay there in the dark and the minutes slipped slowly by. Gradually my ears accustomed themselves to all the various sounds in the docks. It was difficult to distinguish them, for they merged into each other to form a peculiar bustling murmuring sound. But occasionally I could pick out words of comamnd and the sound of boots on rock, and from No. 5 dock came the persistent sound of tumbling rock as they worked to clear the fall and get through into our own dock.

It was an eerie business, lying there waiting for heaven knew what. I kept on mistaking the movement of the water for the sound of a raft being paddled towards us. I found myself praying desperately that Kevan would finish the work before the attack was launched. But I knew it must take him a full half-hour working on his own, and as I lay watching the luminous dial of my wristwatch the minutes seemed to tick by incredibly slowly. A quarter of an hour passed by. Once I raised my rifle and was on the point of firing. But it was nothing. The darkness was absolutely impenetrable. Twenty minutes. Then we heard a new sound, a sound of hammering.

'They're making another raft,' whispered Davies.

At that moment my eyes were attracted by the flickering of a torch from the far end of our own dock. Kevan wanted me. 'I shan't be long,' I said to Davies, and screening a torch, which I had removed from Trevors, I hurried along the deck of the submarine. As soon as I could, I jumped down on to the dock and began to run.

Kevan met me by the oil tank. He said: 'They're almost through the fall.' I could hear the sound of shifting rocks quite clearly.

'Okay,' I said, 'let's pump the oil in.'

There was no time to see whether the basin in the limestone was sufficiently deep. We took hold of the oil tank and dragged it on its trolley to the edge of the debris. Then, while Kevan took the canvas pipe across the debris and laid it over the rampart of rocks so that the nozzle hung down into the basin, I ran back for the smaller petrol tank. Each tank was fitted with a hand pump, and Kevan was already pumping the oil into the basin by the time I had got the pipe of the petrol tank into position. In the light of my torch I could see the black crude oil pouring down amongst the rocks. At the same time I was uncomfortably aware of the sound of voices and falling rocks in the direction of No. 5 dock. At any moment I expected the Germans to break through.

I scrambled back to the petrol tank and began pumping, thankful to have my automatic rifle beside me. When the guage told me I had half-emptied the tank, I went over to help Kevan. The oil tank was still nearly three-quarters full.

I found that Kevan had no need of my assistance, so I looked around and found a length of iron piping and some rags. I tied the rags round one end of the piping and then dipped them first in oil and then petrol. The resultant torch I put down on top of the oil tank. By this time the sound of the Germans coming through the fall was becoming much louder, until by the murmur of their voices I was quite certain that they had broached it.

Kevan straightened his back. The oil tank was empty. I played my torch over the rampart of rock. It seemed to be holding the oil quite satisfactorily. Then, quite distinctly, I heard an exclamation in German. Evidently they had seen the light. Kevan had started the pump of the petrol tank. I could hear the liquid pouring out into the basin. I raised my automatic rifle to cover the spot where the Germans would emerge.

At that moment there was a burst of machine-gun fire from the open end of the dock. I glanced round. Was it another attack? There was no light at all. After the one burst there was silence. Perhaps Davies had made a mistake? Then, faintly, came the sound of Davies's voice speaking. I could not hear what he said, but I was convinced he was speaking to the Germans in the next dock. 'Hurry!' I said to Kevan.

'Nearly finished,' he replied.

Then echoing down the dock came Davies's voice. 'Mr Craig!

Mr Craig!' There was a note of urgency in it.

I took the matches from my pocket and thrust them into Kevan's hand. 'Light the torch and throw it into the basin as soon as you're ready,' I said. 'But for God's sake don't let them get through first.'

'Ar, I'll see to it.' He took the matches, never pausing in his pumping, and I ran down the dock as hard as I could.

'Mr Craig!' Davies's voice again. I clambered on to the deck of the submarine. My shoes rang hollow on the steel plates. At last I put out my torch and felt my way forward to the packing cases. 'What is it?' I asked as I threw myself down beside Davies.

'They've got Miss Weston and your friend Logan.'

'Well?'

'They say they've got them bound and are going to use them as a shield for a machine-gunner unless we surrender. I asked them to wait so that I could consult you.'

At that moment the searchlight of the submarine in the next dock was switched on. Then I understood. Floating just off the entrance to No. 5 dock was a raft, and strapped to it in a kneeling position were Maureen Weston and Big Logan. They were kneeling side by side, and between them poked the muzzle of a machine-gun. It was quite impossible for us to fire at the gunner behind without hitting them. I saw Big Logan's huge body rigid with the effort of trying to tear himself clear of his bonds. The sweat was glistening on his broad forehead and his long brown hair was lank. Maureen looked quite fresh, but the position in which she was held was obviously most uncomfortable. The raft was slowly moving towards us, propelled, I imagine, by at least two ratings swimming in the rear.

'Will you surrender? Or will you risk the lives of your friends?' I recognized the voice as that of Commodore Thepe.

'What are the conditions?' I asked to gain time.

'There will be no conditions,' was the sharp reply.

'Don't be a bloody fool,' said Logan. 'They're going to shoot you.' I saw an arm move from behind him and his body jerked at the sudden pain of a jab from a bayonet.

'You stick to your guns, Walter,' Maureen said. 'Don't worry about us. We'll be shot anyway.'

At that moment I heard the sound of a shot from the dock behind me. I turned to see the distant figure of Kevan stagger, the torch I had left with him blazing in his hand. In the light of it I could just see the figure of a German high up on the rocks above the basin. Then Kevan's arm swung and the blazing torch sailed in a perfect arc into the rock basin. There was an instantaneous flash that lit up the whole dock as the petrol lying on top of the crude oil ignited. Then the whole of the end of the dock seemed suddenly ablaze. What happened to the Germans coming through over the fall from No. 5 dock I cannot imagine. The heat must have been terrific, and the flames were immediately drawn through the gap by the draught. The sound of the flames came down the dock like the roar of a mighty wind. And against their intense light I could see the big ungainly figure of Kevan come stumbling down the dockside, his shadow flickering along the wall of the dock in front of him.

And at that moment the machine-gunner on the raft opened fire on us. I told Davies to make a dash for it. He hesitated an instant, crouching behind the packing cases. Then he darted out and ran as hard as he could down the deck of the submarine. I heard his boots ringing on the deck plates as I opened fire with our own machine-gun. I aimed to the side of the raft, well clear of Maureen and Logan, but it was sufficient to keep the gunner's attention from Davies long enough for him to get into the dock, out of the line of fire.

Almost consciously I forced myself not to think of the possibilities I faced. I had to get for'ard to the conning tower. I bunched my legs up under me and then jumped to my feet and started running as hard as I could down the deck. The light of the flames made it quite easy to see my way without a torch. I remember consciously thinking how little time had passed, for, as I started to run, I saw Kevan's figure still running towards us along the dockside.

Bullets began to whistle to the left of me and I was uncomfortably aware of the persistent clatter of the machine-gun behind me. The gunner had been prepared for my dash and he had swung his gun on me almost before I had broken cover.

I learned later from Maureen that I owed my life at this moment to Logan. As I rose from behind the packing cases he made a superhuman effort to shift himself sufficiently to upset the aim of the gun. He just managed to touch the gun with his elbow and so shift it out of alignment. This occurred, I suppose, just as the gunner swung his gun towards me, for I had not run more than a few yards when I received what felt like a violent kick in the left arm, accompanied immediately by a sharp pain. After that the bullets went wide, and in a few seconds I passed out of the gunner's line of sight.

I saw Kevan struggling on to the deck of the submarine. He

seemed unable to use his right arm, and by the dancing light of the flames I could see the sweat glistening on his face. Davies was standing irresolute at the foot of the conning tower. 'Get inside,' I yelled. He began to swarm up the ladder to the bridge. Kevan reached it just before I did. I followed him up, but when I tried to grasp the rails of the ladder I cried out with the sudden pain in my left arm. The forearm was broken just above the wrist and was bleeding fast.

With my right arm I pulled myself up the ladder. From the bridge of the conning tower I took one brief glance round. In the lurid light, I could just make out a corner of the raft as it slowly approached the end of the dock. At the other end, our improvised tank of oil and petrol was burning furiously. Then I tumbled down the conning tower hatch and closed it after me, fastening it on the inside.

Coming down from the conning tower, I found Davies bandaging Kevan's shoulder. There was a nasty wound just near the arm joint. I ran quickly aft to the store-room bulkhead. I dragged the bulkhead back. The imprisoned Germans were sitting on the packing cases. They sprang up as the door opened. I covered them with my revolver. 'Put your hands above your heads,' I said in German. I backed down the gangway, keeping them covered. 'Follow me!' I backed as far as the engine-room hatch. 'Open that!' I ordered the officer.

He turned back the lever and pulled the hatch open. 'Now get down there – all of you,' I ordered. I saw the officer hesitate, weighing up his chances. 'Wache!' I called. Then I said: 'Get down there.' My call for the guard seemed to settle him, for he went through the hatch and the other followed him. I closed it and fastened it. Then I went back into the store-room. As I climbed the ladder to the hatch I heard the sound of boots moving stealthy along the deck above my head. I fastened the hatch. Then I went for'ard to see about the hatch through which the munitions had been lowered. By the time I had climbed up and fastened this I was feeling pretty faint. Walking back along the gangway, I found myself following a trail of my own blood.

I arrived back in the control room to find Kevan just easing his shoulder into his jacket. 'Better?' I asked. Davies turned at the sound of my voice and then exclaimed: 'Good God in heaven, Mr Craig! Whatever is the matter with you?'

I pointed to my left arm. 'Do you think you can manage a tourniquet?'

'Why, yes, indeed.'

He took my coat off, rolled my sleeve back and then with a strip of material torn from his shirt, he bound my arm just above the elbow. 'You'll want a splint too,' he said, and broke a heavy chart ruler in half. I then spent a most painful five minutes. The force of the bullet had pushed the bone out of place so that splinters were showing through the mess of blood and broken skin. I think I passed out twice whilst Davies was resetting it. 'Lucky it is you are with a miner, Mr Craig,' Davies said, as he bandaged it into place against the splints. 'It's not every one that knows how to set a broken limb properly, is it now?'

I agreed that it wasn't, and sat down on the chart table, feeling rather uncertain of my legs. 'What do we do now?' asked Davies.

'Wait. Just wait,' I said. 'And pray that they don't get into the submarine before the fire had got properly to work on the limestone.'

We stayed in the control room for some time, listening to the sound of footsteps overhead. I could imagine the puzzlement of the Germans. What would they think? One minute we are holding the dock, and the next a huge fire is blazing and we have disappeared inside the submarine. I could imagine the raft plying to and fro between our dock and No. 5 bringing more and more men on to the scene. What would they do about the fire? Would they try to put it out? Even if they had been able to get their fire-fighting equipment into our dock, they hadn't a hope of extinguishing it.

'Let's examine the oxygen supply,' I said. I was feeling a little better now. But the submarine was getting very hot. I could imagine the terrific heat of that fire reddening the bow plates. If we were forced to stay in the submarine any length of time it would become a death trap – a positive oven.

We found the oxygen supply equipment. Davies seemed to know how it worked. It looked very complicated to me. Footsteps kept running backwards and forwards over our heads. It was very eerie in that submarine. All movements on deck came to us as hollow sounds. Very faintly we could hear the sound of voices. The air was already beginning to get stale. I knew we could not have already used up the available air, so I presumed that some of the CO_2 given off by the fire in the limestone basin was beginning to seep into the submarine. The hatches were only fully airtight when subjected to pressure from water outside. Davies switched on the oxygen supply.

I went along the gangway and through the magazine to the spot where I had seen the escape apparatus. From the rack I took five sets of equipment. They consisted of a mask, which clipped over the head and covered the nose and mouth, an air bag which was strapped round the body and a small cylinder of oxygen. To my great relief I discovered that the oxygen cylinders were filled.

As I joined the others I heard a muffled hissing noise coming from the direction of the conning tower. We went into the control room. It was louder there and coming from the hatch. 'Sounds like an oxy-acetylene cutter,' said Davies.

'I'm afraid so,' I said. 'Better stand by to repel boarders.' We found a revolver for Kevan. Davies was the only one capable of using an automatic rifle. As we stood staring up at the conning tower hatch we saw the metal of it suddenly redden at one point. It glowed like a cigarette in the half-darkness, then broadened and whitened. An instant later molten metal was dripping down at our feet and the flame of the cutter had appeared.

We watched the brilliant white flame slowly cutting through the metal. There was a sort of horrible fascination about it. It was a race between the cutter and the gas given off by the fire. Or had the fire been put out? I did not think so for the submarine was so hot. But my mind was so hazy that I could not be certain of anything. Anyway, I was so exhausted that it didn't seem to matter one way or the other.

A large part of the hatch now showed a dull red. The white line of cut metal grew until it showed as a definite segment of a circle. Very slowly I could see the cutting flame moving through the metal. The sound of it was now much louder. Soon the segment had grown to a semi-circle. 'What do we do – fight or surrender?' asked Kevan.

'We'd better take a vote on it,' I said. I was feeling very depressed. My mind kept groping over the formula – $CaCO_3 = CaO + CO_2$. Surely that was right? Or had I made a mistake?

Then suddenly I saw that the cutting flame was no longer moving. 'He's stopped,' I said. We watched. The whiteness of the metal where it had been cut was dimming. It was reddening, and the hatch cover as a whole was becoming black again. Gradually the hiss of the oxy-acetylene blower dwindled until it had stopped altogether.

'Thank God!' I breathed. 'Listen!' Not a sound. I walked down the length of the submarine and back again. There was not a sound from the deck overhead. When I rejoined the others in the control room I said: 'Davies – you and I will go out and bring in Logan and Miss Weston.'

Kevan helped us into the escape apparatus. We blew the air

bags up and switched on the oxygen. Then, wearing a pair of gloves, Davies unfastened the hatch and threw it back. I carried two spare oxygen equipments. We clambered out, breathing through our masks. The fire was still roaring, the flames flickering redly on the rock walls of the dock. Quickly we slammed the hatch back to conserve the pure air in the submarine. As we did so the body of the acetylene cutter rolled face upwards. It was a horrible sight. He had collapsed on to the flame of the blower and his face was burned out of all recognition.

The deck of the submarine presented a most amazing sight. There must have been at least twenty Germans lying huddled where they had collapsed. We hurried to the stern where we found two collapsible rubber boats moored. In one there was a German seated at the oars. He was looking dazed, but was not properly unconscious. But even as we climbed into the other boat, which was empty, he collapsed.

I cast off and Davies rowed quickly round to dock No. 5. Here the sight was even more amazing. The whole dock seemed strewn with the bodies of German sailors. It was like rowing in some fantastic crypt filled with the dead. I looked at Davies, pulling steadily on the oars, his face obscured by the awful futurist mask. So one might depict a modern Charon rowing a new-comer to Hades across the river Styx.

We moored to the flood gates of No. 5 dock and Davies scrambled up on to the dockside. I remained in the boat. In a very short while he returned, dragging Big Logan's unconscious body. I thought I should never be able to get him into the boat safely. But, rocking precariously, I lowered it into the bottom of the boat. Maureen's slight figure was easier to handle. Within less than three minutes of landing we were rowing back to No. 4 dock. Whilst Davies rowed, I fitted the escape apparatus first on to Logan and then on to Maureen. Then I untied their remaining bonds, not an easy procedure since I could use only one hand. Almost as soon as he began to breathe the oxygenized air, Logan showed signs of life. The first thing he did when he recovered consciousness was to try to tear the mask from his face. This I managed to prevent him from doing, and by the time we had reached our own dock, he had recovered sufficiently to lift himself on to the submarine. By that time Maureen had also recovered consciousness, but she needed assistance in climbing up on the deck of the submarine.

Back in the interior of the submarine, we removed their masks and our own. Kevan had plugged the circular cut in the conning tower hatch, and the oxygenized air in the submarine was good to breathe after the mask, which was not at all comfortable. The place was getting very hot indeed, however, and I did not think we should be able to stay there much longer. Kevan had also found a flask of brandy. He passed it first to Maureen. Then on to Logan and so to myself.

Soon after the brandy Maureen lost her dazed look and asked conventionally where she was. I explained what had happened, and she giggled a little uncertainly. 'I never thought I should live to be rescued by you, Walter,' she said. I didn't know quite how to take this, so remained silent. Her dark hair was hanging over her eyes, and flushed with newly regained consciousness, she looked startingly provocative. I saw Logan watching her.

I said: 'I'm afraid you've had rather an unpleasant time.'

But she shook her head. 'No, it wasn't too bad. As soon as Dan here saw the fire he told me what you were up to. You put us to sleep quite comfortably, didn't he?' She turned to Logan.

'Is your name Dan?' I asked.

Logan grinned. 'Yes, they even gave me a Christian name,' he said. 'Where's Trevors?' he added.

'Dead,' I said.

There was a long silence.

By this time every one seemed sufficiently recovered, so I suggested that we started out for the back exit of the base. We put on our oxygen apparatus and each of us took a spare. Also we took one of the submarine's oxygen cylinders, just in case. We had no idea how long our apparatus would keep us going. Then I sent Kevan aft to place a packing case or something fairly heavy over the engine-room hatch and unfasten it. I did not want the men down there to be trapped in this oven.

When we tied up at No. 5 dock and clambered up on to the dockside I was once again conscious of the eeriness of the place. There were men everywhere, but not a soul stirred. It was like a place of the dead. And we five masked figures looked like five horrible ghouls picking our way amongst the dead. The Germans seemed to have been struck down without warning. One still knelt before a piece of wood he had been sawing, kept upright by the saw. It was difficult to believe that they were only unconscious as yet, not dead.

At the end of the dock we found one of the mobile drills. They had been using it to get through the fall that blocked the gallery into our own dock. We then found two more cylinders of oxygen and several picks and placed them on top of the drill. We passed the ends of docks 6 and 7 and then dragged the drill up to the upper galleries. On the ramp and in the galleries we had to skirt unconscious bodies and sometimes they lay so thick that we had to move them in order to get the drill through.

At last we arrived at the guard-room and the cells we knew so well. Logan and Davies, who were armed with automatic rifles, went in front. They threw open the door, their rifles raised in case the gas had not penetrated the closed door. But the guard-room was empty. Davies went straight across to the other side where a rack of rifles stood. He pushed it sideways. A whole section of the cemented wall slid back on rollers to reveal a black cavity in the rock behind.

We hesitated, each looking questioningly from one to the other. Were we to risk everything in a desperate attempt to get through the falls in the mine? That meant blowing up the guard-room and imprisoning ourselves in the mine, for it was impossible to say how long the fire would last and once the men in the base regained consciousness they could come after us in order to prevent us making contact with the outside world. I remembered what Logan had said about falls in tin mines. It seemed pretty hopeless.

'Isn't there some sort of a lookout?' Maureen's voice was muffled by her mask.

'Yes,' I replied, 'but it's like a periscope – just a piece of steel piping thrust through the rock. We'd never get through.'

'Ventilation?'

I shook my head. 'What do you say, Logan?'

'This is our only chance,' was his reply.

'I agree,' I said. 'First, we need some food. And keep that door shut. We don't want to lose any good air there is in the mine.'

Davies pushed the section of wall back across the opening and he and Kevan remained in the guard-room, whilst Logan, Maureen and I went in search of food. In the nearest kitchen we found two of the cooks sprawled across the table and another had burned himself on the stove and slipped to the floor in front of it. We collected enough provisions for a week in a big packing case and a large can of water and dragged them along to the guard-room. We loaded them on to the drill trolley, and after providing ourselves with torches, some spare batteries, an automatic rifle each and magazines, together with several grenades, we went through into the mine.

I think we all felt somewhat chilled at leaving the lighted guard-room for this dark damp tunnel. It was like stepping

straight from the warmth and comfort of civilization into some
aged vault. To me it was like walking into one's grave, for I was
not hopeful for our being able to break through the falls. There
were only two of us properly able-bodied, and I was afraid that
lack of ventilation would kill us long before our food gave out.

As soon as the section of the guard-room wall had been pushed
back behind us we took off our masks. The air smelt damp and
stale. By the light of a torch we walked steadily along the gallery,
the drill trolley, now badly overloaded, jolting on the uneven floor.
After we had gone about two hundred yards we came to a fall.
This was the one that Maureen and her companions had worked
their way through. She pointed to something. It was a piece of
wire that led to one of the larger rocks. Evidently that was what
had give the alarm. The gap they had made was not large and it
proved quite impossible to get the trolley through. We debated
whether to try to widen it or not. I was all for leaving the trolley. I
had suddenly remembered that its engine would pollute the air.
Anyway, it could be brought along later. The others agreed to
this, so we unloaded it and passed all the various articles which we
had loaded on to it through the narrow gap in the fall. It was a
fearful struggle, and by the time everything we wanted had been
transferred I felt completely exhausted. What little I had done
had caused my arm to start bleeding again and I was conscious of
the warm blood trickling down the splints on to my hand.

As soon as everything had been transferred to the farther side of
the fall, I asked Davies if he would go back and demolish the
gaurd-room. 'A few grenades will do the trick,' I said. 'But see that
you leave yourself time to get clear. And keep the door into the
mine as near shut as possible and hold your breath whilst you're
in the guard-room.'

We wished him good luck and he climbed back through the fall.
Gradually the sound of his footsteps died away. Then faintly we
heard the door to the guard-room being slid back. Silence for a
moment. Then the faint rumble of the door sliding to again and
the sound of footsteps running towards us down the mine gallery.
We braced ourselves for the explosion. It came a few seconds later,
a terrific muffled roar that shook the rock in which the gallery
was cut and seemed to rumble through our very bodies. It was not
one explosion, but several very close together, and the roar of
them and the crash of falling rock was continuous. Pieces of rock
fell from the roof of the gallery round us and I felt the fall shift
slightly.

Gradually silence descended on us again. We listened. Not a sound. We called out, but Davies did not answer. 'I'll go back for him,' said Logan.

'No, I will,' I said. I felt sick for fear I had sent the man to his death.

But before I could move Logan was already scrambling over the rocks of the fall. He had to shift great lumps of dislodged rock before he could get through the gap. Again we waited. Two or three minutes later we heard him coming back up the gallery. 'It's all right,' he called from the other side of the fall. 'He got laid out by a lump of rock.'

I felt greatly relieved. And shortly afterwards Davies himself climbed back through the gap in the fall. He had a nasty scalp wound, but otherwise seemed all right. 'The force of it knocked me over,' he said. 'Then a bloody great rock hit me on the side of the head.'

'I went back and had a look at the damage,' Logan said as he climbed through. 'The gallery is completely blocked some yards from the entrance to the guard-room.'

We had burned our boats. I think we all had that sinking feeling. There was no going back. Whatever falls lay ahead, we just had to get through them. Each carrying as much as he could, we went on along the gallery. It sloped gradually upward and bore to the left. There were the remains of sleepers and here and there old lengths of rail on the floor of the gallery. Suddenly it broadened out and we found ourselves emerging from the farthest right of three branches off a main gallery. Logan, who was leading, glanced back at Davies. 'The main gallery,' said the Welshman. 'The other branches are no use whatever. They end in falls, and if you worked through them you'd most likely find yourself back with the submarines.'

So we pushed on up the main gallery. But we had not gone more than a hundred yards or so before we found the gallery completely blocked with rock. 'This is the fall they made yesterday,' said Davies.

'Looks pretty hopeless,' said Maureen rather dully.

'Depends how deep it goes,' was Davies's reply.

We put our things down and set to work immediately. Maureen tried to get Kevan and myself to rest. But I knew the value of time and though we could each use only one arm we were better than nothing.

Davies wielded a pick and the rest of us attacked the fall with our bare hands, pulling the loosened rocks down and piling them up behind us. When we started on it the time was just on four. But after that time had no meaning for me. It was dust and rocks and straining and heaving and sweating. Pain, too, for the exertion brought the blood pumping into my wound. Time went on and I really had no idea what progress we were making. I was just automatically pushing behind me rocks that were thrust at me from above. We took it in turns to rest. Sometimes we had water, sometimes some food, and days seemed to pass.

Nothing seemed real except my intense longing to rest. As in a dream I heard Logan say: 'Listen!' I listened, but I could hear nothing but the pumping of the blood against my ear drums. But still as in a dream I saw the others getting wildly excited and setting to work furiously on the fall again. Once more I began automatically shifting the rocks that were thrust at me. Then I heard faint picking sounds beyond the fall and later I remember Maureen saying: 'It's all right, Walter, they're coming for us.'

I think it was then that I passed out, and I remember nothing until I woke to the lovely cold feel of fresh night air on my face. I had not felt fresh air for a fortnight. I breathed it in – sweet cool stuff smelling of grass and little rock plants. And then I opened my eyes and saw stars and a great round moon floating high in the velvet night. I closed my eyes again and slept.

The following is the report of Captain Marchant, which was forwarded to the War Office by the commanding officer at Trereen:

I proceeded to Pendeen with two companies, arriving there at 22.10 hours. Detective-Inspector Fuller was awaiting my arrrival at the inn, together with an officer of the Intelligence. The latter informed me that the Wheal Garth mine was believed to be occupied and to have some connection with U-boats. A woman reporter and three miners had failed to return from the mine after a visit the previous day.

There were three possible exits at the mine. I detailed a section to guard each of these exits. The fourth section I detailed to watch the cliffs above the mine. Lieutenant Myers took charge of these operations and each section was allotted a local miner as a guide.

With 'B' company I proceeded to the most recent shaft of the mine, which had been opened up by a rescue party. Detective-Inspector Fuller informed me that he had had plant brought over from Wheal Geevor and that thirty miners were working in relays to clear the fall.

We then proceeded down the shaft by rope ladder and through several galleries to the fall. It was then 23.30 hours. At 2.20 hours sounds were heard from the other side of the fall. A way was cleared through and the woman reporter and two of the three miners who had gone down with her were discovered. With them were two men – Craig and Logan – who had disappeared after the landing of a U-boat commander near Cadgwith recently. They reported a complete submarine base with seven docks and accommodation for more than six hundred men. They had fought their way out largely by the ingenious method of causing a fire in a limestone fall and so immobilizing the base with CO_2. They had blocked the gallery behind them.

We proceeded to this fall, and by 5.40 hours had cleared a passage into the base. The gas had cleared and many of the Germans had regained consciousness. But they put up a weak resistance. By 6.50 hours we were in control of the whole base.

Our casualties were two dead – Sgt. Welter and Pte. Gates – and three wounded – Ptes. Morgan, Chapman and Regal. The enemy lost four dead and six wounded in action against us. There were also a further forty-six dead by asphyxiation or by other means. Many were seriously ill as a result of the effects of the gas. A fall in the main gallery by the docks prevented those who resisted from getting at the munition stores and blowing up the whole base. One submarine was, however, destroyed by explosives.

Altogether five ocean-going U-boats have been captured intact and one destroyed, as mentioned above. Also one submarine store ship and a large quantity of war material fell into our hands. Prisoners taken totalled five hundred and sixty-five.

Signed,
MARCHANT.

Following a report by the intelligence officer to M.I.5 the proposed action against Kiel was postponed, it being feared that information concerning this plan might have been transmitted to Germany by a submarine.

After the capture of the base the area of sea immediately off the entrance was closely mined and a phosphorescent float moored in the usual position. By this means four more U-boats were destroyed.

Hammond Innes

The
Mary Deare

PART ONE

I

I WAS tired and very cold; a little scared, too. The red and green navigation lights cast a weird glow over the sails. Beyond was nothing, a void of utter darkness in which the sea made little rushing noises. I eased my cramped legs, sucking on a piece of barley sugar. Above me the sails swung in a ghostly arc, slatting back and forth as *Sea Witch* rolled and plunged. There was scarcely wind enough to move the boat through the water, yet the swell kicked up by the March gales ran as strong as ever and my numbed brain was conscious all the time that this was only a lull. The weather forecast at six o'clock had been ominous. Winds of gale force were reported imminent in sea areas Rockall, Shannon, Sole and Finisterre. Beyond the binnacle light the shadowy outline of the boat stretched ahead of me, merging into the clammy blackness of the night. I had dreamed of this moment so often. But it was March and now, after fifteen hours at sea in the Channel, the excitement of owning our own boat was gone, eaten up by the cold. The glimmer of a breaking wave appeared out of the darkness and slapped against the counter, flinging spray in my face and sidling off into the blackness astern with a hiss of white water. God! It was cold! Cold and clammy – and not a star anywhere.

The door of the charthouse slammed back to give me a glimpse of the lit saloon and against it loomed Mike Duncan's oilskin-padded bulk, holding a steaming mug in either hand. The door slammed to again, shutting out the lit world below, and the darkness and the sea crowded in again. 'Soup?' Mike's cheerful, freckled face appeared abruptly out of the night, hanging disembodied in the light from the binnacle. He smiled at me from the folds of his balaclava as he handed me a mug. 'Nice and fresh up here after the galley,' he said. And then the smile was wiped from his face. 'What the hell's that?' He was staring past my left shoulder, staring at something astern of us on the port quarter. 'Can't be the moon, can it?'

I swung round. A cold, green translucence showed at the edge of visibility, a sort of spectral light that made me catch my breath in a sudden panic with all the old seamen's tales of weird and frightful things seen at sea rushing through my mind.

The light grew steadily brighter, phosphorescent and unearthly – a ghastly brilliance like a bloated glow-worm. And then suddenly it condensed and hardened into a green pin-point, and I yelled at Mike: 'The Aldis – quick!' It was the starboard navigation light of a big steamer, and it was bearing straight down on us. Her deck lights were appearing now, misted and yellow; and gently, like the muffled beat of a tom-tom, the sound of her engines reached out to us in a low, pulsating throb.

The beam of the Aldis lamp stabbed the night, blinding us with the reflected glare from a thick blanket of mist that engulfed us. It was a sea mist that had crept up on me in the dark without my knowing it. The white of a bow wave showed dimly in the brilliance, and then the shadowy outline of the bows themselves took shape. In an instant I could see the whole for'ard half of the ship. It was like a ghost ship emerging out of the mist, and the blunt bows were already towering over us as I swung the wheel.

It seemed an age that I watched *Sea Witch* turn, waiting for the jib to fill on the other tack and bring her head round, and all the time I could hear the surge of that bow wave coming nearer. 'She's going to hit us! Christ! She's going to hit us!' I can still hear Mike's cry, high and strident in the night. He was blinking the Aldis, directing the beam straight at her bridge. The whole superstructure was lit up, the light reflecting back in flashes from the glass windows. And the towering mass of the steamer kept on coming, thundering down on us at a good eight knots without a check, without any alteration of course.

The main and mizzen booms swung over with a crash. The jib was aback now. I left it like that for a moment, watching her head pay off. Every detail of *Sea Witch*, from the tip of her long bowsprit to the top of her mainmast, was lit by the green glow of the steamer's starboard light now high above us. I let go the port jib sheet, hauling in on the starboard sheet, saw the sail fill, and then Mike screamed, 'Look out! Hold on!' There was a great roaring sound and a wall of white water hit us. It swept over the cockpit, lifting me out of my seat, tugging at my grip on the wheel. The sails swung in a crazy arc; they swung so far that the boom and part of the mainsail were buried for a moment in the back of a wave whilst tons of water spilled across our decks; and close alongside the steamer slid by like a cliff.

Slowly *Sea Witch* righted herself as the water poured off her in a white foam. I still had hold of the wheel and Mike was clutching the backstay runner, shouting obscenities at the top of his voice. His words came to me as a frail sound against the solid thumping of the ship's engines. And then another sound emerged out of the night – the steady thrashing of a propeller partly clear of the water.

I shouted to Mike, but he had already realized the danger and had switched the Aldis on again. Its brilliant light showed us plates pitted deep with rust and a weed-grown Plimsoll mark high above the water. Then the plates curved up to the stern and we could see the propeller blades slashing at the waves, thumping the water into a swirling froth. *Sea Witch* trembled, sails slack. Then she slid off the back of a wave into that mill race and the blades were whirling close along our port side, churning white water over the cabin top, flinging it up into the mainsail.

It was like that for a moment and then they flailed off into the darkness beyond the bowsprit and we were left pitching in the broken water of the ship's wake. The Aldis beam picked out her name – *MARY DEARE* – *Southampton*. We stared dazedly at her rust-streaked lettering whilst the stern became shadowy and then vanished abruptly. Only the beat of her engines remained then, throbbing gently and gradually dying away into the night. A faint smell of burning lingered on for a while in the damp air. 'Bastards!' Mike shouted, suddenly finding his voice. 'Bastards!' He kept on repeating the word.

The door of the charthouse slid back, and a figure emerged. It was Hal. 'Are you boys all right?' His voice – a little too calm, a little too cheerful – shook slightly.

'Didn't you see what happened?' Mike cried.

'Yes, I saw,' he replied.

'They must have seen us. I was shining the Aldis straight at the bridge. If they'd been keeping a lookout – '

'I don't think they were keeping a lookout. In fact, I don't think there was anybody on the bridge.' It was said so quietly that for a moment I didn't realize the implication.

'How do you mean – nobody on the bridge?' I asked.

He came out on to the deck then. 'It was just before the bow wave hit us. I knew something was wrong and I'd got as far as the charthouse. I found myself looking out through the window along the beam of the Aldis lamp. It was shining right on to the bridge. I don't think there was anybody there. I couldn't see anybody.'

'But good God!' I said. 'Do you realize what you're saying?'

'Yes, of course, I do.' His tone was peremptory, a little military. 'It's odd, isn't it?'

He wasn't the sort of man to make up a thing like that. H. A.

Lowden – Hal to all his friends – was an ex-Gunner, a Colonel retired, who spent most of the summer months ocean racing. He had a lot of experience of the sea.

'Do you mean to say you think there was nobody in control of that ship?' Mike's tone was incredulous.

'I don't know,' Hal answered. 'It seems incredible. But all I can say is that I had a clear view of the interior of the bridge for an instant and, as far as I could see, there was nobody there.'

We didn't say anything for a moment. I think we were all too astonished. The idea of a big ship ploughing her way through the rock-infested seas so close to the French coast without anybody at the helm . . . It was absurd.

Mike's voice, suddenly practical, broke the silence. 'What happened to those mugs of soup?' The beam of the Aldis lamp clicked on, revealing the mugs lying in a foot of water at the bottom of the cockpit. 'I'd better go and make another brew.' And then to Hal who was standing, half-dressed, his body braced against the charthouse: 'What about you, Colonel? You'd like some soup, wouldn't you?'

Hal nodded. 'I never refuse an offer of soup.' He watched Mike until he had gone below and then he turned to me. 'I don't mind admitting it now that we're alone,' he said, 'but that was a very unpleasant moment. How did we come to be right across her bows like that?'

I explained that the ship had been down-wind from us and we hadn't heard the beat of her engines. 'The first we saw of her was the green of her starboard navigation light coming at us out of the mist.'

'No fog signal?'

'We didn't hear it, anyway.'

'Odd!' He stood for a moment, his long body outlined against the port light, and then he came aft and seated himself beside me on the cockpit coaming. 'Had a look at the barometer during your watch?' he asked.

'No,' I said. 'What's it doing?'

'Going down.' He had his long arms wrapped round his body, hugging his seaman's jersey. 'Dropped quite a bit since I went below.' He hesitated and then said, 'You know, this gale could come up on us pretty quickly.' I didn't say anything and he pulled his pipe out and began to suck on it. 'I tell you frankly, John, I don't like it.' The quietness of his voice added strength to his opinion. 'If the forecast turns out right and the wind backs north-westerly, then we'll be on a lee shore. I don't like gales and I don't like lee shores, particularly when the lee shore is the Channel Islands.'

I thought he wanted me to put back to the French coast and I didn't say anything; just sat there staring at the compass card, feeling obstinate and a little scared.

'It's a pity about the kicker,' he murmured. 'If the kicker hadn't packed up – '

'Why bring that up?' It was the only thing that had gone wrong with the boat. 'You've always said you despise engines.'

His blue eyes, caught in the light of the binnacle, stared at me fixedly. 'I was only going to say,' he put in mildly, 'that if the kicker hadn't packed up we'd be halfway across the Channel by now and the situation would be entirely different.'

'Well, I'm not putting back.'

He took his pipe out of his mouth as though to say something and then put it back and sat there, staring at me with those unwinking blue eyes of his.

'The real trouble is that you're not used to sailing in a boat that hasn't been kept up to ocean racing pitch.' I hadn't meant to say that, but I was angry and my nerves were still tense from the steamer incident.

An awkward silence fell between us. At length he stopped sucking on his pipe. 'It's only that I like to arrive,' he said quietly. 'The rigging is rusty, the ropes rotten and the sails – '

'We went over all that in Morlaix,' I said tersely. 'Plenty of yachts cross the Channel in worse shape than *Sea Witch*.'

'Not in March with a gale warning. And not without an engine.' He got up and went for'ard as far as the mast, bending down and hauling at something. There was the sound of splintering wood and then he came back and tossed a section of the bulwarks into the cockpit at my feet. 'The bow wave did that.' He sat down beside me again. 'It isn't good enough, John. The boat hasn't been surveyed and for all you know the hull may be as rotten as the gear after lying for two years on a French mud bank.'

'The hull's all right,' I told him. I was calmer now. 'There are a couple of planks to be replaced and she needs restopping. But that's all. I went over every inch of her with a knife before I bought her. The wood is absolutely sound.'

'And what about the fastenings?' His right eyebrow lifted slightly. 'Only a surveyor could tell you whether the fastenings – '

'I told you, I'm having her surveyed as soon as we reach Lymington.'

'Yes, but that doesn't help us now. If this gale comes up on us suddenly . . . I'm a prudent mariner,' he added. 'I like the sea, but it's not a creature I want to take liberties with.'

'Well, I can't afford to be prudent,' I said. 'Not right now.' Mike and I had just formed a small salvage company and every day we delayed getting the boat to England for conversion was a day lost out of our diving season. He knew that.

'I'm only suggesting you steer a point off your direct course,' he said. 'Close-hauled we can just about lay for Hanois on Guernsey Island. We'll then be in a position to take advantage of the wind when it backs and run for shelter to Peter Port.'

Of course . . . I rubbed my hand over my eyes. I should have known what he was driving at. But I was tired and the steamer incident had left me badly shaken. It was queer the way the vessel had sailed right through us like that.

'It won't help your salvage venture if you smash the boat up.' Hal's voice cut across my thoughts. He had taken my silence for refusal. 'Apart from the gear, we're not very strongly crewed.'

That was true enough. There were only the three of us. The fourth member of the crew, Ian Baird, had been sea-sick from the time we had left Morlaix. And she was a biggish boat for three to handle – a forty-tonner. 'Very well,' I said. 'We'll head for Guernsey.'

He nodded as though he'd known it all along. 'You'll need to steer North 65° East then.'

I turned the wheel, giving her starboard helm, and watched the compass card swing to the new course. He must have been working out the course in the charthouse just before the steamer came up on us. 'I take it you worked out the distance, too?'

'Fifty-four miles. And at this rate,' he added, 'it'll be daylight long before we get there.'

An uneasy silence settled between us. I could hear him sucking at his empty pipe, but I kept my eyes on the compass and didn't look at him. Damn it, I should have thought of Peter Port for myself! But there'd been so much to do at Morlaix getting the boat ready . . . I'd just about worked myself to a standstill before ever we put to sea.

'That ship.' His voice came out of the darkness at my side, a little hesitant, bridging the gap of my silence. 'Damned queer,' he murmured. 'You know, if there really was nobody on board . . .' He checked and then added, half-jokingly, 'That would have been a piece of salvage that would have set you up for life.' I thought I sensed a serious note underlying his words, but when I glanced

at him he shrugged his shoulders and laughed. 'Well, I think I'll
turn in again now.' He got up and his 'good night' floated back to
me from the dark gap of the charthouse.

Shortly afterwards Mike brought me a mug of hot soup. He
stayed and talked to me whilst I drank it, speculating wildly about
the *Mary Deare*. Then he, too, turned in and the blackness of the
night closed round me. Could there really have been nobody on
the bridge? It was too fantastic – an empty ship driving pell mell
up the Channel. And yet, cold and alone, with the pale glimmer of
the sails swooping above me and the dismal dripping of mist
condensed on the canvas, anything seemed possible.

At three Hal relieved me and for two hours I slept, dreaming of
blunt, rusted bows hanging over us, toppling slowly, everlastingly.
I woke in a panic, cold with sweat, and lay for a moment thinking
about what Hal had said. It would be queer if we salvaged a ship,
just like that, before we'd even . . . But I was asleep again before
the idea had more than flickered through my mind. And in an
instant I was being shaken and was stumbling out to the helm in
the brain-numbing hour before the dawn, all recollection of the
Mary Deare blurred and hazed by the bitter cold.

Daylight came slowly, a reluctant dawn that showed a drab,
sullen sea heaving gently, the steepness flattened out of the swell.
The wind was northerly now, but still light; and some time during
the night we had gone over on to the other tack.

At ten to seven Hal and I were in the charthouse for the weather
report. It started with gale warnings for the western approaches
of the Channel; the forecast for our own area of Portland was:
*Wind light, northerly at first, backing north-westerly later and increasing
strong to gale.* Hal glanced at me, but said nothing. There was no
need. I checked our position and then gave Mike the course to
steer for Peter Port.

It was a queer morning. There was a lot of scud about and
by the time we had finished breakfast it was moving across the sky
quite fast. Yet at sea level there was scarcely any wind so that, with
full main and mizzen set and the big yankee jib, we were creeping
through the water at a bare three knots, rolling sluggishly. There
was still a mist of sorts and visibility wasn't much more than two
miles.

We didn't talk much. I think we were all three of us too
conscious of the sea's menace. Peter Port was still thirty miles
away. The silence and the lack of wind was oppressive. 'I'll go and
check our position again,' I said. Hal nodded as though the
thought had been in his mind, too.

But poring over the chart didn't help. As far as I could tell we were six miles north-north-west of the Roches Douvres, that huddle of rocks and submerged reefs that is the western outpost of the Channel Islands. But I couldn't be certain; my dead reckoning depended too much on tide and leeway.

And then Mike knocked the bottom out of my calculations. 'There's a rock about two points on the starboard bow,' he called to me. 'A big one sticking up out of the water.'

I grabbed the glasses and flung out of the charthouse. 'Where?' My mouth was suddenly harsh and dry. If it were the Roches Douvres, then we must have been set down a good deal further than I thought. And it couldn't be anything else; it was all open sea between Roches Douvres and Guernsey. 'Where?' I repeated.

'Over there!' Mike was pointing.

I screwed up my eyes. But I couldn't see anything. The clouds had thinned momentarily and a queer sun-glow was reflected on the oily surface of the sea, merging it with the moisture-laden atmosphere. There was no horizon; at the edge of visibility sea and air became one. I searched through the glasses. 'I can't see it,' I said. 'How far away?'

'I don't know. I've lost it now. But it wasn't more than a mile.'

'You're sure it was a rock?'

'Yes, I think so. What else could it be?' He was staring into the distance, his eyes narrowed against the luminous glare of the haze. 'It was a big rock with some sort of tower or pinnacle in the middle of it.'

The Roches Douvres light! I glanced at Hal seated behind the wheel. 'We'd better alter course,' I said. 'The tide is setting us down at about two knots.' My voice sounded tense. If it was the Roches Douvres and the wind fell any lighter, we could be swept right down on to the reef.

He nodded and swung the wheel. 'That would put you out by five miles in your dead reckoning.'

'Yes.'

He frowned. He had taken his sou'wester off and his grey hair, standing on end, gave his face a surprised, puckish look. 'I think you're under-rating yourself as a navigator, but you're the boss. How much do you want me to bear up?'

'Two points at least.'

'There's an old saying,' he murmured: 'The prudent mariner, when in doubt, should assume his dead reckoning to be correct.' He looked at me with a quizzical lift to his bushy eyebrows. 'We don't want to miss Guernsey, you know.'

A mood of indecision took hold of me. Maybe it was just the strain of the long night, but I wasn't sure what to do for the best. 'Did you see it?' I asked him.

'No.'

I turned to Mike and asked him again whether he was sure it was rock he'd seen.

'You can't be sure of anything in this light.'

'But you definitely saw something?'

'Yes. I'm certain of that. And I think it had some sort of a tower on it.'

A gleam of watery sunlight filtered through the damp atmosphere, giving a furtive brightness to the cockpit. 'Then it must be the Roches Douvres,' I murmured.

'Look!' Mike cried. 'There it is – over there.'

I followed the line of his outstretched arm. On the edge of visibility, lit by the sun's pale gleam, was the outline of a flattish rock with a light tower in the middle. I had the glasses on it immediately, but it was no more than a vague, misty shape – a reddish tint glimmering through the golden haze. I dived into the charthouse and snatched up the chart, staring at the shape of the Roches Douvres reef. It marked drying rock outcrops for a full mile north-west of the 92-foot light tower. We must be right on the fringe of those outcrops. 'Steer north,' I shouted to Hal, 'and sail her clear just as fast as you can.'

'Aye, aye, skipper.' He swung the wheel, calling to Mike to trim the sheets. He was looking over his shoulder at the Roches Douvres light as I came out of the charthouse. 'You know,' he said, 'there's something odd here. I've never actually seen the Roches Douvres, but I know the Channel Islands pretty well and I've never seen any rock that showed up red like that.'

I steadied myself against the charthouse and focused the glasses on it again. The gleam of sunlight had become more positive. Visibility was improving all the time. I saw it clearly then and I was almost laughing with relief. 'It's not a rock,' I said. 'It's a ship.' There was no doubt about it now. The rusty hull was no longer blurred, but stood out clear and sharp, and what I had taken to be a light tower was its single funnel.

We were all of us laughing with the sense of relief as we turned back on to the course. 'Hove-to by the look of it,' Mike said as he stopped hauling in on the main-sheet and began to coil it down.

It certainly looked like it, for now that we were back on course her position didn't seem to have altered at all. She was lying broadside on to us as though held there by the wind and, as we closed with her and her outline became clearer, I could see that she was stationary, wallowing in the swell. Our course would leave her about half a mile to starboard. I reached for the glasses. There was something about the ship . . . something about her shape and her rusty hull and the way she seemed a little down at the bows.

'Probably pumping out her bilges,' Hal said, his voice hesitant as though he, too, were puzzled.

I focused the glasses and the outline of the vessel leaped towards me. She was an old boat with straight bows and a clean sweep to her sheer. She had an old-fashioned counter stern, an untidy clutter of derricks round her masts, and too much superstructure. Her single smoke stack, like her masts, was almost vertical. At one time she had been painted black, but now she had a rusty, uncared-for look. There was a sort of lifelessness about her that held me with the glasses to my eyes. And then I saw the lifeboat. 'Steer straight for her, will you, Hal,' I said.

'Anything wrong?' he asked, reacting immediately to the note of urgency in my voice.

'Yes. One of the lifeboats is hanging vertically from its davits.' It was more than that. The other davits were empty. I passed him the glasses. 'Take a look at the for'ard davits,' I told him and my voice trembled slightly, the birth of a strange feeling of excitement.

Soon we could see the empty davits with the naked eye and the single lifeboat hanging from the falls. 'Looks deserted,' Mike said. 'And she's quite a bit down by the bows. Do you think – ' He left the sentence unfinished. The same thought was in all our minds.

We came down on her amidships. The name at her bow was so broken up with rust streaks that we couldn't read it. Close-to she looked in wretched shape. Her rusty bow plates were out of true, her superstructure was damaged and she was definitely down by the bows, her stern standing high so that we could see the top of her screw. A festoon of wires hung from her mast derricks. She was a cargo ship and she looked as though she'd taken a hell of a hammering.

We went about within a cable's length of her and I hailed her through our megaphone. My voice lost itself in the silence of the sea. There was no answer. The only sound was the sloshing of the swell against her sides. We ran down on her quickly then, Hal steering to pass close under her stern. I think we were all of us watching for her name. And then suddenly there it was in rust-streaked lettering high above our heads just as it had been during the night: *MARY DEARE – Southampton*.

She was quite a big boat, at least 6000 tons. Abandoned like that she should have had a salvage tug in attendance, ships standing by. But there wasn't another vessel in sight. She was alone and lifeless within twenty miles of the French coast. I glanced up along her starboard side as we came out from under her stern. Both davits were empty, the lifeboats gone.

'You were right then,' Mike said, turning to Hal, his voice tense. 'There wasn't anybody on the bridge last night.'

We stared up at her in silence as we slipped away from her, awed by the sense of mystery. The rope falls hung forlornly from the empty davits. A thin trailer of smoke emerged incongruously from her funnel. That was the only sign of life. 'They must have abandoned ship just before they nearly ran us down,' I said.

'But she was steaming at full ahead,' Hal said, speaking more to himself than to us. 'You don't abandon ship with the engines going full ahead. And why didn't she radio for help?'

I was thinking of what Hal had said half-jokingly last night. If there was really nobody on board . . . I stood there, my hands braced on the guardrail, my body tense as I stared at her, searching for some sign of life. But there was nothing; nothing but that thin wisp of smoke trailing from the funnel. Salvage! A ship of 6000 tons, drifting and abandoned. It was unbelievable. And if we could bring her into port under her own steam . . . I turned to Hal. 'Do you think you could lay *Sea Witch* alongside her, close enough for me to get hold of one of those falls?'

'Don't be a fool,' he said. 'There's still quite a swell running. You may damage the boat, and if this gale – '

But I was in no mood for caution now. 'Ready about!' I called. And then, 'Lee ho!' We came about on to the other tack and I sent Mike below to get Ian out of his bunk. 'We'll jog up to her close-hauled,' I told Hal. 'I'll jump for the ropes as you go about.'

'It's crazy,' he said. 'You've a hell of a height to climb to the deck. And supposing the wind pipes up. I may not be able to get you – '

'Oh, to hell with the wind!' I cried. 'Do you think I'm going to pass up a chance like this? Whatever happened to the poor devils who abandoned her, this is the chance of a lifetime for Mike and myself.'

He stared at me for a moment, and then he nodded. 'Okay. It's your boat.' We were headed back for the ship now. 'When we get under her lee,' Hal said, 'we'll be pretty well blanketed. I may have some difficulty – ' He stopped there and glanced up at the burgee.

I had done the same, for there was a different feel about the boat now. She was surging along with a noise of water from her bows and spray wetting the foredeck. The burgee was streamed out to starboard. I checked with the compass. 'You'll have no difficulty standing off from her,' I said. 'The wind's north-westerly now.'

He nodded, his eyes lifting to the sails. 'You're still determined to go on board?'

'Yes.'

'Well, you'd better not stay long. There's some weight in the wind now.'

'I'll be as quick as I can,' I said. 'If you want to recall me in a hurry signal on the fog-horn.' We were doing all of four knots now and the ship was coming up fast. I went to the charthouse door and yelled to Mike. He came almost immediately. Ian was behind him, white-faced and still sweaty-looking from his bunk. I gave him the boat-hook and told him to stand by in the bows ready to shove off. 'We'll go about just before we get to her. That'll take the way off her and you'll be all set to stand-off again.' I was stripping off my oilskins. Already the rusty sides of the *Mary Deare* were towering above us. It looked a hell of a height to climb. 'Ready about?' I asked.

'Ready about,' Hal said. And then he swung the wheel. *Sea Witch* began to pay off, slowly, very slowly. For a moment it looked as though she was going to poke her long bowsprit through the steamer's rusty plates. Then she was round and I made up the starboard runner as the boom swung over. There was little wind now that we were close under the *Mary Deare*. The sails flapped lazily. The cross-trees were almost scraping the steamer's sides as we rolled in the swell. I grabbed a torch and ran to the mast, climbed the starboard rail and stood there, poised, my feet on the bulwarks, my hands gripping the shrouds. Her way carried me past the for'ard davit falls. There was still a gap of several yards between me and the ship's side. Hal closed it slowly. Leaning out I watched the after davit falls slide towards me. There was a jar as the tip of our cross-trees rammed the plates above my head. The first of the falls came abreast of me. I leaned right out, but they were a good foot beyond my reach. 'This time!' Hal shouted. The cross-trees jarred again. I felt the jolt of it through the shroud I was clinging to. And then my hand closed on the ropes and I let go, falling heavily against the ship's side, the lift of a swell wetting me to my knees. 'Okay!' I yelled.

Hal was shouting to Ian to shove off. I could see him thrusting wildly with the boat-hook. Then the end of the boom hit me between the shoulder-blades, the jar of it almost making me lose my hold. I hauled myself upwards with desperate urgency, afraid that the stern might swing and crush my legs against the ship's side. There was the slam of wood just below my feet and then I saw *Sea Witch* was clear and standing out away from the ship. 'Don't be long,' Hal shouted.

Sea Witch was already heeling to the wind, the water creaming back from her bows and a white wake showing at her stern as she gathered speed. 'I'll be as quick as I can,' I called back to him, and then I began to climb.

That climb seemed endless. The *Mary Deare* was rolling all the time, so that one minute I'd be swung out over the sea and the next slammed against the iron plates of her side. There were moments when I thought I'd never make it. And when, finally, I reached the upper-deck, *Sea Witch* was already half a mile away, though Hal had her pointed up into the wind and was pinching her so that her sails were all a-shiver.

The sea was no longer oil-smooth. Little waves were forming on the tops of the swell, making patterns of white as they broke. I knew I hadn't much time. I cupped my hands round my mouth and shouted: '*Mary Deare!* Ahoy! Is there anybody on board?' A gull shifted his stance uneasily on one of the ventilators, watching me with a beady eye. There was no answer, no sound except the door to the after deck-house slatting back and forth, regular as a metronome, and the bump of the lifeboat against the port side. It was obvious that she was deserted. All the evidence of abandonment was there on the deck – the empty falls, the stray pieces of clothing, a loaf lying in the scuppers, a hunk of cheese trampled into the deck, a half-open suitcase spilling nylons and cigarettes, a pair of sea boots; they had left her in a hurry and at night.

But why?

A sense of unease held me for a moment – a deserted ship with all its secrets, all its death-in-life stillness – I felt like an intruder and glanced quickly back towards *Sea Witch*. She was no bigger than a toy now in the leaden immensity of sea and sky, and the wind was beginning to moan through the empty ship – hurry! hurry!

A quick search and then the decision would have to be made. I ran for'ard and swung myself up the ladder to the bridge. The wheelhouse was empty. It's odd, but it came as a shock to me. Everything was so very normal there; a couple of dirty cups on a ledge, a pipe carefully laid down in an ash-tray, the binoculars set down on the seat of the Captain's chair – and the engine-room telegraph set to *Full Ahead*. It was as though at any moment the helmsman might return to take his place at the wheel.

But outside there was evidence in plenty of heavy weather. All the port wing of the bridge had been stove in, the ladder buckled and twisted, and down on the well-deck the seas had practically stripped the covering from the for'ard holds and a wire hawser was lying uncoiled in loops like dannert wire. And yet that in itself didn't account for her being abandoned; another tarpaulin hatch cover had been partly rigged and fresh timbering lay around as though the watch on deck had just knocked off for a cup of tea.

The chartroom at the back of the wheelhouse shed no light on the mystery; in fact, the reverse, for there was the log book open at the last entry: *20.46 hours – Les Heaux Light bearing 114°, approximately 12 miles. Wind south-east – Force 2. Sea Moderate. Visibility good. Altered course for the Needles – north 33° east.* The date was 18 March, and the time showed that this entry had been made just an hour and three-quarters before the *Mary Deare* had almost run us down. Entries in the log were made every hour so that whatever it was that had made them abandon ship had occurred between nine and ten the previous night, probably just as the mist was closing in.

Checking back through the log I found nothing to suggest that the ship would have to be abandoned. There had been constant gales and they had taken a bad beating. But that was all. *Hove-to on account of dangerous seas, waves sometimes breaking against bridge. Making water in No. 1 hold. Pumps not holding their own.* That entry for 16 March was the worst. Wind strength was given as Force 11 for twelve solid hours. And before then, ever since they had left the Mediterranean through the Straits, the wind had never fallen below Force 7, which is moderate gale, and was several times recorded as Force 10, whole gale. The pumps had been kept going all the time.

If they had abandoned ship in the gale of 16 March it would have been understandable. But the log showed that they had rounded Ushant on the morning of 18 March in clear weather with seas moderate and the wind Force 3. There was even a note – *Pumps making good headway. Clearing wreckage and repairing Number One hatch cover.*

It didn't make sense.

A companion-way led to the upper or boat-deck level. The door to the Captain's cabin was open. The room was neat and tidy, everything in its place; no sign of hurried departure. From the desk a girl's face in a big silver frame smiled at me, her fair hair catching the light, and across the bottom of the picture she had scrawled: *For Daddy – Bons voyages, and come back soon. Love – Janet.* There was coal dust on the frame and more of it on the desk and smudged over a file of papers that proved to be the cargo manifest, showing that the *Mary Deare* had loaded cotton at Rangoon on 13 January and was bound for Antwerp. On top of a filing tray filled with papers were several air mail letter-cards slit open with a knife. They were English letter-cards post-marked London and they were addressed to Captain James Taggart, *s.s. Mary Deare* at Aden, addressed in the same uneven, rather rounded hand that had scrawled across the bottom of the photograph. And below the letters, amongst the mass of papers, I found report sheets written in a small, neat hand and signed James Taggart. But they only covered the voyage from Rangoon to Aden. On the desk beside the tray was a sealed letter addressed to Miss Janet Taggart, University College, Gower Street, London, W.C.1. It was in a different hand and the envelope was unstamped.

All those little things, those little homely details . . . I don't know how to express it – they added up to something, something I didn't like. There was that cabin, so quiet, with all the decisions that had driven the ship throughout her life still there in the atmosphere of it – and the ship herself silent as the grave. And then I saw the raincoats hanging on the door, two blue Merchant Navy officers' raincoats hanging side by side, the one much bigger than the other.

I went out and slammed the door behind me, as though by closing it I could shut away my sudden, unreasoned fear. 'Ahoy! Is there anyone on board?' My voice, high and hoarse, echoed through the vaults of the ship. The wind moaned at me from the deck. Hurry! I must hurry. All I had to do was check the engines now, decide whether we could get her under way.

I stumbled down the dark well of a companion-way, following the beam of my torch, flashing it through the open doorway of the saloon where I had a glimpse of places still laid and chairs pushed hastily back. A faint smell of burning lingered on the musty air. But it didn't come from the pantry – the fire was out, the stove cold. My torch focused on a half-empty tin of bully lying on the table. There was butter, cheese, a loaf of bread with the crust all covered in coal dust; coal dust on the handle of the knife that had been used to cut it, coal dust on the floor.

'Is there anybody about?' I yelled. 'Ahoy! Anyone there?' No answer. I went back to the 'tween-decks alley-way that ran the length of the port-hand midships section. It was as silent and as black as the adit of a mine. I started down it, and then I stopped. There it was again – a sound I had been conscious of, but had not thought about; a sound like the shifting of gravel. It echoed within the ship's hull as though somewhere the steel plates were shifting on the bottom of the sea. It was a strange, uncanny sound, and it stopped abruptly as I walked on down the alley-way so that, in the vacuum of abrupt silence, I heard the wind's howl again.

The door at the end of the alley-way swung open to the roll of the ship, letting in a glimmer of daylight. I started towards it, conscious that the acrid smell of burning had increased until it quite overlaid the fusty mixture of hot oil, stale cooking and sea water dampness that permeates the 'tween-decks of all cargo ships. A fire hose, fixed to a hydrant near the engine-room door, snaked aft through pools of water and disappeared through the open door, out on to the well-deck beyond. I followed it. Out in the day-light I saw that Number Three hatch was burned and blackened, eaten half away by fire, and Number Four had been partly opened up. Fire hoses curled round the deck, disappearing into the open inspection hatch of Number Three hold. I went a few rungs down the vertical ladder, flashing my torch. But there was no smoke, no lurid glow, and the acrid fumes of the fire had a stale, washed-out smell, mixed with the pungent odour of chemicals. An empty foam extinguisher toppled on its side, clattering against the steel of the bulkhead plating. My torch showed the black pit of the hold piled high with charred and sodden bales of cotton and there was the sound of water slopping about.

The fire was out – dead – not even a wisp of smoke. And yet the ship had been abandoned. It didn't make sense. I was thinking of last night, how the smell of burning had lingered in the mist after the ship had gone past us. And there was the coal dust on the captain's desk and in the galley. Somebody must have put that fire out. I ran back to the engine-room door, remembering the grating sound of gravel shifting. Could it have been coal? Was there somebody down in the stokehold? Somewhere in the ship a hatch slammed, or maybe it was a door. I went in, on to the cat-walk that hung over the black abyss of the engine-room, criss-crossed with the steel gratings and vertical ladders. 'Ahoy!' I yelled. 'Ahoy there!'

No answer. My torch showed a glint of polished brass and the duller gleam of burnished steel amidst the shadowy shapes of the engines. No movement either . . . only the sound of water that made little rushing noises as it slopped about to the roll of the ship.

I hesitated, wondering whether to go down to the stokehold, held there by a sort of fear. And it was then that I heard the footsteps.

They went slowly along the starboard alley-way – boots clanging hollow against the steel flooring; a heavy, dragging tread that passed the engine-room door, going for'ard towards the bridge. The sound of the footsteps gradually faded away and was lost in the slapping of the water in the bilges far below me.

It couldn't have been more than twenty seconds that I remained there, paralysed, and then I had flung myself at the door, dragged it open and dived out into the alley-way, tripping over the step in my haste, dropping my torch and fetching up against the further wall with a force that almost stunned me. The torch had fallen into a pool of rusty water and lay there, shining like a glow-worm in the darkness. I stooped and picked it up and shone it down the passage.

There was nobody there. The beam reached the whole shadowy length as far as the ladder to the deck, and the corridor was empty. I shouted, but nobody answered. The ship rolled with a creak of wood and the slosh of water, and above me, muffled, I heard the rhythmic slamming of the door to the after deck-house. And then a faint, far-distant sound reached me, a sound that had a note of urgency in it. It was *Sea Witch*'s fog-horn signalling me to return.

I stumbled for'ard and as I neared the ladder to the deck, the fog-horn's moan was mingled with the noise of the wind soughing through the superstructure. Hurry! Hurry! There was a greater urgency in it now; urgency in the noise of the wind, in the fog-horn's blare.

I reached the ladder, was starting up – when I saw him. He was outlined for an instant in the swinging beam of my torch, a shadowy figure standing motionless in the recess of a doorway, black with a gleam of white to his eyes.

I checked, shocked into immobility – all the silence, all the ghostly silence of that dead ship clutching at my throat. And then I turned the beam of the torch full on him. He was a big man, dressed in reefer and sea boots, and black with coal dust. Sweat had seamed his face, making grime-streaked runnels as though he had wept big tears and the bone of his forehead glistened. All the right side of his jaw was bruised and clotted with blood.

He moved suddenly with great rapidity, came down on me

with a rush. The torch was knocked from my hand and I smelt the stale smell of sweat and coal dust as his powerful fingers gripped my shoulders, turning me like a child, twisting my head to the cold daylight that came down the ladder. 'What do you want?' he demanded in a harsh, rasping voice. 'What are you doing here? Who are you?' He shook me violently as though by shaking me he'd get at the truth.

'I'm Sands,' I gasped out. 'John Sands. I came to see – '

'How did you get on board?' There was a note of authority, as well as violence, in the rasp of his voice.

'By the falls,' I said. 'We sighted the *Mary Deare* drifting and when we saw the lifeboats gone, we came alongside to investigate.'

'Investigate!' He glared at me. 'There's nothing to investigate.' And then quickly, still gripping hold of me: 'Is Higgins with you? Did you pick him up? Is that why you're here?'

'Higgins?' I stared at him.

'Yes, Higgins.' There was a sort of desperate violence in the way he said the man's name. 'But for him I'd have got her safe to Southampton by now. If you've got Higgins with you . . .' He stopped suddenly, his head on one side, listening. The sound of the fog-horn was nearer now and Mike's voice was hailing me. 'They're calling you.' His grip tightened convulsively on my shoulders. 'What's your boat?' he demanded. 'What sort of boat is it?'

'A yacht.' And I added inconsequentially: 'You nearly ran us down last night.'

'A yacht!' He let go of me then with a little gasp like a sigh of relief. 'Well, you'd better get back to it. Wind's getting up.'

'Yes,' I said. 'We'll have to hurry – both of us.'

'Both of us?' He frowned.

'Of course,' I said. 'We'll take you off and when we reach Peter Port . . .'

'No!' The word exploded from his lips. 'No. I'm staying with my ship.'

'You're the Captain, are you?'

'Yes.' He stooped and picked up my torch and handed it to me. Mike's voice came to us faintly, a strangely disembodied shout from the outside world. The wind was a low-pitched, whining note. 'Better hurry,' he said.

'Come on then,' I said. I couldn't believe he'd be fool enough to stay. There was nothing he could do.

'No. I'm not leaving.' And then a little wildy, as though I were a foreigner who had to be shouted at: 'I'm not leaving, I tell you.'

'Don't be a fool,' I said. 'You can't do any good here – not alone. We're bound for Peter Port. We can get you there in a few hours and then you'll be able to – '

He shook his head, like an animal at bay, and then waved an arm at me as though signalling me to go.

'There's a gale coming up.'

'I know that,' he said.

'Then for God's sake, man . . . it's your one chance to get clear.' And because he was the Captain and obviously thinking about his ship, I added, 'It's the one hope for the ship, too. If you don't get a tug out to her soon she'll be blown right on to the Channel Islands. You can do far more good – '

'Get off my ship!' He was suddenly trembling. 'Get off her, do you hear? I know what I have to do.'

His voice was wild, his manner suddenly menacing. I stood my ground for a moment longer. 'You've got help coming then?' I asked. And when he didn't seem to understand, I said, 'You've radioed for help?'

There was a moment's hesitation and then he said, 'Yes, yes, I've radioed for help. Now go.'

I hesitated. But there was nothing else I could say, and if he wouldn't come . . . I paused halfway up the ladder. 'Surely to God you'll change your mind?' I said. His face showed in the darkness below me – a strong, hard face, still young but with deep-bitten lines in it, made deeper by exhaustion. He looked desperate, and at the same time oddly pathetic. 'Come on, man – whilst you've got the chance.'

But he didn't answer; just turned away and left me there. And I went on up the ladder to meet the weight of the wind howling along the deck and find the sea a mass of whitecaps with *Sea Witch* pitching violently two cables off.

2

I HAD stayed too long. I knew that as soon as *Sea Witch* turned to pick me up. She came roaring down-wind, the big yankee jib burying her bows deep into the wind-whipped waters, her long bowsprit thrusting into the backs of the waves, spearing them and coming out in a welter of spray. Hal had been right. I should never have boarded the ship. I ran to the falls, damning the crazy madman who'd refused to be taken off. If he had come with me, there would have been some point.

Sea Witch heeled over in a gust as Hal fought the wheel, bringing her round through the wind, all her sails flogging madly. The big yankee filled with a crack like a pistol shot, heeling the boat over till all the weed-grown boot-topping showed in the trough of a wave; and then the big sail split across and in an instant was blown to tatters. The wind was strong to gale in the gusts and she should have been reefed by now, but they hadn't a hope of reefing, just the three of them. It was madness for them to attempt to come alongside. I had never seen a sea whipped up so quickly. But Mike was waving to me, signalling downwards with his hand, and Hal was braced at the wheel, edging her up towards the ship's side, mainsail shivering, barely filled, the remnants of the yankee fluttering in streamers from the forestay. I caught hold of one of the falls then and swung myself out over the side, slithering down hand over hand until the surge of a wave soaked me to the waist and I looked up and saw that the rusty plates stood above me, high as a cliff.

I could hear *Sea Witch* now, hear the slap of her bows as she hit a wave and the solid, surging noise of her passage through the water. There were shouts and over my shoulder I saw her coming up into the wind, very close now, her head unwilling to pay off, the bowsprit almost touching the steamer's side. A gust of wind buffeted me, the main boom slammed over, sails filling suddenly, and she went surging past me a good twenty yards out from where I clung, swinging sickeningly in mid-air. Hal was shouting at me. 'The wind . . . strong . . . the ship turning round.' That was all I caught and yet he was so close I could see the water dripping off his oilskins, could see his blue eyes wide and startled-looking under his sou'wester.

Mike eased the sheets and the boat roared off down-wind. Hanging there, soaked with sea water thrown up from the wave tops breaking against the ship's side, I felt the weight of the wind pressing me in towards the rusty hull. At each roll I had to brace myself to meet the shock of my body being flung against her. Gradually I realized what had happened. The wind was swinging the *Mary Deare* broadside on; and I was on the windward side, exposed to the full force of the rising gale.

Sea Witch went about again and I wanted to shout to Hal not to be a fool, that it was no good. Now that the *Mary Deare* had swung, it was dangerous to come alongisde with the wind pressing the yacht down on to the ship. But all I did was pray that he'd make it, for I knew I couldn't hang there much longer. The ropes were getting slippery with water and it was bitterly cold.

I don't know how Hal managed it, but despite the lack of head-sails to bring her bow round, he got her about with almost no way on her a short stone's throw from where I was clinging. Then he let her drift down-wind. It was a superb piece of seamanship. There was a moment when her stern was almost within my reach. I think I might have made it, but at that moment the roll of the *Mary Deare* swung me against her sides and I was held fast against the wet chill of her hull, whilst the familiar counter of my boat slid away as Hal got her moving again to prevent her from being battered to pieces against the ship. 'No good . . . daren't . . . too dangerous . . . Peter Port.' The ragged snatches of Hal's shouts reached me through the wind as I was freed from the ship's side and swung out over the water, right over the spot where *Sea Witch*'s stern had been only a few seconds before. I wanted to shout to him to try again, just once more. But I knew it was risking the boat and their lives as well. 'Okay,' I yelled. 'Make Peter Port. Good luck!'

He shouted something back, but I couldn't hear what it was. *Sea Witch* was already disappearing beyond the steamer's bows, going fast with all her sheets eased and the wind driving at the great spread of her mainsail. I glanced up quickly at the towering wall of iron above my head and then I began to climb whilst I still had some strength left.

But each time the ship rolled I was flung against the side. It gave me extra purchase, flattened hard against the rusty plates, but it battered me, knocking the wind out of me. And each time I was swung clear the loss of purchase almost flung me off, for my fingers were numbed with cold and my arms and knees trembled with the strain of clinging there too long. The waves broke, engulfing me in ice-cold spray, and sometimes green water sloshed up the side of the ship and gripped me about the waist, plucking at me as it subsided.

I made only a few feet, and then I was finally halted. I could climb no further. Flattened against the ship's side, I gripped the rope with my shaking legs and, letting go with one hand, hauled up the free end, pulling it up between my legs and wrapping it over my shoulder. It took the strain off my arms. But it didn't get me back on to the ship's deck. I began to shout then, but the sound of my voice was whipped away by the wind. I knew the man couldn't possibly hear me, but I still went on shouting, praying that he'd come. He was my only hope. And then I stopped shouting, for I had no breath left – jarred and bruised, swung one moment out over the tumbled waters, the next slammed against the ship's side, it came to me slowly that this was the end.

It is difficult to be scared of something that is inevitable. You accept it, and that is that. But I remember thinking how ironical it was; the sea was to me a liquid, quiet, unruffled world through which to glide down green corridors to the darker depths, down tall reef walls with the fish, all brilliant colours in the surface dazzle, down to the shadowy shapes of barnacle-crusted wrecks. Now it was a raging fury of a giant, rearing up towards me, clutching at me, foaming and angry.

And then hope came suddenly in the graze of my hand against the rusty plates. Blood oozed in droplets from my knuckles, to be washed away by a blinding sheet of spray, and I stared, fascinated, as a flake of rust was peeled off by the upward scrape of my body. I didn't look up. I didn't move for fear I had imagined that I was being hauled up. But when the sea no longer reached me as it burst against the ship's side, I knew it was true. I looked up then and saw that the davits had been hauled in-board, saw the ropes move, taut, across the rail-capping.

Slowly, a foot at a time, I was hauled up, until at last my head came level with the deck and I looked into the haggard face and the wild, dark eyes of the *Mary Deare's* captain. He dragged me over the side and I collapsed on to the deck. I never knew till then how comfortable iron deck plates could be. 'Better get some dry clothes,' he said.

He pulled me to my feet and I stood there, trying to thank him. But I was too exhausted, too numbed with cold. My teeth chattered. He got my arm round his neck and half dragged me along the deck and down to one of the officers' cabins. 'Help yourself to what you want,' he said as he lowered me on to the bunk. 'Rice was about your height.' He stood over me for a moment, frowning at me as though I were some sort of a problem that had to be worked out. Then he left me.

I lay back, exhaustion weighting my eyelids, drowning consciousness. But my body had no warmth left in it and the cold cling of sodden clothes dragged me up off the bunk, to strip and towel myself down. I found dry clothes in a drawer and put them on; woollen underwear, a shirt, a pair of trousers and a sweater. A glow spread through me and my teeth stopped chattering. I took a cigarette from a packet on the desk and lit it, lying back again on the bunk, my eyes closed, drawing on it luxuriously. I felt better then – not worried about myself, only about *Sea Witch*. I hoped to God she'd get safe to Peter Port.

I was drowsy with the sudden warmth; the cabin was airless and smelt of stale sweat. The cigarette kept slipping from my fingers. And then a voice from a great distance off was saying: 'Sit up and drink this.' I opened my eyes and he was standing over me again with a steaming mug in his hand. It was tea laced with rum. I started to thank him, but he cut me short with a quick, angry movement of his hand. He didn't say anything; just stood there, watching me drink it, his face in shadow. There was a strange hostility in his silence.

The ship was rolling heavily now and through the open door came the sound of the wind howling along the deck. The *Mary Deare* would be a difficult tow if it blew a gale. They might not even be able to get a tow-line across to us. I was remembering what Hal had said about the Channel Islands as a lee shore. The warmth of the drink was putting new life into me; enough for me to consider what faced me, now that I was marooned on board the *Mary Deare*.

I looked up at the man standing over me, wondering why he had refused to leave the ship. 'How long before you expect help to reach us?' I asked him.

'There won't be any help. No call went out.' He leaned suddenly down towards me, his hands clenched and his jaw, thrust into the grey light coming in through the porthole, showing hard and knotted. 'Why the hell didn't you stay on your yacht?' And then he turned abruptly and made for the door.

He was halfway through it when I called after him. 'Taggart!' I swung my legs off the bunk.

He spun round on his heels as though I'd punched him in the

back. 'I'm not Taggart.' He came back through the doorway. 'What made you think I was Taggart?'

'You said you were the captain.'

'So I am. But my name's Patch.' He was standing over me again, a dark shadow against the light. 'How did you know about Taggart? Are you something to do with the owners? Is that why you were out there . . .' The wildness went out of his voice and he wiped his hand across the coal dust grime of his face. 'No. It couldn't be that.' He stared at me for a moment and then he shrugged his shoulders. 'We'll talk about it later. We've plenty of time. All the time in the world. Better get some sleep now.' He turned then and went quickly out.

Sleep! Five minutes ago that was what I'd wanted most in the world. But now I was wide awake. I won't say I was scared; not then. Just uneasy. That the man should behave oddly was not surprising. He had been twelve hours alone on the ship. He'd put out a fire single-handed and he'd stoked furnaces till he was on the brink of exhaustion. Twelve hours of hell; enough to unbalance any man. But if he was the captain, why wasn't he Taggart? And why hadn't the ship radioed for assistance?

I got up stiffly off the bunk, pulled on a pair of sea boots that were lying under the desk and staggered out into the corridor. There was a lot of movement on the ship now. Lying broadside to the seas, she was rolling heavily. A rush of cold air brought with it the battering noise of the wind. I went straight up to the bridge. It was raining and visibility was down to less than a mile; the whole sea was a dirty white of breaking water with the spray smoking from the crests and streaming away before the wind. It was already blowing gale force in the gusts.

The compass showed the ship lying with her bows to the north. The wind had backed into the west then; almost a dead run to Peter Port. I stood there working it out, listening to the thundering of the gale, staring out at that bleak waste of tumbled water. If Hal made it – if he got under the lee of Guernsey and made Peter Port . . . But it would take him several hours and he wouldn't realize at first that no distress signal had been sent out. Even when he did, the lifeboat would have to fight the gale to reach us; it would take them six hours at least, and by then it would be dark. They'd never find us in the dark in this sort of weather.

I turned abruptly and went through into the chartroom. A new position had been marked on the chart; a small cross two miles north-east of the Roches Douvres with 11.06 pencilled against it. It was now eleven-fifteen. I laid off the line of our drift with the parallel rule. If the wind held westerly we should drive straight on to the Plateau des Minquiers. He had discovered that, too, for a faint pencil line had been drawn in and there was a smudge of dirt across the area of the reefs where his fingers had rested.

Well, at least he was sane enough to appreciate the danger! I stood, staring at the chart, thinking about what it meant. It wasn't a pleasant thought. To be driven ashore on the rocky cliffs of Jersey would have been bad enough, but the Plateau des Minquiers . . .

I reached out to the bookshelf above the chart table, searching for Part II of the Channel Pilot. But it wasn't there. Not that it mattered. I knew them by reputation: a fearful area of rocks and reefs that we call The Minkies.

I was thinking about the Minkies and how it would feel to be on board a ship being pounded to pieces in such a maelstrom of submerged rocks when I noticed the door at the back of the chart-room with W/T stencilled on it. There was a steep ladder with no door at the top and as soon as I entered the radio shack I knew why no distress call had been sent out. The place had been gutted by fire.

The shock of it halted me in the doorway. The fire in the hold, and now this! But this was an old fire. There was no smell of burning, and planks of new wood had been nailed over the charred gaps that the fire had burned in roof and walls. No attempt had been made to clear the debris. The emergency accumulators had come through the burned-out roof and lay on the floor where they had fallen; one had smashed down on the fire-blackened table and had crushed the half-melted remains of the transmitter. Bunk and chair were scarcely recognizable, skeletons of blackened wood, and the radio equipment fixed to the walls was distorted beyond recognition and festooned with metal stalactites where solder had dripped and congealed; more equipment lay on the floor, black, twisted pieces of metal in the debris of charred wood. Whatever had caused the fire, it had burned with extraordinary ferocity. Water had seeped in through the gaps in the walls, streaking the blackened wood. The wind stirred the sodden ashes, shaking the rotten structure as it howled round the bridge.

I went slowly back down the ladder to the chartroom. Maybe the log book would tell me something. But it was no longer open on the table. I went through to the wheelhouse and was halted momentarily by the sight of a shaggy comber rearing up out of the murk on the port bow, spindrift streaming from its crest. It crashed down on to the iron bulwarks, and then the whole fore part of the ship, all except the mast and derricks, disappeared beneath a welter of white water. It seemed an age before the shape of the bows appeared again, a faint outline of bulwarks rising sluggishly, reluctantly out of the sea.

I hurried down the companion-way and made straight for the captain's cabin. But he wasn't there. I tried the saloon and the galley, and then I knew he must be down in the stokehold again. There was no doubt in my mind what had to be done. The pumps had to be got going. But there was no light in the engine-room, no sound of coal being shovelled into the furnaces. I shouted from the catwalk, but there was no answer; only the echo of my voice, a small sound lost in the pounding of the waves against the outside of the hull and the swirl of water in the bilges.

I felt a sudden sense of loss, a quite childish sense of loneliness. I didn't want to be alone in that empty ship. I hurried back to his cabin, the need to find him becoming more and more urgent. It was empty, as it had been before. A clang of metal aft sent me pushing through the door to the boat deck, and then I saw him. He was coming towards me, staggering with exhaustion, his eyes staring and his face dead white where he had wiped it clean of sweat and coal dust. All his clothes were black with coal and behind him a shovel slid across the deck. 'Where have you been?' I cried. 'I couldn't find you. What have you been doing all this time?'

'That's my business,' he muttered, his voice slurred with fatigue, and he pushed past me and went into his cabin.

I followed him in. 'What's the position?' I asked. 'How much water are we making? The seas are breaking right across the bows.'

He nodded. 'It'll go on like that – all the time now – until the hatch cover goes. And then there'll only be the shored-up bulkhead between us and the sea bed.' It was said flatly, without intonation. He didn't seem to care, or else he was resigned.

'But if we get the pumps going . . .' His lack of interest checked me. 'Damn it, man,' I said. 'That was what you were doing when I came aboard, wasn't it?'

'How do you know what I'd been doing?' He suddenly seemed to blaze up, his eyes hard and angry and wild. He seized hold of my arm. 'How do you know?' he repeated.

'There was a wisp of smoke coming from the funnel,' I said quickly. 'And then all that coal dust; you were covered with it.' I didn't know what had roused him. 'You must have been down in the stokehold.'

'The stokehold?' He nodded slowly. 'Yes, of course.' He let go
of my arm, his body gradually losing its tautness, relaxing.

'If the pumps could keep her afloat coming up through the
Bay . . .' I said.

'We had a crew then, a full head of steam.' His shoulders
drooped. 'Besides, there wasn't so much water in the for'ard hold
then.'

'Is she holed? I asked. 'Is that the trouble?'

'Holed?' He stared at me. 'What made you . . .' He pushed his
hand up through his hair and then down across his face. His skin
was sallow under the grime; sallow and sweaty and tired-looking.
The ship lurched and quivered to the onslaught of another wave.
I saw his muscles tense as though it were his own body that was
being battered. 'It can't last long.'

I felt suddenly sick and empty inside. The man had given up
hope. I could see it in the sag of his shoulders, hear it in the flat-
ness of his voice. He was tired beyond caring. 'You mean the
hatch cover?' He nodded. 'And what happens then?' I asked.
'Will she float with that hold full of water?'

'Probably. Until the boiler-room bulkhead goes.' His tone was
cold-blooded and without emotion. That hold had been flooded
a long time. The ship had been down by the bows when we had
sighted her through the mist. And last night . . . I was remembering the draught marks high out of the water at her stern and the
blades of the propeller thrashing at the wave tops. He had had
time to get used to the idea.

But I was damned if I was going to sit down and wait for the
end. 'How long would it take to get steam up – enough to drive
the pumps?' I asked. But he didn't seem to hear me. He was
leaning against the deck, his eyes half-closed. I caught hold of his
arm and shook him as though I were waking him out of a trance.
'The pumps!' I shouted at him. 'If you show me what to do, I'll
stoke.'

His eyes flicked open and he stared at me. He didn't say anything.

'You're just about all in,' I told him. 'You ought to get some
sleep. But first you must show me how to operate the furnace.'

He seemed to hesitate, and then he shrugged his shoulders. 'All
right,' he said, and he pulled himself together and went out and
down the companion ladder to the main deck. The weight of the
wind was heeling the ship, giving her a permanent list to starboard. Like that she rolled sluggishly with an odd, uneven motion
that was occasionally violent. His feet dragged along the dark,

echoing alley-way; at times he seemed uncertain of his balance, almost dazed.

We turned in through the engine-room door, crossed the cat-walk and descended an iron ladder into the dark pit of the engine-room, the beams of our torches giving momentary glimpses of vast shadowy machinery, all still and lifeless. Our footsteps rang hollow and metallic on the iron gratings as we made our way for'ard through a litter of smaller machinery. There was a sound of water moving in little rushes and heavy thuds echoed up the tunnel of the propeller shaft.

We passed the main controls with the bridge telegraph repeaters and then we reached the doors leading in to the boiler-room. Both doors were open, and beyond, the shapes of the boilers loomed bulky and majestic, without heat.

He hesitated a moment, and then moved forward again. 'It's this one,' he said pointing to the port-hand of the three boilers. A dull red glow rimmed the furnace door. 'And there's the coal.' He swung the beam of his torch over the black heap that had spilled out of the coal-box opening. He had half-turned back towards the furnace, when he checked and stood staring at the coal as though fascinated, slowly lifting the beam of his torch so that the white circle of it shone on plate after plate, all black with dust, as though he were tracing the line of the coal coming down from the bunkering hatch at deck level. 'We'll work two-hour shifts,' he said quickly, glancing at his watch. 'It's nearly twelve now. I'll relieve you at two.' He seemed suddenly in a hurry to go.

'Just a minute,' I said. 'How do you operate the furnace?'

He glanced impatiently back at the boiler with its temperature gauge and the levers below that operated the furnace doors and the dampers. 'It's quite simple. You'll get the hang of it easily enough.' He was already turning away again. 'I'm going to get some sleep,' he muttered. And with that he left me.

I opened my mouth to call him back. But there seemed no point. I should probably find out easily enough and he needed sleep badly. For a moment, as he passed through the stoke-hold doors, his body was sharply etched against the light of his torch. I stood there listening to the sound of his feet on the steel ladders of the engine-room, seeing the faint reflection of his torch limning the open doorway. Then it was gone and I was alone, conscious suddenly of the odd noises about me – the murmur of water, the queer booming of waves breaking against the ship's hull and the sudden little rushes of coal tipping in the chutes as she rolled;

conscious, too, of a sense of claustrophobia, of being shut in down there below the waterline. Beyond the boilers were the baulks of timber shoring the bulkhead, and beyond the rusty plates was water. I could see it trickling down the seams.

I stripped off my borrowed jersey, rolled up my sleeves and went over to the furnace. It was barely warm. I could put my hands on the casing of it. I found the lever and flung open the furnace door. A pile of ash glowed red. There was no rush of flame, no sign of it having been stoked in hours. I picked up one of the crowbar-like slices that lay about and prodded the glowing mass. It was all ash.

I had a look at the other two furnaces then, but their draught vents were all wide open, the fires burned out, the boilers cold. There was just that one furnace still alive, and it was alive because the dampers were shut right down. I remembered then how his footsteps had dragged past the engine-room door that first time I had stood on the catwalk calling into the abyss below. He hadn't been down here – then or at any time. Yet he was covered in coal dust. I stood there, leaning on my shovel, thinking about it until the noise of the waves booming against the hollow hull reminded me that there were other, more urgent matters, and I began shovelling in coal.

I piled it in until it was heaped black inside the furnace. Then I shut the door and opened all the dampers. In a few minutes the furnace was roaring, the bright light of flames showing round the edges of the door and lighting the stoke-hold with a warm glow, so that the shapes of the boilers emerged, dim and shadowy, from the darkness that surrounded me. I opened the door again and began shovelling hard, the shovel and the black coal lit by the lurid glow. Soon I was stripped to the waist and the sweat was rolling off me so that my arms and body glistened through their coating of coal dust.

I don't know how long I was down there. It seemed like hours that I shovelled and sweated in the cavernous inferno of the stoke-hold. The furnace roared and blazed with heat, yet it was a long while before I noticed any change in the pressure gauge. Then slowly the needle began to rise. I was standing, leaning on my shovel, watching the needle, when faint above the furnace roar I heard the slam of metal against metal and turned.

He was standing in the rectangle of the stoke-hold doors. He didn't move for a moment and then he advanced towards me, reeling drunkenly to the movement of the ship. But it wasn't the rolling that made him stagger. It was exhaustion. I watched him as he came towards me with a sort of fascination. The furnace door was open and in the glow I saw his face sweating and haggard, the eyes sunk into shadowed sockets.

He stopped as he saw me staring at him. 'What's the matter?' he asked. There was a nervous pitch to his voice, and his eyes, turned now to catch the furnace glow, had a wild look in them. 'What are you staring at?'

'You,' I said. 'Where have you been?'

He didn't answer.

'You haven't been to sleep at all.' I caught hold of his arm. 'Where have you been?' I shouted at him.

He shook me off. 'Mind your own damn' business!' He was staring at me wildly. Then he reached for the shovel. 'Give me that.' He snatched it out of my hand and began to feed coal in through the open furnace door. But he was so exhausted he could hardly balance himself to the roll of the ship. His movements became slower and slower. 'Don't stand there watching me,' he shouted. 'Go and get some sleep.'

'It's you who need sleep,' I told him.

'I said we'd take it in two-hour shifts.' His voice was flat, his tone final. Coal spilled suddenly out of the chute, piling over his feet to a heavy roll. He stared at it with a sort of crazy fascination. 'Get out of here,' he said. And then, shouting: 'Get out! Do you hear?' He was leaning on the shovel, still staring down at the coal spilling out of the chute. His body seemed to sag and he brushed his arm across his sweaty face. 'Go and get some sleep, for God's sake. Leave me here.' The last almost a whisper. And then he added, as though it were a connected thought: 'It's blowing full gale now.'

I hesitated, but he looked half-crazed in that weird light and I picked up my jersey and started for the door. I checked once, in the doorway. He was still watching me, the furnace-glow shining full on his haggard face and casting the enormous shadow of his body on the coal chute behind him.

Clambering up through the gloom of the engine-room I heard the scrape of the shovel and had one last glimpse of him through the open door; he was working at the coal, shovelling it into the furnace as though it were some sort of enemy to be attacked and destroyed with the last reserves of his energy.

The sounds of the gale changed as I climbed up through the ship; instead of the pounding of the waves against the hull, solid and resonant, there was the high-pitched note of the wind and the hissing, tearing sound of the sea. Cold, rushing air hit me in a blast as I stepped out into the corridor and made my way for'ard to my borrowed cabin. I had a wash and then lay back on the bunk, exhausted.

But though I was tired and closed my eyes, I couldn't sleep. There was something queer about the man – about the ship, too; those two fires and the half-flooded hold and the way they had abandoned her.

I must have dozed off, for, when I opened my eyes again, I was suddenly tense, staring at the dim-lit unfamiliarity of the cabin, wondering where I was. And then I was thinking of the atmosphere in that other cabin and, in the odd way one's mind clings to a detail, I remembered the two raincoats hanging on the door, the two raincoats that must belong to two different men. I sat up, feeling stale and sweaty and dirty. It was then just after two. I swung my feet off the bunk and sat there staring dazedly at the desk.

Rice! That was the name of the man. Less than twenty-four hours ago he had been on board, here in his cabin, perhaps seated at that desk. And here was I, dressed in his clothes, occupying his cabin – and the ship still afloat.

I pulled myself up and went over to the desk, drawn by a sort of fellow-feeling for the poor devil, wondering whether he was still tossing about on the sea in one of the lifeboats. Or had he got safe ashore? Maybe he was drowned. Idly I opened the desk top. There were books on navigation; he'd been an orderly man with a sense of property for he had written his name on the fly-leaf of each – John Rice, in the same small, crabbed hand that had made most of the entries in the bridge log book. There were paperbacks, too, mostly detective fiction, exercise books full of trigonometrical calculations, a slide rule, some loose sheets of graph paper.

It was under these that I found the brand-new leather writing case, the gift note still inside – *To John. Write me often, darling. Love – Maggie.* Wife or sweetheart? I didn't know, but staring up at me was the last letter he had written her. *My darling Maggie* it began, and my eyes were caught and held by the opening of the second paragraph: *Now that the worst is over, I don't mind telling you, darling, this has been a trip and no mistake. Nothing has gone right.*

The skipper had died and they had buried him in the Med. And out in the Atlantic they had run into heavy weather. On 16 March they were hove-to – *a real buster* – the pumps unable to hold their own, Numbers One and Two holds flooded, and a fire in the radio shack whilst they were trying to shore up the boiler-room bulkhead, with the crew near panic *because that bastard*

Higgins, had told them that explosives formed part of the cargo, whatever the manifest said. A Mr Dellimare, whom he referred to as *the owner*, had been lost overboard that same night.

Patch he described as having joined the ship at Aden as first officer in place of *old Adams who was sick.* And he added this: *Thank God he did or I don't think I'd be writing this to you. A good seaman, whatever they say about his having run the* BELLE ISLE *on the rocks a few years back.* And then this final paragraph: *Now Higgins is first officer and honestly, Maggie, I don't know. I've told you how he's been riding me ever since we left Yokohama. But it isn't only that. He's too thick with some of the crew – the worst of them. And then there's the ship. Sometimes I think the old girl knows she's bound for the knacker's yard. There's some ships when it comes to breaking up . . .*

The letter ended abruptly like that. What had happened? Was it the shout of Fire? There were questions racing through my mind, questions that only Patch could answer. I thrust the letter into my pocket and hurried down to the stoke-hold.

I had got as far as the engine-room before I stopped to think about the man I was going to question. He'd been alone on the ship. They'd all abandoned her, except him. And Taggart was dead – the owner, too. A cold shiver ran through me, and on the lower catwalk I stopped and listened, straining my ears – hearing all the sounds of the ship struggling with the seas, all magnified by the resonance of that gloomy cavern, but unable to hear the sound I was listening for, the sound of a shovel scraping coal from the iron floors.

I went down slowly then, a step at a time, listening – listening for the scrape of that shovel. But I couldn't hear it and when I finally reached the door to the stoke-hold, there was the shovel lying on the coal.

I shouted to him, but all I got was the echo of my own voice, sounding thin against the pounding of the seas. And when I flung open the furnace door, I wondered whether he existed at all outside of my imagination. The fire was a heap of white-hot ash. It looked as though it hadn't been stoked since I had left it.

In a frenzy, I seized the shovel and piled on coal, trying to smother my fears in physical exertion, in satisfaction at the sound of the coal spilling out of the chute, at the roar of the furnace.

But you can't just blot out fear like that. It was there inside me. I suddenly dropped the shovel, slammed the furnace door shut and went rushing up through the ship. I had to find him. I had to convince myself that he existed.

You must remember I was very tired.

He wasn't on the bridge. But there were pencil marks on the chart, a new position. And the sight of the seas steadied me. They were real enough anyway. God! they were real! I clung to the ledge below the glass panels of the wheelhouse and stared, fascinated, as a wave built up to port, broke and burst against the ship's side, flinging up a great column of smoking water that crashed down on the foredeck, blotting everything out. The sea rolled green over the bows. And when the outline of the bulwarks showed again and she struggled up with thousands of tons of water spilling off her, I saw that the for'ard hatch was a gaping rectangle in the deck.

There was no litter of matchwood. The deck was swept clear of all trace of the hatch covers. They had been gone some time. I watched the water spilling out of the hold as the ship rolled. But as fast as it spilled, the angry seas filled it up again. The bows were practically under water. The ship felt heavy and sluggish under my feet. She didn't feel as though she could last much longer.

I glanced round the bridge, rooted to the spot by the strange emptiness of it and the sudden certainty that the ship was going to go down. The spokes of the wheel were flung out in a forlorn circle. The brass of the binnacle gleamed. The telegraph pointers still stood at Full Ahead. The emptiness of it all . . . I turned and went down to the captain's cabin. He was there, lying back in the arm-chair, his body relaxed, his eyes closed. A half-empty bottle of rum stood on the desk at his elbow. The glass was on the floor, spilling a brown wet stain across the carpet. Sleep had smoothed out the lines of his face. Like that he seemed younger, less tough; but he still looked haggard and his right hand twitched nervously where it lay against the dark leather arm of the chair. The two blue raincoats still hung incongruously side-by-side on the back of the door. The girl still smiled at me sunnily from her silver frame.

A big sea broke against the ship's side, darkening the portholes with upflung water. His eyelids flicked back. 'What is it?' He seemed instantly wide awake, though his face was still puffed with sleep, flushed with the liquor he'd drunk.

'The for'ard hatch covers have gone,' I said. I felt a strange sense of relief. He was real and it was his responsibility, not mine. I wasn't alone after all.

'I know that.' He sat up, pushing his hand across his face and up through his black hair. 'What do you expect me to do about it – go out and rig new ones?' His voice was a little slurred. 'We did that once.' He pulled himself up out of the chair and went over to the porthole and stood there, looking at the sea. His back was towards me, his shoulders slightly hunched, hands thrust into his pockets. 'It was like this all the way up through the Bay – heavy seas and the ship making water all the time.' The daylight filtering through the porthole shone cold and hard on his exhausted features. 'And then that storm! God! What a night!' He stared out through the porthole.

'You'd better get some more sleep,' I said.

'Sleep?' His hand went to his eyes, rubbing them, and then pushing up through his hair again. 'Mabye you're right.' His forehead wrinkled in a frown and he smiled so that his face had a surprised look. 'You know, I can't remember when I last slept.' And then he added: 'There was something . . .' He was frowning. 'God! I can't remember. Something I was going to look up.' He stared down at the chart and books that lay on the floor beside the arm-chair. The chart was Number 2100, the large-scale chart of the Minkies. And then he was looking at me again and in an odd voice he said, 'Who exactly are you?' He was a little drunk.

'I told you that earlier,' I replied. 'My name is – '

'To hell with your name,' he shouted impatiently. 'What were you doing out there in that yacht? What made you board the ship?' And then before I had time to say anything, he added, 'Are you something to do with the Company?'

'What company?'

'The Dellimare Trading and Shipping Company – the people who own the *Mary Deare*.' He hesitated. 'Were you out there, waiting to see if – ' But then he shook his head. 'No, it couldn't have been that. We weren't steaming to schedule.'

'I'd never heard of the *Mary Deare* until last night,' I told him. And I explained how we'd almost been run down. 'What happened?' I asked him. 'How was it that the crew abandoned her with the engines still running and you on board? Was it the fire?'

He stared at me, swaying a little on his feet. And then he said, 'She was never meant to make the Channel.' He said it with a sort of smile, and when I asked him what he meant, he shrugged his shoulders and turned back to the porthole, staring out at the sea. 'I thought we were in the clear when I'd got her round Ushant,' he murmured. 'God damn it! I thought I'd taken all the knocks a man could in the course of a single voyage. And then that fire.' He turned and faced me again then. He seemed suddenly to want to talk. 'It was the fire that beat me. It happened about nine-thirty last night. Rice rushed in here to say that Number Three hold was ablaze and the crew were panicking. I got the hoses run out and part of Number Four hatch cleared so that we could play water on the bulkhead. And then I went down the inspection ladder into Number Four to check. That's how they got me.' He pointed to the bloodied gash on his jaw.

'You mean somebody hit you – one of the crew?' I asked in astonishment.

He nodded, smiling. It wasn't a pleasant smile. 'They battened the inspection hatch down on top of me when I was unconscious and then they drove the crew in panic to the boats.'

'And left you there?'

'Yes. The only thing that saved me was that they forgot we'd cleared part of the hatch cover. By piling bales of cotton up – '

'But that's mutiny – murder. Are you suggesting Higgins . . .'

He lurched towards me then, sudden violence in his face. 'Higgins! How did you know it was Higgins?'

I started to explain about the letter Rice had written, but he interrupted me. 'What else did he say?' he demanded. 'Anything about Dellimare?'

'The owner? No. Only that he'd been lost overboard.' And I added, 'The Captain died, too, I gather.'

'Yes, damn his eyes!' He turned away from me and his foot struck the overturned glass. He picked it up and poured himself a drink, his hands shaking slightly. 'You having one?' He didn't wait for me to reply, but pulled open a drawer of the desk and produced a glass, filling it almost to the brim. 'I buried him at sea on the first Tuesday in March,' he said, handing the drink to me. 'And glad I was to see the last of him.' He shook his head slowly. 'I was glad at the time, anyway.'

'What did he die of?' I asked.

'Die of?' He looked up at me quickly from under his dark brows, suddenly suspicious again. 'Who the hell cares what he died of?' he said with sudden truculence. 'He died and left me to face the whole . . .' He made a vague gesture with the hand that held his glass. And then he seemed suddenly to notice me again, for he said abruptly: 'What the hell were you doing out there in that yacht of yours last night?'

I started to tell him how we'd bought *Sea Witch* in Morlaix and were sailing her back to England for conversion into a diving tender, but he didn't seem to be listening. His mind was away on some thought of his own and all at once he said: 'And I thought it was decent of the old bastard to get out and make room for a younger man.' He was laughing again as though at some joke. 'Well, it's all the same now. That bulkhead will go soon.' And he looked at me and added, 'Do you know how old this ship is? Over forty years old! She's been torpedoed three times, wrecked twice. She's been rotting in Far Eastern ports for twenty years. Christ! She might have been waiting for me.' And he grinned, not pleasantly, but with his lips drawn back from his teeth.

A sea crashed against the ship's side and the shudder of the impact seemed to bring him back to the present. 'Do you know the Minkies?' He lunged forward and came up with a book which he tossed across to me. 'Page three hundred and eight, if you're interested in reading the details of your own graveyard.' It was the Channel Pilot, Part II.

I found the page and read: *PLATEAU DES MINQUIERS. – Buoyage. – Caution. – Plateau des Minquiers consists of an extensive group of above-water and sunken rocks and reefs, together with numerous banks of shingle, gravel and sand . . . The highest rock, Maîtresse Île, 31 feet high, on which stand several houses, is situated near the middle of the plateau . . .* There were details that showed the whole extent of the reefs to be about $17\frac{1}{2}$ miles long by 8 miles deep, and paragraph after paragraph dealt with major rock outcrops and buoyage.

'I should warn you that the so-called houses on Maîtresse Île are nothing but deserted stone shacks.' He had spread the chart out on the desk and was bending over it, his head in his hands.

'What about tide?' I asked.

'Tide?' He suddenly seemed excited. 'Yes, that was it. Something to do with the tide. I was going to look it up.' He turned and searched the floor again, swaying slightly, balanced automatically to the roll of the ship. 'Well, it doesn't matter much.' He downed the rest of his drink and poured himself another. 'Help yourself.' He pushed the bottle towards me.

I shook my head. The liquor had done nothing to the chill emptiness inside me – a momentary trickle of warmth, that was all. I was cold with weariness and the knowledge of how it would end. And yet there had to be something we could do. If the man were fresh; if he'd had food and sleep . . . 'When did you feed last?' I asked him.

'Oh, I had some bully. Sometime this morning it must have been.' And then with sudden concern that took me by surprise, he said, 'Why, are you hungry?'

It seemed absurd to admit to hunger when the ship might go down at any moment, but the mere thought of food was enough. 'Yes,' I said. 'I am.' Anyway, it might get him away from the bottle, put something inside him besides liquor.

'All right. Let's go and feed.' He took me down to the pantry, holding his glass delicately and balancing himself to the sluggish roll. We found a tin of ham – bread, butter, pickles. 'Coffee?' He lit a Primus stove he'd found and put a kettle on. We ate ravenously by the light of a single, guttering candle; not talking, just stuffing food into our empty bellies. The noise of the storm was remote down there in the pantry, overlaid by the roar of the Primus.

It's surprising how quickly food is converted into energy and gives a man back that desperate urge to live. 'What are our chances?' I asked.

He shrugged his shoulders. 'Depends on the wind and the sea and that bulkhead. If the bulkhead holds, then we'll be driven on to the Minkies sometime during the night.' The kettle had boiled and he was busy making the coffee. Now that the Primus was out, the pantry seemed full of the noise of the gale and the straining of the ship.

'Suppose we got the pumps working, couldn't we clear that for'ard hold of water? There was a good deal of pressure in the boiler when I was down there and I stoked before I left.'

'You know damn' well we can't clear that hold with the hatch cover gone.'

'Not if we ran her off before the wind. If we got the engines going . . .'

'Look,' he said. 'This old ship will be weeping water at every plate joint throughout her whole length now. If we ran the pumps flat out, they'd do no more than hold the water that's seeping into her, let alone clear Number One hold. Anyway, how much steam do you think you need to run the engines and the pumps as well?'

'I don't know,' I said. 'Do you?'

'No. But I'm damn' sure it would need more than one boiler; two at least. And if you think we could keep two boilers fired . . .' He poured the coffee into tin mugs and stirred sugar in. 'With one boiler we could have the engines going intermittently.' He seemed to consider it, and then shook his head. 'There wouldn't be any point in it.' He passed me one of the mugs. It was scalding hot.

'Why not?' I asked.

'For one thing the wind's westerly. Keeping her stern to the wind would mean every turn of the screw would be driving her straight towards the Minkies. Besides . . .' His voice checked, ceased abruptly. He seemed to lose himself in some dark thought of his own, his black brows furrowed, his mouth a hard, bitter line. 'Oh, to hell with it,' he muttered and poured the rest of his rum into his coffee. 'I know where there's some more liquor on board. We can get tight, and then who the hell cares?'

I stared at him, my bowels suddenly hot with anger. 'Is that what happened last time? Did you just give up? Is that what it was?'

'Last time?' He was frozen to sudden immobility, the mug of coffee halfway to his lips. 'What do you mean – last time?'

'The *Belle Isle*,' I said. 'Did she go down because . . .' I stopped there, checked by the sudden, blazing fury in his eyes.

'So you know about the *Belle Isle*. What else do you know about me?' His voice was shrill, uncontrolled and violent. 'Do you know I was on the beach for damn' near a year? A year in Aden! And this . . . The first ship in a year, and it has to be the *Mary Deare*, a floating bloody scrap-heap with a drunken skipper who goes and dies on me and an owner . . .' He pushed his hand up through his hair, staring through me, back into the past. 'Fate can play dirty tricks, once she's got her claws into you.' And then, after a pause: 'If I could keep this old tramp afloat . . .' He shook his head. 'You wouldn't think it would happen to a man twice, would you,' he murmured. 'Twice! I was too young and green to know what they were up to when I got command of the *Belle Isle*. But I knew the smell of it this time. Well, they got the wrong man.' He gave a bitter laugh. 'A lot of good it did me, being honest. I got her up through the Bay. God knows how I did it, but I did. And round Ushant I headed for Southampton.' His eyes focused on me again and he said, 'Well, now I don't care any more. You can't go on fighting a thing. This gale has finished me. I know when I'm licked.'

I didn't say anything, for there wasn't anything I could say. It had to come from him. I couldn't drive him. I knew that. I just sat there and waited and the silence tightened between us. He finished his coffee and put the mug down and wiped his mouth with the back of his hand. The silence became unbearable, full of the death-struggle sounds of the ship. 'Better come and have a drink,' he said, his voice tense.

I didn't move. I didn't say anything either.

'It's tough on you, but you didn't have to come on board, did you?' He stared at me angrily. 'What the hell do you think I can do?'

'I don't know,' I said. 'You're the captain. It's for you to give the orders.'

'Captain!' He laughed without mirth. 'Master of the *Mary
Deare!*' He rolled it round his tongue, sneeringly. 'Well, at least
I'll have gone down with the ship this time. They said she was
jinxed, some of them.' He seemed to be speaking to himself. 'They
were convinced she'd never make it. But we're all jinxed when
times get hard; and she's been kicked around the world for a
good many years. She must have been a crack cargo liner in her
day, but now she's just a rusty old hulk making her last voyage.
We'd a cargo for Antwerp, and then we were taking her across
the North Sea to Newcastle to be broken up.' He was silent after
that, his head on one side, listening. He was listening to the
sounds of the ship being pounded by the waves. 'What a thing it
would be – to steam into Southampton with no crew and the ship
half-full of water.' He laughed. It was the drink in him talking,
and he knew it. 'Let's see,' he said, still speaking to himself. 'The
tide will be turning against us in a few hours. Wind over tide.
Still, if we could hold her stern-on to the wind, maybe we could
keep her afloat a little longer. Anything could happen. The
wind might shift; the gale might blow itself out.' But there was
no conviction in the way he said it. He glanced at his watch.
'Barely twelve hours from now the tide will be carrying us down
on to the rocks and it'll still be dark. If visibility is all right, we
should be able to see the buoys; at least we'll know – ' His voice
checked abruptly. 'The buoys! That's what I was thinking about
before I went to sleep. I was looking at the chart . . .' His voice
had become animated, his eyes suddenly bright with excitement.
And then his fist crashed against the palm of his hand and he
jumped to his feet. 'That's it! If we were to hit the tide just
right . . .' He pushed by me and I heard his feet take the steps of
the ladder leading to the bridge two at a time.

I followed him up and found him in the chartroom, poring over
a big book of Admiralty tide-tables. He looked up and for the first
time I saw him as a leader, all the fatigue wiped out, the drink
evaporated. 'There's just a chance,' he said. 'If we can keep her
afloat, we might do it. It means working down in that stoke-
hold – working like you've never worked in your life before; turn-
and-turn about – the stoke-hold and the wheelhouse.' He seized
hold of my arm. 'Come on! Let's see if we've got sufficient head of
steam to move the engines.' A wave hit the side of the ship.
Sheets of water fell with a crash, sluicing into the wheelhouse
through the broken doorway leading to the port wing of the
bridge. Out of the tail of my eye I saw water thundering green
across the half-submerged bows. And then I was following him

down the ladder again into the body of the ship and he was shouting: 'By God, man, I might cheat them yet.' And his face, caught in the light of my torch as it was turned momentarily up to me, was filled with a sort of crazy vitality.

3

THE DARKNESS of the engine-room was warm with the smell of hot oil and there was the hissing sound of steam escaping, so that the place seemed no longer dead. In my haste I let go at the bottom of the last ladder and was pitched a dozen feet across the engine-room deck, fetching up against a steel rail. There was a prolonged hiss of steam as I stood there, gasping for breath, and the pistons moved, thrusting their arms against the gleaming metal of the crankshaft, turning it – slowly at first, and then faster and faster so that all the metal parts gleamed in the light of my torch and the engines took on that steady, reassuring thump-thump of vitality and power. The hum of a dynamo started and the lights began to glow. The humming became louder, the lights brighter, and then abruptly they snapped full on. Brass and steelwork gleamed. The whole lit cavern of the engine-room was alive with sound.

Patch was standing on the engineer officer's control platform. I staggered down the catwalk between the two big reciprocators. 'The engines!' I shouted at him. 'The engines are going!' I was beside myself with excitement. For that one moment I thought we could steam straight into a port.

But he was already shutting off the steam, and the beat of the engines slowed and then stopped with a final hiss. 'Don't stand there,' he said to me. 'Start stoking. We want all the steam we can get.' For the first time he looked like a man in control of the situation.

But stoking was more difficult now; dangerous, too. The movements of the ship were unpredictable. One moment I would be flinging a shovelful of coal high up against the thrust of gravity, the next I would be pitched towards the flaming mouth of the furnace and the coal would seem to have no weight in it at all as it left the shovel.

I don't know how long I was working there alone before he

joined me. It seemed a long time. I didn't see him enter. All my mind was concentrated on the coal and that gaping furnace door, concentrated on gauging the pitch of the ship, avoiding being flung against the red-hot fire. I felt a hand on my arm and I looked up to find him standing over me. I straightened up and faced him, panting, with the sweat pouring off my body. 'I've got the pumps going,' he said.

I nodded, too short of breath to waste it in speech.

'I've just been up on the bridge,' he went on. 'Half the time the bows are right under. Any moment that bulkhead may go. Do you think you could hear the engine-room telegraph from in here?'

'I don't know,' I said. 'I expect so.'

He took me through into the engine-room then and showed me the engine controls and the voice pipe that connected with the bridge. 'I'll go up to the bridge now,' he said. 'You go back to the boiler-room and start stoking. I'll give you a ring on the engine-room telegraph. If you don't hear it after two minutes come to the voice pipe. Okay?'

I nodded and he went clambering up the ladder, whilst I returned to the stoke-hold. Even in that short time my arms and back had stiffened. I had to force myself to start shovelling again. I was beginning to get very tired and I wondered how long we could keep this up. Faint above the roar of the furnace and the sounds of the engine-room came the jangling of the bridge telegraph. I flung the furnace door to and went through to the engineer's control platform. The pointer stood at Full Ahead. I spun the control wheel, opening up the steam valves, and for the first time I understood the thrill and pride an engineer officer must feel; the hiss of steam, the pistons moving and the engines taking up a steady, pulsating beat, vibrant with power. The heart of the ship had come alive, and it was I who had made it alive. It was satisfying.

Back in the stoke-hold the shovel felt strangely light. I barely noticed the aching of my arms. Confidence and the will to fight back had returned. I was suddenly full of energy.

It worked out that about every ten minutes or so the engines had to be run; it took about three minutes to get her stern-on again. Those three minutes produced a big drop in the pressure gauge. Only by keeping the furnace full and roaring could that pressure be built up again in time to meet the next demand from the bridge.

At 15.30 he called me up to take over the wheel. 'Watch the

spindrift,' he said. 'That will tell you the wind direction. Lay her exactly along the direction of the wind. If you're a fraction out the stern will swing almost immediately. And have full rudder on from the moment you order me to start the engines – and don't forget she'll carry way for a good five minutes after the engines have stopped.' He left me then and I was alone at the wheel.

It was a welcome relief to be able to stand there with nothing heavier than the wheel to shift. But whereas in the stoke-hold, with the roar of the furnace and the periodic sound of the engines, there had been a sense of security and normality, here I was face to face with the reality of the situation. A grim half light showed the bows so badly down in the water that they barely lifted above the marching wave tops even when running dead before the wind, and, as soon as the ship swung and I had to use the engines, the whole deck for'ard of the bridge became a seething welter of water. The sweat cooled on my body, an ice-cold, clammy coating to my skin, and I began to shiver. I found a duffle coat in the chartroom and put it on. A new position had been marked in on the chart. We were lying just about halfway between the Roches Douvres and the Minkies. The congested areas of submerged reefs was looming rapidly nearer.

At 16.30 he relieved me. He stood for a moment looking out across the bows into the faded daylight of that wretched, gale-swept scene. His face and neck glistened with sweat and his eyes were deep-sunk in their sockets, all the bone formation of his face standing out hard and sharp. 'Come through into the chartroom a minute,' he said, taking hold of my arm – whether out of a need for the companionship of physical contact or to steady himself against the roll of the ship, I don't know. 'The wind is westerly now,' he said, pointing to our position on the chart. 'It will probably back further into the south-west. If we're not careful we're going to be driven slap into the middle of the Minkies. What we've got to do now is to inch our way to the south'ard. Every time we run the engines we've got to make full use of them.'

I nodded. 'Where are you heading for – St Malo?'

He looked at me. 'I'm not heading anywhere,' he said. 'I'm just trying to keep afloat.' He hesitated and then added, 'In four hours the tide will start running against us. It'll be wind over tide then and throughout most of the night. It'll kick up a hell of a sea.'

I glanced out of the chartroom window and my heart sank, for it didn't seem possible that the sea could be worse than it was now. I watched him work out the dead reckoning and mark in

another cross about five miles west and a little south of the other.
'We can't have moved that much in an hour,' I protested.

He flung down the pencil. 'Work it out for yourself if you don't
believe me,' he said. 'The tide's running south-easterly three
knots. Allow two miles for wind and engines, and there you are.'

I stared at the chart. The Minkies were getting very close.
'And in the next two hours?' I asked.

'In the next two hours the tide slacks off considerably. But my
reckoning is that we'll be within a mile or so of the south-west
Minkies buoy. And there we'll stay for the first half of the night.
And when the tide turns . . .' He shrugged his shoulders and went
back again into the wheelhouse. 'Depends whether we've
managed to edge south at all.'

With this cheerful prospect I went below again, back to the
familiar, aching grind and blazing heat of the stoke-hold. One
hour in the stoke-hold; one on the bridge. Turn and turn about;
it became a routine. Dazed with tiredness we did it automatically,
unconsciously adjusting ourselves to the greater movement of the
bridge and then readjusting ourselves to the quicker, less pre-
dictable and much more dangerous motion of the stokehold.

I remember being at the wheel when darkness fell. It seemed to
steal up on us almost imperceptibly. And then suddenly I couldn't
see the bows, couldn't tell where the wind was because I couldn't
see the spume flying off the wave tops. All I could see was darkness
shot with the white-tumbling wave tops. The deck sloped forward
under my feet and, with broken water all round the ship, it was as
though we were running the rapids of a giant river, slipping down-
hill at tremendous speed. I steered by the compass and the feel of
the ship then, all the time pushing her towards the south with
every burst of the engines.

At the helm just after midnight a glimmer of light showed for
an instant in the rushing, wind-torn darkness beyond the bows.
I hoped to God I had imagined it. I was very tired by then and it
had just been a momentary gleam, indistinct and ephemeral. But
a little later I saw it again, a flash of light about two points off the
starboard bow. It showed intermittently, often obscured by the
backs of the waves.

By the end of my watch it was possible to identify it as group-
flashing two. The chart showed the south-west Minkies buoy as
Gp.fl.(2). 'About what we expected,' Patch said when he relieved
me. His voice showed no lift of interest; it was flat and slurred
with weariness, his face gaunt in the light of the binnacle.

And after that the light was always with us, getting a little nearer, a little clearer until it began to fade with the first grey glimmer of dawn as I took over the wheel at five-thirty in the morning. I was almost dead with exhaustion then, hardly able to stand, my knees trembling. The night in the stoke-hold had been hell, the last hour almost unendurable, shovelling coal with rivulets of water spilling across the floor and spitting steam as they swirled round the hot base of the furnace.

The tide had turned now and the double flash of the Minkies buoy began to come down on us fast, and on the wrong side of us. Soon, as the daylight strengthened, I could see the buoy itself, one of those huge pillar buoys that the French use, and, even above the wind, I thought now and then I could catch the mournful, funeral note of its whistle. We were going to pass at least half a mile inside it. I had a look at the chart and then got Patch on the voice pipe and told him to come up.

It seemed a long time before he appeared on the bridge, and when he came he moved slowly, his feet dragging as though he were just out of a sick bed. Changing watches during the night, he had been just a shadowy shape in the pale, reflected glow of the binnacle light. Now, seeing him suddenly in the cold light of day, I was shocked. He looked ghastly. 'You're just about out on your feet,' I said.

He stared at me as though he hadn't understood. I suppose I looked pretty bad myself. 'What is it?' he asked.

I pointed to the Minkies buoy, now almost four points on the starboard bow. 'We're passing too far inside it,' I said. 'At any moment we may hit the Brisants du Sud rocks.'

He went into the chartroom and I waited, expecting him to send me running below to get the engines going. He was gone a long time. Once I shouted to him, afraid that he must have gone to sleep. But he answered immediately that he was watching the buoy through the window and working something out. The tide had got a firm hold of us now. I watched the bearing of the buoy altering rapidly. It was almost abeam of us before he emerged from the chartroom. 'It's all right,' he said. 'There's water enough at this stage of the tide.' His voice was quite calm.

The wind had caught our stern now and we were swinging. Not two cables' length away an eddy marked a submerged rock and the heavy overfalls broke against each other in violent collision, sending up great gouts of water. And beyond was a cataract of broken water where the waves spilled in tumbled confusion, raging acres of surf. A big sea hit us, thudding against the ship's side and rolling in a white tide across the foredeck. Tons of water crashed down on the bridge. The whole ship shuddered. 'Aren't you going to get the engines started?' I demanded.

He was standing with his back to me, staring out to starboard. He hadn't heard me. 'For God's sake!' I cried. 'We're being carried right on to the Minkies.'

'We're all right for the moment.' He said it quietly, as though to soothe me.

But I didn't believe him. How could we be all right? All ahead of us was nothing but reefs with the seas pouring white across miles of submerged rock. Once we struck . . . 'We've got to do something,' I said desperately.

He didn't answer . He was staring through the glasses out beyond the starboard bow, his legs straddled against the sickening lunges of the ship.

I didn't know what to do. He seemed calm and in control of the situation, and yet I knew that he had gone physically beyond the limits of endurance – mentally, too, perhaps. 'We've got to get clear of the Minkies,' I told him. 'Once we're clear of the Minkies we're all right.' I let go of the wheel and started for the companion ladder. 'I'm going to start the engines.'

But he grabbed hold of my arm as I passed him. 'Don't you understand?' he said. 'We're sinking.' His face was as stony as the gaze of his dark eyes. 'I didn't tell you before, but water is flooding through that bulkhead. I had a look at it just before I relieved you.' He let go of my arm then and stared through the glasses again, searching for something in the grey, scud-filled dawn.

'How long – ' I hesitated, unwilling to put it into words. 'How long before she goes down?'

'I don't know. A few minutes, an hour, maybe two.' He lowered the glasses with a little grunt of satisfaction. 'Well, it's a slender chance, but . . .' He turned and stared at me as though assessing my worth. 'I want pressure in that boiler for ten to fifteen minutes' steaming. Are you prepared to go below and continue stoking?' He paused and then added, 'I should warn you that you'll stand no chance at all if that bulkhead goes whilst you're down there.'

I hesitated. 'For how long?'

'An hour and a half I should say.' He glanced quickly away to starboard, half nodded his head and then caught hold of my arm. 'Come on,' he said. 'I'll give you a hand for the first hour.'

'What about the ship?' I asked. 'If she strikes on one of these reefs . . .'

'She won't strike,' he answered. 'We're drifting down just

about a mile inside the buoys.'

Down in the stoke-hold there was a strange sense of remoteness from danger. The warmth and the furnace glow and the blaze of the lights were comfortingly normal. Now that I could no longer see the seas thundering over the reefs I was enveloped in a false sense of security. Only the boom of the waves crashing against the hollow sides of the ship and the bright rivulets of water streaming from the started rivet holes reminded us of the danger we were in; that and the forward slant of the decks and the water sluicing up out of the bilges, black with coal dust, filthy with oil.

We stoked like madmen, shoulder-to-shoulder, flinging coal into the furnace with utter disregard of exhaustion. It seemed an eternity, but the bulkhead held and finally Patch looked at his watch and flung his shovel down. 'I'm going up to the bridge,' he said. 'You'll be on your own now. Keep on stoking until I ring for full speed. Then, when you've got the engines going, come straight up to the bridge. All right?'

I nodded, not trusting myself to speak. He was pulling his clothes on and I watched him as he staggered through to the engine-room and disappeared. The sound of the waves thundering against the hull seemed louder now. I looked down at my wrist watch. It was twenty past seven. I started to shovel coal again, conscious all the time of the hull plates towering above me and of the slope of the decks; conscious that at any moment this lit world might plunge below the seas. Water was sloshing about in the bilges, spilling over on to the plates and swirling round my feet.

Half-past seven! Quarter to eight! Would he never ring for the engines? Once I paused, leaning on my shovel, certain that the deck below my feet was at a steeper angle, watching that streaming bulkhead and wondering what the hell he was doing up there on the bridge. What was this slender chance he had talked of? Exhausted, my nerves strung taut with fear and the long wait, I suddenly wasn't sure of him any more. What did I know about him? My first impressions – of a man unbalanced by circumstances – returned, stronger now because more dangerous.

And then suddenly, faint above the booming of the waves, came the jangle of the telegraph. It was almost eight o'clock. I flung my shovel down, slammed the furnace door shut and, with my clothes in my hand, staggered quickly through into the engine-room. The telegraph indicator was at Full Ahead. I turned the steam full on and as I raced up the ladders, the whole steel-traceried vault of the engine-room became alive with the pounding of the engines.

He was standing at the wheel, steering the ship, as I panted up the ladder on to the bridge. 'Are we clear of the Minkies yet?' I gasped.

He didn't answer. His hands were gripped tight on the wheel, his whole body tense as he stared out ahead. The ship heeled in a long agonizing roll and I staggered down the slope of the bridge-deck to the starboard windows. A buoy, painted red and white, was sliding past us. The bows were completely submerged.

'Almost there now.' His voice was taut, barely audible. His eyes looked out of their sunken sockets, staring fixedly. And then he shifted the balance of his feet and the wheel spun under his hands. I couldn't believe it for a moment. He was turning the wheel to port. He was turning the ship to port, turning her in towards the rock outcrops of the Minkies. 'Are you crazy?' I shouted at him. 'Turn to starboard! To starboard, for God's sake!' And I flung myself at the wheel, gripping the spokes, trying to turn it against the pressure of his hands.

He shouted something at me, but it was lost in the noise of a big sea crashing against the bridge. I wouldn't have heard him anyway. St Malo was only twenty miles away and the beat of the engines throbbed through the deck plates, beating a message of hope against the soles of my feet. We had to turn to starboard – away from the Minkies, towards St Malo. 'For Christ's sake!' I screamed at him.

Fingers gripped my hair, forcing my head back. He was shouting at me to let go of the wheel, and my eyes, half-closed with pain, caught a glimpse of his face, set and hard and shining with sweat, the lips drawn back from his teeth and the muscles of his jaw knotted. 'It's our only chance.' His voice was barely audible above the roar of the seas. And then the muscles of my neck cracked as he flung me back and I was caught on a downward plunge and fetched up against the window ledge with such force that all the breath was knocked out of me. A patch of broken water slid past on the port side and almost ahead of us the sea flung a curling wave-top round a little huddle of rocks that were just showing their teeth. I felt suddenly sick.

'Will you take the wheel now?' His voice was distant, quite cool. I stared at him, dazed and not understanding. 'Quick, man,' he said. 'Take the wheel.' He was on his own bridge, giving an order, expecting it to be obeyed. The acceptance of obedience was implicit in his tone. I dragged myself to my feet and he handed over to me. 'Steer north ten degrees east.' He fetched the hand-bearing compass from the chartroom and went out with it on to the starboard wing of the bridge. For a long time he stood there, quite motionless, occasionally raising the compass to his eye and taking a bearing on some object behind us.

And all the time I stood there at the wheel, holding the ship to ten degrees east of north and wondering what in God's name we were doing sailing straight in towards the reefs like this. I was dizzy, still a little sick, too scared now to do anything but hold on to the course I had been told, for I knew we must be in among the rocks and to try to turn the ship would mean certain disaster. And through the windows, out in that maelstrom of white water that filled all my horizon, there gradually emerged the shapes of more rocks, whole masses of rocks, getting nearer and nearer every minute.

'Steer due north now.' His voice was still calm. Yet all ahead of us was nothing but waves tumbling and falling and cascading on the half-exposed reefs. There was one lone island of rock nearer than the rest and, as the ship drove towards it, he was back at my side. 'I'll take her now.' There was a gentleness in the way he spoke and I let him have the wheel, not saying anything, not asking any questions, for his face had a strange, set look as though he were withdrawn inside himself, out of the reach of any human.

And then we struck – not suddenly with an impact, but slowly, gently, a long grinding to a halt that sent me staggering forward until I was brought up against the window ledge. The ship checked, her keel making a noise that was felt in vibration rather than heard above the roar of the storm. For a moment she seemed to tear herself loose and go reeling on through the water; then she struck again and ground to a sudden, sickening halt. The engines continued without pause as though the heart of her had refused to recognize death.

It was a queer moment. Patch was still standing there at the wheel, still staring out ahead with set face and the knuckles of his hands white with the violence of his grip on the wheel spokes. The wheelhouse looked exactly the same, and for'ard, through the glass windows, the bows remained submerged with the waves rolling across them. The deck under my feet still pulsed with life. Nothing had changed; only that we were now motionless and at rest.

Trembling, I wiped the cold sweat from my forehead with my hand. We were aground on the Minkies now. I felt a sense of finality. I turned and looked at him. He seemed dazed. His face, where it had been wiped clear of coal dust, was chalk-white, his dark eyes staring. He was gazing out across the tumbled waste of the sea. 'I did what I could,' he breathed. And then again, louder: 'God in heaven, I did what I could.' There was no blasphemy in the way he said it; only the sense of a man in torment. And finally his hands dropped slackly from the spokes of the wheel as though relinquishing at last his command of the ship and he turned away and walked, slowly and deliberately in the manner of a sleep-walker, through into the chartroom.

I pulled myself together then and followed him.

He was bent over the chart and he didn't look up. A wave crashed against the ship's side, throwing a solid mass of water against the chartroom window, momentarily blocking out the daylight. As it fell away he pulled the log book towards him and, picking up the pencil, began to write. When he had finished, he closed the book and straightened up, as though he had written *Finis* to that section of his life. His eyes came slowly round and met mine. 'I'm sorry,' he said. 'I should have explained what I was going to do.' He was like a man woken from a dream and suddenly rational. 'It was a question of hitting the tide just right.'

'But we should have headed towards St Malo.' I was still dazed, a little stupid – I didn't understand.

'In just over two hours, if we'd lasted that long, the tide would have turned and driven us north across the reefs.' He slid the chart along the table towards me. 'See for yourself,' he said. 'The only chance was to beach her here.' And he put his pencil on the spot where the ship was lying.

It was about a mile south of the main body of the reefs in an area showing 2¼ fathoms depth at low water. 'That rock away on the port bow is Grune à Croc,' he said. It was marked as drying 36 ft. 'And you'll probably find the Maîtress Île just visible away to starboard.' His pencil point rested for a moment on the high point to the east of the main reefs. 'At low water it should be reasonably sheltered in here.' He threw the pencil down and straightened up, stretching himself and rubbing his eyes. 'Well, that's that.' There was finality and the acceptance of disaster in the way he said it. 'I'm going to get some sleep.' He went past me then without another word, through into the wheelhouse. I heard his feet on the companion ladder descending to the deck below. I hadn't said anything or tried to stop him. I was too tired to question him now. My head throbbed painfully and the mention of sleep had produced in me an intense desire to close my eyes and slide into oblivion.

I paused on my way through the wheelhouse and stood looking out on the grey, desolate sea-scape of rock and broken water. It was queer to stand there by the wheel with the feel of the engines under my feet, knowing all the time that we were hard aground on the worst reef in the English Channel. Everything in the wheelhouse seemed so normal. It was only when I looked out through the windows and saw the rocks emerging from the tide and the ship's bows no more than a vague outline below the creaming break of the waves that I was able to comprehend what had happened.

But for six hours or more we should be safe; until the rising tide exposed us again to the full force of the seas. I turned and made my way below, moving as though in a dream, like a sleep-walker. Everything seemed vague and a little remote and I staggered slightly, still balancing automatically to the roll of a ship which was now as steady as a rock. As I reached my cabin I felt the beat of the engines slow and stop. Either we had exhausted the steam or else he had gone below and stopped the engines himself. It didn't seem to matter either way. We shouldn't be wanting the engines again, or the pumps. Nothing seemed to matter to me then but sleep.

That sleep should have been possible in those circumstances may seem incredible, but having thought him mad and then found him, not only sane, but capable of an extraordinary feat of seamanship, I had confidence in his statement that we should be sheltered as the tide fell. In any case, there was nothing I could do – nothing either of us could do; we had no boats, no hope of rescue in the midst of those reefs, and the gale was at its height.

I woke to complete darkness with water running like a dark river down the corridor outside my cabin. It came from a broken porthole in the saloon – probably from other places, too. The seas were battering against the ship's side and every now and then there was a grumbling, tearing sound as she shifted her bottom on the shingle bed. I moved up to Patch's cabin then. He was lying on his bunk, fully clothed, and even when I shone my torch on him he didn't stir, though he had been asleep for over twelve hours. I made two trips below to the galley for food and water and the Primus stove, and it was on the second of these that I noticed the little white rectangle of a card pinned to the mahogany of the door just aft of the captain's cabin. It was a business card: *J. C. B. Dellimare*, and underneath – *The Dellimare Trading and Shipping Company Ltd.* The address was St Mary Axe in the City of London. I tried the door, but it was locked.

It was daylight when I woke again. The wind had died down and the seas no longer crashed against the ship's side. A gleam of watery sunlight filtered in through the salt-encrusted glass of the porthole. Patch was still asleep, but he had taken off his boots and some of his clothes and a blanket was pulled round his body. The companion ladder leading to the saloon and the deck below was a black well of still water in which things floated. Up on the bridge, the sight that met my eyes was one of utter desolation. The tide was low and the rocks stood up all round us like the stumps of rotten teeth, grey and jagged with bases blackened with weed growth. The wind was no more than Force 5 or 6 and, though I could see the seas breaking in white cascades over the further rocks that formed my horizon, the water around was relatively quiet, the broken patches smoothed out as though exhausted by their passage across the reefs.

I stood there for a long time watching the aftermath of the storm whirl ragged wisps of thin grey cloud across the sun, staring at the chaos of rocks that surrounded us, at the seas breaking in the distance. I felt a deep, satisfying joy at the mere fact that I was still alive, still able to look at sunlight glittering on water, see the sky and feel the wind on my face. But the davits were empty arms of iron uplifted over the ship's side and the boat that had been hanging by one of its falls was a broken piece of splintered wood trailing in the sea at the end of a frayed rope.

Patch came up and joined me. He didn't look at the sea or the the sky or the surrounding rocks. He stood for a moment gazing down at the bows which now stood clear of the sea, the gaping hole of the hatch black and full of water. And then he went out to the battered port wing and stood looking back along the length of the ship. He had washed his face and it was white and drawn in the brittle sunlight, the line of his jaw hard where the muscles had tightened, and his hands were clenched on the mahogany rail-capping.

I felt I ought to say something – tell him it was bad luck, that at least he could be proud of an incredible piece of seamanship in beaching her here. But the starkness of his features checked me. And in the end I went below, leaving him alone on the bridge.

He was there for a long time and when he did come down he only said, 'Better get some food inside you. We'll be able to leave in an hour or two.' I didn't ask him how he expected to leave with all the boats smashed. It was obvious that he didn't want to talk. He went and sat on his bunk, his shoulders hunched, going through his personal belongings in a sort of daze, his mind lost in its own thoughts.

I got the Primus going and put the kettle on whilst he wandered over to the desk, opening and shutting drawers, stuffing papers into a yellow oilskin bag. He hesitated, looking at the photograph, and then he took that, too. The tea was made by the time he had finished and I opened a tin of bully. We breakfasted in silence, and all the time I was wondering what we were going to do, how we were going to construct a boat. 'It's no good waiting to be taken off,' I said at length. 'They'll never find the *Mary Deare* here.'

He stared at me as though surprised that anybody should speak to him in the dead stillness of the ship. 'No, it'll be some time before they find her.' He nodded his head slowly, still lost in his own thoughts.

'We'll have to build some sort of a boat.'

'A boat?' He seemed surprised. 'Oh, we've got a boat.'

'Where?'

'In the next cabin. An inflatable rubber dinghy.'

'A rubber dinghy – in Dellimare's cabin?'

He nodded. 'That's right. Odd, isn't it? He had it there – just in case.' He was laughing quietly to himself. 'And now we're going to use it.'

The man was dead and I saw nothing funny about his not being here to use his dinghy. 'You find that amusing?' I asked angrily.

He didn't answer, but went to the desk and got some keys, and then he went out and I heard him unlock the door of the next cabin. There was a scrape of heavy baggage being moved and I went to give him a hand. The door was opened and, inside, the cabin looked as though a madman had looted it – drawers pulled out, suitcases forced open, their hasps ripped off, their contents strewn over the floor; clothes and papers strewn everywhere. Only the bed remained aloof from the chaos, still neatly made-up, un-slept-in, the pillows stained with the man's hair oil.

He had the keys. He must have searched the cabin himself. 'What were you looking for?' I asked.

He stared at me for a moment without saying anything. Then he shifted the big cabin trunk out of the way, toppling it on to its side with a crash. It lay there, a slab of coloured hotel labels – Tokyo, Yokohama, Singapore, Rangoon. 'Catch hold of this!' He had hold of a big brown canvas bundle and we hauled it out into the corridor and through the door to the open deck. He went back then and I heard him lock the door of Dellimare's cabin. When he returned he brought a knife with him. We cut the canvas straps, got the yellow dinghy out of its wrappings and inflated it.

The thing was about twelve feet long and five feet broad; it had paddles and a rudder and a tubular telescopic mast with nylon rigging and a small nylon sail. It even had fishing tackle. 'Was he a nervous sort of man?' I asked. For a shipowner to pack a collapsible dinghy on board one of his own ships seemed odd behaviour – almost as though he suffered from the premonition that the sea would get him.

But all Patch said was, 'It's time we got moving.'

I stared at him, startled at the thought of leaving the comparative security of the ship for the frailty of the rubber dinghy. 'The seas will be pretty big once we get clear of the reefs. Hadn't we better wait for the wind to drop a bit more?'

'We need the wind,. He sniffed at it, feeling for its direction with his face. 'It's veered a point or two already. With luck it will go round into the north-west.' He glanced at his watch. 'Come on,' he said. 'There's four hours of tide with us.'

I tried to tell him it would be better to wait for the next tide and get the whole six hours of it, but he wouldn't listen. 'It would be almost dark then. And suppose the wind changed? You can't beat to windward in this sort of craft. And,' he added, 'there may be another depression following on behind this one. You don't want to be caught out here in another gale. I don't know what would happen at high water. The whole bridge deck might get carried away.'

He was right, of course, and we hurriedly collected the things we needed – food, charts, a hand-bearing compass, all the clothes we could clamber into. We had sou'westers and sea boots, but no oilskins. We took the two raincoats from the cabin door.

It was nine forty-five when we launched the dinghy from the for'ard well-deck. We paddled her clear of the ship and then hoisted sail. The sun had disappeared by then and everything was grey in a mist of driving rain, the rocks appearing further away, vague battlement shapes on the edge of visibility; many of them were already covered. We headed for Les Sauvages and in a little while the flashing buoy that marked the rocks emerged out of the murk. By then the *Mary Deare* was no more than a vague blur, low down in the water. We lost her completely as we passed Les Sauvages.

There was still a big sea running and, once we cleared the shelter of the Minkies, we encountered the towering swell left by the gale. It marched up behind us in wall upon wall of steep-fronted, toppling water, and in the wet, swooping chill of that grey day I lost all sense of time.

For just over four hours we were tumbled about in the after-math of the storm, soaked to the skin, crammed into the narrow space between the fat, yellow rolls of the dinghy's sides, with only an occasional glimpse of Cap Frehel to guide us. And then, shortly after midday, we were picked up by the cross-Channel packet coming in from Peter Port. They were on the look-out for sur-vivors, otherwise they would never have sighted us, for they were passing a good half mile to the west of us. And then the packet suddenly altered course, coming down on us fast, the bows almost hidden by spray flung up by the waves. She hove-to a little up-wind of us, rolling heavily, and as she drifted down on to us rope ladders were thrown over the side and men came down to help us up, quiet, English voices offering words of encouragement, hands reaching down to pull us up.

People crowded us on the deck – passengers and crew, asking questions, pressing cigarettes and chocolate on us. Then an officer took us to his quarters and the packet got into her stride again, engines throbbing gently, effortlessly. As we went below I caught a glimpse of the dinghy, a patch of yellow in the white of the ship's wake as it rode up the steep face of a wave.

4

A HOT shower, dry clothes and then we were taken into the officers' saloon and a steward was bustling about, pouring tea, bringing us plates of bacon and eggs. The normality of it – the incredible normality of it! It was like waking from a nightmare. The *Mary Deare* and the gale and the tooth-edged rocks of the Minkies seemed part of another life, utterly divorced from the present. And then the Captain came in. 'So you're survivors from the *Mary Deare*.' He stood, looking from one to the other of us. 'Is either of you the owner of the yacht *Sea Witch*?'

'Yes,' I said. 'I'm John Sands.'

'Good. I'm Captain Fraser. I'll have a radio message sent to

Peter Port right away. A Colonel Lowden brought her in. He was very worried about you. He and Duncan were on board yesterday, listening to the radio reports of the search. They had planes out looking for you.' He turned to Patch. 'I take it you're one of the *Mary Deare*'s officers?' His voice was harder, the Scots accent more pronounced.

Patch had risen. 'Yes. I'm the master of the *Mary Deare*. Captain Patch.' He held out his hand. 'I'm most grateful to you for picking us up.'

'Better thank my first officer. It was he who spotted you.' He was staring at Patch, small blue eyes looking out of a craggy face. 'You say your name is Patch?'

'Yes.'

'And you're the master of the *Mary Deare*?'

'Yes.'

The iron-grey brows lifted slightly and then settled in a frown. 'I understood that a Captain Taggart was master of the *Mary Deare*.'

'Yes, he was. But he died.'

'When was that?' There was a sharpness in the way the question was put.

'Just after we cleared Port Said – early this month.'

'I see.' Fraser stared at him stonily. And then, consciously relaxing: 'Well, don't let me interrupt your meal. You must be hungry. Sit down. Sit down, both of you.' He glanced at his watch and then called to the steward to bring another cup. 'I've just time before we go into St Malo.' He sat down, leaning his elbows on the table, his little blue eyes staring at us, full of curiosity. 'Well, now, what happened, Captain Patch? The air has been thick with messages about the *Mary Deare* for the last twenty-four hours.' He hesitated, waiting. 'You'll be glad to know that a boatload of survivors was washed up on Île de Bréhat yesterday afternoon.' Patch still said nothing. 'Oh, come; you can't expect me not to be curious.' His tone was friendly. 'The survivors report that there was a fire and you ordered the crew to abandon ship. That was Thursday night and yet Lowden told me – '

'I ordered them to abandon ship?' Patch was staring at him. 'Is that what they say?'

'According to a French report, yes. They abandoned ship shortly after 22.30 hours. Yet at 09.30 the following morning Lowden saw the *Mary Deare* . . .' He hesitated, silenced by Patch's hard, uncompromising stare. 'Damn it, man!' he said in sudden exasperation. 'What happened? Is the *Mary Deare* afloat or sunk or what?'

Patch didn't say anything for a moment. He seemed to be thinking it out. Finally he said, 'A full statement will be made to the proper authorities. Until then – ' He was still staring at Fraser. 'Until then you'll excuse me if I don't talk about it.'

Fraser hesitated, unwilling to let it go at that. Then he glanced at his watch again, drank up his tea and rose to his feet. 'Very proper of you, Captain,' he said, his voice formal, a little huffed. 'Now I must go. We're just coming into St Malo. Meantime, please accept the hospitality of my ship. Anything you want, ask the steward.' As he went out, he paused in the doorway. 'I think I should tell you, Captain, that we have a young lady on board – a Miss Taggart. She's Captain Taggart's daughter. She flew out to Peter Port yesterday, and when she heard survivors had come ashore on the coast of France, she came on with us.' He paused, and then came back a few steps into the saloon. 'She doesn't know her father is dead. She's hoping he's amongst the survivors.' Again a slight hesitation. 'I presume you notified the owners?'

'Of course.'

'I see. Well, it's a pity they didn't see fit to inform his next-of-kin.' He said it angrily. 'I'll have my steward bring her to you.' And then in a softer tone: 'Break it to her gently, man. She's a nice wee thing and she obviously adored her father.' He left then and a silence descended on the room. Patch was eating with the concentration of a man shovelling energy back into his body. There was nothing relaxed about him.

'Well, what did he die of?' I asked him.

'Who?' He looked at me with a quick frown.

'Taggart.'

'Oh, Taggart. He died of drink.' He resumed his eating, as though dismissing the matter from his mind.

'Good God!' I said. 'You can't tell her that.'

'No, of course not,' he said impatiently. 'I'll just tell her he died of heart failure. That was probably the medical cause anyway.'

'She'll want to know details.'

'Well, she can't have them.' I thought he was being callous and got up and went over to the porthole. The engines had been slowed. We were coming into the *Rade* and I could see the tourist hotels of Dinard climbing the hill from the quay, deserted and forlorn in the rain. 'He was running around the ship, screaming like a soul in torment.' He pushed his plate away from him. 'I had to lock him in his cabin, and in the morning he was dead.' He pulled out the packet of cigarettes he had been given and opened it with trembling fingers, tearing at it viciously. His face was deathly pale in the flare of the match.

'DTs?' I said.

'No, not DTs. I only discovered afterwards . . .' He dragged on his cigarette, pushing his hand up through his hair. 'Well, it doesn't matter now.' He pulled himself to his feet. 'We're nearly in, aren't we?'

The ship was moving very slowly now. Lock gates glided past. Boots rang on the deck overhead and there was the clatter of a donkey engine. 'I think we're going into the basin now,' I told him.

'You're lucky,' he said. 'You're through with the *Mary Deare* now.' He had started pacing restlessly up and down. 'God! I almost wish I'd gone down with the ship.'

I stared at him. 'It's true then . . . You did order the crew to take to the boats. That story about your being knocked out – '

He turned on me, his face livid. 'Of course, I didn't order them to take to the boats. But if they stick to that story . . .' He flung away towards the other porthole, staring out at the grey daylight.

'But why should they?' I demanded. 'If it isn't true – '

'What's truth got to do with it?' He stared at me angrily. 'The bastards panicked and now they're saying I ordered them to abandon ship because they've got to cover themselves somehow. A bunch of damned cowards – they'll cling together. You'll see. When it comes to the Formal Enquiry . . .' He gave a little shrug of his shoulders. 'I've been through all this before.' He said it slowly, half to himself, his head turned away, staring out through the porthole again at the waste ground with the rusty railway wagons. He muttered something about it being a strange co-incidence, and then a door slammed and there was the sound of voices, a medley of French and English. He swung round, staring at the door and said, 'You will, of course, confine yourself to a statement of the reasons for your presence on board the *Mary Deare*.' He spoke quickly, nervously. 'You are in the position of a passenger and any comments – ' The door opened and he half turned, facing it.

It was Captain Fraser, and with him were two French officials. Smiles, bows, a torrent of French, and then the shorter of the two said in English: 'I regret, Monsieur le Capitaine, I have bad news for you. Since half an hour I have heard on the radio that some bodies have been washed ashore on Les Heaux. Also some wreckage.'

'From the *Mary Deare*?' Patch asked.

'Mais oui.' He gave a little shrug. 'The lighthouse men on Les Heaux have not identified them, but there is no other ship in distress.'

'Les Heaux is an island just north of the Île de Brehat – about forty miles west of here,' Fraser said.

'I know that.' Patch moved a step towards the official. 'The survivors,' he said. 'Was there a man called Higgins amongst them?'

The officer shrugged. 'I do not know. No official list of survivors is yet completed.' He hesitated. 'Monsieur le Capitaine, if you will come to the Bureau with me it will assist me greatly. Also it will be more simple. The formalities, you understand . . .' He said it apologetically, but it was clear he had made up his mind.

'Of course,' Patch said, but I could see he didn't like it. His eyes glanced quickly from one to the other of them, and then he went across the room and passed through the lane they opened out for him to the door.

The official turned to follow him, but then stopped and looked back at me. 'Monsieur Sands?' he enquired.

I nodded.

'I understand your boat is waiting for you in Saint Peter Port. If you will give my friend here the necessary particulars and your address in England, I do not think we need detain you at all.' He gave me a quick, friendly smile. 'Bon voyage, mon ami.'

'Au revoir, monsieur,' I said. 'Et merci, mille fois.'

His assistant took the particulars, asked a few questions and then he, too, departed. I was alone, and I sat there in a sort of coma, conscious of the bustle and hubbub of passengers descending to the quay, yet not sure that it was real. I must have dozed off for the next thing I knew the steward was shaking me. 'Sorry to wake you, sir, but I've brought Miss Taggart. Captain's orders, sir.'

She was standing just inside the door; a small, neat girl, her hair catching the light from the porthole just the way it had done in that photograph. 'You're Mr Sands, aren't you?'

I nodded and got to my feet. 'You want Captain Patch.' I started to explain that he had gone ashore, but she interrupted. 'What happened to my father, please?'

I didn't know what to say. She should have been asking Patch, not me. 'Captain Patch will be back soon,' I said.

'Was my father on the *Mary Deare* when you boarded her?' She stood there, very straight and boyish, and quite determined.

'No,' I said.

She took that in slowly, her eyes fixed steadfastly on mine. They were grey eyes, flecked with green; wide and startled-looking. 'And this Captain Patch was in command?' I nodded. She stared at me for a long time, her lip trembling slightly. 'My father would never have abandoned his ship.' She said it softly and I knew she had guessed the truth, was bracing herself for it. And then: 'He's dead – is that it?'

'Yes,' I said.

She took it, dry-eyed, standing there, stiff and small in front of me. 'And the cause of death?' She tried to keep it formal, impersonal, but as I hesitated, she made a sudden, small feminine movement, coming towards me: 'Please, I must know what happened. How did he die? Was he ill?'

'I think it was a heart attack,' I said. And then I added, 'You must understand, Miss Taggart, I wasn't there. I am only passing on what Captain Patch told me.'

'When did it happen?'

'Early this month.'

'And this Captain Patch?'

'He was the first mate.'

She frowned. 'My father didn't mention him. He wrote me from Singapore and Rangoon and the only officers he mentioned were Rice and Adams and a man named Higgins.'

'Patch joined at Aden.'

'Aden?' She shook her head, huddling her coat close to her as though she were cold. 'My father always wrote me from every port he stopped at – every port in the world.' And then she added, 'But I got no letter from Aden.' Tears started to her eyes and she turned away, fumbling for a chair. I didn't move and after a moment she said, 'I'm sorry. It's just the shock.' She looked up at me, not bothering to wipe away the tears. 'Daddy was away so much. It shouldn't hurt like this. I haven't seen him for five years.' And then in a rush: 'But he was such a wonderful person. I know that now. You see, my mother died . . .' She hesitated and then said, 'He was always coming back to England to see me. But he never did. And this time he'd promised. That's what makes it so hard. He was coming back. And now – ' She caught her breath and I saw her bite her lip to stop it trembling.

'Would you like some tea?' I asked.

She nodded. She had her handkerchief out and her face was turned away from me. I hesitated, feeling there ought to be something I could do. But there was nothing and I went in search of the steward. To give her time to recover, I waited whilst he made the tea and brought it back to her myself. She was composed now and though her face still looked white and pinched, she had got back some of the vitality that there had been in that photograph. She began asking me questions and to keep her mind off her father's death I started to tell her what had happened after I boarded the *Mary Deare*.

And then Patch came in. He didn't see her at first. 'I've got to leave,' he said. 'A question of identification. They've picked up twelve bodies.' His voice was hard and urgent, his face strained. 'Rice is dead. The only one I could rely on – '

'This is Miss Taggart,' I said.

He stared at her. For a second he didn't know her, didn't connect her name; his mind was concentrated entirely on his own affairs. And then the hardness slowly left his face and he came forward, hesitantly, almost nervously. 'Of course. Your face . . .' He paused as though at a loss for words. 'It – it was there on his desk. I never removed it.' And then, still looking at her, as though fascinated, he added almost to himself: 'You were with me through many bad moments.'

'I understand my father is dead?'

The forthright way in which she put it seemed to shock him, for his eyes widened slightly as though at a blow. 'Yes.'

'Mr Sands said you thought it was a heart attack?'

'Yes. Yes, that's right – a heart attack.' He said it automatically, not thinking about the words, all his mind concentrated in his eyes, drinking her in as though she were some apparition that had suddenly come to life.

There was an awkward pause. 'What happened? Please tell me what happened?' She was standing facing him now and there was a tightness in her voice that betrayed her nervousness. I suddenly felt that she was afraid of him. A sort of tension stretched between them. 'I want to know what happened,' she repeated and her voice sounded almost brittle in the silence.

'Nothing happened,' he answered slowly. 'He died. That's all.' His voice was flat, without feeling.

'But how? When? Surely you can give me some details?'

He pushed his hand up through his hair. 'Yes. Yes, of course. I'm sorry. It was 2nd March. We were in the Med. then.' He hesitated as though searching in his mind for the words he wanted.

'He didn't come up to the bridge that morning. And then the steward called me. He was lying in his bunk.' Again a pause and then he added, 'We buried him that afternoon, at sea.'

'He died in his sleep then?'

'Yes. That's right. He died in his sleep.'

There was a long silence. She wanted to believe him, wanted to desperately. But she didn't. Her eyes were very big and her hands were pressed tightly together. 'Did you know him well?' she asked. 'Had you sailed with him before?'

'No.'

'Had he been ill at all – during the voyage, or before you joined the ship at Aden?'

Again the slight hesitation. 'No. He hadn't been ill.' He seemed to pull himself together then. 'I gather the owners didn't inform you of his death. I'm sorry about that. I notified them by radio immediately, but I received no reply. They should have notified you.' He said it without any hope that they would have done so.

'What did he look like – before his death? Tell me about him please. You see, I hadn't seen him – ' The pleading sound of her voice trailed away. And then suddenly in a firmer voice she said, 'Can you describe him to me?'

He frowned slightly. 'Yes, if you want me to.' His tone was reluctant. 'I — don't quite know what you want me to tell you.'

'Just what he looked like. That's all.'

'I see. Well, I'll try. He was small, very small – there was almost nothing of him at all. His face was red – sun-burned. He was bald, you know, but when he had his cap on and was up on the bridge he looked much younger than – '

'Bald?' Her voice sounded shocked.

'Oh, he still had some white hair.' Patch sounded awkward. 'You must understand, Miss Taggart, he wasn't a young man and he'd been a long time in the tropics.'

'He had fair hair,' she said almost desperately. 'A lot of fair hair.' She was clinging to a five-year-old picture of him. 'You're making him out to be an old man.'

'You asked me to describe him,' Patch said defensively.

'I can't believe it.' There was a break in her voice. and then she was looking at him again, her chin up, her face white. 'There's something more, isn't there – something you haven't told me?'

'No, I assure you,' Patch murmured unhappily.

'Yes, there is. I know there is.' Her voice had suddenly risen on a note of hysteria. 'Why didn't he write to me from Aden?

He always wrote me . . . every port . . . and then dying like that
and the ship going down . . . He'd never lost a ship in his life.'

Patch was staring at her, his face suddenly hard and angry.
Then abruptly he turned to me. 'I've got to go now.' He didn't
look at the girl again as he turned on his heels and walked quickly
out.

She looked round at the sound of the door closing, staring at
the blankness of it with wide, tear-filled eyes. And then suddenly
she slumped down into her chair and buried her head in her arms,
her whole body racked by a paroxysm of sobs. I waited, wondering what I could do to help her. Gradually her shoulders ceased to
shake. 'Five years is a long time,' I said gently. 'He could only tell
you what he knew.'

'It wasn't that,' she said wildly. 'All the time he was here I
felt – ' She stopped there. She had her handkerchief out and she
began dabbing at her face. 'I'm sorry,' she whispered. 'It was silly
of me. I – I was just a schoolgirl when I last saw my father. My
impression of him is probably a bit romantic.'

I put my hand on her shoulder. 'Just remember him as you last
saw him,' I said.

She nodded dumbly.

'Shall I pour you some more tea?'

'No. No, thanks.' She stood up. 'I must go now.'

'Is there anything I can do?' I asked. She seemed so lost.

'No. Nothing.' She gave me a smile that was a mere con-
ventional movement of her lips. She was more than dazed; she
was raw and hurt inside. 'I must go – somewhere, by myself.' It
was said fugitively and in a rush, her hand held out to me automatically. 'Good-bye. Thank you.' Our hands touched, and she
was gone. For a moment her footsteps sounded on the bare wood
of the deck outside, and then I was alone with the sounds of the
ship and the dock. Through the porthole I saw the bare, grey
walls of St Malo glistening wet in a fleeting gleam of sunlight –
the old walls of the city and above them the new stone and roofing
of buildings faithfully copied to replace the shattered wreckage
that the Germans had left. She was walking across the cobbled
roadway, walking quickly, not seeing the passengers or the French
or the sombre, fortress-like beauty of the ancient city; a small, neat
figure whose mind clung to a girl's memories of a dead father.

I turned away and lit a cigarette, slumping wearily into a chair.
The crane, the gangway, the passengers in their raincoats and the
French dock men in their blue smocks and trousers; it all seemed

so ordinary – the Minkies and the *Mary Deare* were a vague dream.

And then Captain Fraser came in. 'Well,' he said, 'what *did* happen? Do you know?' The curiosity in his blue eyes was unveiled now. 'The crew say that he ordered them to abandon ship.' He waited and when I didn't say anything, he added, 'Not just one of them; it's what they all say.'

I remembered then what Patch had said: *They'll cling together . . . because they've got to cover themselves somehow.* Who was right – Patch or the crew? My mind went back to that moment when we had grounded, when he had relinquished the wheel from the grip of his hands in the midst of that waste of sea and rock.

'You must have some idea what really happened.'

I was conscious of Fraser again and was suddenly and for the first time fully aware of the ordeal that Patch now faced. I pulled myself stiffly up out of the chair. 'I've no idea,' I said. And then, because I sensed in the man a sort of hostility towards Patch, I added quickly, 'But I'm quite certain he never ordered the crew to take to the boats.' It was an instinctive rather than a reasoned statement. I told him I was going ashore then to find a hotel, but he wouldn't hear of it and insisted on my accepting the hospitality of his ship, ringing for the steward and putting a cabin at my disposal.

I saw Patch once more before I took the plane for Guernsey. It was at Paimpol, twenty or thirty miles to the west of St Malo, in a little office down by the *bassin*. There were fishing vessels there, packed two and three-deep along the walls – tubby wooden bottoms, all bitumen-black, nudging each other like charladies, with mast-tops nodding, gay with paint – and the water of the *bassin* was poppled with little hissing waves, for it was blowing half a gale again. As the police car that had brought me from St Malo drew up I saw Patch framed in the fly-blown office window; just his face, disembodied and white as a ghost, looking out like a prisoner on to the world of the sea.

'This way plees, monsieur.'

There was an outer office that served as a waiting-room with benches round the wall and a dozen men were seated there, dumb, apathetic and listless – flotsam washed in by the sea. I knew instinctively that they were all that remained of the *Mary Deare's* crew. Their borrowed clothes breathed shipwreck and they huddled close together, like a bunch of frightened, bewildered sheep; some that were clearly English, others that might be any race under the sun. One man, and one man alone, stood out from the motley bunch. He was a great hunk of a brute with a bull's neck and a bull's head, all hard bone and folds of flesh. He stood with his legs spread wide, solid as a piece of sculpture on the pedestal of his feet, his huge, meaty hands thrust inside his trousers, which were fastened with a broad leather belt that was stained white with a crust of salt and had a big square brass buckle that had turned almost green. He held his hands there as though trying to prevent the great roll of fat, like a rubber tyre, that was his belly escaping entirely from the belt. His clothes were borrowed – a blue shirt that was too small for him and blue trousers that were too short. His thighs and legs tapered away like a bull terrier's hind quarters so that they looked on the verge of buckling under the weight of that great barrel of a body.

He started forward as though to bar my way. Tiny eyes, hard as flint, stared at me unwinking over heavy pouches of flesh. I half-checked, thinking he was going to speak to me, but he didn't; then the gendarme opened the door to the inner office and I went in.

Patch turned from the window as I entered. I couldn't see his expression. His head and shoulders were outlined against the window's square of daylight and all I could see was the people in the road outside and the fishing boats moving restlessly in the *bassin* beyond. There were filing cabinets ranged against the walls under faded charts of the harbour, a big, old-fashioned safe in one corner, and, seated at an untidy desk facing the light, was a ferrety little man with twinkling eyes and thinning hair. 'Monsieur Sands?' He held out a thin, pale hand. He didn't rise to greet me and I was conscious of the crutch propped against the wooden arm of his chair. 'You will excuse me please for the journey you make, but it is necessary.' He waved me to a seat. 'Alors, monsieur.' He was staring at the sheet of foolscap in front of him that was covered with neat, copper-plate writing. 'You go on board the *Mary Deare* from your yacht. C'est ça?'

'Oui, monsieur.' I nodded.

'And the name of your yacht, monsieur?'

'*Sea Witch.*'

He began to write slowly and with meticulous care, frowning slightly and biting softly at his underlip as the steel nib scratched across the surface of the paper. 'And your name – your full name?'

'John Henry Sands.' I spelt it for him.

'And your address?'

I gave him the name and address of my bank.

'Eh bien. Now, you boarded the *Mary Deare* how long after the crew had abandoned the ship?'

'Ten or eleven hours after.'

'And Monsieur le Capitaine?' He glanced at Patch. 'He was still on the ship, eh?'

I nodded.

The official leaned forward. 'Alors, monsieur. It is this that I have to ask you. In your opinion, did Monsieur le Capitaine order the crew to abandon ship or did he not?'

I looked across at Patch, but he was still just a silhouette framed in the window. 'I can't say, monsieur,' I replied. 'I wasn't there.'

'Of course. I understand that. But in your opinion. I want your opinion, monsieur. You must know what had happened. He must have talked about it with you. You were on that ship through many desperate hours. It must have occurred to you both that you might die. Did he not say anything that would enable you to form some opinion as to what really happened?'

'No,' I said. 'We didn't talk very much. There wasn't time.' And then, because it must seem extraordinary to him that we hadn't had time to talk in all the hours we had been on board together, I explained exactly what we had had to do.

He kept on nodding his small head whilst I was talking, a little impatiently as though he weren't listening. And as soon as I had finished, he said, 'And now, monsieur, your opinion. That is what I want.'

By then I had had time to make up my mind. 'Very well,' I said. 'I am quite convinced that Captain Patch never ordered his crew to abandon ship.' And I went on to explain that it was impossible to believe that he had done so since he himself had remained on board and, single-handed, had put out the fire in the after hold. All the time I was talking the steel pen scratched across the surface of the paper, and when I had finished the official read it through carefully and then turned the sheet towards me. 'You read French, monsieur?' I nodded. 'Then please to read what is written there and sign the deposition.' He handed me the pen.

'You understand,' I said, when I had read it through and signed it, 'that I wasn't there. I do not *know* what happened.'

'Of course.' He was looking across at Patch. 'You wish to add anything to the statement you have made?' he asked him. And when Patch merely shook his head, he leaned forward, 'You understand, Monsieur le Capitaine, that it is a very serious charge that you make against your crew – your officers also. Monsieur 'Iggins has sworn that you gave the order to him, and the man at the wheel – Yules – has confirmed that he heard you give the order.' Patch made no comment. 'I think perhaps it will be best if we have Monsieur 'Iggins and the other man in here so that I can – '

'No!' Patch's voice trembled with sudden violence.

'But, monsieur.' The official's voice was mild. 'I must understand what – '

'By Christ! I tell you, no!' Patch had come forward to the desk in two strides, was leaning down over it. 'I won't have my statement queried in front of those two.'

'But there must be some reason – '

'No, I tell you!' Patch's fist crashed down on the desk. 'You have my statement and that's that. In due course there will be an Enquiry. Until then neither you nor anybody else is going to cross-examine me in front of the crew.'

'But, Monsieur le Capitaine, do you understand what it is you accuse them of?'

'Of course, I do.'

'Then I must ask you – '

'No. Do you hear me? No!' His fist slammed the desk again. And then he turned abruptly to me. 'For God's sake, let's go and have a drink. I've been in this wretched little office . . .' He caught hold of my arm. 'Come on. I need a drink.'

I glanced at the official. He merely shrugged his shoulders, spreading his hands out palm upwards in a little gesture of despair. Patch pulled open the door and strode through the outer office, not glancing to left or right, walking straight through the men gathered there as though they didn't exist. But when I started to follow him, the big man blocked my path. 'Well, wot did you tell 'em?' he demanded in a throaty voice that was like steam wheezing up from the great pot of his belly. 'I suppose you told 'em that he never ordered us to abandon ship. Is that wot you said?'

I tried to push past him, but one of his great paws shot out and gripped me by the arm. 'Come on. Let's have it. Is that wot you told 'em?'

'Yes,' I said.

He let go of me then. 'God Almighty!' he growled. 'Wot the hell do you know about it, eh? You were there I s'pose when we took to the boats?' He was grinning, truculent, and the stubble mat of his face, thrust close to mine, was still grey with salt and dirt. For a man who had been shipwrecked he looked oddly pleased with himself. He oozed self-confidence like a barrel oozes lard and his small, blood-shot eyes glittered moistly, like a pair of oysters, as he said again, 'You were there, eh?' And he guffawed at his own heavy humour.

'No,' I told him. 'Of course I wasn't there. But I don't – '

'Well, we was there.' His voice was raised and his small eyes darted to the half-open door behind me. 'We was there an' we know dam' well wot orders were given.' He was saying it for the benefit of the French official in the inner office. 'It was the right order, too, with the ship half full of explosives and a fire on board. That's wot we felt at the time – me and Rice and the old Chief . . . everybody.'

'If it was the right order,' I said, 'how was it possible for Captain Patch to put the fire out on his own?'

'Ah. You'd better ask him that.' And he turned and looked at Patch.

Patch came slowly back from the street door. 'What exactly do you mean by that, Higgins?' he demanded. His voice was quiet, but it trembled slightly and his hands were clenched.

'Wot a man's done once, he'll do again,' Higgins said, and there was a little gleam of triumph in his eyes.

I thought Patch was going to hit him. So did Higgins, for he stepped back, measuring the distance between them. But Patch didn't hit him. Instead, he said, 'You deserve to be strung up for murder. You killed Rice and those others as surely as if you'd taken a gun to them and shot them down in cold blood.' He said it through clenched teeth and then turned abruptly to walk out.

And Higgins, stung, shouted hoarsely after him: 'You won't get away with it at the Enquiry – not with your record.'

Patch swung round, his face white, and he was trembling as he looked at the pitiful little gathering, his eyes passing from face to face. 'Mr Burrows.' He had picked on a tall, thin man with a sour, dissipated face. 'You know damn' well I never gave any orders to abandon ship.'

The man shifted his feet nervously, not looking at Patch. 'I only know what was passed down to me on the blower,' he muttered. They were all nervous, doubtful, their eyes on the floor.

'Yules.' Patch's gaze had switched to an under-sized little runt of a man with a peaked, sweaty face and shifty eyes. 'You were at the wheel. You heard what orders I gave up there on the bridge. What were they?'

The man hesitated, glancing at Higgins. 'You ordered the boats swung out and the men to stand by to abandon ship,' he whispered.

'You damned little liar!' Patch started to move towards him, but Higgins stepped forward. And Yules said, 'I don't know what you mean.' His voice was high-pitched on a note of sudden spite.

Patch stared at him a moment, breathing heavily. And then he turned and went out quickly. I followed him and found him waiting for me on the pavement outside. His whole body was shaking and he looked utterly drained. 'You need some sleep,' I said.

'I need a drink.'

We walked in silence up to the square and sat at a little *bistro* that advertised *crêpes* as a speciality. 'Have you any money?' he asked. And when I told him Fraser had lent me some, he nodded and said, 'I'm a distressed seaman and a charge on the Consul. It doesn't run to drinks.' There was a note of bitterness in his voice. And then, when we had ordered cognac, he suddenly said, 'The last body wasn't brought in until two o'clock this morning.' His face looked haggard as it had done on the *Mary Deare*, the bruise along his jaw even more livid against the clean-shaven pallor of his face.

I gave him a cigarette and he lit it with trembling hands. 'They got caught in the tide-rip off the entrance to Lezardrieux.' The drinks came and he knocked his back and ordered two more. 'Why the hell did it have to be Rice's boat?' The palm of his hand slapped viciously against the table. 'If it had been Higgins . . .' He sighed and relapsed into silence.

I didn't break it. I felt he needed that silence. He lingered over his second drink and every now and then he looked at me as though trying to make up his mind about something. The little square bustled with life, full of the noise of cars hooting and the quick, excited chatter of French people as they hurried along the pavement outside. It was wonderful just to sit there and drink cognac and know that I was alive. But my mind couldn't shake itself free of the *Mary Deare*, and watching Patch as he sat, staring down at his drink, I wondered what had really happened on that ship before I boarded her. And that little huddle of survivors in the office overlooking the *bassin* . . . 'What did Higgins mean – about your record?' I asked. 'Was he referring to the *Belle Isle*?'

He nodded, not looking up.

'What happened to her?'

'Oh, she ran aground and broke her back . . . and people talked. That's all. There was a lot of money involved. It's not important.'

But I knew it was. He'd kept on talking about it, saying you wouldn't think it could happen to the same man twice. 'What's the connection between the *Belle Isle* and the *Mary Deare*?' I asked.

He looked up at me quickly. 'How do you mean?'

'Well . . .' It wasn't easy to put it into words with him staring at me like that. 'It's a pretty strange story, you know – the crew saying you ordered them to abandon ship and you saying you didn't. And there's Taggart's death,' I added. 'Dellimare, too.'

'Dellimare?' The sudden violence of his voice shook me. 'What's Dellimare got to do with it?'

'Nothing,' I said. 'But . . .'

'Well, go on. What else are you thinking?'

It was a question that had been in my mind for a long time. 'That fire . . .' I said.

'Are you suggesting I started it?'

The question took me by surprise. 'Good God, no.'

'What are you suggesting then?' His eyes were angry and suspicious.

I hesitated, wondering whether he wasn't too exhausted to answer rationally. 'It's just that I can't understand why you put the fire out and yet didn't bother to get the pumps going. I thought you'd been stoking that boiler. But it hadn't been touched.' I paused there, a little uncertain because of the strange look on his face. 'What had you been doing?'

'God damn you!' His eyes suddenly blazed. 'What's it got to do with you?'

'Nothing,' I said. 'Only . . .'

'Only what? What are you getting at?'

'It was just the coal dust. You were covered with it and I wondered . . .' I saw his hand clench and I added quickly, 'You can't expect me not to be curious.'

His body relaxed slowly. 'No. No, I suppose not.' He stared down at his empty glass. 'I'm sorry. I'm a little tired, that's all.'

'Would you like another drink?'

He nodded, sunk in silence again.

He didn't speak until the drinks came, and then he said, 'I'm going to be quite honest with you, Sands. I'm in a hell of a spot.' He wasn't looking at me. He was looking down at his glass, watching the liquor cling to the sides of it as he swirled it gently round and round.

'Because of Higgins?'

He nodded. 'Partly. Higgins is a liar and a blackguard. But I can't prove it. He was in this thing right from the start, but I can't

235

prove that either.' He looked at me suddenly. 'I've got to get out to her again.'

'To the *Mary Deare*?' It seemed odd that he should think that it was his responsibility. 'Why?' I asked. 'Surely the owners will arrange – '

'The owners!' He gave a contemptuous little laugh. 'If the owners knew she was on the Minkies . . .' And then abruptly he changed the subject and began questioning me about my own plans. 'You said something about being interested in salvage and converting that yacht of yours into a diving tender.' That had been up in his cabin when he'd been half-doped with liquor and exhaustion. I was surprised he remembered it. 'You've got all the equipment, have you – air pumps and diving suits?'

'We're aqualung divers,' I said. His sudden interest had switched my mind to the problems that lay ahead – the conversion, the fitting out, all the business of starting on our first professional salvage operation.

'I've been thinking . . .' He was drumming nervously on the marble-topped table. 'That boat of yours – how long will it take to convert her?'

'Oh, about a month,' I said. And then it dawned on me. 'You aren't suggesting that we take you out to the *Mary Deare*, are you?'

He turned to me then. 'I've got to get back to her,' he said.

'But, good God – why?' I asked. 'The owners will arrange for the salvage – '

'Damn the owners!' he snarled. 'They don't know she's there yet.' He leaned urgently towards me. 'I tell you, I've got to get out to her.'

'But why?'

His eyes gradually dropped from my face. 'I can't tell you that,' he muttered. And then he said, 'Listen, Sands. I'm not a salvage man. But I'm a seaman, and I know that ship can be refloated.'

'Nonsense,' I said. 'Another gale and she'll be flooded – she'll probably break up.'

'I don't think so. She'll have water in her, but she won't be flooded. It isn't as though she's sunk,' he added. 'At low water you could get pumps operating from her deck and, with all the apertures sealed up . . .' He hesitated. 'I'm trying to put it to you as a business proposition. That ship is lying out there and you and I are the only people who know she's there.'

'Oh, for God's sake!' I said. The effrontery of the proposition staggered me. He didn't seem to understand that there were laws of salvage, that even if it were possible to refloat the *Mary Deare*, it involved agreement between the owners, the insurance people, the shippers – everybody.

'Think it over,' he said urgently. 'It may be weeks before some fisherman finds her there.' He gripped hold of my arm. 'I need your help, Sands. I've got to get into that for'ard hold. I've got to see for myself.'

'See what?'

'That hold didn't flood because the ship was unseaworthy. At least,' he added, 'that's what I believe. But I've got to have proof.'

I didn't say anything, and he leaned towards me across the table, his eyes on mine, hard and urgent. 'If you won't do it . . .' His voice was hoarse. 'I've nobody else who'll help me. Damn it, man! I saved your life. You were dangling at the end of that rope. Remember? I helped you then. Now I'm asking you to help me.'

I looked away towards the square, feeling a little embarrassed, not understanding what it was that he was so worried about. And then the police car that had brought me to Paimpol drew up at the curb and I watched with relief as the gendarme got out and came into the *bistro*.

'Monsieur – if you wish to catch your aeroplane . . .' He nodded towards the car.

'Yes, of course.' I got to my feet. 'I'm sorry. I've got to go now.'

Patch was staring up at me. 'What's your address in England?' he asked.

I gave him the name of the boatyard at Lymington. He nodded, frowning, and looked down at his empty glass. I wished him luck then and turned to go.

'Just a minute,' he said. 'You've got a bank, I suppose?' And when I nodded, he reached into his pocket and pulled out a package and tossed it on to the table. 'Would you have them lock that up for me?'

'What is it?' I asked as I picked it up.

He moved his hand in a vague, impatient gesture. 'Just some personal papers. Afraid they may get lost.' And then, without looking up at me, he added, 'I'll collect them when I see you.'

I hesitated, wanting to tell him it was no good his coming to see me. But he was sitting there, slumped in his chair, lost apparently in his own thoughts. He looked drawn and haggard and ghastly tired. 'You better get some sleep,' I said, and my words took me back again to the *Mary Deare*. He didn't answer, didn't look up. I slipped the package into my pocket and went out to the car. He was still sitting there slumped over the table as I was driven away.

Two hours later I was in the air, high up over the sea. It was like a corrugated sheet of lead and out beyond the starboard wingtip was an area all flecked with white.

The Frenchman in the next seat leaned across me to peer out. 'Regardez, regardez, monsieur,' he whispered eagerly. 'C'est le Plateau des Minquiers.' And then, realizing I was English, he smiled apologetically and said, 'You will not understand, of course. But there are rocks down there – many, many rocks. Trés formidable! I think it better we travel by air. Look, monsieur!' He produced a French paper. 'You 'ave not seen, no?' He thrust it into my hands. 'It is terrible! Terrible!'

It was opened at a page of pictures – pictures of Patch, of Higgins and the rest of the survivors, of a dead body lying in the sea, and of officials searching a pile of wreckage washed up on some rocks. Bold black type across the top announced: MYS-TÈRE DE VAISSEAU BRITANNIQUE ABANDONNÉ.

'Interesting, is it not, monsieur? I think it is also a very strange story. And all those men . . .' He clicked his tongue sympathetically. 'You do not understand how terrible is this region of the sea. Terrible, monsieur!'

I smiled, overwhelmed by a desire to laugh – to tell him what it had been like down there in the Minkies. But by now I was reading the statement made to the authorities by *le Capitaine Gideon Patch*, and suddenly it was borne in on me that he had not stated the *Mary Deare*'s position. He hadn't even mentioned that the ship was stranded and not sunk. '. . . *and you and I are the only people who know she's there.*' His words came back to me and I sat, staring down at the paper, knowing suddenly that this wasn't going to be the end of the *Mary Deare*.

'A strange affair, is it not, monsieur?'

I nodded, not smiling now. 'Yes,' I said. 'Very strange.'

PART TWO

I

THE FORMAL ENQUIRY into the loss of the *Mary Deare* was finally fixed for Monday, 3 May, at Southampton. For a Ministry of Transport Enquiry, this must be considered unusually expeditious, but I learned later that the date had been brought forward at the urgent request of the insurance companies. The sum involved was a very large one and right from the start it was the question of insurance that was the vital factor.

In fact, we had only been in Lymington a few days when I had a visit from a Mr F. T. Snetterton representing the H. B. & K. M. Insurance Corporation of San Francisco. It was that section of the cargo consigned by the Hsu Trading Corporation of Singapore that interested him. Could I testify as to the nature of it? Had I been down into any of the holds? Had Patch talked to me about it?

There was a devil of a racket going on. *Sea Witch* had just been slipped and the yard men were drawing keel bolts for inspection and Mike and I were stripping the old engine out of her. I took him down to the waterfront, where we could talk in peace.

'You understand, Mr Sands,' he explained earnestly, 'I have to be sure that the cargo was exactly what the Hsu Trading Corporation claim. I have to establish the manifest, as it were. Now surely you must have seen something that would enable you to give an opinion as to the nature of the cargo? Think, sir. Think.' He was leaning forward, blinking in the bright sunshine, quite over-wrought by the urgency of his problem.

I told him I had been down the inspection hatch of Number Three hold. I described the charred bales to him. 'Please, Mr Sands.' He shook his head impatiently. 'It's the aero engines I am interested in. Only the aero engines.'

That was the first time anyone had mentioned aero engines to me. 'I heard she had a cargo of explosives.'

'No, no – aero engines.' He sat down on the railing of one of the pontoons where the boats were laid up, a neat, dapper man dressed in black with a brief-case. He looked entirely out of place. 'The ship herself,' he said in his precise way, 'is not important –

239

twice the break-up value, that's all. And the cotton was insured by a Calcutta firm. No, it's the aero engines we're worried about. There were a hundred and forty-eight of them – surplus American stores from the Korean war – and they were insured for £296,000. I must be certain that they were on board at the time the ship went down.'

'What makes you think they weren't?' I asked him.

He looked at me quickly, hesitating and fidgeting with his brief-case. 'It's a little difficult,' he murmured. 'But perhaps – since you're not an interested party . . . perhaps if I explain, it may help you to remember something – some little thing . . . an unguarded word, perhaps.' He looked at me again, and then said, 'Shortly after the claim was filed, we heard from our agent in Aden that a man named Adams had been talking about the *Mary Deare* and her cargo in a Steamer Point bar. He was reported to have given it as his opinion that she contained nothing but bales of cotton at the time she went down.' And he added hastily, 'You understand, sir, this is in the strictest confidence.' And then he asked me again whether I couldn't remember some little detail that would help him. 'Surely if you were on that ship for forty-eight hours you must have learned something about the cargo?'

'There was a gale blowing,' I said. 'The ship was sinking.'

'Yes, yes, of course. But you must have talked with Mr Patch. You were with him through a critical period. A man will often say things in those circumstances that he would be reluctant . . .' He let the sentence go, staring at me all the time through his glasses. 'You're sure he said nothing about the cargo?'

'Quite sure.'

'A pity!' he murmured. 'I had thought . . .' He shrugged his shoulders and stood up. I asked him then how he thought it was possible for a cargo consigned to a ship not to be on board her at a later date? He looked at me. 'All things are possible, Mr Sands, where a great deal of money is involved.' I remembered Patch saying the same thing about the loss of the *Belle Isle*. And then he suddenly asked me whether Patch had mentioned the name of another boat whilst we were together on the *Mary Deare*?

'I don't think so,' I said quickly. If Snetterton wanted to find out about the *Belle Isle*, he could find it out from somebody else.

But he wasn't to be put off so easily. 'You don't think so?' He was peering at me. 'I want you to be quite certain about this, Mr Sands. It may be vitally important.'

'I am quite certain,' I said irritably.

'Mr Patch never mentioned the name of another ship to you?'

Damn it, the man had no right to come here questioning me about what Patch had said. No, I told him. And I added that if he wanted to find out what ships Patch had been connected with why the devil didn't he go and ask him.

He stared at me. 'This isn't a ship that Mr Patch ever sailed in.'

'Well, what ship is it then?'

'The *Torre Annunziata*. Now please think back very carefully. Did Mr Patch ever mention the name *Torre Annunziata* to you?'

'No,' I said. 'Definitely not.' I felt relieved and angry. 'What's the *Torre Annunziata* got to do with it?'

He hesitated. 'It's a little delicate, you understand . . . so much supposition . . .' Then he suddenly made up his mind and said, 'The Dellimare Company owned only two ships – the *Mary Deare* and the *Torre Annunziata*. The *Torre Annunziata* was in the Rangoon River at the same time that the *Mary Deare* put in to load her cotton cargo.' He glanced at his watch and then rose to his feet. 'Well, sir, I won't trouble you any further for the moment.'

He turned then and began to walk back towards the slip, and as we negotiated the wooden duck-boards of the pontoons, he said, 'I'll be quite honest with you. This is a matter that might in certain circumstances . . .' He hesitated there and seemed to change his mind. 'I am waiting for a report now from our agent in Rangoon. But . . .' He shook his head. 'It is all very disturbing, Mr Sands. The *Torre Annunziata* has been sold to the Chinese. She has vanished behind what I believe is called the Bamboo Curtain – not only the ship, but her crew as well. And Adams has disappeared, too. We are almost certain that he shipped out in a dhow bound for Zanzibar. It may be weeks before we can contact him. And then there are these two fires on the *Mary Deare* and the loss of Mr Dellimare. A fire in the radio room is most unusual, and Mr Dellimare had been in the Navy. The possibility of suicide . . . small firm, you know . . . might be in difficulties . . .' He tucked his brief-case more firmly under his arm. 'You see what I mean, Mr Sands. Little things in themselves, but together . . .' He glanced at me significantly. And then he added, 'The trouble is the time factor. The H. B. & K. M. are making great efforts to increase their business in the Pacific. And Mr Hsu is a big man in Singapore – considerable influence in Eastern ports. They feel it calls for prompt settlement of the claim unless . . .' He shrugged.

We had reached the slip and he paused for a moment to admire

Sea Witch's lines, asking questions about our diving plans, the aqualungs we were using and the depths at which we could work. He seemed genuinely interested and I explained how we had financed ourselves by salvaging bits and pieces from the wreck of a tanker in the Mediterranean and that we were now going to work on the wreck of an LCT in Worbarrow Bay off the Dorset coast. He wished us luck and gave me his card. 'Think about what I've said, Mr Sands. If you remember anything – well, you have my card, sir.'

It was only after Snetterton had gone – when I had had time to think over what he had told me – that I began to understand what the loss of the *Mary Deare* was going to lead to. There would be other people besides Snetterton coming to ask me questions. He was just the breeze before the storm. The newspaper reports I had read had all taken it for granted that the ship was sunk – so had Snetterton and the two reporters who had come to see me when I had arrived with *Sea Witch*. Everybody thought she was sunk. But sooner or later they would start probing, and before then I had to see Patch and find out his reasons for concealing her position.

I thought it must be connected in some way with his past record and when I was in London two days later to sign our salvage contract with the underwriters, I made a few enquiries about the *Belle Isle*. She had been wrecked on the Anambas Islands north-east of Singapore nearly ten years ago, and she was entered in the records as a 'total loss'. Her master was given as Gideon S. Patch. An Enquiry had been held in Singapore and the Court had found the stranding to be due to default of the Master and had suspended his Certificate for a period of five years. That was all. There were no details. But, discussing it with one of my friends in the marine section of Lloyd's, who specialized in the Far East, I learned that some ugly rumours had got about afterwards to the effect that the stranding had been a put-up job. The ship had been very heavily insured.

I was very close to St Mary Axe and I decided to have a look at the Dellimare Company office. It was partly that I was curious to see the sort of company it was, and also I wanted to find out where I could contact Patch. Their offices were at the Hounds-ditch end, on the fourth floor of a dingy building full of small trading businesses. I found myself in a poky little room with a desk and a gas fire and some filing cabinets. The single typewriter had its cover on and dirt-grimed windows looked out across a litter of chimney pots to the white-tiled rear of a big office block. There was a bell on the counter and amongst a litter of papers

was some Dellimare Company notepaper. It gave the directors as
J. C. B. Dellimare, Hans Gundersen and A. Petrie. When I rang
the bell, the door of an inner office was opened and a full-bosomed,
fleshy-looking woman appeared, dressed in black with a lot of
cheap jewellery and blonde hair that was startling because it was
clearly natural.

When I gave her my name, she said, 'Oh, are you the Mr
Sands who was on board the *Mary Deare*? Then perhaps you can
help me.' She took me through into the other office. It was a
much brighter room with cream walls and a red carpet and a big
green and chromium steel desk that was littered with press
clippings, mostly from French newspapers. 'I'm trying to find out
what really happened to him,' she said. 'To Mr Dellimare, that
is.' And she glanced involuntarily at a big photograph in an
ornate silver frame that stood beside her on the desk. It was a
head and shoulders portrait, showing a rather hard, deeply-lined
face with a small, straight mouth under the thin pencil-line of a
moustache.

'You knew him well?' I asked.

'Oh, yes. We formed the Company. Of course, after Mr
Gundersen joined, it was all different. Our main office became
Singapore. Mr Dellimare and I just looked after the London end.'
There was something entirely personal about the way she said
'Mr Dellimare and I', and after that she began asking me ques-
tions. Had Captain Patch said anything to me about how Mr
Dellimare had been lost? Did I go into his cabin? Had I talked
to any of the survivors? 'He had been in the Navy. He couldn't
just have gone overboard like that?' Her voice trembled slightly.

But when she realized I could tell her nothing that she didn't
already know, she lost interest in me. I asked her then for Patch's
address, but she hadn't got it. 'He came in about three days ago
to deliver his report,' she said. 'He's coming back on Friday,
when he'll be able to see Mr Gundersen.' I gave her the address
of the boatyard and asked her to tell Patch to contact me, and
then I left. She came with me to the door. 'I'll tell Mr Gundersen
you've been,' she said with a quick, brittle smile. 'I'm sure he'll be
interested.'

Mr Gundersen! Perhaps it was the inflection of her voice, but I
got the impression that she was a little nervous of him, as though
he were entirely remote from the Dellimare Company office that
she knew with its silver-framed photograph and its view over the
chimneys.

It never occurred to me that I should meet Gundersen, but on

Friday afternoon the boy from the yard's office came down to the slip to say that a Mrs Petrie was calling me from London. I recognized the slightly husky voice at once. Mr Gundersen had just arrived by plane from Singapore and would like to have a talk with me. He was coming down to Southampton tomorrow, would it be convenient for him to call on me at the yard at eleven o'clock?

I couldn't refuse. The man had come all the way from Singapore and he was entitled to find out all he could about the loss of the Company's ship. But, remembering the things Snetterton had hinted at, I had a feeling of uneasiness. Also, my time and all my energies were concentrated on the conversion of *Sea Witch* and I resented anything which took my mind off the work that Mike and I had planned and struggled for over years of wreck-hunting. I was worried, too, about what I was going to tell him. How was I to explain to him that nobody had been notified of the position of the wreck?

And then early next morning Patch came on the phone from London. No, they hadn't given him any message from me. I thought then that he was ringing me about the package I had brought over for him and which I realized was still on board, locked away in my brief-case. But it wasn't that. It was about Gundersen. Had Gundersen been to see me? And when I told him that I was expecting him at eleven o'clock, he said, 'Thank God! I tried to get you last night – to warn you.' And then he added, 'You haven't told anybody where the *Mary Deare* is lying, have you?'

'No,' I said. 'Not yet.' I hadn't told anybody, not even Mike.

'Has a man called Snetterton been to see you – a marine insurance agent?'

'Yes.'

'You didn't tell him?'

'No,' I said. 'He didn't ask me. He presumed the ship was sunk.' And then I said, 'Haven't you notified the authorities yet? If you haven't, I think it's time – '

'Listen,' he said. 'I can't come down now. I've got to see somebody. And on Monday I've got to go to the Ministry of Transport. But I'll be able to come down and see you on Tuesday. Will you promise to say nothing until then?'

'But why?' I said. 'What's the point in concealing her position?'

'I'll explain when I see you.'

'And what about Gundersen? What am I to say to him?'

'Say anything you like. But for God's sake don't tell him where she is. Don't tell anybody. I ask you as a favour, Sands.'

'All right,' I said doubtfully.

He thanked me then and rang off.

An hour later Gundersen arrived. The boy came down to say that he was waiting for me in the yard manager's office. A big chauffeur-driven limousine stood outside and I went in to find Gundersen seated on the edge of the desk smoking a cigarette and the manager standing in front of him in uneasy silence. 'You're Mr Sands, are you?' Gundersen asked. He didn't offer me his hand or get up or make any move. The manager gave us the use of his office and slipped out. As soon as the door was shut Gundersen said, 'You know why I'm here, I imagine?' He waited until I had nodded and then said, 'I saw Mr Patch yesterday. I understand you were with him during the last forty-eight hours on the *Mary Deare*. Naturally I wanted to hear your version of what happened on our ship.' He asked me then to go through the whole sequence of events. 'I want every detail, please, Mr Sands.'

I went through the whole story for him, leaving out only the details about Patch's behaviour and what had happened at the end. He listened in complete silence, not interrupting once. His long, immobile face, tanned by the sun, showed no flicker of expression, and his eyes, behind their horn-rimmed glasses, watched me all the time I was talking.

Afterwards he asked me a series of questions – straightforward, practical questions concerning course and wind strength and the length of time we had run the engines. The ordeal we had gone through seemed to mean nothing to him and I got the impression of a cold personality.

Finally, he said, 'I don't think you have yet understood, Mr Sands, what it is I wish to know.' His slight accent was more noticeable now. 'I want to discover the exact position in which the ship went down.'

'You don't seem to realize the conditions prevailing at the time,' I said. 'All I can tell you is that she was close to the Roches Douvres at the time I boarded her.'

He got up then. He was very tall and he wore a light-coloured suit of smooth material draped in the American fashion. 'You are not being very helpful, Mr Sands.' A signet ring on his finger flashed in the pale April sunlight. 'It seems odd that neither you nor Patch can say where the ship was at the time you abandoned her.' He waited, and then he said, 'I have also talked to Higgins. He may not have a Master's Certificate, but he's an experienced seaman. You may be interested to know that his calculations, based on wind strength, probable drift and tide, put the *Mary Deare*'s final position a good deal to the east of where you and Patch seem to think you were. Have you any comment to make?' He stood facing me, his back to the window.

'None,' I said, nettled and a little angry at his manner. And then, because he was still staring at me, waiting, I said, 'I'd remind you, Mr Gundersen, that I am not concerned in this. I was on board your ship by accident.'

He didn't answer for a moment. Finally he said, 'That remains, perhaps, to be seen.' And he added, 'Well, at least I have got something out of you. Now that we have some idea of the length of time the engines were running and the course steered whilst they were in use, it should be possible to arrive at an approximation of the position.' He paused again. 'Is there anything further you would care to add to what you have already told me, Mr Sands?'

'No,' I said. 'Nothing.'

'Very well.' He picked up his hat. And then he paused. 'The manager here tells me that you're interested in salvage. You've formed a company – Sands, Duncan & Company, Ltd.' He stared at me. 'I think I should warn you that this man Patch has a bad record. Unfortunately our Mr Dellimare was inexperienced in matters connected with shipping. He employed this man when nobody else would, and the result has proved disastrous.'

'He did his best to save the ship,' I said angrily.

For the first time his face moved. An eyebrow lifted. 'After he had caused the crew to panic and take to the boats. I have yet to discover his precise motives, but if you're mixed up in this, Mr Sands . . .' He put his hat on. 'You can contact me at the Savoy Hotel if you should find you have some further information to give me.' He went out of the office then and I watched him drive away with an uneasy feeling that I was getting myself dangerously involved.

This feeling persisted, and it came between me and my work so that I was not in a particularly sympathetic mood when Patch finally arrived. We were living on board *Sea Witch* by then, which was fortunate because he didn't arrive until the evening. I had expected him to look rested, the lines in his face smoothed out. It came as a shock to me to find him looking just as haggard. We had only one light on board, an inspection lamp clamped to a half-erected bulkhead, and in its harsh glare he looked ghastly, his face quite white and a nervous tic at the corner of his mouth.

We cleared the saloon table of tools and wood-shavings, and I sat him down and gave him a drink and a cigarette and introduced him to Mike. It was neat rum I gave him and he knocked it straight back, and he drew on his cigarette as though it were the first he'd had in days. His suit was old and frayed and I remember wondering whether the Dellimare Company had paid him. Oddly enough, he accepted Mike at once and, without attempting to get me alone, asked straight out what Gundersen had wanted, what he had said.

I told him, and when I had finished, I said, 'Gundersen suspects something. He hinted as much.' I paused, waiting for the explanation he had promised me. But all he said was, 'I'd forgotten that Higgins might work it out.' He was speaking to himself.

'What about that explanation?' I asked him.

'Explanation?' He stared at me blankly.

'You surely don't imagine,' I said, 'that I can be a party to a piece of deception that involves the owners, the insurance people, everybody with a financial interest in the ship, unless I know that there is some good reason?' I told him I considered that my duty was clear. 'Either you explain why you've withheld this vital information or I go to the authorities.' An obstinate, shut look had come over his face. 'Why pretend the ship went down, when at any moment she may be sighted lying there in the middle of the Minkies?'

'She could have been carried there by the tides,' he murmured.

'She could have been, but she wasn't.' I lit a cigarette and sat down opposite him. He looked so desperately tired of it all. 'Listen,' I said more gently. 'I've been trained in marine insurance. I know the procedure after the loss of a ship. Any moment now the Receiver of Wreck will start taking depositions under oath from everybody connected with the loss. And under oath I've no alternative but to give the full – '

'You won't be called on to make a deposition,' he said quickly. 'You weren't connected with the ship.'

'No, but I was on board.'

'By accident.' He pushed his hand up through his hair in a gesture that brought it all back to me. 'It's not for you to make any comment.'

'No, but if I have to make a statement under oath . . .' I leaned across the table towards him. 'Try and see it from my point of view,' I said. 'You made me a certain proposition that day in Paimpol. A proposition which, in the light of your failure to notify the owners of the present whereabouts of the ship, was entirely crooked. And Gundersen is beginning to think – '

'Crooked?' He began laughing and there was a note of hysteria in his voice. 'Do you know what cargo the *Mary Deare* carried?'

'Yes,' I said. 'Aero engines. Snetterton told me.'

'And did he tell you that the other Dellimare ship was moored next to the *Mary Deare* for four days in the Rangoon River? Those aero engines are in China now – sold to the Chinks for a mint of money.'

The positiveness of his accusation took me by surprise. 'How can you be certain?' I asked him.

He looked at me, hesitating for a moment. 'All right. I'll tell you. Because Dellimare offered me five thousand quid to wreck the *Mary Deare*. Cash – in fivers.'

In the sudden silence I could hear the lapping of the water at the bottom of the slip. 'Dellimare? Are you serious?' I asked.

'Yes, Dellimare.' His voice was angry and bitter. 'It was after old Taggart died. Dellimare was desperate then. He had to improvise. And, by the luck of the devil, I was on board. He knew my record. He thought he could buy me.' He leaned back and lit another cigarette, his hands shaking. 'Sometimes I wish to God I'd accepted his offer.'

I poured him another drink. And then I said, 'But I still don't understand why you should conceal the *Mary Deare*'s position. Why haven't you told all this to the authorities?'

He turned and looked at me. 'Because if Gundersen knows where she is, he'll go out there and destroy her.'

That was nonsense, of course. You can't destroy a 6000-ton ship just like that. I told him so. He'd only got to go to the authorities, demand an examination of the vessel and the whole thing would be decided. But he shook his head. 'I have to go back myself – with somebody like you that I can trust.'

'You mean you're not sure about what you just told me – about the cargo?'

He didn't say anything for a moment, but just sat there, hunched over his drink, smoking. You could feel his nerves in the stillness of the cabin. 'I want you to take me out there,' he said finally. 'You and Duncan.' He turned, leaning towards us. 'You've been in marine insurance, haven't you, Sands? You know how to fix up a salvage contract. Now listen. When will your boat be ready?'

'Not till the end of the month,' Mike said, and the way he said it was a warning to me that he didn't want to have anything to do with it.

'All right. The end of the month. I'll come back then. Have you got an underwater camera?' And when I nodded, he leaned forward earnestly. 'You could take a picture then of the damage to the for'ard holds. The insurance people would give you a lot of money for that – and for pictures of the cargo.' And then he added, 'And if I'm wrong, then there's quarter of a million pounds' worth of aero engines – enough salvage to set you up in a big way. Well?' His eyes moved quickly, nervously, from one to the other of us.

'You know very well I can't agree to a proposition like that,' I said. And Mike added, 'I think you should put the whole matter in the hands of the authorities.'

'No. No, I can't do that.'

'Why not?' I asked.

'Because I can't.' The tension was building up in him again. 'Because I'm up against a company. I've a record behind me and they'll twist things . . . I've been through all this before.' Sweat was shining in beads on his forehead. 'And there's Higgins and the crew. Everything is against me.'

'But if the Receiver of Wreck made an examination – '

'I tell you, No. I'm not having the Receiver of Wreck out there – or anybody.' He was staring at me wildly. 'Can't you understand – I've got to go back there myself.'

'No, I can't,' I said. 'If you refused Dellimare's offer, you've nothing to worry about. Why conceal the fact that you beached her on the Minkies?' And when he didn't answer, I said, 'Why do you have to go back? What the devil is there on that ship that you've got to go back for?'

'Nothing. Nothing.' His voice quivered in tune with his nerves.

'Yes there is,' I said. 'There's something drawing you back to her as though – '

'There's nothing,' he shouted at me.

'Then why not tell the authorities where she is? What is it you're afraid of?'

His fist crashed down on the table top. 'Stop it! Questions . . . questions . . . nothing but questions. I've had enough of it, do you hear?' He got abruptly to his feet and stood, staring down at us. He was trembling all over.

I think he was on the verge of telling us something. I think he wanted to tell us. But instead he seemed to get a grip of himself. 'Then you won't take me out there?' There was a note of resignation in his voice.

'No,' I said.

He seemed to accept that and he stood there, his body slack, staring down at the table. I got him to sit down again and gave him another drink. He stayed on to supper. He was very quiet and he didn't talk much. I didn't get anything more out of him. He seemed shut away inside himself. When he left he gave me his address. He was in lodgings in London. He said he'd come down at the end of the month and see if we'd changed our minds. I saw him out across the darkened yard and then walked slowly back through the dark shapes of the slipped boats.

'Poor devil!' Mike said, as I went below again. 'Do you think Dellimare really offered him five thousand to wreck the ship?'

'God knows!' I said. I didn't know what to think. It seemed to me that perhaps Patch might be a psychological case – a man whose balance had been destroyed because of the ship he had lost before. 'I know almost nothing about the man,' I murmured. But that wasn't true. You can't live through what we'd lived through together without knowing a good deal about a man. He was tough. He had great reserves. And I admired him. I almost wished I'd agreed to take him out to the Minkies – just to discover the truth.

I told Mike the whole story then, all the little details I'd left out when I rejoined *Sea Witch* in Peter Port. And after I had finished, he said, 'It's a hell of a situation for him if the cargo really has been switched.'

I knew what he meant. He was thinking of the insurance companies, and, having worked for seven years in the marine section of Lloyd's, I knew very well that once they got their teeth into a claim, they'd never let go.

I worried a lot about this during the fitting out. But a few days after Patch had visited us, I received notification of the date of the Formal Investigation and I comforted myself with the thought that it would all be resolved then.

Sea Witch was ready sooner than we had dared to hope. We sailed on Tuesday, 27 April, motoring down to the Solent and then heading westwards under full canvas with a light northerly wind. I hadn't seen Patch again, but I couldn't help thinking that the wind was fair for the Channel Islands. Twenty-four hours' sailing would have taken us to the Minkies, and the forecast couldn't have been better – continental weather with a belt of high pressure over the Azores. We had Mike's old diving friend, Ian Baird, with us again, and with three of us working we could have got into the *Mary Deare*'s holds and checked that cargo and still got back for the Investigation. And as *Sea Witch* leaned to the breeze, her new sails gleaming white in the sunlight, I felt none of the elation that I should have felt at the start of this venture that Mike and I had dreamed about for so long.

The devil of it was that, now I was at sea, I remembered things I had forgotten in the bustle of fitting out. Patch had saved my life and, though he hadn't referred to it that night he had come to see us at Lymington, I could remember the desperation that had prompted him to remind me of it in Paimpol. I had the sense of a debt owed, but not paid.

It wasn't only that I felt I had failed in an obligation. Sitting there, with my hands on the wheel, feeling the ship lift to the swell and hearing the water creaming past, I wondered whether it wasn't fear that was directing my course west towards Worbarrow Bay, instead of south to the Minkies. I had seen the Plateau des Minquiers in bad conditions, and deep down in my heart I knew I was scared of the place.

And the irony of it was that for four days we dived in Worbarrow Bay in conditions that were as perfect as I have ever seen them in the Channel – clear blue skies and a calm sea ruffled by only the slightest of breezes. The only limiting factor was the coldness of the water which affected us after a time, even though we were using our heaviest foam rubber suits. In those four days we located and buoyed the wreck of the LCT, cut through into the engine-room and cleared the way for lifting out the main engines, work that we had feared might take anything up to a month.

In the same time, if I had had the nerve to take the gamble, we could have cut our way into each of the *Mary Deare*'s holds. I thought about it sometimes as I worked down in the green depths with *Sea Witch*'s hull a dark shape in the translucent sea above me, and at night the tally of the day's work seemed a reproach and I turned into my bunk in a mood of depression.

It was almost with relief that I woke on the Sunday to a grey dawn misted with rain and a forecast that announced a deep depression over the Atlantic moving eastwards. By midday the seas were beginning to break; we got the anchors up and plugged it on the engine against a strong westerly wind for the shelter of Lulworth Cove.

I left early next morning for Southampton. It was stormy, and the downland hills, that crooked chalk fingers round the natural lagoon of the cove, were a gloomy green, shrouded in curtains of driving rain. Big seas piled up in the narrow entrance, filling the cove with an ugly swell, which broke in a roar on the shingle beach. Gusts of wind funnelled into the cove from the tops of the downs, flattening the water in sudden, violent swirls. Nobody was about. The whole chalk basin – so regular in its circle that it might have been the flooded crater of an extinct volcano – was deserted. There was only *Sea Witch*, rolling heavily, and the gulls, like scraps of paper, whirled about by the wind.

'Better set an anchor watch if it gets any worse,' I told Mike as he rowed me ashore. 'It's not very good holding ground here.'

He nodded, his face unnaturally solemn under his sou'wester. 'What are you going to do if things go against him at this Enquiry?' he asked.

'Nothing,' I replied and my voice sounded peevish against the blatter of the wind. I was tired. I think we were both pretty tired. We had been diving hard for four days. 'If I'd been going to do anything,' I added, 'the time to do it was last week, when we sailed from Lymington. The worst that can happen to him is that they'll cancel his Master's Certificate again.' Mike didn't say anything. His yellow oilskins gleamed with water in the grey light as he moved rhythmically back and forth to the swing of the oars, and over his shoulders the houses of Lulworth stood silent, with a grey, shut look, on the flank of the hill.

The dinghy grounded with a sudden jar and Mike jumped out into the backwash of a wave and hauled it up so that I could step out dry-footed in my shore-going clothes. We stood there in the rain for a moment, talking about ordinary, mundane things, things that had to be done around the boat. And then, as I turned to climb the beach, he checked me. I just want you to know, John . . .' He hesitated, and then said, 'As far as I'm concerned you're free to make any decision you like – whatever the risk.'

'It's very decent of you, Mike,' I said. 'But I don't think – '

'It's not a question of being decent.' He was grinning. 'I just don't like working with a man who's got something on his mind.' He left me then and pushed out in the dinghy, and I climbed the steep slope of the beach to the road where the bus was waiting for me.

2

It was almost eleven when I reached the court. I was late and the corridor leading to the courtroom was almost empty. The letter requesting my attendance gave me the guidance of one of the officials and as we reached a small door leading into the court, it opened and Snetterton came out. 'Ah, Mr Sands.' He blinked at me. 'Come to see the fun, eh?'

'I'm here as a witness,' I said.

'Yes, yes, of course. Pity to drag you away from your diving. Heard you had started work on that wreck in Worbarrow Bay.' He hesitated and then said, 'You know, we seriously considered approaching you over the question of the *Mary Deare*. We were going to try an asdic search. But then some new information came up and it became unnecessary.'

'What new information?' I was wondering whether the *Mary Deare* had been found. The weather had been bad during most of April, but there was always the chance . . .

'You'll see, Mr Sands. Interesting case, most interesting . . .' And he hurried off down the corridor.

The official opened the door for me then and I went into the court. 'The seats for witnesses are on the right, sir,' he whispered. There was no need for him to have whispered. The room was full of the murmur of voices. I stood there in the doorway, a little dazed. There were many more people than I had expected. The whole court seemed crammed to overflowing; only in the public gallery was there any vacant space. The witnesses were crowded into the seats usually occupied by jurymen called but not serving and some of them had spilled over into the jury box itself. Patch I saw at once, sitting well down towards the front, his face pale and taut, but harder now, like a man who knows what is coming and has nerved himself to meet it. Behind him, and to the right, the crew were clustered in a little hard knot round Higgins's solid bulk. They looked awkward and ill-at-ease, a little exotic in their new shore-going clothes. Fraser, the captain of the Channel packet that had picked us up, was there, too, and sitting beside him was Janet Taggart. She gave me a quick smile, tight-lipped and a little wan, and I wondered why the devil they needed to drag her in as a witness.

And then somebody was signalling me from just behind her and, as he craned his neck up, I saw it was Hal. I pushed my way down the row and squeezed in beside him. 'I didn't expect to find you here,' I whispered.

'Very important witness,' he said. 'Don't forget that it was I who first reported the ship as a derelict hulk containing the person of my erstwhile and somewhat foolhardy skipper.' He smiled at me out of the corners of his eyes. 'Anyway, I wouldn't have missed it for the world. Going to be a damned interesting case if you ask me.'

At the time I had entered, men in various parts of the court, but chiefly on the side across from me, were standing up to give their names and state their business and who they represented. There were a surprising number of them, for, besides the insurance companies and the owners, the builders of the *Mary Deare* were represented, the Marine Officers' Association, the Radio Operators' Association, the various unions; there was even a solicitor appearing for the relatives of Captain Taggart deceased.

The atmosphere was very informal by comparison with a court of law – no wigs, no gowns, no police, no jury. Even the judge and his three assessors wore lounge suits. Across the court from where I sat the desks were occupied by the various counsel appearing for interested parties. They were very crowded. The witness box nearby stood empty and beyond was the Press desk with two reporters at it. On our side of the court the desks were occupied by the Treasury counsel and his junior and the Treasury solicitors and assistants.

Hal leaned towards me. 'Do you know who's representing the insurance people?' he whispered.

I shook my head. I had no information about the legal representatives. All I knew was that a Mr Bowen-Lodge QC was chairman of the Enquiry.

'Sir Lionel Falcett. About the most expensive man they could have got.' His blue eyes darted me a quick glance. 'Significant, eh?'

I glanced down at Patch. And then I was remembering that I, too, might have to go into the witness box, and all the counsel had the right to cross-examine.

A hush slowly spread through the room. The Chairman, who had been engaged in earnest discussion with his assessors, had turned and faced the court. As soon as there was complete silence he began his opening address. 'Gentlemen. This Court meets here today, as you are well aware, to investigate the loss of the steamship *Mary Deare*. It will be the duty of the Court to examine, not only the circumstances of the loss itself, but all the relevant factors that may possibly have contributed to that loss. The scope of this investigation, therefore, covers the state of the ship at the time she started on her ill-fated voyage from Yokohama, her sea-worthiness, the condition of her machinery, the nature of her cargo and the manner of its stowage, and, in particular, the state of her fire-fighting equipment. It covers also the behaviour and conduct of all those concerned in the running of the vessel to the extent that they may or may not have contributed to the disaster.

'For disaster it was, gentlemen. Out of a total crew of thirty-two, no less than twelve men – over a third of the ship's complement – lost their lives. Moreover, the captain died during the voyage and a director of the company owning the vessel is reported missing. It is a sad business that we are investigating and it is possible that relatives of men who lost their lives may be present in this courtroom today. I, therefore, consider it my duty to remind you that this is a Formal Enquiry to determine the cause of this disaster and, whilst I am anxious that proper respect should be paid to the dead and that no advantage should be taken of men who, through death, are unable to testify, I would impress upon you that we are here to investigate this whole terrible business thoroughly and impartially.' Bowen-Lodge leaned a little forward. 'I will now call on Mr Holland to open proceedings on behalf of the Ministry of Transport.'

Holland might have been a banker or perhaps a stockbroker. Whereas the judge, despite his sour, dyspeptic-looking features, had comprehended the tragedy that lay behind the Enquiry and had filled the court with the drama of it, this tall, smooth-faced barrister with the sleek head of black hair had a cold-blooded urbanity of manner that suggested an interest in figures rather than the frailties of human behaviour

'Mr Learned Chairman.' He had risen and was facing the judge and the three assessors, his hands thrust into the pockets of his jacket. 'I think I should bring to your notice at the outset that the Receiver of Wreck, in his report to the Minister, stressed that in several particulars the evidence of the survivors was conflicting. As you know, in cases of this nature, the Receiver of Wreck prepares his report on the basis of depositions in writing. These depositions are made under oath. I do not propose, therefore, to outline in detail the events leading up to the disaster or the disaster itself. I will confine myself to a brief statement of the established facts concerning the voyage and leave the details – the story as it were – to emerge from the evidence of the various witnesses.'

He paused and glanced down at his notes. Then he faced the courtroom itself and in a smooth, rather bored voice summarized the events of the voyage.

The *Mary Deare* had been purchased by the Dellimare Trading and Shipping Company in June of the previous year. She had belonged to a Burmese company and for two years had been laid-up in a creek near Yokohama. On completion of the purchase she had been towed into Yokohama for a complete overhaul. On 18 November she had been granted a seaworthy certificate to cover a single voyage to Antwerp and thence to England where she was to be broken up. On 2 December she completed coaling. On 4 December she began loading her cargo. This consisted of 148 war surplus aircraft engines of American manufacture, including 56 jet engines for a particular fighter in use with NATO forces. In addition to this cargo, which was destined for Antwerp and was distributed fairly equally over the four holds, a large quantity of Japanese cotton and rayon goods were loaded. This part of the cargo was destined for Rangoon and was, therefore, loaded on top of the aircraft engines. The whole of the cargo, including the engines, was the property of the Hsu Trading Corporation, a very large and influential Chinese merchanting organization in Singapore.

The *Mary Deare* sailed from Yokohama on 8 December. On 6 January she reached Rangoon and off-loaded her cargo of Japanese goods. A cargo of raw cotton for England, also the property of the Hsu Corporation, was not ready at the docks for loading. The ship, therefore, proceeded to bunker and then moved out into the river, where she moored to a buoy already occupied by the *Torre Annunziata*, another of the Dellimare Company ships. Four days later she moved into the docks again and loaded her cargo of cotton, the bulk of it in Numbers Two and Three holds.

She sailed from Rangoon on 15 January, reaching Aden on 4 February. There she landed Mr Adams, the first officer, who was sick. Mr Patch was accepted to fill this vacancy. The ship sailed on 6 February. On 2 March, the Master, Captain James Taggart, died, and Mr Patch assumed command of the ship. The *Mary Deare* was then in the Mediterranean, four days out from Port Said. On 9 March she passed through the Straits of

Gibraltar, out into the Atlantic. Almost immediately she ran into heavy weather. She was making a certain amount of water and the pumps were kept going intermittently. On 16 March conditions worsened and it blew full gale.

'And now,' Holland said, his voice lifting slightly from the smooth monotone in which he had been addressing the Court – 'Now we come to the series of incidents – mysteries you might almost call them – that are the subject of this Investigation.'

Briefly he enumerated them: the damage sustained by the ship in the for'ard holds, the water making headway against the pumps, the shoring of the stoke-hold bulkhead, the fire in the radio shack, the disappearance of Dellimare; and then, after rounding Ushant, the fire in Number Three hold, the abandonment of the ship by all except the captain, the discovery of the ship still afloat the following morning, her final abandonment. He punched these events home to the packed courtroom one after another in terse, hard sentences, so that the effect of them was cumulative.

'Twelve men went to their death, gentlemen,' he added, after a pause, his voice now very quiet. 'Went to their death in a mad scramble to get away from a ship that, in point of fact, was in no immediate danger of sinking. That in itself is significant.' He had turned and was facing the Chairman of the Court. 'It is not for me to attempt to influence the Court in any way, merely to present the facts. But I am entitled to draw your attention to certain points, and the points, Mr Learned Chairman, to which I wish to draw the attention of the Court are – firstly, the succession of incidents affecting the safety and sea-keeping ability of the ship, and secondly, the abandonment of a ship that was to stay afloat in gale conditions for more than 48 hours. I submit that this is one of the most extraordinary cases to come before a Formal Enquiry and one that may, as a result of your decision, have far-reaching consequences for one or more of the people here in this courtroom today.'

In making that pronouncement his eyes had roved the room – to the lawyers representing the various interested parties across the floor of the court, to the public gallery, and, finally, he had turned his body round and had stared at the witnesses. His gaze was cold and hard and accusing.

Still facing the witnesses, he went on: 'I have referred to a lack of consistency in the evidence given on oath in depositions made by the various witnesses. Those same witnesses, and some others, will be giving evidence on oath before this Court. But here there is a difference; you can be cross-examined on your evidence in the witness box by myself or by any or all of the representatives of the interested parties.' He paused and then added, 'I would remind you that perjury is a serious offence.'

There was complete silence as he stared at us, and some of the *Mary Deare*'s crew shifted uneasily in their seats. Abruptly, he sat down. For perhaps thirty seconds he let the silence his speech had produced hang over the court, and then he got slowly to his feet again and called 'Gideon Patch'.

Patch was sitting quite still, his eyes fixed across the court – fixed on nothing – and he didn't move. I thought for a moment that he hadn't heard his name called. But then he turned his head and looked at Holland, and quietly, like a man who cannot believe that the moment has finally come, he got to his feet. He seemed to brace himself to meet the situation and, with a firm, decisive tread, he crossed the floor of the court and took his stand in the witness box.

The movement released the tension in the court so that there was a sudden murmur of voices and shifting of feet that continued whilst the oath was being administered and then gradually died away as Holland began his questions, Patch answering them in a voice that was barely audible.

His name was Gideon Stephen Patch. He had been educated at Pangbourne, joined the Merchant Service as a cadet in 1935, Mate's Certificate 1941, Master's Certificate 1944, first command 1945, the *Belle Isle* incident, the years on the beach; the wasted, frustrated years – Holland took him through it all, fact after fact in that same bored voice as though he were tracing the history of a parcel sent through the post. And then the technical details: Did he consider the *Mary Deare* seaworthy? Had he examined the fire-fighting equipment? Had he inspected the boats himself? Did he regard the crew as efficient? Were the officers, in his opinion, competent?

And Patch, once over the hurdle of the *Belle Isle* sinking and the suspension of his Master's Certificate, began noticeably to relax and to gain confidence. It was all so impersonal. Yes, the boats were all right, he had inspected them personally. The crew were average – he had sailed with worse. The officers? He would rather not comment. Some were good, some were not.

'And the captain?' The question was put in the same flat, bored voice.

Patch hesitated, and then said, 'I imagine he was a good seaman.'

'You imagine?' Holland's dark brows lifted slightly.

'Captain Taggart was a sick man, sir.'

'Then why was he not put ashore?'

'I don't know.'

'The first officer, Adams, was put ashore because he was sick. Why wasn't Captain Taggart put ashore, if he was also sick?'

'I imagine the owners thought him fit enough to complete the voyage.'

'By the owners you mean Mr Dellimare?'

'Yes.'

'Tell me, what was the nature of Captain Taggart's illness?'

Patch had clearly been expecting that question, and, now it had come, he looked unhappy about it and for a moment his eyes glanced towards the waiting witnesses. He was looking towards Janet Taggart. And then he was facing Holland again. 'I'm sorry, sir, but I do not think I can answer that.'

Holland made a little impatient gesture. It was obvious that he intended to press the point, but the Chairman intervened. 'Mr Holland.' He was leaning forward. 'It seems hardly necessary for us to pursue this matter. I do not feel that the nature of Captain Taggart's illness can have any bearing on the subject of this Investigation.'

Holland had turned and was facing the judge's chair, his hands gripping the lapels of his jacket as though he were, in fact, wearing a gown. 'I submit, Mr Learned Chairman, that everything connected with the *Mary Deare* is relevant to your Investigation. I am endeavouring to present a complete picture. To do so I must give you the facts – all the facts.'

'Quite so, Mr Holland.' Bowen-Lodge's mouth was a trap-shut line. 'But I see here' – and he glanced at his papers – 'that Miss Taggart is amongst the witnesses in this court. I would ask you to bear that in mind, Mr Holland, and, in your references to her father, to avoid as far as possible giving her any further cause for pain.'

'Unfortunately . . .' But Holland checked himself before Bowen-Lodge's cold, official stare, and then turned to face Patch. 'I will content myself at the moment with asking you whether, in fact, you knew what was wrong with Captain Taggart?'

'Yes, I knew,' Patch answered. And then added quickly, 'But I had no idea that it would prove fatal.'

'Quite so.' Holland turned to the cargo then. 'As first officer you would assume responsibility for the state of loading of the holds. Did you examine the holds yourself?'

'I satisfied myself they were properly loaded.'

'All four holds?'

'Yes.'

'You actually went into each of the holds yourself?'

'Numbers One and Four holds, yes. The other two were full of cargo, but I was able to get some idea of the stowage by looking in through the inspection hatches.'

'Before or after sailing from Aden?'

'Before.'

'Would you tell the Court exactly how these holds were loaded.'

Patch started with Number One hold and worked aft. He gave the dimensions of each – they ran the full width of the ship throughout their depth. The floor of each hold was covered by cases. He gave the approximate dimensions of the cases and the USAAF code numbering painted on them.

'You knew that those cases contained aero engines?' Mr Holland asked.

'Yes, I did.'

'From personal observation? By that I mean, did you at any time examine the contents of one of those cases yourself?'

'No. I had no occasion to. In any case, it would have been very difficult to get one opened – they were tightly packed and, except in Numbers One and Four holds, the cotton cargo completely covered them.'

'I see. So that when you say you knew the cases contained aero engines, you are really saying that that was how the contents were described on the manifest?' Patch nodded. 'Did Captain Taggart show you the manifest before you made your inspection of the holds?'

'I had a look at the manifest before I made my inspection.'

Holland stared at him. 'That wasn't what I asked you. Did Captain Taggart show you the manifest before you made your inspection?'

Patch hesitated and then said, 'No.'

'Had you seen Captain Taggart at that time?'

'Yes.'

'Did you ask him for the manifest?'

'No.'

'Why not? Surely if you were going to inspect the holds – '

'Captain Taggart wasn't well, sir.'

Holland hesitated. Then he half-shrugged his shoulders and turned to the ship herself. There followed nearly half an hour of technical details – her dimensions, construction, date of building, repairs, alterations, characteristics and behaviour, and her history.

She had been built on the Clyde in 1910 for the Atlantic trade. Patch had got her history from some old notebook he had found on board. He had even discovered the origin of her name; the result of some long-dead chairman's dry sense of humour, his wife being called Mary and his own second name being Deare. The ship had been torpedoed twice in the first World War, patched up and kept at sea in convoy after convoy, and then in 1922 she had hit a growler off the Gulf of St Lawrence and after that she'd been sold and for ten years had tramped the seas. The Depression caught her in a Far Eastern port where she lay rotting until the shadow of another war raised shipping freights and she changed hands again and was put to work in the Indian Ocean and the China Seas. She was torpedoed again in 1941, just outside Singapore, packed with troops. She limped into Rangoon, was patched up and sailed to San Francisco. There she had the only decent overhaul in twenty years and went back to work again in the Far Eastern theatre. And then in the last days of the Japanese war, she was stranded on a coral reef under shell-fire. Half her bottom was torn out, her keel permanently kinked, part of her superstructure shot away.

'Any modern ship would have broken her back,' Patch said, and there was a sort of pride in the way he said it.

He went on to tell how she had changed hands again in 1947 – a Burmese owner this time; how she had gone on struggling from port to port throughout the Far East with a twisted back and botched-up repairs until she had been discarded in Yokohama, four years later, and left there to rot until the Dellimare Company purchased her.

In telling her story, he somehow invested the *Mary Deare* with personality. If he had laid stress on the fact that she was a broken-down old hulk on her way to the scrap-heap he could have demonstrated his ability as a seaman and as a Master in bringing her up through the Bay in one of the worst storms of the year. Instead, he told the Court that she was a fine ship, easy to handle, and explained that it was only the repairs, carried out in poorly-equipped Far Eastern ports, that caused her to leak. His loyalty to the ship was impressive, but it lost him the sympathy he might so easily have had.

After that Holland was taking him over the details of the voyage – up through the Red Sea and the Suez Canal and into the

Mediterranean; and all the time he questioned him about the crew, the officers, the relations between Dellimare and Taggart; and the picture that emerged was not a pleasant one – the crew ill-disciplined, the chief engineer incompetent, a poker addict, gambling indiscriminately with crew and officers, the captain keeping to his cabin, never on the bridge, and Dellimare roaming restlessly round the ship, feeding alone in his cabin, occasionally with Higgins, and sometimes shut up with the captain for hours on end.

The court was very still as Holland reached the point at which Patch had assumed command. 'According to your entry in the ship's log, Captain Taggart died some time in the early hours of 2nd March. Is that correct?'

'Yes.'

'You had no doctor on board?'

'No.'

Janet Taggart was leaning forward, her face very pale, the knuckles of her hands white as they gripped the back of the seat in front of her.

'Did you treat Captain Taggart yourself?'

'I did what I could.'

'And what was that?'

'I got him to bed. I tried to get him to take a sedative, but he wouldn't.' Patch's voice trailed off and he glanced quickly across the court at Janet Taggart.

'Did you lock him in his cabin?'

'Yes.' His voice was scarcely above a whisper.

'Why?'

Patch did not reply.

'You state in the log that, in your opinion, Captain Taggart died of heart failure. Would you please explain to the Court what it was that caused his heart – if it was his heart – to fail?'

'Mr Holland.' Bowen-Lodge's voice cut in, sharp and high. 'I must remind you of what I said before. I do not consider this relevant or necessary.'

But Holland was obstinate this time. 'With all due deference, Mr Learned Chairman, I consider it highly relevant. The witness is showing commendable restraint regarding the nature of Captain Taggart's illness. That illness, however, has a considerable bearing on the efficiency of the command he inherited and in fairness to him the Court must be informed.' And, without waiting for permission, he swung round on Patch and said, 'Now that you know the reason for the question, perhaps you will answer it.

What was the basic cause of death?'

Patch stood there, obstinately silent, and Holland became suddenly impatient. 'The man died locked in his cabin. Isn't that correct?'

It was brutally put and there was a shocked look on Patch's face as he nodded dumbly.

'Why did you lock him in his cabin?' And when Patch didn't answer, Holland put a leading question. 'Is it true that you locked him in his cabin because he was raving?'

'He was delirious, yes,' Patch murmured.

'He was upsetting the crew?'

'Yes.'

'Making wild accusations?'

'Yes.'

'What accusations?'

Patch glanced unhappily round the court, and then said, 'He was accusing the officers of stealing liquor from his cabin.'

'Now, will you please answer this question.' Holland was leaning forward. 'What was the basic cause, as far as you know, of Captain Taggart's death?'

Patch might have remained obstinate on this point, but Bowen-Lodge's voice cut in from high up on the judge's seat. 'Witness will kindly answer the question put to him by Counsel. I will repeat it for his benefit – what was the basic cause of death?'

Patch hesitated. 'Drink, sir,' he said reluctantly.

'Drink? Do you mean he died of drink?'

'Because of it – yes.'

The stunned silence that enveloped the court was broken by a girl's voice. It was shrill and high and quavering as she cried out, 'That's not true. How can you say a thing like that – when he's dead?'

'Please, Miss Taggart.' Holland's voice was gentle, almost fatherly. 'The witness is under oath.'

'I don't care whether he's under oath or not, he's lying,' she sobbed wildly. Patch's face had gone very white. Fraser was trying to pull her back into her seat. But she had turned towards the Chairman. 'Please stop him,' she sobbed. And then, flinging up her head, she declared. 'My father was a fine man, a man anybody here would be proud to have known.'

'I understand, Miss Taggart.' Bowen-Lodge's voice was very quiet and soft. 'But I must remind you that this Court is investigating a disaster in which many men lost their lives. The witness is under oath. Moreover, he is not the only witness. You may rest assured that this accusation will be probed and the truth revealed. Will you please be seated now. Or if you prefer it, you may leave the court and wait outside until you are called to give evidence.'

'I'll stay,' she answered in a small, tight voice. 'I'm sorry.' She sat down slowly, her face completely white, her hands fumbling for a handkerchief.

Holland cleared his throat. 'Only one more question on this subject and then we will leave it. About how much liquor was Captain Taggart in the habit of consuming each day?'

'I cannot answer that. I don't know.' Patch's voice was scarcely audible.

'You mean you didn't actually see him consume any set quantity?'

Patch nodded.

'But you must have some idea. What was it he habitually drank – whisky?'

'Yes.'

'Anything else?'

'Sometimes a bottle of cognac. Occasionally rum.'

'How much?'

'I don't know.'

'Had this been going on ever since the start of the voyage?'

'Yes, I think so.'

'Then, since it affected you directly as first officer, you must have made enquiries as to how much he drank. How much did you gather he consumed each day?'

Patch hesitated, and then reluctantly: 'The steward said a bottle, a bottle and a half – sometimes two.' The court gasped.

'I see.' The sound of suppressed sobbing was distinctly audible in the stillness of the court. 'So that he was completely incapable as the Master of the ship?'

'Oh, no.' Patch shook his head. 'Towards the end of the day he would become a little fuddled. But otherwise I would say he was reasonably in command of the situation.'

'You mean to say' – Bowen-Lodge was leaning forward ' – that he was in full command of his faculties when he was steadily drinking one or two bottles a day?'

'Yes, sir. That is to say, most of the time.'

'But you admitted that he was raving and you had to lock him in his cabin. If he was raving, then surely . . .' the Chairman's brows lifted in a question.

'He wasn't raving because he was drunk,' Patch answered slowly.

'Then why was he raving?'

'He had run out of liquor.'

A shocked silence gripped the court. Janet Taggart had stopped sobbing. She was sitting quite rigid, staring at Patch with a sort of fascinated horror.

'I would like to get this point perfectly clear before we go any further,' Bowen-Lodge said in a quiet, controlled voice. 'What you're suggesting is that Captain Taggart did not die of drink, but the lack of it. Is that correct?'

'Yes, sir.'

'Do you really think absence of liquor can kill a man?'

'I don't know,' Patch answered wretchedly. 'All I know is that he lived on nothing else, and when he hadn't got it, he went raving mad and died. He never seemed to have anything in the way of food.'

Bowen-Lodge considered for a moment, his pencil tracing lines on the paper in front of him. At length he looked down at Counsel. 'I think, Mr Holland, we should call medical evidence to establish the point one way or another.'

Holland nodded. 'I have already arranged for that – it seemed necessary after reading his deposition.'

'Good. Then we can leave the matter in abeyance till then.' He sounded relieved. 'Please proceed with the examination of the witness.'

The next stage of the voyage was uneventful, but Patch was taken through it in detail and the picture that emerged was of a conscientious officer doing his best to pull a ship's company together with the presence of the owner a constant irritant. The incidents that came to light under Holland's steady questioning were trivial enough in themselves – the crew's mess table uncleaned between meals, cockroaches, several men lousy, the galley dirty, a lifeboat without provisions, a man injured in a fight, the engines stopped for the replacement of a bearing that had been allowed to run hot – but together they produced an impression of a ship that was badly served by the men who ran her.

Other things emerged, too. The log was improperly kept, the wells not sounded regularly, water consumption unchecked, and as often as not it was Higgins, by then acting as first officer, who was responsible. Patch showed that he was coming to depend more and more on his second officer, John Rice, and the growing sense of comradeship between the two men ran like a strong thread through the evidence.

Twice Patch referred to Dellimare. Once of his own accord, when he was dealing with the lack of supervision of the engine-room staff. 'He was encouraging Mr Burrows, my chief engineer, in his poker playing. I had to insist that he stopped entertaining Mr Burrows in his cabin. They were playing cards together till all hours of the night and it was throwing undue responsibility upon Mr Raft, the second engineer.'

'Did Mr Dellimare raise any objection?' Holland asked.

'Yes.'

'What did he say?'

'He said it was his ship and he would do what he damn' well liked and entertain any of the officers he pleased when he pleased.'

'And what did you say to that?'

'That it was endangering the safety of the ship and the morale of the engine-room and that I was the captain, not him, and the ship would be run the way I wanted it run.'

'In other words you had a row?'

'Yes.'

'And did he agree to stop playing poker with the chief engin-eer?'

'In the end, yes.'

'In the end? You used some persuasion?'

'Yes. I told him I had given Mr Burrows a direct order and that, if it wasn't obeyed, I should know what action to take. And I made it a direct order as far as he was concerned.'

'And he accepted that?'

'Yes.'

'Will you tell the Court what your relations with Mr Dellimare were at this stage?'

Patch hesitated. He had revealed that his relations with the owner were strained. He could in one sentence explain the reason for those strained relations and in doing so gain the sympathy of the whole court. But he let the opportunity go, merely saying, 'We did not see eye-to-eye on certain matters.' And Holland left it at that.

A further reference to Dellimare occurred almost accidentally. Patch had just assured the Court that he had personally checked all four holds as the ship ran into heavy weather off the coast of Portugal, and Holland, again being scrupulously fair to him, drew attention to the fact that he hadn't relied on his first officer's report to make sure that there could be no shifting of the cargo.

'You didn't trust him, in other words?'

'To be honest, no.'

'Did Mr Higgins, in fact, check the holds?'

'I don't know.'

'You thought so little of him that you didn't even ask whether he had checked them?'

'Yes, I suppose that is correct.'

'Did anybody, other than yourself, check the holds?'

Patch paused a moment before replying. Then he said, 'I think Mr Dellimare checked them.'

'You think he checked them?'

'Well, he was in Number One hold when I went in through the inspection hatch to check. I presumed that he was there for the same purpose as myself.'

Holland seemed to consider this for a moment. 'I see. But this was the duty of one of the ship's officers. It seems odd that the owner should find it necessary to check the cargo himself. Have you any comment to make on that?'

Patch shook his head.

'What sort of man was Mr Dellimare?' Holland asked. 'What was your impression of him?'

Now, I thought – now he'll tell them the truth about Dellimare. It was the opening he needed. But he stood there, without saying anything, his face very pale and that nerve twitching at the corner of his mouth.

'What I am trying to get at is this,' Holland went on. 'We are coming now to the night of 16 March. On that night Mr Dellimare disappeared – lost overboard. Did you know that Mr Dellimare had been in the Navy during the war?'

Patch nodded and his lips framed the word 'Yes.'

'He served in corvettes and frigates, mainly in the Atlantic. He must have been through a great many storms.' There was a significant pause, and then Holland said, 'What was your impression of him, at this time, when you knew you were running into very heavy weather? Was he normal in every way?'

'Yes, I think so.' Patch's voice was very low.

'But you're not certain.'

'I didn't know him very well.'

'You had been on this ship with him for over a month. However much he kept to his cabin, you must have had some idea of his mental state. Would you say he was worried?'

'Yes, I think you could say that.'

'Business worries or private worries?'

'I don't know.'

'I'll put it quite bluntly. When you found him checking the cargo, what interpretation did you put on his action?'

'I didn't put any interpretation on it.' Patch had found his voice again and was answering factually and clearly.

'What did you say to him?'

'I told him to stay out of the holds.'

'Why?'

'He shouldn't have been there. The cargo wasn't his responsibility.'

'Quite. I'll put it to you another way. Would you say that his presence there indicated that he was getting scared, that his nerves were going to pieces? He had been torpedoed once during the war and was a long time in the water before being picked up. Would you say that his war experience was in any way affecting him?'

'No, I would . . . I don't know.'

Holland hesitated and then he gave a little shrug. He had been a man seeking after the truth, using the depositions already made as a base from which to probe. But now he changed his tactics and was content to let Patch tell the story of the night the *Mary Deare* was hove-to in the wind-spun waters of the Bay of Biscay, not questioning, not interrupting – just letting it run.

And Patch told it well, gaining from the rapt silence of the court, telling it in hard, factual sentences. And the *Mary Deare* floated into that court, rusty and battered, with the seas bursting like gunfire against the submerged reef of her bows. I watched his face as he told it straight, man-to-man – from the witness box to the Court – and I had the odd feeling that all the time he was skating round something. I looked up at the Chairman. He was sitting slightly forward with his chin cupped in his right hand, listening with a shut, tight-lipped, judicial face that told me nothing of his reactions.

The facts, as Patch presented them, were straightforward enough: the glass falling steadily, the seas rising, the wind increasing, the ship rolling, rolling steady and slow, but gradually rolling her bulwarks under as the mountains of water lifted her on to their streaming crests and tumbled her down into the valleys between. He had been on the bridge since dusk. Rice had been there, too. Just the two of them and the helmsman and a lookout. It had happened about 23.20 hours – a slight explosion, a sort of shudder. It had sounded like another wave breaking and slamming against the bows, except that there was no white water at that particular moment and the ship did not stagger. She was down in a trough and rising slowly. The break of the wave came later and, with it, the hesitation, the crash of the impact, and the sudden blur of white hiding all the fore part of the ship.

Nothing had been said for a moment, and then Rice's voice had cut through the gale's roar as he shouted, 'Did we hit something, sir?' And then he had sent Rice to sound the wells and back had come the report – making water in both the for'ard holds, particularly in Number One. He had ordered the pumps to be started in both Number One and Number Two holds, and he had stood on the bridge and watched the bows become heavy and the seas start to break green over all the for'ard part of the ship. And then Dellimare had come on to the bridge, white-faced and scared-looking. Higgins, too. They were talking about abandoning ship. They seemed to think she was going down. And Rice came back to say the crew were panicking.

He had left the bridge to Higgins then and had gone out on to the upper-deck with Rice. Four men in life-jackets were starting to clear Number Three boat. They were scared and he had to hit one man before they would leave the boat and go back to their duties. He had taken all the men he could find, some ten of them, and had set them to work under the bos'n and the third engineer to shore up the bulkhead between Number Two hold and the boiler-room just in case. And it was whilst he was supervising this that the helmsman had reported to the engine-room that the bridge was full of smoke.

He had taken half a dozen men and when he reached the bridge there was only the helmsman there, his eyes streaming, racked with coughing, as he clung to the wheel, nursing the ship through the crowding storm-breakers, the whole place filled with a fog of acrid smoke.

The fire had been in the radio shack, a little above and behind the bridge. No, he had no idea how it had started. The radio operator had gone below to get his life-jacket. He had stayed below to relieve himself and to have a mug of cocoa. Higgins had gone aft to inspect the steering which seemed slack. No, he didn't know where Dellimare was. He regretted that the helmsman was not among the survivors.

They had used foam extinguishers on the fire. But the heat had been so intense that they hadn't been able to get inside the room. What had finally put the fire out was the partial collapse of the roof, which had allowed the water from a breaking wave to engulf the flames.

The wind was now Force 12 in the gusts – hurricane force. He had hove-to then, putting the ship's bows into the wind with the engines at slow ahead, just holding her there, and praying to God that the seas, piling down in white cascades of water on to the bows, wouldn't smash the for'ard hatch covers. They had stayed hove-to like that, in imminent danger of their lives, for fourteen hours, the pumps just holding their own, and all the time he and Rice had kept moving constantly through the ship, to see that the bulkhead – which was leaking where the weight of water was bulging it, low down near its base – was properly shored, to keep the crew from panicking, to see that they kept to their stations and helped the ship in its struggle against the sea.

About 06.00 hours, after twenty-two hours without sleep, he had retired to his cabin. The wind was dropping by then and the glass beginning to rise. He had gone to sleep fully clothed and two hours later had been woken by Samuel King, the Jamaican steward, with the news that Mr Dellimare could not be found.

The whole ship had been searched, but without success. The man had vanished. 'I could only presume that he had been washed overboard,' Patch said, and then he stood silent, as though waiting for Holland to question him, and Holland asked him if he had held any sort of enquiry.

'Yes. I had every member of the crew make a statement before Mr Higgins, Mr Rice and myself. As far as we could determine, the last man to see Mr Dellimare alive was the steward. He had seen him leave his cabin and go out through the door on to the upper-deck leading aft. That was at about 04.30 hours.'

'And nobody saw him after that?'

Patch hesitated, and then said, 'As far as anybody could find out – no.'

'The upper-deck was the boat-deck?'

'Yes.'

'Was there any danger in going out on to that deck?'

'I don't know. I was on the bridge dealing with the fire.'

'Yes, but in your opinion – was there danger in crossing that deck?'

'No, I don't think so. It's difficult to say. Spray and some seas were sweeping right across all the decks.'

'Right aft?'

'Yes.'

'And Mr Dellimare was going aft?'

'So King said.'

Holland paused and then he asked, 'Have you any idea where

Mr Dellimare was going?'

'No.'

'In view of what you have told us before, would it be reasonable to assume that he might be going aft to check that the hatches of the after-holds were still secure?'

'Possibly. But there was no need. I had checked them myself.'

'But if he had gone to check those hatches, it would have meant going down on to the after well-deck?'

'He could have seen the state of the hatches from the after end of the upper-deck.'

'But if he had gone down, would it have been dangerous?'

'Yes. Yes, I think so. Both well-decks were being swept by the seas.'

'I see. And that was the last anyone saw of him?' The court was very still. The old ship, with her water-logged bows pointed into the gale and a man's body tossed among the spindrift out there in the raging seas; there wasn't anybody in the room who couldn't see it for himself. The puzzle of it, the mystery of it – it held them all enthralled. And behind me somebody was crying.

Then Patch's voice was going on with his story, nervous and jerky, in tune with the sense of tragedy that was seen only in the imagination and not in the cleansing, healing atmosphere of salt wind and spray.

The wind had fallen, and the sea with it, and at 12.43 hours, according to the entry in the log, he had rung for half-ahead on the engines and had resumed course. As soon as it was practicable he had ordered the hand pumps manned, and, as the bows slowly emerged from the sea, he had set a working party under Rice to repair the damage to the for'ard hatches.

He had considered putting into Brest. But, with the weather improving and the pumps holding their own, he had finally decided to hold his course, and had rounded Ushant early on the morning of the 18th. By then he had increased the engine revolutions to economical speed. There was still a big swell running, but the sea was quiet, almost dead calm, with very little wind. Nevertheless, he had hugged the French coast just in case there was some sudden change in the state of the for'ard holds. Île de Batz was abeam at 13.34, Triagoz light at 16.12, Sept Îles at 17.21. He read these times out to the Court from the log. At 19.46 the group occulting light on Les Heaux was just visible through a light mist four points on the starb'd bow. He had then altered course to North 33 East. This would take him outside the Barnouic and Roches Douvres reefs and leave Les Hanois, the light on the south-western tip of Guernsey, about four miles to starb'd. After altering course he had informed his officers that he had decided to take the ship into Southampton for inspection and repairs.

At approximately 21.20, when the steward was clearing his evening meal, which he had taken, as usual, alone in his cabin, he had heard shouts, and then Rice had rushed in to say that the after hold was on fire and that the crew were in a state of panic.

'Any particular reason for their panic?' Holland asked.

'Well, I think they thought the ship was jinxed,' Patch answered. 'In the last two days I had heard that word often.'

'And what did you think? Did you think the ship was jinxed?'

Patch faced the Chairman and the assessors. 'No,' he said. 'I thought there had been a deliberate attempt to wreck her.'

There was a stir of interest throughout the courtroom. But he didn't punch it home with any direct accusation. He just said: 'It was too coincidental – the damage to the holds and then the fire in the radio shack.'

'You were convinced that there had been some sort of explosion in Number One hold?' Holland asked.

Patch hesitated. 'Yes. Yes, I think so.'

'And the radio shack?'

'If it was an explosion, then the radio shack had to be put out of action – it was my means of communication with the rest of the world.'

'I see.' Holland paused, and then he said, 'What you are saying, in fact, is that there was somebody on board who was trying to destroy the ship.'

'Yes.'

'And when you heard that Number Three hold was on fire – did you immediately think that this was another attempt to destroy the ship?'

'Yes, I did.'

'And is that still your opinion?'

Patch nodded. 'Yes.'

'You realize that this is a very serious accusation you are making?'

'Yes, I realize that.'

Holland held the court in utter silence for a moment. And then he said, 'There were thirty-one men on board the *Mary Deare*. If the fire were deliberately started, it endangered all those lives. It was tantamount to murder.'

'Yes.'

'And you still say that the fire was started deliberately?'

'Yes, I do.'

The next question was inevitable. 'Who did you suspect of starting it?' Holland asked, and Patch hesitated. To produce the story of Dellimare's offer now was pointless. Dellimare was dead. He couldn't have started that fire, and all Patch could say was that he hadn't had much time for formulating suspicions – he had been too busy trying to save the ship.

'But you must have thought about it since?'

'Yes, I have.' Patch was facing the judge and the assessors. 'But I think that is a matter for the Court to decide.'

Bowen-Lodge nodded his agreement and Holland then got Patch back to the events following the outbreak of the fire. He and Rice had organized a fire-fighting party. No, Higgins wasn't there. It was his watch. But the second engineer was there and the radio operator and the bos'n. They ran out hoses and got them playing on to the flames through the inspection hatch whilst they cleared part of the main hatch cover. They also cleared a section of Number Four hatch cover in case it was necessary to play the hoses on the bulkhead between the two holds. He had then gone down into Number Four hold through the inspection hatch.

'Why did you do that?'

'I wanted to see how hot the bulkhead plates had become. I didn't want the fire to spread aft. Also, because that hold was only partly filled with cargo, I hoped to be able to tell from the heat of the plates just how serious the fire was – what hold it had got.'

'And what did you discover?'

'It had clearly only just broken out. The bulkhead wasn't even hot. But I didn't discover that until later.'

'How do you mean?'

He explained then how he had been knocked unconscious just as he had reached the bottom of the vertical ladder. He told it in the same words that he had told it to me in his cabin on the *Mary Deare* and when he had finished Holland said, 'You're sure it wasn't an accident – that you didn't slip?'

'Quite sure,' Patch answered.

'Perhaps something fell on you – a loose piece of metal?'

But Patch pointed to his jaw where the scar still showed, maintaining that it was quite impossible for it to have happened accidentally.

'And when you came to, was there any sort of weapon near you that your assailant might have used?'

'No, I don't think so. But I couldn't be certain. The place was full of smoke and I was dazed, half-asphyxiated.'

'I put it to you that one of the crew – a man, say, who had a grudge against you – could have followed you down . . . hit you perhaps with his fist?'

'He would have had to be a very powerful man.' Patch was looking across at Higgins. And then he went on to describe how, when he had come to, he could still hear the men shouting as they got the boats away. He had crawled back up the vertical ladder to the inspection hatch, but the cover had been closed and clamped down. What saved him was the fact that the main hatch had been cleared at one corner and after a long time he had managed to stack enough bales of cotton up to be able to reach this opening and crawl out on to the deck. He had found Number Three boat hanging from its bow falls, the other davits empty. The engines were still running, the pumps still working and the hoses were still pouring water into Number Three hold. But not a single member of the crew remained on board.

It was an incredible, almost unbelievable story. And he went on to tell how, alone and unaided, he had put the fire out. And then in the morning he had found a complete stranger wandering about the ship.

'That would be Mr Sands, from the yacht *Sea Witch*?'

'Yes.'

'Would you explain why you didn't accept his offer to take you off?'

'I saw no reason to abandon ship. She was badly down by the bows, but she wasn't in imminent danger. I thought he would notify the authorities and that it would help the salvage tug if I were on board to organize the tow.'

He told them then how he had seen me fail to regain my yacht, how he had pulled me on to the deck, and then he was telling them of our efforts to save the ship in the teeth of the rising gale, how we had got the engines going and the pumps working and kept her stern to the wind. But he made no mention of the Minkies. According to him, we had finally abandoned the ship in a rubber dinghy taken from Dellimare's cabin when she was on the verge of sinking. No, he couldn't say exactly what the position was, but it was somewhere to the east of the Roches Douvres. No, we hadn't seen her go down. The rubber dinghy? Well, yes, it did seem to indicate that Dellimare had been nervous, had not trusted the boats or the seaworthiness of the ship.

'Two final questions,' Holland said. 'And they are very important questions for you and for everybody connected with the ship.' He paused and then said, 'On reflection, are you quite convinced that it was an explosion that caused the flooding in Number One hold? I put it to you that in the conditions prevailing it was almost impossible to be certain that it wasn't some submerged object that you hit or a wave breaking against the bows.'

Patch hesitated, glancing round the court. 'It definitely wasn't a sea breaking,' he said quietly. 'It was afterwards that the next sea broke over the bows. As to whether we hit something or an explosive charge was set off, only an inspection of the actual damage could prove it one way or the other.'

'Quite. But since the ship is probably lying in at least twenty fathoms of water and we don't know quite where, inspection of the damage is out of the question. I want your opinion.'

'I don't think I can say any more than I have. I can't be certain.'

'But you think it was an explosion?' Holland waited, but getting no reply, he added, 'Having regard to the fire in the radio shack and, later, the fire in the after hold – taking them all together, you incline to the theory that it was an explosion?'

'If you put it that way – yes.'

'Thank you.' Holland sat down and even then nobody moved. There was no whispering, no shuffling of feet. The whole court was held in the spell of the evidence.

And then Sir Lionel Falcett rose. 'Mr Learned Chairman, I would be glad if you would put one or two additional questions to the witness.' He was a small man with thinning hair and a high forehead, a very ordinary-seeming man except for his voice, which had great depth of tone and was vibrant, so that one was conscious of the power of great energy and vitality behind it. It was his voice, not the man, that instantly dominated the court. 'Witness has made it clear that he is convinced, in his own mind, that some attempt was made to wreck the *Mary Deare*. And indeed, the incidents he has related to the Court, in the absence of any natural explanation, would appear to support this conclusion. I would, however, point out to the Court that the value of the ship herself was not such as to justify so elaborate a plot and that we must, therefore, presume that, if such a plot existed, it was directed towards fraudulently obtaining the insurance value of the cargo. I would respectfully point out to you, Mr Learned Chairman, that there would only be financial gain in such a dastardly and murderous endeavour if, in fact, the cargo had been removed prior to the loss of the ship.'

Bowen-Lodge nodded. 'I quite understand your argument,

Sir Lionel.' He glanced at the clock at the far end of the court, above the public gallery. 'What is your question?'

'It concerns the time the ship was moored alongside the *Torre Annunziata* in the Rangoon River,' Sir Lionel said. 'My information is that the *Mary Deare*'s crew were given shore leave, and that during that period the *Torre Annunziata* was a blaze of lights with all her winches in operation.' He looked across at Holland. 'I understand that a deposition to this effect will be introduced later and that it states that the official concerned was informed by the Master of the *Torre Annunziata* that he had been shifting cargo to make room for some steel tubing he was due to load.' He turned back to face Bowen-Lodge. 'I should like to know, Mr Learned Chairman, whether the witness heard any of his officers speak of this after he had joined the ship – whether, in fact, it had been the subject of some comment?'

The question was put and Patch answered that he had heard of it from Rice. He hadn't at the time attached any significance to it.

'But you do now?' Sir Lionel suggested.

Patch nodded. 'Yes.'

'Just one more question, Mr Learned Chairman. Can the witness tell us whether Mr Dellimare at any time made any reference to the cargo?'

The question was put and, when Patch answered, no, Sir Lionel said, 'You had no indication from anyone that the cargo might be other than that stated on the manifest?'

'No.'

'I will put it to you another way – a ship is a very tight little company of men, and in any enclosed community like that a thing popularly known as the grapevine operates. Did you hear any rumours about the cargo after you joined the ship?'

'Some men seemed to think that we had a cargo of explosives on board,' Patch answered. 'It was a rumour that persisted despite the fact that I posted a copy of the manifest on the crew's notice board.'

'You thought it dangerous that they should think they were sitting on top of a lot of explosives?'

'I did.'

'Having regard to the sort of crew you had?'

'Yes.'

'Would you say that this rumour would be sufficient in itself to cause panic amongst the crew as soon as they knew a fire had broken out?'

'Probably.'

'In point of fact Rice reported that they were panicking.' Sir Lionel leaned forward, staring at Patch. 'How did this extraordinary rumour get around the ship?'

Patch glanced involuntarily towards the waiting witnesses. 'I don't think Mr Higgins was ever convinced that we were carrying the cargo declared on the manifest.'

'He thought it was a cargo of explosives, eh? What gave him that idea?'

'I don't know.'

'Did you ask him?'

'Yes, I did.'

'When?'

'Just after we had rounded Ushant.'

'And what did he say?'

'He refused to answer.'

'What were his exact words when you put the question to him?'

'His exact words?'

'Yes.'

'He said I could bloody well try and get the answer out of Taggart or Dellimare and stop bothering him. They were both dead, of course.'

'Thank you.' Sir Lionel folded himself delicately into his seat. Bowen-Lodge looked at the clock again and adjourned the court. 'Two o'clock please, gentlemen.' He rose and the court rose with him, standing whilst he left by the door at the rear of the judge's chair, followed by his three assessors.

When I turned to leave I found that Mrs Petrie had been sitting right behind me. She gave me a little brief smile of recognition. Her face was puffy and pallid under her make-up and her eyes were red. Gundersen was there, too. He had been sitting beside her, but now he had moved along the row and was talking to Higgins. She went out on her own. 'Who's that woman?' Hal asked me.

'One of the Dellimare directors,' I replied, and I told him about my visit to the company's offices. 'I rather think she may have been living with Dellimare,' I told him.

Outside, the sun shone on rain-wet pavements, and it came as something of a shock to discover that there were people – ordinary people who knew nothing of the *Mary Deare* – hurrying about their everyday affairs. Patch was standing alone on the pavement's edge. He had been waiting for me and he came straight across.

'I'd like a word with you, Sands.' His voice was hoarse with talking and his face looked drained.

Hal said he would go on to the hotel where we had decided to lunch and Patch watched him go, fidgeting with the coins in his pocket. As soon as Hal was out of ear-shot, he said, 'You told me your boat wouldn't be ready until the end of the month.' He said it accusingly, anger and resentment in his voice.

'Yes,' I said. 'It was ready a week earlier than I expected.'

'Why didn't you let me know? I went down to the yard last Wednesday and you'd already gone. Why didn't you tell me?' And then he suddenly burst out, 'All I needed was one day. Just one day out there.' He stared at me, literally grinding his teeth. 'Don't you realize – one look at that hole in the ship's hull and I'd have known. I'd have been able to tell the truth then. As it is – ' his eyes were a little wild, like something brought to bay and not knowing which way to turn. 'As it is I don't know what the hell I'm saying, what God-damn pit I'm digging for myself. One day! That was all I wanted.'

'You didn't tell me that,' I said. 'In any case, you know very well that an inspection of that sort would have to be carried out by the authorities.' But I could understand how he had wanted to be certain, to prove that his suspicions were justified. 'It'll work out,' I said, patting his arm.

'I hope you're right,' he said between his teeth. 'I hope to God you're right.' He was looking at me and his eyes were bright like coals. 'All that effort . . . to put her on the Minkies . . . wasted. My God! I could – ' And there he stopped and his eyes, looking past me, widened, and I turned to find Janet Taggart coming straight towards us.

I once saw a painting entitled 'Vengeance'. I can't remember the artist's name and it doesn't matter now, because I know it wasn't any good. Vengeance should be painted the way Janet Taggart looked. She was pale as death, and in the pallor of her frozen face her eyes were enormous. She stopped just in front of him and struck out at him blindly.

I don't remember her words now – they came in a great over-whelming torrent of cutting, lacerating sentences. I saw Patch's eyes go dead as he flinched before the whip-lash of her tongue, and then I left them, walking quickly, wanting to get the picture of the two of them right out of my mind. I wondered if she knew what power she had to hurt the man.

We had a quick lunch and returned to the court, and on the stroke of two Bowen-Lodge took his place on the judge's seat.

There were five men at the Press desk now. They were gathering like vultures at the smell of news. 'With your permission, Mr Chairman,' Holland said, rising, 'I propose to proceed with the other evidence in order that the Court shall have a complete picture.'

Bowen-Lodge nodded. 'I think that a very proper course, Mr Holland. Your first witness must, however, remain in the court. Those representing the various interested parties will, I know, wish to put further questions to him.'

I had expected Higgins to be the next witness. Instead, Holland called for 'Harold Lowden' and I suddenly realized that I still hadn't made up my mind what I was going to say. Hal stood in the witness box, very erect, very much the soldier, and in short, clipped sentences told of our encounter with the *Mary Deare* and how we had found her abandoned the following morning. And when he stepped down it was my turn and I found myself automatically crossing the court and taking my stand in the witness box. I was in a cold sweat.

I repeated the oath and then Holland was facing me, smooth and urbane, asking me in that soft, bored voice of his whether I was John Henry Sands, my business and background and why I was sailing the yacht *Sea Witch* in that area of the Channel on the night of 18 March. And as I gave the answers, I could hear the nervousness in my voice. The court was very silent. Bowen-Lodge's small gimlet eyes watched me and Holland stood there in front of me, waiting to prompt me with questions, to probe if necessary.

Across the court I saw Patch, sitting a little forward, his hands clasped, his body tense and rigid. His eyes were fixed on my face. I was telling them what the *Mary Deare* had looked like that morning when I boarded her, and suddenly my mind was made up. To tell them that the ship was stranded on the Minkies would prove him a liar. It would cut the ground from under his feet. I couldn't do it. I think I had known that all along, but the strange thing was that, once I had made the decision, all nervousness left me. I knew what I was going to say and I set out to present Patch to the Court as I had seen him through those desperate hours – a man, staggering with exhaustion, who had put out a fire single-handed and could still go on fighting to save his ship.

I told them about the bruise on his jaw, about the coal dust and the smoke-blackened haggardness of his face. I told them how we'd sweated down there in the stoke-hold to raise steam on that one boiler, how we'd got the pumps going, how we'd used the engines to keep her stern to the wind and how the seas had swept across her submerged bows in thundering cataracts of white water. And I left it at that, simply saying that we had finally abandoned her on the morning of the second day.

The questions started then. Had Patch made any comments to me about the crew having abandoned ship? Could I give the Court any idea of the *Mary Deare*'s position at the time we had taken to the dinghy? Did I think that, if there had been no gale, the ship could have safely got to some port?

Sir Lionel Falcett rose to his feet and put the same questions that Snetterton had asked me – about the cargo, the holds, Patch. 'You lived with this man through a desperate forty-eight hours. You shared his fears and his hopes. Surely he must have said something, made some comment?' And I replied that we had had little opportunity for talking. I told them again of our exhaustion, the fury of the seas, the moment-to-moment fear that the ship would go down under us.

And then suddenly it was over and I walked back across the floor of the court, feeling like a rag that has been squeezed dry. Hal gripped my arm as I sat down. 'Magnificent!' he whispered. 'You've damn' near made a hero of the man. Look at the Press desk.' And I saw that it was emptying hurriedly.

'Ian Fraser!' Holland was on his feet again and Captain Fraser was making his way across the court. It was routine evidence of how he had picked us up, and then he was released and Janet Taggart was called.

She went into the witness box pale as death, but with her head up and her face a tight little defensive mask. Holland explained that he had called her at this stage in order to release her from the painful ordeal of listening to any further statements that might be made by witnesses about her father. He then took her gently through a description of her father as she had known him – his letters, coming unfailingly from every port he visited, his presents, the money to take her on from college to university, his care of her after the death of her mother when she was seven. 'I never knew how wonderful he had been as a father until these last few years, when I was old enough to understand how he must have scraped and saved and worked to give me the education I've had.' She described him as she had last seen him, and then she read the letter he had written her from Rangoon. She read it in a small, trembling voice, and his love and concern for her were there in every line of it.

It was very painful to hear her, knowing the man was dead, and when she had finished there was a murmur of men clearing their throats and shifting uneasily in their seats.

'That will be all, Miss Taggart,' Holland said with that gentleness that he had used with her throughout her evidence. But she didn't move from the witness box. She had taken a picture postcard from her bag and she stood with it clutched in her hand, looking across at Patch. And the look on her face sent a cold shiver through me as she said, 'A few days ago I received a post-card from Aden. It had been delayed in the post.' She shifted her gaze to Bowen-Lodge. 'It's from my father. May I read part of it please?'

He nodded his permission and she went on: 'My father wrote: "The owner has engaged a man called Patch to be my first officer in place of poor old Adams".' She wasn't reading it. She was staring straight at Bowen-Lodge, the postcard still gripped in her hand. She knew it by heart. ' "I do not know what will come of this. Rumour has it that he stranded a ship once, deliberately. But whatever happens I promise you it shall not be of my doing. God go with you, Janie, and think of me. If all goes well, I shall keep my promise this time and see you again at the end of the voyage".' Her voice broke on a whisper. The court held its breath. She was like a spring coiled too tight and near to breaking.

She held the card out to Holland and he took it. 'Witness is excused,' Bowen-Lodge said. But she had turned and was facing Patch across the court. Wildly she accused him of dragging her father's name in the mud to save himself. She had checked on the loss of the *Belle Isle*. She knew the truth now and she was going to see that the Court knew it. Bowen-Lodge beat on his desk with his gavel. Holland was at her side, remonstrating with her. But she ignored him, and Patch sat there, white-faced and appalled, as she blamed him for the fires, for the flooded holds, for the whole wreckage of her father's ship. 'You're a monster,' she sobbed as they dragged her from the witness box. And then she went suddenly limp and allowed herself to be hurried out of the court, her whole body convulsed with the passion of her tears.

The courtroom eased itself a little self-consciously. Nobody looked at Patch. Nobody looked anywhere until Bowen-Lodge's matter-of-fact voice lifted the tension from the room. 'Call the next witness.'

'Donald Masters!' Holland was in his place again. The Court began to get back into its stride. Technical witnesses followed, giving details of the ship and its equipment, passing judgement on its age and condition, with depositions sworn by the surveyor in Yokohama and the Lloyd's official who had issued her load-line certificate. Another by the Docks Superintendent at Rangoon giving information about the *Torre Annunziata* and the adjustments to her cargo. And then Holland called 'Angela Petrie' and the court, so predominantly male, stirred with interest as Mrs Petrie went into the witness box.

She explained that the Dellimare Trading and Shipping Company had been formed as a private limited company in 1947 with Mr Dellimare, a Mr Greenly and herself as directors. It had been entirely a trading concern, specializing in the import-export business, chiefly with India and the Far East. Later Mr Greenly had ceased to be a director and Mr Gundersen, who operated a similar type of business in Singapore, had joined the board, the capital had been increased and the business considerably expanded. She gave figures, producing them from memory with quiet efficiency.

'And the position of the Company now?' Holland asked.

'It's in process of being wound-up – a voluntary liquidation.'

'And that was arranged before Mr Dellimare's death?'

'Oh yes, it was decided some months back.'

'Any particular reason?'

She hesitated, and then said, 'There were certain tax advantages.'

A little murmur of laughter ran round the court and Holland sat down. Almost immediately Patch's lawyer was on his feet, a thin, dried-up man with a reedy voice. 'Mr Learned Chairman, I should like to ask the witness whether she is aware that Mr Dellimare was involved, just before the formation of this Company, in a case of fraudulent conversion?'

Bowen-Lodge frowned. 'I do not regard that as relevant, Mr Fenton,' he said acidly.

'I should like to answer that question.' Mrs Petrie's voice was bold and clear and vibrant. 'He was acquitted. It was a malicious accusation with no shred of evidence to support it.'

Fenton sat down a little hurriedly and Sir Lionel Falcett rose. 'Mr Learned Chairman, I should like to know from the witness whether any ships were purchased by the Company at the time of its formation?'

Bowen-Lodge put the question and Mrs Petrie answered none.

'You hadn't the capital, is that it?' Sir Lionel asked. And when she agreed, he said, 'In point of fact, it was quite a small business?'

'Yes.'

'Then why call it the Dellimare Trading and Shipping Company? Surely it was a rather unnecessarily grandiose title?'

'Oh, well, you see, Mr Dellimare was always very keen about ships, and being ex-Navy and all that, he hoped one day . . . Anyway,' she added, with a flash of pride, 'we did finish up by owning ships.'

'You had the *Mary Deare* and the *Torre Annunziata*. Any others?'

She shook her head. 'No. Just the two.'

Sir Lionel glanced down at his papers. 'The purchase of the *Mary Deare* was completed on 18 June of last year. When was the *Torre Annunziata* purchased?'

For the first time Mrs Petrie showed a slight hesitation. 'I can't remember exactly.'

'Was it in April of last year?'

'I don't remember.'

'But you are a director of the Company and this must have involved a considerable amount of finance. Do you mean to say you have no records of the transactions?' Sir Lionel's voice had sharpened slightly.

'I may have. I don't know.' And then she added quickly, 'We were expanding fast at that time and it was all fixed up at the Singapore end.'

'And you were not kept fully informed, is that it?' She nodded and he then asked, 'At what date did Mr Gundersen join the board?'

'On 2 March of last year.'

'So that these shipping transactions were a result of his joining the board?'

'Yes, I suppose so.'

Sir Lionel turned to the Chairman. 'There is just one more question I should like to put to the witness. As the Court is already aware, the *Mary Deare* was making just this one voyage and was then being sold for scrap. The *Torre Annunziata* made only two voyages and then she was sold to the Chinese. I should like to know what the margin of profit was on these transactions.'

Bowen-Lodge put the question, but she shook her head. She didn't know.

'What was the cost of acquiring these ships, then?' Sir Lionel put the question to her direct.

'No figures have yet been passed across to our office.'

'And I suppose you have no idea who put up the money?'

She shook her head. 'I'm afraid I don't know. It was all arranged at the Singapore end.'

Sir Lionel nodded and sat down. Mrs Petrie was released from the witness box and she walked back across the court. I saw that her eyes were fixed on someone just behind me, and I guessed it must be Gundersen. Her face was very white and she looked scared.

Hal leaned across to me. 'Looks as though Lionel is mounting an attack on the Company,' he whispered, and I nodded, thinking that perhaps Patch was saving his announcement of Dellimare's offer until he was questioned by Sir Lionel. It seemed reasonable. And that question by his lawyer, Fenton – it had been clumsily done, but he had made his point.

Perfume wafted over me as Mrs Petrie resumed her seat, and I heard Gundersen's voice, cold and angry, say, 'Why didn't you tell him? I gave you those figures weeks back.' And she answered him in a whisper: 'How can I think of figures now?'

And then Holland called 'Hans Gundersen.'

He described himself as a financier and company director and he made a strong impression on the Court. He was a business man and he had all his facts and figures at his finger-tips. Without any prompting from Holland he explained to the Court exactly why he had joined the Company, why they had acquired the *Mary Deare* and the *Torre Annunziata*, how the purchases had been financed and what the expected profits were.

He explained his interest in the Dellimare Company in the cold, hard language of business. He had many interests in Singapore and other ports in the Far East. It suited his interests at that time to take a hand in the affairs of this small company. He had the chance to acquire two old ships at a very low figure. He had taken the view that freight rates were on the mend and that in a year's time it would be possible to sell the ships at a handsome profit. He had chosen the Dellimare Company as the medium through which to make the purchase because he knew Mr Dellimare and discovered that he was willing to have the Company wound up at the end of the transaction. 'In my experience,' he added, 'that is much the most remunerative way of engaging in these operations.' In the case of the *Torre Annunziata* his object had been achieved. They had sold the ship to the Chinese at a figure much higher than the purchase price. The *Mary Deare*, however, had not proved such a good proposition. Her condition had been worse than he had been led to believe. The result was that he had decided that she should make one voyage and then be sold for scrap in England. Break-up price less purchase price and overhaul would have given the Dellimare Company a small margin of profit plus the profits of the voyage. He handed Holland a slip of paper. 'Those are the figures, actual and estimated,' he said.

Holland passed them up to Bowen-Lodge and then sat down. The Chairman checked through the figures, nodded and glanced towards Sir Lionel, who rose and said, 'I should like to know from the witness who financed the acquisition of these ships and how exactly he stood to gain from the deal.'

Bowen-Lodge put the question and Gundersen replied, 'Of course. I financed the operation myself. In return I was allotted all the shares of the increased capital of the Company.'

'In other words,' Sir Lionel said, 'your motive for becoming a director of this company was profit?'

'Naturally. I am a business man, sir.'

'I appreciate that.' Sir Lionel smiled drily. 'Now, about the *Mary Deare*. You have admitted that she was not in the condition you had hoped. How was it that such a valuable cargo was entrusted to her? Did Mr Dellimare arrange that?'

'No. I arranged it through my contacts in Singapore. You must understand that I am very well known in business circles there.'

'One further question. For what reason were these two ships – the *Mary Deare* and the *Torre Annunziata* – routed in such a way that they were in the Rangoon River together from 7 to 11 January?'

'I don't understand the reason for your question, sir,' Gundersen replied. 'Mr Dellimare looked after all the details of the Company management. If a ship is sailing from England to China and another from Japan to Antwerp, then they will cross somewhere.'

Sir Lionel asked him a number of further questions, but Gundersen refused to admit any responsibility for the details of ships' schedules. 'You must understand that I have many calls on my time. This was a very small business. I do not concern myself with the day-to-day management of affairs of companies I am interested in.'

'But you flew all the way from Singapore as soon as you heard what had happened to the *Mary Deare* and have remained in this country ever since.'

'Of course. I am a director of the Company and this is a serious business. When something goes wrong, then it is necessary to be on the spot. Particularly as Mr Dellimare is dead.'

'One final question; why was it necessary for Mr Dellimare to travel on the *Mary Deare* as supercargo. Surely in these days it is very unusual?'

Gundersen shrugged his shoulders. 'Mr Dellimare was in Yokohama to arrange all the details. I don't think he was a rich man, and it is cheaper to travel a long distance like that in your own ship.'

There were no further questions and Gundersen stood down. He was dressed now in a dark-grey double-breasted suit, obviously cut by a London tailor, and he looked a typical English business man – quiet, remote, competent.

More technical evidence followed, and then Bowen-Lodge adjourned the Court. 'Tomorrow at ten-thirty, gentlemen.'

As I followed Hal into the corridor, a hand plucked at my sleeve. 'You're Mr Sands, aren't you?' A little, grey-haired woman was smiling up at me a little uncertainly.

'Yes,' I said. There was something about her face that I seemed to recognize.

'I thought you were, but I'm never quite certain about people – my eyes, you know. I just wanted to tell you how glad I am he has one good friend in all this terrible business. You were splendid, Mr Sands.'

I saw the likeness then. 'You're his mother, aren't you?' I was looking round for Patch, but she said, 'Please. He doesn't know I'm here. He'd be terribly angry. When he came down to see me at Bridgwater, he didn't tell me anything about it. But I knew at once that he was in trouble.' She gave a little sigh. 'It was the first time I had seen him in seven years. That's a long time, Mr Sands, for an old body like me. I only had the one, you see – just Gideon. And now that his father's dead . . .' She smiled and patted my arm. 'But there, you don't want to hear about my troubles. I just wanted you to know that I'm glad he's got one good friend.' She looked up at me. 'It will be all right this time . . . you do think so, don't you, Mr Sands?'

'I'm sure it will,' I murmured. 'Sir Lionel Falcett is obviously concentrating on the cargo and the Company.'

'Yes. Yes, that's what I thought.'

I offered to see her to her hotel, but she wouldn't hear of it and left me with a brave little smile, moving along with the crowd. Hal joined me then and we went out to his car. I caught a glimpse of her standing, waiting for a bus. She was off-guard then, and she looked lonely and a little frightened.

Hal had offered to put me up for the night and we collected my suitcase from the station and drove down to his house at Bosham, a small, thatched place with a lawn running down to the water. I had bought an evening paper in Southampton; it was all over the front page and three columns of it inside – *Captain's Daughter Breaks Down at Enquiry; Strange Story of Loss of Mary Deare.*

It wasn't until after dinner that Hal began to ask me specific questions about Patch. At length he said, 'That day you rejoined us at Peter Port – you didn't say very much about him.' He was standing by the window, looking out across the lawn to where the water was a milky blur in the dusk. There were a couple of yachts moored out there and their masts were bobbing to the lop and the wind gusts. He turned and looked at me. 'You knew about the *Belle Isle* business then, didn't you?'

I nodded, wondering what was coming. It was very cosy in that room with its lamps and its glimmer of Eastern brass and the big tiger skins on the floor, very remote from all that I had lived with during the past two months. Even the glass of port in my hand seemed part of the illusion of being in another world.

He came and sat down opposite me. 'Look, old chap,' he said. 'I don't want to pry into what, after all, is your concern. But just how sure are you about this fellow?'

'How do you mean?'

'Well, you've got to be damn' sure about a man . . . I mean . . .' He hesitated, searching for the words he wanted. 'Well, put it this way. If Patch wrecked that ship – deliberately wrecked her – then it was murder. They may only be able to pin a charge of manslaughter on him in law, but before God he'd be guilty of murder.'

'He didn't do it,' I said.

'You're sure of that?'

'Absolutely.' And having said that, I sat back, wondering why I'd said it, why I was so certain?

'I'm glad,' Hal said. 'Because, you know, all the time you were in the witness box, I was conscious that you were defending him. You were selecting your evidence, keeping things back, and at times you were a little scared. Oh, you needn't worry. I don't think anybody else noticed it. I noticed it because I know you and because at Peter Port, when you'd had less time to think it all out, you were so obviously covering up.' He paused and sipped his port. 'Go carefully, though,' he added. 'I know Lionel Falcett. Member of my club. Seen him in action, too. Don't let him get his claws into you.'

3

IT WAS still blowing and the streets were wet as we drove to the court the following morning. Proceedings started sharp at ten-thirty with evidence about the cargo. And then a doctor was called who showed that it was quite possible for a man who lived on nothing but liquor to die for lack of it. Through all this the courtroom was restless as though waiting for something. The public gallery was packed, the Press desk crammed. And then at last Holland called 'Alfred Higgins' and, as Higgins thrust his huge bulk into the witness box, there was a sudden, expectant hush, so that the sound of a clock striking eleven was quite audible through the taking of the oath.

He was forty-three years old, Higgins told the Treasury Counsel, and, when asked for his qualifications, he explained that he'd started life on his father's barge, sailing the East Coast ports until he was fifteen; then he'd got mixed up in some smuggling racket and had stowed away on a banana boat. He'd stayed at sea after that, moving from ship to ship across the traffic lanes of the world – square-riggers, tramps and liners, tugs and coasters; he rolled the names of them out of his great barrel of a body like pages picked at random from Lloyd's Register.

He began his story back where the *Mary Deare* steamed out of Yokohama. According to him, the ship was a floating death-trap of rattling rivets and clanging plates, a piece of leaking iron-mongery taken off the junk-heap of the China Seas. Of the captain, he simply said, 'The 'ole ship knew 'e was drinking 'isself ter death.' The first mate was sickening for jaundice and the third officer, Rice, was only a kid of twenty-four on his second voyage with a watch-keeper's certificate. The implication was that he, Higgins, was the only reliable deck officer on board, and though he looked like a bull about to charge, there was something impressive about him as he stood there and gave his evidence in a throaty rumble.

Singapore, Rangoon, Aden – and then he was covering the same ground that Patch had covered, but from a different angle. He thought the crew 'not bad considerin' the moth-eaten sort o' a tub she was.' Patch he regarded as 'a bit pernickity-like' and added, 'But that's ter be expected when a man wiv 'is record gets command again.'

And then up through the Bay of Biscay the Court got little glimpses of Patch, nervous, over-bearing, at odds with the owner, with his officers – 'All 'cept Rice. 'E was the white-headed boy, as the sayin' is.' And when it came to the gale itself and the ship down by the bows and the radio shack gutted by fire, Higgins didn't give it graphically as Patch had done, but baldly, factually. He had been asleep in his bunk when the hold had started to flood. He had taken over the bridge and had remained on watch until 10.00 hours the following morning – eleven solid hours. He had then organized a more thorough search for Dellimare. No, Mr Patch hadn't ordered him to. He'd done it on his own initiative, having been relieved. He couldn't believe that Dellimare 'who was Navy an' a good bloke on a ship' could have gone overboard. Altogether he had been forty-two hours without sleep.

'You liked Mr Dellimare?' Holland asked him.

'I didn't like or dislike 'im. I jus' said 'e was a good bloke, an' so 'e was.'

'Did you advise Mr Patch at one stage to abandon ship?'

'Well, yes, in a manner o' speakin'. We considered it, Mr Dellimare an' me.'

'Why?'

' 'Cos we knew the sort o' ship she was. We'd bin through two gales already comin' across from Singapore. Patch 'adn't. An' the one in the Bay was a lot worse than wot we'd gone through before.'

'And you thought an explosion had occurred in the for'ard hold?'

'I didn't think nothin' of the kind. I knew she was rotten an' we were takin' a helluva pounding. We didn't think she'd stand much more.' And then he said, 'If you're suggesting we were scared, just remember what it was like out there. Ten to one the boats wouldn't 've got launched in that sea, let alone stayed afloat. It took guts to even think 'o takin' ter the boats, pertikly fer Mr Dellimare who'd had a basinful o' that sort o' thing during the war. Later, when we 'ove-to, things was easier an' I thought maybe we had a chance.'

And then he was dealing with the night the fire had broken out in the after hold and they had abandoned ship. Yes, it had been about 21.20 hours. It was a stoker who had discovered it, a man called West. He'd come out of the after deck-house and had seen smoke coming from the hatch of Number Three hold. He'd reported at once to the bridge by phone. Rice had been there at the time and Higgins had sent him to check the report and notify Mr Patch. Not once in his evidence did he refer to Patch as the captain.

'And what happened then?' Holland asked him.

'I didn't hear nothin' further for about quarter of an hour. But I knew it was fire orl right 'cos the after derrick lights was switched on an' there was a lot of activity with men running about the deck. Then Mr Patch comes up to the bridge lookin' very wild and all covered in smoke grime an' says he's ordered the boats swung out just in case. I asked him whether he'd like me ter take charge of the fire-fighting party and he said No, Mr Rice was in charge. He stood aba't fer a bit after that as though he couldn't make up his mind aba't somethin'. An' after a bit Rice comes runnin' up to the bridge in a bit of a panic an' says the fire's getting worse. And at that Patch orders him to pass the word to stand by to abandon ship. "You notify the engine-room, Mr Higgins," he says. "Then take charge of the fire-fighting party. Mr Rice, you'll have charge of the upper-deck. See there's no panic when I give the word." An' that's the last I saw of him,' Higgins added.

The rest was a pattern of disaster that comes from absence of command. Higgins and his men had fought the fire for a further fifteen minutes or so, and all the time it seemed to be gaining on them. The men were scared. They believed the ship was jinxed, that the cargo was explosives. Higgins sent Rice to tell Patch he couldn't hold the men much longer and Rice came back to say he couldn't find Patch anywhere. 'By then the men were near ter panic. Some were already on the upper-deck, piling into Number Three boat. There weren't nothing I could do 'cept give the order to abandon ship.'

The order had resulted in a stampede for the boats. When he reached the upper-deck, Higgins saw Number Three boat hanging by its bow falls with one man clinging to it. Number One boat had also been cleared. She was empty and being battered to pieces against the ship's side. By using his fists he'd got some sort of order out of the chaos on deck and he and the officers had organized the men into the two remaining boats. He had put Rice in charge of Number Four boat and had waited to see him safely clear. He had then lowered and released his own boat. Owing to the speed at which the ship was travelling he had lost contact with Rice by the time his boat hit the water and he never regained it.

'Do you mean to say,' Holland asked, 'that you took to the boats with the ship still steaming?'

'Yes. Acting on Mr Patch's instructions I had ordered the engine-room staff to stand by to take to the boats. When I gave the order to abandon, they didn't 'ave no instructions about stopping the engines an' afterwards none o' 'em would go below to do it.'

'But surely if you gave the order – '

'What the hell use were orders?' Higgins growled. 'Patch'd gone – vanished. One boat was already hanging in her davits, the men in her all tipped into the sea; another was bein' smashed up alongside. The men were panicking. Anybody who went below stood a good chance of coming up and finding the last two boats gone. It was as much as Rice an' I could do ter get those boats away orderly-like.'

'But good heavens!' Holland exclaimed. 'Surely, as an experienced officer, you had some control over your – '

But Higgins interrupted him again. 'Ain't you got no imagination?' he burst out. 'Can't you see what it was like – Patch gone and the crew in a panic and a fire raging on top of a cargo of explosives.'

'But it wasn't explosives.'

' 'Ow were we ter know?'

'You've heard the evidence proving that the cases loaded at Yokohama contained aero engines. There was no justification for believing – '

'We know now they was full of aero engines,' Higgins said quickly. 'But I'm telling you wot we thought at the time. We thought they was full of explosives.'

'But you'd seen the manifest,' Holland reminded him. 'Mr Patch even posted a copy of it on the crew's notice board.'

'What difference does that make?' Higgins demanded angrily. 'A crew don't 'ave ter believe everything that's posted on their notice board. An' let me tell you, mister, men that sail in ships like the *Mary Deare* don't go much by the manifest, pertickly in the China Seas. We may be uneddicated, but we ain't stupid. A manifest is just a piece of paper somebody's written what he wants believed on. Least, that's the way I look at it – an' I've me reasons for doin' so.'

There was no answer to that. The outburst called for a rebuke from the Chairman, but it was given mildly. Higgins was accepted for what he was, a piece of human flotsam speaking with the voice of experience. In a sense he was magnificent. He dominated that drab court. But not by the power of his personality, which was crude. He dominated it because he was different, because he was the obverse of the coin of human nature, a colourful, lawless buccaneer who didn't give a damn for authority.

'In other words,' Holland said, 'you've known a lot of strange things happen aboard ships around the world. Now, have you ever known a stranger set of circumstances than those that happened aboard the *Mary Deare*?'

Higgins pursed his lips, then shook his head. 'No, I can't say I 'ave.'

'Take the flooding of the for'ard holds. You say you didn't think it was an explosion of some sort.'

'I didn't say nuthing of the kind. I said I didn't think about it, not at the time. There was a lot of other things ter think aba't. Anyway, I wasn't on the bridge.'

'And what's your opinion now?'

Higgins shook his head. 'I don't know wot ter think.'

'And what about the fires? Were they natural outbreaks?'

'Ah, the fires – that's different.' His cunning little eyes darted a glance to where Patch sat, watching him with a tense face.

'You think they were started deliberately?'

'Yes, I reckon so.'

'You suspect somebody then?'

'I don't know about that. But,' he added, 'I knew we was in fer trouble as soon as 'e come aboard.' And he nodded his hard bollard of head towards Patch. 'Stands ter reason, a man wiv 'is record don't get the job fer nuthing – and then the skipper dying so convenient-like.'

'Are you blaming somebody for Captain Taggart's death?' There was a note of censure in Holland's voice.

'I ain't blamin' anyone. But somebody swiped the poor devil's liquor and all I say is it only did one man any good.'

An excited buzz ran round the court as Holland sat down. Fenton was immediately on his feet. It was a disgraceful allegation, made without a shred of evidence to support it. And the Chairman agreed, leaning forward and asking Higgins whether it wasn't true that Taggart had accused several of the officers. And when Higgins admitted that it was, he said, 'Yourself as well?'

'The poor devil was ravin',' Higgins declared angrily.

'So he's raving when he accuses you, but not when he accuses Mr Patch, is that it?' Bowen-Lodge's voice was icy.

'Well, it didn't do me no good, him dying,' Higgins muttered.

'I put it to you that Captain Taggart just ran out of liquor.'

But Higgins shook his head. 'There was a lot of stuff brought off to 'im by a ship's chandler in Aden. 'E couldn't 've drunk it all in the time. It weren't 'umingly possible.'

'What did you think about it at the time? Did you take his accusations seriously?'

'No, why should I? When a man's ravin' the way he was, you don't know wot ter believe.' Higgins had a baffled look as though he wasn't sure where the questions were leading. 'Mebbe 'e 'ad liquor, an' mebbe 'e didn't,' he muttered hoarsely. 'Mebbe somebody pinched it – I dunno. All I know is, we searched the 'ole bloomin' ship fer 'im, jus' ter make 'im 'appy, 'an we didn't find a single bottle wot belonged to 'im. 'Course,' he added, 'if we'd known as 'ow 'e was goin' ter die fer lack of the stuff, there's some of us, as was plannin' ter smuggle the odd bottle through the Customs, who'd 've chipped in ter 'elp 'im, as the sayin' is.'

Bowen-Lodge nodded and Fenton started to question Higgins, trying to get him to admit that Patch had never given the order to stand-by to abandon ship, trying to confuse him and break him down over little details. But Higgins was a dangerous witness to cross-examine. He made it clear with every answer that he didn't trust Patch, and he didn't budge an inch from his original testimony.

But with Sir Lionel it was different. His interest was the cargo. What had led the witness to believe that the cases loaded at Yokohama contained explosives? Had he discovered something whilst he was loading the cases? But when the Chairman put the question, Higgins said he hadn't been a member of the ship's company at the time the cases were loaded.

'When did your employment as second officer commence then?' Bowen-Lodge asked.

'The day before the ship sailed,' Higgins answered. 'By then she was all loaded up, hatches battened down an' lying out in the fairway.'

'You were shown the manifest?'

'No. I never saw the manifest, not till later.'

'Then what gave you the idea that the cargo contained explosives?'

'There was rumours around the docks.'

'And amongst the crew?'

'Yes.'

'Have you ever known explosives packed in cases clearly marked as aero engines?'

'Not exactly. But I've heard of explosives bein' packed and marked as other things, to avoid the regulations as you might say.'

'But you had no definite indication that the cases might contain other than what was stated on the manifest?'

'No.'

'And you did your utmost to scotch this rumour?'

For the first time Higgins showed uncertainty. 'Well, no, to be honest I can't say I did.'

'Why not?'

The muscles along Higgins's neck thickened. 'Well, if it comes ter that, why should I? Wasn't none of my business.'

Bowen-Lodge glanced across at Sir Lionel with one eyebrow raised. The next question concerned the four days the ship was moored in the Rangoon River. Yes, Higgins admitted, he had gone ashore with the rest. Well, why not? It wasn't every day the owners gave a ship's company forty-eight hours ashore, expenses paid. The reason? Mr Dellimare was a good bloke, that's why – knew how to treat a crew, believed in a happy ship.

'When you got back to the ship – ' Sir Lionel was now putting his questions direct to the witness again – 'did you talk to any of the officers or men of the *Torre Annunziata*?'

'Yes. The first officer, a bloke called Slade, came aboard for a drink wiv me and the Chief.'

'Did you ask them why they had been shifting cargo around?'

'No. But Slade tol' me they'd 'ad ter do it because of some clerical mess-up over the destination of the steel tubes they were due to load.'

'Did you talk to Adams about it?'

'No.'

'But you saw him when you got back on board?'

'Yes.'

'Did he suggest that the crew of the *Torre Annunziata* had been tampering with the *Mary Deare*'s cargo?'

'No.' And then he added quickly, 'An' if they 'ad, 'e'd 've known about it 'cos when I saw 'im, 'e was up an' about an' feelin' better fer 'is two days in bed.'

'Adams being sick, I take it you were in charge of the loading of the cotton cargo?' Higgins nodded and Sir Lionel then asked him, 'Did you notice any change in the disposition of the cargo?'

'No, can't say I did.'

'You're quite certain?'

' 'Course I'm certain.'

Sir Lionel's small head shot forward and his voice was suddenly crisp and hard as he said, 'How could you be? You said you joined the ship after she was loaded?'

But Higgins wasn't easily put out. His tongue passed over the dry line of his lips. But that was the only sign of uneasiness he gave. 'I may not 've bin there when she was loaded. But I was when we discharged our top cargo of Japanese cotton an' rayon goods. I took special note of 'ow the cases was stowed 'cos I guessed I'd 'ave to load the bales of raw cotton when they was ready.'

Sir Lionel nodded. 'Just one more question. You say you didn't go aboard the *Mary Deare* until the day before she sailed. How was that?'

'Well, I wasn't took on till then.'

'Who engaged you – Captain Taggart?'

'No, Mr Dellimare. Oh, Captain Taggart signed the papers. But it was Dellimare wot engaged me.'

'Why?'

Higgins frowned. ' 'Ow d'you mean?'

'I asked you why he engaged you. Were you the only man who applied for the vacancy?'

'Well, not exactly. I mean . . .' Higgins glanced round the court and again his tongue passed along his lips. 'It didn't 'appen like that.'

'You mean the job wasn't offered in the usual way? You were engaged by Mr Dellimare privately?'

'I suppose so.' Higgins sounded reluctant.

'Perhaps you would be good enough to explain to the Court how it happened.'

Higgins hesitated. 'Well, we 'appened ter meet, as you might say, an' 'e was short of a second officer an' I wanted a berth, an' that's all there was to it.'

'Where did you meet?'

'Some bar da'n by the waterfront. Don't remember the name of it.'

'By arrangement?'

Higgins's face was reddening, the muscles on his neck swelling. 'Yes, by arrangement.' He said it angrily as though challenging Sir Lionel to make something of it.

But Sir Lionel only said, 'Thank you. That was what I wanted to know.' And sat down. He had established two things: that, if the Dellimare Company were planning to wreck the *Mary Deare*, the vital shift of cargo was a possibility, and that Higgins could have been the instrument of their choice. But he had nothing definite against Higgins and that, he admitted to Hal long afterwards, was the real trouble. To justify his clients in withholding payment of the insurance claim he had to have something more positive.

It was the evidence of the other survivors that finally decided him, and the most damaging evidence was that of the helmsman, Yules, who had been on the bridge with Higgins when the fire broke out. He was timid and he gave his evidence with a slight stutter. He wasn't a very strong witness, but he clung to his statement that Patch had given the order to stand by to abandon ship with unshakeable obstinacy. He even had the words off pat, and though Patch's counsel rose to the occasion and had him so terrified that he kept on looking to Higgins for support, he never budged.

He was the last witness before lunch and I didn't need Hal to tell me that Patch would have a bad time of it when he took the stand for examination by the various counsel. The Court hadn't begun to get at the truth yet. But what was the truth? Hal asked me that over lunch and all I could say was, 'God knows.'

'Dellimare couldn't have started that fire in the hold,' he said, and I agreed. Dellimare was dead by then. It had to be Higgins. Evidently Bowen-Lodge had also considered this possibility over his lunch, for, when the Court reassembled, he had Yules recalled and questioned him closely about the movements of the officer of the watch. And Yules swore that Higgins had been on the bridge from 20.00 hours and hadn't once left it. Later, Burrows, the chief engineer officer, testified that Higgins had been playing poker with him and two members of the crew who had been drowned, from 17.00 hours to 20.00 hours with only a brief break for food.

One after the other the survivors went into the witness box, each from his different angle corroborating what had gone before – the certainty that the ship was jinxed, that she carried explosives and that she was destined to go to the bottom. It was the story of men carrying within themselves the seeds of inevitable tragedy.

And then at last Holland called 'Gideon Patch' and he was standing there in the witness box again, slightly stooped, his hands gripping the rail, knuckles as white as the pallor of his face. He looked worried sick and the twitch was there at the corner of his mouth.

Bowen-Lodge questioned him first – questioned him in minute detail about the orders he had given after the fire broke out. He had him go through the whole thing again from the moment Rice had rushed into his cabin to report the outbreak. Then, when Patch had told it exactly as he'd told it before, Bowen-Lodge gave a little shrug and Holland took up the questioning again. And all the time it was obvious that something was being kept back. You could sense it in the way the man stood there with that hunted look on his face and his body all tense and trembling. And the questions went back and forth with nobody making any sense out of it and Patch sticking to his statement that he had been knocked out and that the fire had been started deliberately.

'Yes, but by whom?' Bowen-Lodge demanded.

And Patch had answered in a flat, colourless voice, 'That is for the Court to decide.'

After that the ball had been tossed to the counsel representing the interested parties and they hounded him with questions about Taggart and Dellimare, about his handling of the crew, about the seaworthiness of the ship, and then finally the counsel for the Marine Officers' Association was on his feet, going back once again over the orders he'd given the night the ship was abandoned, and Bowen-Lodge was beginning to glance at the clock.

At last Sir Lionel rose, and his questions were all about the cargo. If Patch could have said that those cases were empty or contained something other than aero engines, that would have been that and Sir Lionel would have been satisfied. But he couldn't say it and the questions went on and on until Sir Lionel had exhausted all the possibilities. He paused then and seemed on the point of sitting down. He was bending forward, peering at some notes and he looked up over his reading glasses and said, 'Perhaps Mr Learned Chairman, you would ask the witness to tell me how he came to be on the *Mary Deare*.'

The question was put and Patch answered, quite unsuspecting, that he thought he had already explained that he had replaced Mr Adams who had been taken to hospital suffering from jaundice.

'Yes, yes, quite,' Sir Lionel said impatiently. 'What I meant was, who signed you on – Captain Taggart or Mr Dellimare?'

'Captain Taggart.'

'He came ashore and made the choice himself?'

'No.'

'Who did come ashore then and make the choice?' Sir Lionel's voice still sounded bored. He gave the impression that he was dealing with a small routine point.

'Mr Dellimare.'

'Mr Dellimare?' Sir Lionel's face was suddenly expressive of surprise. 'I see. And was it done privately, a meeting in some bar – by arrangement?' His tone carried the bite of sarcasm in it.

'No. We met at the agents'.'

'At the agents'? Then there were probably other unemployed officers there?'

'Yes. Two.'

'Why didn't Mr Dellimare choose one of them? Why did he choose you?'

'The others withdrew when they heard that the vacancy was for the *Mary Deare*.'

'But you did not withdraw. Why?' And when Patch didn't answer, Sir Lionel said, 'I want to know why?'

'Because I needed the berth.'

'How long had you been without a ship?'

'Eleven months.'

'And before that you hadn't been able to get anything better than the job of second mate on a miserable little Italian steamer called the *Apollo* working the coastal ports of East Africa. Didn't you think it strange that a man with your record should suddenly find himself first officer of a 6000-ton ocean-going ship?' And when Patch didn't say anything, Sir Lionel repeated, 'Didn't you think it strange?'

And all Patch could say, with the eyes of the whole Court on him, was, 'I never considered it.'

'You – never – considered it!' Sir Lionel stared at him – the tone of his voice, the carriage of his head all indicating that he thought him a liar. And then he turned to Bowen-Lodge. 'Perhaps, Mr Learned Chairman, you would ask the witness to give a brief resumé of the events that occurred on the night of 3rd/4th February nine years ago in the region of Singapore?'

Patch's grip on the rail in front of him tightened. His face looked ghastly – trapped. The courtroom stirred as though the first breath of a storm had rustled through it. Bowen-Lodge looked down at the questioner. 'The *Belle Isle*?' he enquired. And then, still in the same whisper of an aside, 'Do you consider that necessary, Sir Lionel?'

'Absolutely,' was the firm and categorical reply.

Bowen-Lodge glanced up at the clock again and then he put the question to Patch. And Patch, rigid, and tight-lipped, said, 'There was a report issued at the time, sir.'

Bowen-Lodge looked across at Sir Lionel, a mute question to discover whether he wished to pursue the matter. It was obvious that he did. You could see it in the stillness with which he watched the man in the witness box, his small head thrust a little forward as though about to strike. 'I am well aware that there is a report available,' he said in a cold, icy voice. 'Nevertheless, I think it right that the Court should hear the story from your own lips.'

'It's not for me to give my views on it when a Court has already pronounced judgement,' Patch said in a tight, restrained voice.

'I was not asking for your views. I was asking for a resumé of the facts.'

Patch's hand hit the rail involuntarily. 'I cannot see that it has any bearing on the loss of the *Mary Deare*.' His voice was louder, harsher.

'That is not for you to say,' Sir Lionel snapped. And then – needling him – 'There are certain similarities.'

'Similarities!' Patch stared at him. And then, beating with his hand on the rail, he burst out: 'By God, there are.' He turned to face the Chairman – still angry, goaded beyond the limits of what a man will stand. 'You want the sordid details. Very well. I was drunk. Dead drunk. That's what Craven said in evidence, anyway. It was hot like the inside of an oven that day in Singapore.' He was still staring at the Chairman, but not seeing him any more, seeing only Singapore on the day he'd smashed up his career. 'Damp, sweaty, torrid heat,' he murmured. 'I remember that and I remember taking the *Belle Isle* out. And after that I don't remember a thing.'

'And were you drunk?' Bowen-Lodge asked. His voice was modulated, almost gentle.

'Yes, I suppose so . . . in a sense. I'd had a few drinks. But not enough,' Patch added violently. 'Not enough to put me out like a light.' And then, after a pause, he added, 'They ran her aground on the Anambas Islands at 02.23 hours in the morning with a thundering surf running and she broke her back.'

'You are aware,' Sir Lionel said quietly, 'that there has been a lot of talk since . . . suggesting that you did it for the insurance.'

Patch rounded on him. 'I could hardly be unaware of it,' he said with wild sarcasm, 'seeing that all these years I've barely been able to scratch a living in my own chosen profession.' He turned back to the Chairman, gripping hold of the rail. 'They said I ordered the course and they had the log to prove it. It was there in my own handwriting. Craven – he was the second officer – swore that he'd been down to my cabin to query it and that I'd bawled him out. Later he took a fix and then came down to my cabin to warn me again, but I was in a drunken stupor – those were his words – and when he couldn't wake me, he went back to the bridge and altered course on his own responsibility. By then, of course, it was too late. That was his story, and he stuck to it so well that everybody believed him, even my own counsel.' He had turned his head and was looking across the courtroom at Higgins. 'By God,' he repeated, 'there are similarities.'

'What similarities?' Sir Lionel asked in a light tone of disbelief.

Patch turned to face him. It was pitiful to see how easily he was goaded. 'Just this,' he almost shouted. 'Craven was a liar. The log entry was forged. The *Belle Isle* was owned by a bunch of Greek crooks in Glasgow. They were on the verge of bankruptcy. The insurance money just about saved them. It was all in the papers six months later. That was when the rumours started.'

'And you had nothing to do with it, I suppose?' Sir Lionel asked.

'No.'

'And this man Craven had slipped a micky into your drink. Is that what you're suggesting?'

It took away from him and destroyed his defence. His muttered 'Yes' was painful anti-climax. Bowen-Lodge intervened then. 'Are you suggesting a similarity between this Greek company and the Dellimare Trading and Shipping Company?' he asked.

And Patch, fighting back, cried, 'Yes. Yes, that's exactly what I am suggesting.'

It brought the Dellimare Company's counsel on to his feet, protesting that it was a monstrous allegation, an unwarranted aspersion on a man who was dead at the time the fire broke out in the hold. And Bowen-Lodge nodded and said, 'Quite, Mr Smiles – unless there is some justification.' He turned to Patch then and said, 'Have you any reason for making such an allegation?'

Now, I thought – now he must tell them about Dellimare's offer. Whether he had evidence to support it, or not, it was the only thing for him to do. But, instead, he drove home his accusation on the basis of motive and opportunity; the Company in liquidation and the only people who would benefit by the loss of the ship. 'Why else should the owner have been on board?' he demanded. A voyage of almost five months! It was a ridiculous waste of a director's time, unless there was a reason for his being on the ship. 'And I say there was,' he declared.

Smiles jumped to his feet again, but Bowen-Lodge forestalled him. 'You seem to be forgetting the cause of the ship being abandoned and finally lost. Are you accusing Mr Dellimare of causing the fire in that after hold?'

It brought Patch up with a jolt. 'No,' he said.

'He was dead by then?'

'Yes.' Patch's voice had dropped to a whisper.

And then Smiles, still on his feet, asked what possible motive the Company could have in destroying the ship. 'She was bound for the scrap yards and in the figures Mr Gundersen has given you, Mr Learned Chairman, you will find that the scrap value was fixed at a little over £15,000. She was insured for £30,000. Is the witness suggesting that a mere £15,000 was sufficient motive to induce a company to endanger the lives of a whole ship's crew?'

'The question of motive,' Bowen-Lodge said, 'does not come within the scope of this Investigation. We are concerned solely with the facts.' He glanced towards Sir Lionel as though expecting something further from him.

'I think at this stage, Mr Learned Chairman,' Sir Lionel said, 'I should ask you to put this very serious question to the witness – Did he, or did he not, on the night of 18 March, set fire to Number Three hold of the *Mary Deare*, or cause it to be set on fire?' A sort of gasp like an eager shudder ran through the courtroom.

The eyes of the two men, Counsel and Chairman, remained fixed on each other for a moment, and then Bowen-Lodge nodded slowly and turned to face the witness. Looking down on him and speaking quietly, but with great distinctness, he said, 'I think it my duty to tell you that in my opinion this whole matter of the loss of the *Mary Deare* will be the subject of a case in another Court and to advise you that you need not answer this very direct question if you do not wish to. Having so advised you, I will now put the question.' And he repeated it.

'No, I did not,' Patch declared, and his voice was clear and firm. And then he added, turning to face Sir Lionel Falcett, 'If I'd set fire to the ship, why should I go to the trouble of putting it out?'

It was a good point, but Sir Lionel only shrugged. 'We have to consider that she might have gone aground on the nearby reefs, perhaps the coast of France, only partially burned out. The evidence would be better sunk in twenty fathoms of water. There was a gale coming up and then you had Mr Sands' arrival to consider – '

Bowen-Lodge gave a discreet little warning cough and Sir Lionel murmured his apologies. The Chairman looked up at the clock again and then leaned over and conferred with his assessors. Finally he adjourned the Court. 'Until ten-thirty tomorrow, gentlemen.'

Nobody moved for a moment, and even when they did, I sat there, stunned and angry at the injustice of it. To take a man's record and fling it in his face like that, to damn him without a shred of evidence . . . and there was Patch still standing stiff and rigid in the witness box – and Sir Lionel, picking up his papers and smiling at some little joke made by one of the other lawyers.

Patch was moving now, crossing the floor of the court. Without thinking I started forward to meet him, but Hal put his hand on my arm. 'Better leave him now,' he said. 'He needs to think it out, poor devil.'

'Think what out?' I asked angrily. I was still wrought up by the injustice of it.

'What he's going to say tomorrow,' Hal answered. And then he added, 'He hasn't told the whole story yet and Lionel Falcett knows it. He can tell it tomorrow, or he can tell it in the criminal courts! But he's got to tell it some time.'

The criminal courts. 'Yes, I suppose it will come to that,' I murmured. But before that, the truth had to be uncovered. And the truth, whatever it was, lay out on the Minkies. 'I must have a word with him,' I said. I had suddenly made up my mind and was forcing my way through the crowd towards Patch.

He didn't hear me when I called to him. He seemed oblivious to everything but the need to get out of the place. I caught hold of him, and he turned abruptly with a nervous start. 'Oh, it's you.' He was trembling. 'Well, what is it?'

I stared at him, horrified by the haggard, hunted look in his face. There were beads of sweat still on his forehead. 'Why in God's name didn't you tell them?' I said.

'Tell them what?' His eyes had suddenly gone blank of all expression.

'About Dellimare,' I said. 'Why didn't you tell them?'

His eyes flickered and slid away from me. 'How could I?' he breathed. And then, as I started to tell him that the Court had a right to the truth, he said, 'Leave it at that, can't you? Just leave it at that.' And he turned on his heel and walked quickly away towards the exit.

I went after him then. I couldn't leave it like that. I had to give him the chance he'd asked for. I pushed through a little knot of the *Mary Deare*'s crew and caught him up in the corridor outside. 'Listen,' I said. 'I'll take you out there – as soon as the Enquiry is over.'

He shook his head, still walking towards the freedom of the main doors. 'It's too late now,' he said.

His attitude exasperated me and I caught hold of his arm, checking him. 'Don't you understand? I'm offering you my boat,' I said. '*Sea Witch* is lying in Lulworth Cove. We could be over there in twenty-four hours.'

He rounded on me then. 'I tell you it's too late.' He almost snarled the words at me. And then his eyes slid past me, narrowing suddenly and blazing with anger. I felt his muscles tense, and then he had freed himself from me and was walking away. I turned to find Higgins standing there. He had Yules with him and they were both staring after Patch. All around me people were moving, whispering, watching Patch walking down the corridor, fascinated by the thought that he might be guilty of sending a lot of men to their death.

I turned to look for Hal, but Higgins caught hold of my arm, so that I was instantly conscious of the colossal brute strength of the man. 'I 'eard wot you said just then.' His throaty voice was full of the smell of stale beer as he thrust his head close to mine. 'If you think you're goin' ter take 'im a't there . . .' He checked himself quickly, his small, blood-veined eyes narrowed, and he let go of my arm. 'Wot I mean is . . . well, you steer clear of 'im,' he rasped. ' 'E's a wrong 'un – yer can take my word fer it. You'll only get yerself inter trouble.' And he turned quickly and went ploughing off down the corridor, little Yules hurrying after him.

A moment later Hal joined me. His face was serious. 'I've been talking to Lionel Falcett,' he said, as we moved off towards the entrance. 'It's as I thought. They think he's hiding something.'

'Who – Patch?' I was still shaken by what Higgins had said, wondering if he'd guessed that I'd been referring to the *Mary Deare*.

'Yes. It's only an impression, mind you. Lionel didn't say anything, but . . .' He hesitated. 'Do you know where Patch is staying?' And when I nodded, he said, 'Well, if you're absolutely certain of the chap, I'd get hold of him and tell him what the form is. It's the truth, and the whole truth now, if he wants to keep clear of trouble. That's my advice, anyway. Get hold of him tonight.'

We went into the pub across the road and had a drink. I phoned Patch from there. It was a lodging house down by the docks and the landlady told me that he'd come in, got his coat and gone out again. I phoned him later when we arrived at Bosham and once after dinner, but he still hadn't returned. It worried me and, going to bed early, I found it difficult to sleep. Rain was lashing at the window and in the twilight of half-consciousness Patch and Higgins wandered through my mind. I pictured Patch walking the streets of Southampton, walking endlessly to a decision that would justify his cry that my offer was too late and leave him just something to be identified in a mortuary.

In the morning, of course, it all seemed different. The sun was shining and there was a blackbird singing, and as we drove into Southampton, the world was going about its prosaic, everyday life – delivery vans and postmen on bicycles and kids going to school. It was ten-fifteen when we reached the court. We had arrived early so that I could have a word with Patch before the Investigation was resumed. But he hadn't arrived yet. Only a few of the witnesses were there, Higgins among them, his big body slewed round in his seat, watching the entrance.

Across the court several of the lawyers had come in and were standing together in a little knot, talking in low voices. The Press desk was filling up; the public gallery, too. Hal left me and went to his seat, and I moved out into the corridor and stood there, watching the people filing slowly in, searching for Patch amongst the faces that thronged the narrow passage-way.

'Mr Sands.' A hand touched my arm, and I turned to find Janet Taggart standing beside me, her eyes unnaturally large in the pallor of her face. 'Where is he? I can't find him.'

'Who?'

'Mr Patch. He's not in the courtroom. Do you know where he is, please?'

'No.'

She hesitated, unsure of herself. 'I'm terribly worried,' she murmured.

I stared at her, wondering how it was she had come to share my own fears. 'You should have thought of that before,' I said brutally and watched the muscles of her face contract so that the features looked small and pinched. She was different now from the sunny-smiling kid of the photograph, and the light wasn't shining on her hair any more. She looked grown up, a woman. 'He'll be here in a moment,' I said more gently, trying to calm her fears, and my own.

'Yes,' she said. 'Yes, of course.' She stood there, hesitating, her face taut. 'I went to see him last night. I didn't understand – not until I read the evidence of Higgins and the others.' She stared at me, her eyes big and scared-looking. 'He told me everything then. He was so – ' She stopped there with a little shrug, uncertain of herself and what she was saying. 'You do think he's all right, don't you?' And then, because I didn't answer, she said, 'Oh God! I could kill myself for the things I said.' But she wasn't speaking to me. She was speaking to herself.

I heard the Court rise. The corridor was empty. There was still no sign of Patch. 'We'd better go in,' I said gently.

She nodded, not saying anything more, and we went into the courtroom together and took our seats. Holland was on his feet. He had a piece of paper in his hand and he turned to face Bowen-Lodge as silence descended on the room. 'Mr Learned Chairman. I have just received information from the Receiver of Wreck to the effect that the *Mary Deare* is not sunk. The Harbour Master at St Helier, Jersey Island, has reported that the vessel lies stranded on the Plateau des Minquiers and that a French salvage company is endeavouring to refloat her.'

The gasp of surprise that greeted this news swept through the courtroom, gathering force as people gave voice to their astonishment. Men in the Press desk were on their feet. I caught sight of Higgins, sitting with a dazed look on his face. There was still no sign of Patch.

Bowen-Lodge leaned forward over his desk. 'This alters the situation entirely, Mr Holland. I take it that it means that the Receiver of Wreck will be able to make a full examination of the wreck.' And when Holland nodded, he added, 'I presume you have discussed it with him. How long before he can report to the Court?'

'He's not sure about that,' Holland answered. 'He doesn't yet know the exact position of the *Mary Deare* on the reefs nor has he any information as to the identity of the salvage company. He is making enquiries. But he informs me that the legal position may be complicated – the Minkies being part of the Channel Islands and the company concerned being French. It is a question of the Crown's rights and the rights of the salvage company. He also stated that the tides in this area, which rise and fall by over thirty feet, made the reefs particularly dangerous and, as far as the cargo was concerned, any examination might have to wait on the successful refloating of the vessel.'

'I see. Thank you, Mr Holland.' Bowen-Lodge nodded and turned to his assessors. He conferred with them, heads close together, whilst the sound of people talking broke like a wave again over the court. The Press desk was empty now. 'Well, that's that,' Hal whispered to me. 'He'll adjourn the Court now.' And then he said, 'Did you know she wasn't sunk?' And when I nodded, he said, 'Good God man! You must be daft.'

Bowen-Lodge had separated from his assessors now and he tapped with his gavel to silence the court. 'There are one or two questions, Mr Holland, arising out of the discovery that the ship is not sunk. Please recall your last witness.'

Holland nodded and called, 'Gideon Patch.'

The court was still, nobody moved.

'Gideon Patch!' And when he still didn't appear, Holland turned to the usher on the door and said, 'Call Gideon Patch.' The name was repeated, echoing in the emptiness of the corridors outside. But still nothing happened. Necks craned in the public gallery; the buzz of conversation rose again.

They waited several minutes for him, and the silence in the court was so absolute that you could almost hear the ticking of the clock. And then, after a brief discussion with the assessors, Bowen-Lodge adjourned the Court for one hour. 'At twelve o'clock please, gentlemen.' The court stood and then everybody was talking at once, and down by the jury box Higgins, Yules and Burrows stood in a little bunch with their heads close together. And then Higgins broke away from them suddenly and came lumbering towards the door. His eyes met mine for a second, and they had the dead, flat look of a man who is scared.

The wait seemed a long one. There was no news. All we could learn was that enquiries were being made at Patch's lodgings. 'A fat lot of good that will do,' was Hal's comment. 'A warrant and the police is the only thing now.' We had nothing to say to each other as we waited. He had accepted Patch's guilt as proved. Others took the same view. Scraps of comment came to me from the waiting crowd: 'Wot I say is, he's no better than a murderer . . . You can always tell, old boy. It's the eyes that give them away every time . . . And what about Dellimare and that poor Captain Taggart? . . . 'Course 'e did. Wouldn't you do a bunk if you'd killed 'alf the crew . . .' And all the time I was trying to reconcile the sort of man they thought he was with the man I had known on the *Mary Deare*.

At length the crowd began to drift back into the courtroom. As they did so a rumour ran from mouth to mouth – Patch hadn't been seen since the previous evening. Bowen-Lodge and the assessors entered and there was silence as Holland rose to say that he regretted he was not able to produce his chief witness.

'Have the police been requested to take action?' Bowen-Lodge asked.

'Yes. A search has been instituted.' There was a moment's silence as Bowen-Lodge fiddled with the papers on his desk.

'Would you care to re-examine any of the witnesses?' Holland asked.

Bowen-Lodge hesitated. He was looking over the available witnesses and for a moment I thought his cold, searching gaze was fixed on me. Finally he leaned over in conference with his assessors. I felt the shirt sticking to my body. What the hell was I going to say if he recalled me? How was I going to explain my failure to tell them the ship was on the Minkies?

The minute I was kept in suspense seemed a long time. And then Bowen-Lodge said, 'I don't think there is any point in recalling any of the witnesses now, Mr Holland.' He looked up at the court. 'In view of the fact that the *Mary Deare* has been located, the assessors and I are agreed that no further purpose can be served by continuing this Investigation, particularly as the chief witness is no longer available. I am, therefore, adjourning the Court indefinitely pending examination of the wreck. All witnesses are released. You will be notified in due course should further evidence be required of you. Thank you, gentlemen, for your attendance.'

It was over, the Chairman and assessors gone, the courtroom emptying. As I made my way towards the door, Higgins stepped forward, blocking my path. 'Where is 'e?' he demanded. 'Where's 'e gone?'

I stared at him, wondering why he should be so worked up over Patch's disappearance. He ought to have been pleased. 'What's it got to do with you?' I asked him.

Beady eyes searched my face, peering at me over sagging pouches. 'So you do know, eh? I said you would.'

'As it happens,' I said, 'I don't know. I wish I did.'

'To hell with that!' The violence inside him bubbled to the surface. 'You think I don't know what yer up to – you with your boat lyin' in Lulworth, waiting for 'im. Well, I tell yer, if that's yer game, wotch a't, that's all.' He stared at me, his small eyes narrowed, and then he turned abruptly and left us.

As we walked down the corridor, Hal said, 'You're not going to be a fool and try and slip him out of the country, are you?' He was looking at me, his face serious, a little worried.

'No,' I said. 'I don't think it ever occurred to him that that was a way out.'

He nodded, but I don't think he was convinced. He would have pressed the point further, but as we went out into the sunshine, he was greeted by a man in a reefer with a little pointed beard and greying hair. He had a high, rather strident voice, and, as I waited, I heard him say to Hal, 'Oh, not your type, Colonel – definitely not.' There was something about a motor boat, and then: '. . . rang up about an hour and a half ago. They had her on charter a month back . . . Yes, old *Griselda*. You remember. Dry rot in the keel and rolls like a bastard.' He went off with a high-pitched laugh and Hal rejoined me. Apparently the man was a yacht broker down at Bosham. 'Odd place, this, for him to do business,' Hal said. And then he added, 'I wonder if it's the Dellimare Company, chartering a boat to go out and see what the French salvage people are up to. I wouldn't be surprised.'

We started to walk to the car and he went on talking, giving me some advice about not leaving it too late. But I was thinking of Higgins. Why had Patch's disappearance scared him?

'John. You're not listening.'

'No. I'm sorry.'

'Well, that's not surprising. Nobody listens to advice.' We had reached the car. 'But if it comes to a criminal case, see that you give them the full story, just as it happened. Don't leave it to be dragged out of you in cross-examination. They'll play hell with you, and you may find yourself in real trouble.'

'All right,' I said.

We drove down to the police station then to see if there was any news of Patch. But all the sergeant at the desk could tell us was that he had been seen in a number of pubs in the dock area and had spent part of the night at an all-night café out on the Portsmouth road. He had got a lift about four in the morning in a truck headed back towards Southampton. They were now trying to trace the truck driver.

We hung around for a little, but there was no further news. 'And it's my opinion,' the sergeant added darkly, 'that there won't be any – 'cept for the finding of the body as you might say. The people at the café described him as desperate – looked like death, the report says.'

Hal drove me to the railway station then, and when he had gone I bought an evening paper. Without thinking I found myself looking at the forecast. Winds moderate, north-westerly. As I stood waiting for my train I was thinking of Higgins and the Dellimare Company and the fact that the Minkies were only a day's sail from Lulworth.

PART THREE

I

'*Sea Witch!* Ahoy! Ahoy, *Sea Witch!*'

Gulls wheeled, screaming, and my voice came back to me, a lonely shout in the drizzling rain. The yacht lay motionless in the crater of the cove, the reflection of her black topsides shattered every now and then as cat's-paws of wind riffled the mirror-surface of the water. The waves of a swell broke in the entrance and, all round, the hills loomed ghostly and grey in the mist, all colour lost, their grass slopes dropping to the dirty white of the chalk cliffs. There wasn't a soul about.

'Ahoy! *Sea Witch!*' A figure moved on the deck, a splash of yellow oilskins; the clatter of oars and then the dinghy was coming to meet me. It grounded with a crunch on the wet shingle and I climbed in and Mike rowed me out. I was relieved to find that I didn't have to tell him about the Enquiry; he had followed it all in the newspapers. But once we were on board with the dinghy made fast and my gear stowed, he began to ask questions – what had happened to Patch, why hadn't he turned up at the Court this morning? 'You know they've issued a warrant for his arrest?'

'A warrant? How do you know?' I asked. I don't know why, but it shocked me. It seemed so pointless.

'It was on the six o'clock news.'

'Did it say what the charge was?'

'No. But they've got police checks on all the roads leading out of Southampton and they're keeping watch on the ports.'

We discussed it during the meal. There were only the two of us. Ian had gone home to visit his people. Mike was to phone him as soon as we were ready to start operations again, but he hadn't done so yet because the latest forecast was wind moderate north-westerly, backing westerly later and becoming fresh, with the outlook unsettled. The thing that puzzled Mike most about the whole business was why Patch hadn't told the Court about Delli-mare's offer. Not having been present at the Enquiry, but only reading the reports, it was natural, I suppose, that he should still retain a vivid impression of Patch's visit, and over coffee he suddenly reminded me of the package I had been given at Paim-

309

pol. 'I suppose it couldn't contain some vital piece of evidence?'
he said.

Until that moment I had forgotten all about it. 'If it had,' I
said, 'he would have asked me to produce it.'

'Have you still got it?'

I nodded and got up and went into the after cabin. It was still
there in my brief-case and I took it through into the saloon. Mike
had cleared a space on the table and I reached for a knife and cut
the string, feeling as I had done during the war on the occasions
when I had to deal with the effects of some poor devil who'd been
killed.

'Looks like a book of some sort,' Mike said. 'It couldn't be the
log, could it?'

'No,' I answered. 'The log was in Court.'

Inside the brown paper wrapping was an envelope. The name
J. C. B. Dellimare was typed on it and below, in blue pencil, was
scrawled the one word *Collect*. The envelope had been ripped open,
the tear crossing the stamped impress of a City bank. I had a
vague hope then that perhaps Mike was right – that it was some
sort of an account book belonging to Dellimare or the Company,
something that would reveal a financial motive. And then I slid
the contents on to the table and stared incredulously.

Lying amongst the supper things was a thick wad of five-pound
notes.

Mike was gazing at the pile, open-mouthed with astonishment.
He'd never seen so much cash in his life; neither of us had. I split
it between us. 'Count it!' I said.

For several seconds there wasn't a sound in the saloon except
the crackle of those Bank of England notes. And when we had
totalled it all up, it came to exactly £5,000, and Mike looked up at
me. 'No wonder he didn't want to bring it out through the
Customs himself,' he said. And then, after a pause, he added, 'Do
you think he accepted Dellimare's offer after all?'

But I shook my head. 'If he'd accepted, why put out the fire,
why beach her on the Minkies?' I was remembering the state of
that cabin when I'd gone in to help him get out the rubber
dinghy. 'No, he must have taken it afterwards – after the man
was dead.'

'But why?'

'God knows!' I shrugged my shoulders. There were so many
things I didn't understand. I gathered the notes together and put
them back in the envelope. 'If this were his payment for wrecking

the ship,' I said, 'he'd have been down here to collect it the instant he landed in England.'

'Yes, that's true.' Mike took the envelope from me, frowning and turning it over in his hand. 'Odd that he should have failed to collect it. It's almost as though he'd forgotten all about it.'

I nodded slowly. And then I went up on deck and lit the riding light. It wasn't really necessary; we were the only boat in the anchorage, and nobody was likely to come in on such a reeking night. But it gave me something to do. I lit a cigarette. It was quite dark now and we lay in a little pool of light, hemmed in by the iridescent curtain of the drizzle. The wind seemed to have died away. The water was very black and still. No ripples slapped against the topsides. The only sound was the faint murmur of wavelets on the beach. I stood there, smoking in the feeble glow of the riding light and wondering what the hell I was going to do with all that money. If I took it to the authorities, I should have to account for my possession of it. Or should I send it anonymously to form the basis of a fund for the dependants of those who had lost their lives? I certainly couldn't send it to his mother, and I was damned if I was going to return it to the Dellimare Company.

I stayed there, thinking about it, until my cigarette was a sodden butt. I threw it in the water then and went below. Mike was checking over one of the aqualungs. 'Care for a drink?' I asked him.

He nodded. 'Good idea.'

I got out the bottle and the glasses.

I didn't say anything. I didn't want to talk about it. I just sat there with my drink and a cigarette, going over the whole thing in my mind. We sat for a long time in silence.

I don't know who heard it first, but we were suddenly staring at each other, listening. It came from the bows, a sort of splashing sound. 'What is it?' Mike had got to his feet. The splashing ceased and then footsteps sounded on the deck above our heads. They came slowly aft, whilst we stood waiting, frozen into immobility. They reached the hatch. The cover was slid quietly back and bare feet appeared, followed by dripping trouser legs and then the body of a man all sodden with water; he was standing suddenly at the foot of the ladder, blinking in the light, his face pale as death, his black hair plastered to his skull and water streaming from his clothes on to the grating.

'Good God!' I breathed. I was too astonished to say anything else. He was shivering a bit and his teeth were chattering, and I

stood there, staring at him as though he were a ghost. 'If somebody would lend me a towel . . .' Patch began to strip off his wet
clothes.

'So Higgins was right,' I said.

'Higgins?'

'He said you'd make for *Sea Witch*.' And then I added, 'What
have you come here for? I thought you were dead.' God! I almost
wished he were as I realized the impossible position he'd put me
in. 'What the devil made you come here?'

He ignored my outburst. It was as though he hadn't heard or
had shut his mind to it. Mike had found him a towel and he began
to dry himself, standing naked, his hard, sinewy body still brown
with the heat of Aden. He was shivering and he asked for a
cigarette. I gave him one and he lit it and started to dry his hair.
'If you think we're going to slip you over to France, you're wrong,'
I said. 'I won't do it.'

He looked at me then, frowning a little. 'France?' The muscles
of his jaw tightened. 'It's the Minkies I want to get to,' he said.
'You promised to take me there. You offered me your boat.' A
sudden urgency was in his voice.

I stared at him. Surely to God he didn't still want to go out to
the Minkies? 'That was last night,' I said.

'Last night – tonight . . . what difference does it make?' The
pitch of his voice had risen. He had stopped towelling himself and
suddenly there was doubt in his face. It was as though he had
come here in the certainty that when he had arrived everything
would be all right, and suddenly he knew it wasn't.

'You probably don't know it,' I said, trying to soften the blow,
'but there's a warrant out for your arrest.'

He showed no surprise. It was as though he had expected it.
'I was walking for a long time last night,' he said, 'trying to make
up my mind. In the end I knew I'd never reach the *Mary Deare*
if I went into that Court this morning. So I came here. I walked
from Swanage and I've been up on the hills half the day, waiting
for it to get dark.'

'Have you seen a paper?' I asked him.

'No. Why?'

'The *Mary Deare* has been located and a French salvage
company is endeavouring to refloat her. A full examination is to
be made of the wreck, and if you think there's any point – '

'A full examination.' He seemed shocked. 'When?' And then
he added, 'It was announced in Court, was it?'

'Yes.'

'Who told them where the ship was. Did Gundersen?'

'Gundersen? No. It was the Harbour Master at St Helier reporting to the Receiver of Wreck. I imagine a Jersey Island fisherman sighted the wreck. He must have seen the salvage people working on her.'

'That's all right.' He seemed relieved. 'But we'll have to hurry.' He picked up the towel. 'Have you got a drink?'

I reached into the locker and got him the rum bottle and a glass. His hands shook as he poured it out. 'I'll need some clothes, too.' He knocked the drink back at one gulp and stood gasping for breath. 'Now that they know there's going to be an official examination of the boat, we'll have to move fast.'

Mike had produced some clothes out of a locker. He put them on the table and Patch picked up a vest. 'How soon can you leave?' he asked.

I stared at him. 'Don't you understand?' I said. 'There's a warrant out for your arrest. I can't possibly take you.'

He was halfway into the vest and he stopped, his eyes fixed on me. For the first time, I think, he realized that we weren't going to take him. 'But I was relying on you.' His tone was suddenly desperate. And then he added angrily, 'It was only yesterday you offered to take me. It was the one chance and – '

'But you didn't accept it,' I said. 'You told me it was too late.'

'So it was.'

'If it was too late then,' I said, 'it's certainly too late now.'

'How could I accept your offer? They were going to arrest me. I was quite certain of that, and if I'd gone back into that Court this morning – '

'But you didn't.'

'No.'

'Why not? Can't you see you've put yourself in an impossible situation.' I leaned forward, determined to get at the truth. 'You've got the police hunting for you now – everybody against you. What in God's name made you decide to run for it?'

He pulled the vest down over his head and came to the edge of the table, leaning down over it. 'Something I learned last night – something that made me realize I had to get out to the *Mary Deare* as soon as possible.' There was silence for a moment, whilst we looked at him, waiting. And then he said, 'That salvage company – it's under contract to the Dellimare Company.'

'How do you know?' It seemed the wildest piece of guesswork. 'How can you possibly know when it's only just been announced that a salvage company is working on the wreck?'

'I'll tell you.' He began to get into the rest of Mike's clothes. 'Last night, when I got back to my rooms – I went up and got my coat. I was going for a walk – to think things over. And outside – I found Janet – Miss Taggart – waiting for me there in the street. She'd come . . .' He gave a quick shrug. 'Well, it doesn't matter, but it made a difference. I knew she believed in me then, and after that I searched the pubs all through the dock area. I was certain I'd find Burrows in one of them. He couldn't keep away from the booze so long as he had money. And he had money all right. I found him down in the old part of the town, and he told me the whole thing – drunk and truculent and full of confidence. He hated my guts. That's why he told me about the salvage company. He was gloating, knowing I'd never prove anything after they'd sunk her. And all because I'd told him he was incompetent and that I'd see to it he never had charge of an engine-room again.'

He paused and took a quick drink. The wind was rising, and in the silence the sound of it whining through the rigging was suddenly loud. Then he pulled on Mike's sweater and came and sat down opposite me. He was still shivering. 'Higgins must have worked out the course of our drift for Gundersen. Anyway, they were convinced she was on the Minkies and they chartered a boat and went over there. And when they'd found her, Gundersen signed up this French outfit to salvage her.'

'But what difference does that make to you?' Mike asked. 'It's perfectly natural for the Dellimare Company to want to salvage her.'

Patch turned on him, his lips drawn back in a smile. 'They're not going to salvage her,' he said. 'They're going to have the French pull her off and then they're going to sink her in deep water.'

I saw Mike looking at him as though he were crazy and I said, 'Do you seriously imagine they could get away with that?'

'Why not?' he demanded.

'But no salvage company – '

'It's nothing to do with the salvage company. But the contract is for refloating and towing the hulk to Southampton, and Higgins and Burrows will be on board the tow. Gundersen will insist on that. And with those two on board, it's simple. Burrows has only got to open the sea cocks and the *Mary Deare* will quietly founder at the end of her tow line. They'll wait till they're past the Casquets, I imagine, and sink her in the Hurd Deep. She'll go down in sixty fathoms or more, and everybody will think it a stroke of bad luck and put it down to the state of the hull after

being pounded for a couple of months on the Minkies.' He turned
and stared at me. 'Now perhaps you understand. I've got to get
out to her, Sands. It's my only hope. I must have proof.'

'Of what?' Mike demanded.

He looked from one to the other of us, a quick, uncertain
movement of the eyes. 'I must know for certain that there was an
explosion in those for'ard holds.'

'I should have thought that was a matter for the authorities,'
Mike said.

'The authorities? No. No, I must be certain.'

'But surely,' I said, 'if you went to the authorities and told them
the truth . . . if you told them about Dellimare's offer – '

'I can't do that.' He was staring at me and all the vitality in his
eyes seemed to have burned itself out.

'Why not?' I asked.

'Why not?' His eyes dropped and he fiddled with his glass.
'You were with me on that ship,' he whispered. 'Surely to God
you must have guessed by now.' And then he added quickly.
'Don't ask me any more questions. Just take me out there. Afterwards . . .' He hesitated. 'When I know for certain – ' He didn't
finish, but looked directly at me and said, 'Well? Will you take
me?'

'I'm sorry,' I said. 'But you must realize it's impossible now.'

'But – ' He reached out his hand and gripped hold of my arm.
'For Christ's sake! Don't you understand? They'll refloat her and
then they'll sink her out in deep water. And after that I'll never
know . . .' He had a beaten look and I was sorry for him. And then
a spark of anger showed in his eyes. 'I thought you'd more guts,
Sands,' he said, and his voice quivered. 'I thought you'd take a
chance – you and Duncan. God damn it! You said you'd take
me.' He was coming up again, the muscles of his arm tightening,
his body no longer sagging . . . unbelievably there was strength in
his voice again as he said, 'You're not scared, are you, just because
there's a warrant out for my arrest?'

'No,' I said. 'It isn't only that.'

'What is it then?'

I reached across the table for the envelope. 'This for one thing,'
I said and I threw it down on the table in front of him so that the
fivers spilled out of it and lay there, white and crisp, black-inked
like funeral cards. 'You let me bring that back for you, not knowing what it was.' I watched him staring down at them uncomfortably and I went on, 'Now suppose you tell us the truth – why you
took that money, why you didn't tell the Court about Dellimare's

offer.' I hesitated, still staring at him, but he wouldn't meet my gaze. 'You took that money from his cabin after he was dead, didn't you?'

'Yes.' His voice sounded weary, exhausted.

'Why?'

'Why?' He lifted his eyes then, staring straight at me, and they were suddenly the eyes of the man I had first met on the *Mary Deare*. 'Because it was there, I suppose. I didn't reckon it belonged to him any more . . . Oh, I don't know.' He was frowning, as though trying to concentrate on something that didn't interest him. He seemed to be lost in some private hell of his own creation. 'I suppose I was a fool to take it. It was dangerous. I realized that afterwards. But at the time . . . well, I was broke, and when you know you've got to fight a company to prove you did your best to bring a ship home that they didn't want brought home . . .' He let it go at that, his mind still on something else.

'Is that why you didn't tell the Court about Dellimare's offer?' I asked.

'No.' He got suddenly to his feet. 'No, it wasn't that.' He stood for a moment looking out through the open hatch and then he came back to the table. 'Don't you understand yet?' His eyes were fixed on my face. 'I killed him.'

'Dellimare?' I stared at him in shocked silence.

'He didn't go overboard,' he said. And then, after a pause, he added, 'His body is still there on the *Mary Deare*.'

I was so staggered I could think of nothing to say. And then suddenly he began to pour out the whole story.

It had happened on the night of the gale, just after the fire in the radio shack had been reported to him. He had gone out on to the wing of the bridge, to see whether the fire could be tackled from there, and he'd seen Dellimare making his way aft along the upper-deck. 'I'd warned him I'd kill him if I found him trying to monkey with the ship. There was no reason for him to be going aft.' He had rushed down from the bridge then and had reached the after end of the deck just in time to see Dellimare disappearing through the inspection hatch of Number Four hold. 'I should have slammed the lid shut on him and left it at that.' But instead he'd followed Dellimare down into the hold and had found him crouched by the for'ard bulkhead, his arm thrust down into the gap between the top case of the cargo and the hull plates. 'I can remember his face,' he breathed. 'Startled and white as hell in the light of my torch. I believe he knew I was going to kill him.'

Patch's voice trembled now as he relived the scene that had

been pent-up inside him too long. Dellimare had straightened himself with a cry, holding some sort of a cylinder in his hand, and Patch had moved in with a cold, dynamic fury and had smashed his fist into the man's face, driving his head back on to the steeel of the hull, crashing it against an angle iron. 'I wanted to crush him, smash him, obliterate him. I wanted to kill him.' He was breathing heavily, standing at the end of the table, staring at us with the light shining down on his head, deepening the shadows of his face. 'There were things happening to the ship that night – the for'ard holds flooding, the fire in the radio shack, and then that little rat going down into the hold . . . and all the time a gale blowing hurricane force. My God! What would you have done? I was the Captain. The ship was in hellish danger. And he wanted her wrecked. I'd warned him . . .' He stopped abruptly and wiped his forehead.

Then he went on, more quietly, describing what had happened after Dellimare had crumpled up, lying in a heap on one of the aero engine cases with blood glistening red in his pale thin hair. He hadn't realized he'd killed him – not then. But the anger had drained out of him and somehow he had managed to get him up the vertical ladder to the deck. He had nearly been knocked down by a sea that had come surging in-board, but he had made the ladder to the upper-deck. That way he wouldn't meet any of the crew. But when he had almost reached the bridge-housing the lights shining out of the after portholes showed him Dellimare's head and he knew then that the man was dead. 'His neck was broken.' He said it flatly, without emotion.

'But surely you could have said he'd had an accident – fallen down the hold or something?' I suggested. I was remembering the coal dust and the sound of shifting coal in the bunker, knowing what was coming.

He reached for the packet and lit a cigarette. Then he sat down opposite me again. 'I panicked, I suppose,' he said. 'Poor devil, he wasn't a pretty sight – all the back of his head smashed in.' He was seeing the blood and the lolling head again, and the sweat glistened on his forehead. 'I decided to dump him over the side.'

But he had set the body down to examine it and when he bent to pick it up, he'd seen Higgins coming out through the starboard doorway from the bridge-housing. He hadn't dared carry the body to the rail then. But just beside him the hatch of the port bunkering chute stood open for some strange reason and, without thinking, he pitched the body down the chute and slammed the lid on it. 'It wasn't until hours later that I realized what I'd done.'

He took a pull at his cigarette, dragging at it, his hands trembling. 'Instead of getting shot of the man, I'd hung his body round my neck like a millstone.' His voice had fallen to a whisper and for a moment he sat in silence. Then he added, 'When you came on board, I'd slung a rope ladder down into that bunker and was in there, trying to get at the body. But by then the rolling of the ship had buried him under tons of coal.'

There was a long silence after that and I could hear the wind in the rigging, a high, singing note. The anchor chain was grating on the shingle as the boat yawed. And then, speaking to himself, his head lowered: 'I killed him, and I thought it was justice. I thought he deserved to die. I was convinced I was saving the lives of thirty-odd men, my own included.'

And then he looked at me suddenly. 'Well, I've told you the truth now.'

I nodded. I knew this was the truth. I knew now why he had to get back there, why he couldn't reveal Dellimare's offer to the Court. 'You should have gone to the police,' I said, 'as soon as you reached England.'

'The police?' He was staring at me, white-faced. 'How could I?'

'But if you'd told them about the offer Dellimare made you . . .'

'Do you think they'd have believed me? It was only my word. I'd no proof. How could I possibly justify . . .' His gaze switched to the envelope lying on the table. 'You see this money?' He reached out and grabbed up a handful of the fivers. 'He offered it to me, the whole lot. He had it there in his cabin and he spilled the whole five thousand out in front of me – out of that envelope that's lying there; and I picked it up and threw it in his face and told him I'd see him in hell before I did his dirty work for him. That's when I warned him that I'd kill him if he tried to lose me the ship.' He paused, breathing heavily. 'And then that gale and the for'ard holds suddenly making water and the fire in the radio shack . . . when I found him down in that hold – ' He was still staring at me and his features were haggard and drawn, the way I'd first seen them. 'I was so sure I was justified – at the time,' he whispered.

'But it was an accident,' Mike said. 'Damn it, you didn't mean to kill him.'

He shook his head slowly, pushing his hand up through his hair. 'No, that's not true,' he said. 'I did mean to kill him. I was mad at the thought of what he'd tried to make me do – what he was doing to the ship. The first command I'd had in ten years . . .'

He was looking down at his glass again. 'I thought when I put her on the Minkies, that I could get back to her, get rid of his body and prove that he was trying to sink her – ' He was staring at me again. 'Can't you understand, Sands . . . I had to know I was justified.'

'But it was still an accident,' I said gently. 'You could have gone to the authorities . . .' I hesitated, and then added, 'There was a time when you were prepared to – when you altered course for Southampton after rounding Ushant.'

'I still had the ship then,' he muttered, and I realized then what his ship meant to a man like Patch. So long as he'd had the *Mary Deare*'s deck under his feet and he was in command he'd still had confidence in himself, in the rightness of his actions.

He reached out his hand for the bottle. 'Mind if I have another drink?' His tone was resigned.

I watched him pour it, understanding now how desperate was his need to justify himself. I remembered how he'd reacted to the sight of the crew huddled like sheep around Higgins in the office at Paimpol. His first command in ten years and the whole thing repeating itself. It was an appalling twist of fate. 'When did you feed last?' I asked him.

'I don't know. It doesn't matter.' He swallowed some of the drink, his hand still trembling, his body slack.

'I'll get you some food.' I got up and went through into the galley. The stew was still hot in the pressure-cooker and I put some on a plate and set it in front of him. And then I asked Mike to come up on deck. The freshening wind had thinned the mist, so that the hills were dim, humped-up shapes, their shadows thrown round the cove and falling away to the narrow gap of the entrance. I stood there for a moment, wondering how I was going to persuade him. But Mike had guessed what was in my mind. 'You want *Sea Witch*, is that it, John?'

I nodded. 'For four days,' I said. 'Five at the most. That's all.'

He was looking at me, his face pale in the faint glow of the riding light. 'Surely it would be better to put the whole thing in the hands of the authorities?' I didn't say anything. I didn't know how to make him understand the way I felt. And after a while, he said, 'You believe him then – about the Dellimare Company planning to sink the ship in deep water?'

'I don't know,' I murmured. I wasn't sure. 'But if you accept that the cargo has been switched, that the whole thing was planned . . .' I hesitated, remembering how scared Higgins had been. If Higgins had started that fire and knocked Patch out and panicked the crew . . . 'Yes,' I said. 'I think I do believe him.'

Mike was silent for some time then. He had turned away from me and was staring out towards the entrance. At length he said, 'You're sure about this, John? It's a hell of a risk you're taking for the fellow.'

'I'm quite sure,' I said.

He nodded. 'Okay. Then the sooner we get under way the better.'

'You don't have to come,' I said.

He looked at me with that slow, rather serious smile of his. '*Sea Witch* and I go together,' he said. 'You don't get the one without the other.' He glanced up at the masthead. The burgee hadn't been taken down and it showed the wind westerly. 'We'll be able to sail it.' He was thinking we'd make better time under sail, for our engine was geared for power, not speed.

Down below I found Patch leaning back, the glass in his hand, smoking a cigarette. He hadn't touched the food. His eyes were half closed and his head lolled. He didn't look up as we entered.

'We're getting under way,' I told him.

He didn't move.

'Leave him,' Mike said. 'We can manage. I'll go and start the engine.' He was already pulling on a sweater.

But Patch had heard. His head came slowly round. 'Where are you making for – Southampton?' His voice had no life in it.

'No,' I said. 'We're taking you out to the Minkies.'

He stared at me. 'The Minkies.' He repeated it slowly, his fuddled mind not taking it in. 'You're going out to the *Mary Deare*?' And then he was on his feet, the glass crashing to the floor, his body jarring the table. 'You mean it?' He lurched across to me, catching hold of me with both his hands. 'You're not saying that just to keep me quiet. You mean it, don't you?'

'Yes,' I said. 'I mean it.' It was like trying to convince a child.

'My God!' he said. 'My God, I thought I was finished.' He was suddenly laughing, shaking me, gripping Mike's hand. 'I think I'd have gone mad,' he said. 'The uncertainty. Ten years and you get a ship and you're in command again, and then . . . You don't know what it's like when you suddenly lose confidence in yourself.' He pushed his hands up through his hair, his eyes alight and eager. I'd never seen him like that before. He turned and scrabbled up a whole pile of the fivers that were lying on the table. 'Here. You take them.' He thrust them into my hand. 'I don't want them. They're yours now.' He wasn't drunk, just a little crazed – the reaction of nerves strung too taut.

I pushed the notes away. 'We'll talk about that later,' I said. 'Can you navigate into the Minkies without a chart?'

His mind seemed to snap suddenly into place. He hesitated – a seaman considering a nautical problem. 'You mean from Les Sauvages to the *Mary Deare*?'

'Yes.'

He nodded slowly. He was frowning, his mind groping for the bearings. 'Yes. Yes, I'm sure I can remember. It's only a question of the tide. You've got a nautical almanac?'

I nodded and it was settled. I had charts for the Channel. All I lacked was the large-scale chart of the Minkies. 'We'll hoist sail in here, before we get the hook up,' I said. I reached for my monkey jacket and slipped it on, and then we went up on deck and got the covers off the main and mizzen. I sent Mike to get the engine going whilst Patch and I put the battens in and hoisted the mainsail, tacking it down so that the luff was set up taut. The starter whined and the engine caught, throbbing at the deck under my feet. *Sea Witch* was suddenly alive. We hoisted the dinghy on board then and the ship bustled with activity as we got her ready for sea.

It was whilst I was up for'ard, hanking the big yankee jib on to the forestay, that I heard it – the beat of an engine coming in from the sea. I stood there for a moment, listening, and then I extinguished the riding light and ran aft, shouting to Mike to get the hook up. It might be just another yacht coming in, but it wasn't the night for yachtsmen to be risking their boats, feeling their way into a place like Lulworth, and I had no desire to be caught in here with Patch on board. We were outside the law and I wanted to get clear of the cove without being seen. I switched off the lights below and sent Patch for'ard to help Mike, and then I was at the wheel and the chain was coming in with a run as I manœuvred *Sea Witch* up to her anchor on the engine.

The sound of the boat coming in was quite clear now, the beat of its engines throbbing back from the cliffs. The white of her masthead light appeared in the gap, bobbing to the swell. The green eye of a starboard light showed, and then the red as she turned in.

'Up and down,' Mike called.

'Leave it there,' I called to him. 'Hoist the yankee.'

The big jib floated up, a blur of white in the darkness. I hauled in the sheet and *Sea Witch* began to glide through the water as I swung her bows towards the gap. The in-coming boat was right in the entrance now. 'What do you think it is – the police?' Mike asked as he came back aft to help trim the sheets.

'I don't know,' I said. 'Get the mizzen hoisted.' For an instant I saw Patch's face, a white glimmer in the darkness as he stared seaward, and then he went aft to help Mike. I was keeping the engine throttled right back so that they wouldn't hear it above the noise of their own engine, hoping I could slip out without their seeing us in the darkness.

There wasn't a great deal of wind in the cove, but we were moving, steadily gathering way. The other boat came in slowly. She had a spotlight and she flashed it on the rocks by the entrance, holding a middle course between them. And then she was inside and we were bearing straight down on her. Under sail I had no chance of giving her a wide berth. I just had to hold my course and hope that she'd turn away.

But she held straight on and we passed her so close that I could see the whole shape of her, a big sea-going motor boat with flared bow and a long sloping deck-house. I even caught a glimpse of the man in the wheelhouse, a dim figure peering at us out of the night.

And then their spotlight stabbed the darkness, momentarily blinding me, picking out the triangle of our mainsail in glaring white, and a voice hailed us. I think he was asking the name of our ship, but the words were lost in the roar of the engine as I opened the throttle wide, and we went steaming out through the gap. The sails flapped wildly as we came under the lee of the cliffs and the boat heaved to the swell. Then we were through and the sails filled. *Sea Witch* heeled, the water creaming back from her bows and sliding white past the cockpit as she surged forward under the thrust of power and sail.

'She's turning,' Mike shouted down to me.

I glanced over my shoulder. The motor boat's masthead steaming light and the red and green of her navigation lights were showing in the black outline of the land behind us. She was coming out through the gap.

Mike tumbled into the cockpit, hardening in the main sheet for me as I headed south on a broad reach. With the ship blacked-out – not even a binnacle light – I sailed by the wind, my head turned every now and then over my shoulder to watch the motor boat. Her masthead light began to dance as she met the swell in the entrance, and then it was swinging steadily, rhythmically as she pitched to the sea, and the red and green of her navigation lights remained fixed on us like two eyes. Her spotlight stabbed the darkness, showing glimpses of black, lumpy water as it probed the night.

'If we'd got away half an hour earlier . . .' Patch was staring aft.

'And if we'd been five minutes later,' Mike snapped, 'you'd be under arrest.' His voice sounded on edge and I knew he didn't like it any more than I did. 'I'll go and get the anchor on board.' He disappeared for'ard and I sent Patch to help him.

It was cold in the cockpit now that we were under way. But I don't think I noticed it. I was wondering about the boat behind us. It had gained on us slightly and the spotlight, reaching out to us across the tumbled waters, lit our sails with a ghostly radiance. It didn't probe any longer, but was held on us, so that I knew they'd picked us out. The drizzle had slackened again and our white sails made us conspicuous.

Up for'ard Mike was coiling down the halyards, whilst Patch lashed the anchor. They came aft together. 'John. Hadn't we better heave-to?'

'They haven't ordered you to.' Patch's voice was hard and urgent. 'You don't have to do anything till they signal instructions.' He was back at sea again and a man doesn't easily give up in his own element. He came down into the cockpit. His face had tightened so that there was strength in it again. 'Well, are you going on or not?' It wasn't exactly a challenge, certainly not a threat, and yet the way he said it made me wonder what he'd do if I refused.

Mike jerked round, his body bunched, his quick temper flaring. 'If we want to heave-to, we will.'

The spotlight was switched off. Sudden blackness descended on us. 'I was asking Sands.' Patch's voice trembled out of the darkness.

'John and I own this boat jointly,' Mike flung out. 'We've worked and planned and slaved our guts out to have our own outfit, and we're not going to risk it all to get you out of the mess you're in.' He stepped down into the cockpit, balancing himself to the pitch of the boat. 'You've got to heave-to,' he said to me. 'That boat is gradually coming up on us and when the police find we've got Patch on board, it's going to be damned hard to prove that we weren't slipping him out of the country, especially with all that cash sculling around below.' He leaned forward, gripping hold of my shoulder. 'Do you hear me, John?' He was shouting at me above the noise of the engine. 'You've got to heave-to before that police boat comes up on us.'

'It may not be the police,' I said. I had been thinking about it all the time they'd been up for'ard. 'The police would have sent a patrol car. They wouldn't have come by boat.'

'If it's not the police, then who the hell is it?'

I glanced over my shoulder, wondering whether perhaps imagination hadn't got the better of reason. But there was the boat, still following us. The white steaming light was swaying wildly, showing the slender stick of her mast and the outline of the deck-house. 'She certainly rolls,' I murmured.

'What's that?'

I turned to him then. 'Did you get a good look at her, Mike, as we came out?'

'Yes. Why?'

'What sort of a boat was she – could you see?'

'An old Parkhurst, I should say.' Mike's training as a marine engineer had given him a quite remarkable knowledge of power craft.

'You're certain of that?'

'I think so. Yes, I'm sure she was.'

I asked him to go down below then and look up *Griselda* in Lloyd's Register. 'And if she's in the book and her description fits, then I'd like an estimate of her speed.'

He hesitated, glancing quickly from me to Patch, and then he disappeared for'ard towards the main hatch. 'And if it is *Griselda*?' Patch asked.

'Then she was chartered this morning,' I said. 'By somebody who was in that Court.'

The spotlight was on us again and he was staring at me. 'Are you sure?'

I nodded and I could see him working it out for himself. *Sea Witch* heeled to a gust of wind and I felt the drag of the prop. Spray splashed my face. And then Mike was back. 'How did you know it was *Griselda*?' he asked me.

'I was right, was I?'

'Yes – it's either *Griselda* or a sister ship. Fifty-foot over all. Built by Parkhurst in 1931.'

'And her top speed?'

'Hard to say. She's got two six-cylinder Parkhurst engines. But they're the original engines and it depends how they've been maintained. Flat out, I'd say she might do a little over eight knots.'

Sea Witch was heeling further now and the wave-tops were lopping over on to the foredeck. 'In calm water.'

'Yes, in calm water.'

The wind was rising and already the seas were beginning to break. I was thinking that in a little over two hours the tide would turn. It would be west-going then and the freshening wind would kick up a short, steep sea. It would reduce *Griselda*'s speed by at least a knot. 'I'm standing on,' I told Mike. 'We'll try and shake them off during the night.' And then I explained about the yacht broker I had met with Hal and how Higgins had warned me. 'Higgins even guessed you'd come down to Lulworth,' I said, turning to Patch.

'Higgins!' He turned and stared aft. The spotlight was on his face and there was something in the way his eyes shone – it might have been anger or fear or exultation; I couldn't tell. And then the spotlight was switched off and he was just a black shape standing there beside me.

'Well, if it's only the Dellimare Company – ' Mike's voice sounded relieved. 'They can't do anything, can they?'

Patch swung round on him. 'You don't seem to realize . . .' His voice came hard and abrupt out of the darkness, the sentence bitten off short. But I had caught his mood and I looked back over my shoulder. Was it my imagination or was the motor boat nearer now? I found myself looking all round, searching for the lights of another ship. But there was nothing – only the blackness of the night and the white of the breaking wave-tops rushing at us out of the darkness. 'Well, we go on. Is that right?' I wasn't sure what I ought to do.

'You've no alternative,' Patch said.

'Haven't we?' Mike stepped down into the cockpit. 'We could run for Poole. That boat's following us and . . . Well, I think we should turn the whole thing over to the authorities.' His voice sounded nervous.

A wave broke against the weather bow, showering spray aft, and we heeled to a gust so that our lee decks were awash. The sea was shallower here. There were overfalls and *Sea Witch* pitched violently with a short, uncomfortable motion, the screw juddering under the stern and the bows slamming into the waves so that water was sluicing across the foredeck. 'For God's sake cut that engine!' Patch shouted at me. 'Can't you feel the drag of the prop?'

Mike swung round on him. 'You don't run this boat.'

'It's stopping our speed,' Patch said.

He was right. I had been conscious of it for some time. 'Switch it off, will you, Mike?' I asked.

He hesitated and then dived into the charthouse. The noise of the engine died, leaving a stillness in which the sound of the sea seemed unnaturally loud. Under sail alone, the boat merged with the elements for which she had been designed, fitting herself to the pattern of wind and wave. The movement was easier. Waves ceased to break over the foredeck.

But though Patch had been right, Mike came back out of the charthouse in a mood of blazing anger. 'You seem bloody certain we're going to try and race that boat for you,' he said. And then, turning to me, he added, 'Take my advice, John. Turn down-wind and head for Poole.'

'Down-wind,' Patch said, 'the motor boat will be faster than you.'

'Well, head up-wind then and make for Weymouth.'

'It's a dead beat,' I said.

And Patch added, 'Either way she'll overhaul you.'

'What's that matter?' Mike demanded. 'They can't do anything. They've got the law on their side. That's all. They can't do anything.'

'God Almighty!' Patch said. 'Don't you understand yet?' He leaned forward, his face thrust close to mine. 'You tell him, Sands. You've met Gundersen. You know the set-up now.' He stared at me, and then he swung round to face Mike again. 'Listen!' he said. 'Here was a plan to clean up over a quarter of a million pounds. The cargo was switched and sold to the Chinks. That part of it went all right. But all the rest went wrong. The captain refused to play his part. They tried to sink her in a gale and they failed. Higgins was left to do the job on his own and he botched it.' His voice was pitched high in the urgency of his effort to communicate what he believed. 'Can't you see it from their point of view . . . twelve men drowned, an old man dead, possibly murdered, and the ship herself lying out there on the Minkies. They daren't let me reach the *Mary Deare*. And they daren't let you reach her either. They daren't even let you get into port now – not until they've disposed of the *Mary Deare*.'

Mike stared at him. 'But that's fantastic,' he breathed.

'Why fantastic? They must know I'm on board. And you wouldn't have sailed if you hadn't believed my story. Imagine what they face if the truth comes out.'

Mike turned to me. 'Do you believe this, John?' His face was very pale. He sounded bewildered.

'I think we'd better try and shake them off,' I said. Patch had his own reasons for driving us on. But I knew I didn't want that boat to catch up with us in the dark.

'But good God! This is the English Channel. They can't do anything to us here.' He stared at Patch and myself, waiting for us to answer him. 'Well, what the hell can they do?' And then he looked out at the blackness that surrounded us, realizing gradually that it made no difference that we were in the Channel. There were just the three of us alone in a black waste of tumbled water that spilled to white on the crests, and without another word he got the log line out of the locker and went aft to stream it astern.

'We go on then,' Patch said. The sudden relief from tension made his voice sound tired. It reminded me that he had had no sleep the night before and no food, that for days he'd been under a great strain.

Mike came back into the cockpit. 'I think we're holding them now,' he said. I glanced back at *Griselda*. Her navigation lights were masked every now and then by the marching wave-tops. 'When the tide turns,' I said, 'we'll beat up to windward and see if that will shake them off.' I got up stiffly from behind the wheel. 'Will you take the first watch, Mike?' It would have to be two hours on and four off, with one man alone at the wheel and the other two on call. We were desperately short-handed for a hard sail like this. I gave him the wheel and went through into the charthouse to enter up the log.

Patch followed me in. 'Have you thought about who will be on board that motor boat?' he asked me. I shook my head, wondering what was coming, and he added, 'It won't be Gundersen, you know.'

'Who will it be then?'

'Higgins.'

'What's it matter which of them it is?' I asked. 'What are you trying to tell me?'

'Just this,' he said earnestly. 'Gundersen is a man who would only take calculated risks. But if Higgins is in control of that boat . . .' He stared at me, watching to see whether I had understood his point.

'You mean he's desperate?'

'Yes.' Patch looked at me for a moment. 'There's no need to tell young Duncan. If Higgins doesn't stop us before we get to that salvage tug, he's done for. When he's arrested, the others will panic. Burrows, for one, will turn Queen's evidence. You understand?' He turned away then. 'I'll go and get some food inside me.' But in the doorway he hesitated. 'I'm sorry,' he said. 'I didn't mean to land you in a thing like this.'

I finished entering up the log and turned in, fully-clothed, on the charthouse bunk. But I didn't sleep much. The movement was uncomfortable, and every time I looked out through the open doorway I could see *Griselda*'s lights bobbing in the darkness astern of us, and then I would listen to the sound of the wind in the rigging, alert for the slightest indication that it was slackening. Twice Mike had to call me out to help him winch in the sheets, and at two o'clock I took over the helm.

The tide had turned and the seas were steep and breaking. We altered course to south-west, sheeting in the sails till they were almost flat as we came on to the wind. It was cold then with the wind on our faces and the spray slatting against our oilskins as *Sea Witch* beat to windward, bucking the seas and busting the wave-tops open, water cascading from her bows.

Behind us, *Griselda*'s navigation lights followed our change of course and the white of her masthead light danced crazily in the night as she wallowed and pitched and rolled in our wake. But a power boat doesn't fit herself to the pattern of the water the way a boat under sail does and gradually the red and green lights dipped more frequently below the level of the waves, until at last all we could see was her steaming light dancing like a will-o'-the-wisp on the wave-tops.

Mike's voice reached out to me through the noise of wind and sea: 'We've got them now.' He was excited. 'If we go about . . .' The rest of it was lost to me, whipped away by the wind, drowned in the crash of a wave bursting against the bows. But I knew what was in his mind. If we went on to the other tack, sailing north-west, instead of south-west, there was a good chance that they wouldn't notice our change of course, even though the night had become brilliant with stars. And once clear of them we could turn down-wind, get to the east of them and make for the Alderney Race.

There is no doubt in my mind now that Mike was right and, had I done as he suggested, the disaster for which we were headed might have been avoided. But the changed motion induced by our heading into the wind had brought Patch on deck. I could see him sitting on the main hatch, staring aft for glimpses of *Griselda*, and I wondered what his reaction would be if we went over on to the port tack, heading back towards the English coast. Also, we were over-canvassed, and when you go about there are backstays to set up as well as the sheets to handle; one slip and we could lose our mast!

'I don't like it,' I told Mike. We were short-handed and it was night. Also, of course, in those conditions, when you are tired and cold and wet, there is a great temptation to sit tight and do nothing. I thought we were drawing ahead of them.

Apparently Mike had the same thought, for, instead of pressing his point, he shrugged his shoulders and went into the charthouse to turn in. It seems extraordinary to me now that I didn't appreciate the significance of the fact that *Griselda*'s light was no longer showing astern of us, but way out on the port quarter. Had I done so, I should have known that we were not gaining on her, merely diverging from her. She was steering a more southerly course, maintaining her speed by avoiding the head-on battering of the seas. And I for my part – as so often happens at night – thought our own speed was greater than it was.

By the end of my watch it was clouding over and the wind was slackening. I called Patch and when he came up, we eased the sheets and altered course to sou'-sou'-west. We were no longer butting into the seas then, but following the lines of the waves with a wild, swooping movement. The wind was free and *Sea Witch* was going like a train.

I heated some soup then and we drank it in the cockpit, watching the dawn break. It came with a cold, bleak light and Patch stood, staring aft. But there was nothing to be seen but a waste of grey, tumbled water. 'It's all right,' I said. 'We've left them way behind.'

He nodded, not saying anything. His face looked grey. 'At this rate we'll raise the Casquets inside of two hours,' I said, and I left him then and went below to get some sleep.

An hour later Mike woke me, shouting to me to come up on deck, his voice urgent. 'Look over there, John,' he said as I emerged from the hatch. He was pointing away to port and, at first, I could see nothing. My sleep-dimmed eyes absorbed the cold daylight and the drabness of sea and sky, and then on the lift of a wave I thought I saw something, a stick maybe or a spar-buoy raised aloft out there where the march of the waves met the horizon. I screwed up my eyes, focusing them, and the next time I balanced to the upward swoop of the deck, I saw it clearly – the mast of a small ship. It lifted itself up out of the waves and behind it came the hull of the boat itself, drab white in the morning light.

'*Griselda*?' I said.

Mike nodded and passed me the glasses. She was certainly rolling. I could see the water streaming off her and every now and then a wave burst against her bows, throwing up a cloud of spray. 'If we'd gone about last night . . .'

'Well, we didn't,' I said. I glanced aft to where Patch sat

hunched over the wheel in borrowed oilskins. 'Does he know?' I
asked.

'Yes. He saw her first.'

'What did he say?'

'Nothing. He didn't seem surprised.'

I stared at the boat through the glasses again, trying to estimate
her speed. 'What are we doing?' I asked. 'Did you get a log
reading at six?'

'Yes. We did eight in the last hour.'

Eight knots! I glanced up at the sails. They were wind-bellied
out, tight and hard, solid tons of weight pulling at the mast, hauling the boat through the water. My God! it was hard that we
hadn't shaken them off after a whole night of sailing.

'I've been thinking,' Mike said. 'If they come up with us . . .'

'Well?'

'There's not much they can do really, is there? I mean . . .' He
hesitated, glancing at me uncertainly.

'I hope you're right,' I said and went into the charthouse. I was
tired and I didn't want to think about it. I worked out our dead-
reckoning, based on miles logged, courses sailed and tides, and
found we were ten miles north-north-west of the Casquets. In two
hours' time the tide would be east-going, setting us in towards
Alderney and the Cherbourg Peninsula. But that damned boat
lay between us and the coast, and there was no getting away from
her, not in daylight.

I stayed on in the charthouse and got the forecast: wind
moderating later, some fog patches locally. A depression centred
over the Atlantic was moving slowly east.

Shortly after breakfast we raised the Casquets – the north-
western bastion of the Channel Islands. The tide turned and
began to run against us and we had the Casquets with us for a long
time, a grey, spiked helmet of a rock against which the seas broke.
We thrashed our way through the steamer lane that runs up-
Channel from Ushant, seeing only two ships, and those hull-down
on the horizon. And then we raised Guernsey Island and the
traffic in the steamer lane was just smudges of smoke where sky and
sea met.

All morning Patch remained on deck, taking his trick at the
helm, dozing in the cockpit or sitting staring at the grey acres that
separated us from *Griselda*. Sometimes he would dive into the
charthouse and work frenziedly with parallel rule and dividers,
checking our course and our ETA at the Minkies. Once I suggested that he went below and got some sleep, but all he said was

'Sleep? I can't sleep till I see the *Mary Deare*.' And he stayed there, grey and exhausted, existing on his nerves, as he had done all through the Enquiry.

I think he was afraid to go below – afraid that when he couldn't see her *Griselda* would somehow creep up on us. He was frighteningly tired. He kept on asking me about the tides. We had no tidal chart and it worried him. Even when the tide turned around midday, pushing us westward again, he kept on checking our bearing on the jagged outline of Guernsey Island.

I should perhaps explain that the tidal surge of six hours flood and six hours ebb that shifts the whole body of water of the English Channel builds up to an extraordinary peak in the great bight of the French coast that contains the Channel Islands. At 'springs', when the tides are greatest, it sluices in and out of the narrow gap between Alderney and the mainland at a rate of up to 7 knots. Its direction in the main body of the Channel Islands rotates throughout the twelve hours. Moreover, the rise and fall of tide is as much as from 30 to 40 feet.

I mention this to explain our preoccupation with the tide and because it has a bearing on what followed. Moreover, the whole area being strewn with submerged reefs, rock outcrops and islands, there is always a sense of tension when navigating in this section of the Channel.

Holding to our course, we were headed direct for the central mass of Guernsey. I was relying on the westward thrust of the tide to push us clear, and as we closed with the broken water that marked the submerged rocks known as Les Frettes, we were all of us watching to see what *Griselda* would do. In fact, she had no alternative, and when the rock cliffs of the island were close to port she altered course to come in astern of us.

The westernmost tip of Guernsey is marked by Les Hanois, a lighthouse set seaward on a group of rocks. We passed so close that we could see every detail of it – the cormorants standing like vultures on the rocks and the swell breaking white all along the edge; and dead astern of us *Griselda* followed in our wake, pitching and rolling with the spray flying from her bow wave. She was less than a quarter of a mile away and Patch stood with his body braced against the charthouse, staring at her through the glasses.

'Well,' I said, 'is it Higgins?' I could see a figure moving on the deck.

'Yes,' he said. 'Yes, it's Higgins all right. And Yules, too. There's another of them in the wheelhouse, but I can't see who it is.'

He handed me the glasses. I could recognize Higgins all right. He was standing by the rail, staring at us, his big body balanced to the movement of the boat. Higgins and Yules and Patch – three of the men who had sailed the *Mary Deare*! And here we were, within forty miles of where the ship was stranded.

Mike was at the wheel and he suddenly called to me. 'If we turn now, we could make Peter Port ahead of them.'

It was a straight run before the wind along the southern coast of the island. We could make St Martin's Point without their gaining on us and then a few miles under engine and we should be in Peter Port. I glanced at Patch. He had stepped down into the cockpit. 'I'll relieve you,' he said. It wasn't a suggestion. It was an order.

'No.' Mike was staring at him, anger flaring up into his eyes.

'I said I'll relieve you.' Patch reached for the wheel.

'I heard what you said.' Mike swung the wheel over, shouting to me to ease the sheets. But Patch had his hands on the wheel, too. Standing, he had more purchase and he slowly got it back, holding it there whilst Mike shouted obscenities at him. Their two faces were within a foot of each other – Patch's hard and tense, Mike's livid with rage. They were like that for a long two minutes, held immobile by the counteracting force of their muscles like two statues.

And then the moment when we had any choice of action was past. *Griselda*, clear of Les Hanois rocks, was altering course to get between us and Peter Port. Patch had seen it and he said, 'You've no choice now.' He hadn't relaxed his grip of the wheel, but the tension was out of his voice. Mike stopped cursing at him. He seemed to understand, for he turned his head and stared at the motor boat. Then he let go of the wheel and stood up. 'Since you appear to be skippering this boat, you'd better bloody well steer her. But by Christ!' he added, 'if anything happens to her . . .' He stared coldly at me, still trembling with anger, and went below.

'I'm sorry,' Patch said. He had seated himself at the wheel and his voice was weary.

'This isn't your boat,' I reminded him.

He shrugged his shoulders, looking round at *Griselda*. 'What else did you expect me to do?'

There was no point in discussing it. We were committed now to go on until we reached the *Mary Deare*. But if the wind dropped . . . 'Suppose Higgins catches up with us?' I said.

He looked at me quickly. 'He mustn't.' And then he added,

'We've got to get there first.'

'Yes, but suppose he does?' I was thinking that after all Higgins had got to keep within the law. 'He can't do very much.'

'No?' He laughed a little wildly. 'How do you know what Higgins can do? He's frightened.' He looked at me, sideways out of the corners of his eyes. 'Wouldn't you be frightened if you were Higgins?' And then he glanced up at the sails and his voice was quiet and practical again as he asked me to ease the sheets and he altered course for the north-west Minkies buoy.

After that we didn't talk any more and gradually I became conscious of the sound of the motor boat's engine. It was very faint at first, a gentle undertone to the swish of the sea going past, but it warned me that the wind was easing. The overcast had thinned and a humid glare hung over the water so that the outline of Jersey Island away to port was barely visible. I started the engine and from that moment I knew *Griselda* would overtake us.

The forecast announced that the depression over the Atlantic was deepening, moving eastwards faster. But it wouldn't help us. All the time the wind was dropping now and *Griselda* was coming up abeam of us, keeping between us and Jersey Island. The glare faded, leaving sea and sky a chill, luminous grey. There was no horizon any more. Patch went below to get some more clothes. It had suddenly become much colder and the wind was fluky, blowing in sudden puffs.

I sat at the wheel and watched *Griselda* draw steadily ahead of the beam, wallowing in the swell. I wondered what Higgins would do, what I would do in his place. I tried to think it out rationally. But it's difficult to think rationally when you're cold and tired and sitting alone, almost at water level, isolated in an opaque void. That sense of isolation! I had felt it at sea before, but never so strongly. And now it chilled me with a feeling of foreboding. The sea had an oily look as the big swells lumbered up from the west and rolled beneath us.

I didn't notice the fog at first. I was thinking of Higgins – and then suddenly a grey-white plasma was creeping towards us across the sea, shrouding and enveloping the water in its folds. Mike came up from below and I gave him the wheel, shouting for Patch to come on deck. *Griselda* had seen the fog, too, and she had turned in towards us. I watched her coming, waiting for the fog to close round us and hide us from her. 'We'll go about as soon as we lose sight of her,' I said as Patch came up through the hatch.

She wasn't more than two cables away when her outline blurred and then she vanished, swallowed abruptly. 'Lee-ho!' Mike called and spun the wheel. *Sea Witch* turned into the wind and through it, the big yankee flapping as I let go the jib sheet. And then the main boom was across and Patch and I were winching in the starboard jib sheet as we gathered way on the port tack.

We were doubling back on our tracks through a cold, dead, clammy world and I straightened up, listening to the beat of the motor boat's engines, trying to estimate her position, wondering whether the fog was thick enough for us to lose her.

But Higgins must have guessed what we'd do, or else we had lost too much time in going about, for the sound of *Griselda's* engines was abeam of us and, just as I realized this, the shape of her reappeared. Her bows seemed to rip the curtain of fog apart and suddenly the whole of her was visible, coming straight for us.

She was coming in at right-angles, her engines running flat out and her sharp bows cutting into the swell, spray flying up past her wheelhouse. I shouted to Mike to go about again. We were heeled over, going fast and I knew that if both boats held their course we must hit. And when he didn't do anything, my throat was suddenly dry. 'Put her about!' I yelled at him. And at the same moment Patch shouted, 'Turn, man! For God's sake turn!'

But Mike stood there, his body braced against the wheel, staring at the on-coming boat with a set expression on his face. 'Let him turn,' he said through his clenched teeth. 'I'm holding on.'

Patch jumped down into the cockpit. 'He's going to ram you.'

'He wouldn't dare.' And Mike held obstinately to his course, watching *Griselda* through narrowed eyes, his face suddenly white. Out of the corner of my eye I saw Higgins lean out of his wheelhouse. He was shouting and his powerful voice reached across to us through the roar of engines – 'Stand by! I'm coming alongside.' And then *Griselda* was turning, swinging to come in on our bows and crowd us up into the wind.

Everything happened very fast then. Mike shouted at us to ease the sheets. 'I'm going to cut under her stern.' He turned the wheel and *Sea Witch* began to swing her bows in towards the motor boat. *Griselda* was halfway through her turn. There was just room for us to pass astern of her if we turned quickly.

But things went wrong. I eased out on the jib sheet, but Patch, unaccustomed to sail, failed to ease out on the main. And at the same moment we heeled to a puff of wind. It was that unlucky puff of wind that did it. With the full weight of it on the mainsail, *Sea Witch* failed to come round fast enough. And Higgins had throttled down to bring his boat alongside us. We drove straight into *Griselda*'s counter, drove straight into it with all the force of our powerful engines and tons of wind-driven canvas. We caught her on the port side just a few feet from her stern as it was swinging in towards us on the turn. There was a rending, splintering crash; our bows reared up as though to climb over her and then we stopped with a horrible, jarring shudder. I caught a glimpse of Yules, staring open-mouthed, and then I was flung forward against the charthouse. The boom jerked free of the mast and swung in towards me. I threw up my arm and it caught my shoulder a shattering blow, wrenching it from its socket and flinging me against the guardrails.

I remember clutching at the guardrails, blinded with pain, and then I was lying on the deck, my face pressed close against a metal jib sheet lead and the noise of rending wood was still there and somebody was screaming. I shifted myself and pain stabbed through me. I was looking down into the water and a man's body drifted past. It was Yules and he was thrashing wildly at the water, his face white and scared with a lock of hair washed over his eyes.

The deck vibrated under me. It was as though compressed-air drills had been put to work on the hull. I could feel the juddering all through my body. 'You all right?' Mike reached a hand down and dragged me to my feet. My teeth clenched on my lip.

'The bastard!' He was staring for'ard, his face paper-white, all the freckles showing a dull orange against his pasty skin, and his hair flaming red. 'I'll kill him.' He was shaking with anger.

I turned to see Higgins erupt from *Griselda*'s wheelhouse. He was shouting something, his great, bellowing voice audible above the noise of the engines and the continuing, rending sound of wood. The two boats were locked together and he caught hold of our bowsprit, his teeth bared like an animal, his head sunk into his bull neck and his shoulder muscles bunched as he tried to tear the boats apart with his bare hands.

Mike moved then. He had the grim, avenging look of a man who has seen something he loves and has worked for wantonly smashed up. I called to him, for the fool was running for'ard up the sloped deck, yelling at Higgins, cursing him; and he flung himself from the bowsprit, straight at the man, hitting out at him in a blind fury of rage.

The boats separated then with a tearing of wood and bubbling of water and I didn't see any more. Patch had put our engine into reverse and I staggered into the cockpit, shouting at him to stop. 'Mike is still there. You can't leave him.'

'Do you want the belly torn out of your boat?' he demanded, turning the wheel as *Sea Witch* began to go astern. 'Those props were drilling the guts out of her.' Dimly I realized that he meant *Griselda*'s props and understood what had caused the deck planks to vibrate under my body.

I turned and watched as the gap between us and the motor boat widened. *Griselda* was down by the stern with a hole torn out of her port quarter as though a battering-ram had hit her. Higgins was going back into the wheelhouse. There was nobody else on her deck. I suddenly felt sick and tired. 'What happened to him?' I asked. The sickly-sweet taste of blood was in my mouth where I'd bitten through my lip. My arm and all that side of my body was heavy and numb with pain. 'Did you see what happened?'

'He's all right,' Patch said. 'Just knocked cold.' He started to ask me about my shoulder, but I was telling him to get into forward gear and start sailing again. 'Don't lose her!' Already *Griselda*'s outlines were fading and a moment later she disappeared. Patch had put the gear lever into neutral and we could hear her engines then, racing with an ugly, grinding noise. There was a sharp report and, a little later, another. After that we couldn't hear her any more.

'Prop shafts by the sound of it,' Patch said.

Sails and mast and boat began to spin before my eyes and I sat down. Patch seemed immensely tall, standing at the wheel, and his head swung dizzily over me. I steadied myself and the roll of a swell lapped into the cockpit. I stared at it stupidly, watching the water roll back down the forward, sloping deck. And then the engine spluttered and gave out.

I shook my head, bracing myself against the dizziness that threatened to overwhelm me. There was nobody at the helm. I called to Patch and struggled to my feet. He came up out of the main hatch, his trousers dripping. 'It's up to the galley already.' And then my eyes took in the tilt of the deck, following it down to where the bowsprit was buried in the back of a wave. All the foredeck was awash. I stared at it, taking it in slowly, whilst he pushed past me into the charthouse. He came out with a jack-knife in his hand. 'She's going down,' I said. My voice sounded dead and hopeless in my ears.

'Yes,' he said. 'Not much time.' And he began slashing at the dinghy tie-ers. I watched him hoist the praam over so that she fell with her keel on the guardrails and he was able to slide her into the water.

We were still sailing, moving sluggishly through the water, and over Patch's back, as he bent to secure the dinghy painter, I caught a glimpse of *Griselda* again, a vague shape rolling sluggishly on the edge of visibility.

'Is there any food up here?' Patch was gathering up things from the charthouse and tossing them into the dinghy – blankets, duffle coats, torches, flares, even the hand-bearing compass.

'Some chocolate.' I got it from the drawer of the chart table – three small slabs and some sweets. I got life-jackets, too, from the locker aft. But my movements were slow and clumsy and by the time I had dropped them in the dinghy the whole length of the deck was awash, the mast tilted forward and the foot of the yankee below the water.

'Quick!' Patch said. 'In you get.' He was already untying the painter. I clambered in. It wasn't difficult. The dinghy rode level with the deck. He followed me and pushed off.

I never saw her go down. As we rowed away from her, she slowly disappeared into the fog, her stern a little cocked-up, the big jib and the mizzen still set, and nothing but sea for'ard of the charthouse. She looked a strange sight – like a ghost of a ship doomed everlastingly to sail herself under. I could have wept as she faded and was suddenly gone.

I turned then to look at *Griselda*. She was lying like a log, badly down by the stern and rolling slowly to the long swell – as useless as only a motor boat can be when her engines are out of action. 'Pull on your right,' I told Patch.

He stared at me, not saying anything, his body moving rhythmically to the swing of the oars. 'For God's sake pull on your right,' I said. 'You're still not headed for *Griselda*.'

'We're not going to *Griselda*.'

I didn't understand for a moment. 'But where else . . .' My voice broke off abruptly and I felt suddenly deadly scared. He had the box of the hand-bearing compass set up at his feet, the lid open. His eyes were watching it as he rowed. He was steering a compass course. 'My God!' I cried. 'You're not going to try and make it in the dinghy?'

'Why not?'

'But what about Mike?' I was suddenly desperate. I could see Higgins struggling to get his dinghy into the water. 'You can't do it.' I seized hold of his hand as he leaned forward, gripping hold of one of the oars, pain bursting like an explosive charge in my body. 'You can't do it, I tell you.'

He stared at me, his face only a foot or two from mine. 'No?' His voice grated in the stillness, and faint across the water came a cry for help – a desperate, long-drawn-out cry. He wrenched the oar free of me and began to row again. 'If you don't like it, you can get out and swim for it like that poor bastard.' He nodded across his left shoulder and at the same moment the cry came again. This time I was able to pick him out on the lift of a swell, a black head and two dripping arms thrashing their way towards us. 'H-e-lp!'

Patch rowed on, ignoring the cry. 'Are you going to leave him to drown?' I said, leaning forward, trying with my voice to touch some spark of humanity in him.

'It's Yules,' he answered. 'Let Higgins pick him up.'

'And Mike?' I said. 'What about Mike?'

'He'll be all right. That boat isn't going to sink.'

The oars dipped and rose, dipped and rose, his body swinging back and forth. And I sat there and watched him row away from the man. What else could I do? My shoulder had been driven out of its socket; he had only to touch it to send pain searing through me, and he knew it. I thought maybe he was right about the boat. It was only the stern that was damaged. All the fore part would be water-tight. And Higgins would pick Yules up. He had his dinghy launched now and was pulling away from *Griselda*. In the weird, fog-belt light he looked like a giant specimen of those insects that are called water-boatmen. Yules had seen him coming and had ceased to thrash about in the water. He was directly between us and Higgins and he lay still in the water, not crying out any more, just waiting to be picked up.

I don't know why I should have stayed, twisted round like that, in a position that gave me a lot of pain. But I felt I had to see him picked up. I had to know that there was no justification for the feeling of horror that had suddenly gripped me.

Higgins was rowing fast, a long, sweeping stroke that was full of power, and at each pull a little froth of white water showed at the dinghy's blunt bows. Every now and then he turned and looked over his shoulder, and I knew that it was at us he was looking and not at the man in the water.

We were pulling away from Yules all the time and I couldn't be sure how near Higgins was to him. But I heard Yules call out. 'Alf!' And he raised one hand. 'I'm here.' The words were distinct and very clear in the stillness of the fog. And then suddenly he was shouting and swimming with frantic desperation, his arms flailing the water, his feet kicking at the surface.

But Higgins never checked, never spoke a word to him. He left him to drown and the oars dipped and rose with terrible regularity, the water streaming from them at every stroke as he came after us.

There was one last despairing cry, and then silence. Sickened, I turned to look at Patch. 'It's a bigger dinghy than ours,' he said. He meant it as an explanation. He meant that Higgins couldn't afford to stop – not if he was to catch up with us. His face was quite white. He was rowing harder now, the sweat glistening on his forehead. His words sent a cold shiver through me, and I sat there, rigid, all pain momentarily forgotten.

After that I was conscious all the time of the dinghy behind us. I can see it still, like a deadly water-beetle crawling after us across the sea, everlastingly following us through an unreal miasma of fog; and I can hear the creak of the rowlocks, the dip and splash of the oars. And I can see Patch, too, his set face leaning towards me and then pulling back, endlessly moving back and forth as he tugged at the oars, tugged till his teeth were clenched with the pain of his blistered hands, until the blisters broke and the blood dripped on the oars – hour after wretched hour.

At one time Higgins was less than fifty yards behind us and I could see every detail of his boat. It was a gay blue metal dinghy, a little battered, with the paint flaking and dulled with age, and round the gunn'ls was a heavy canvas fend-off. The thing was meant to hold five or six people and it had bluff bows so that every time he pulled it smiled an ugly, puffy smile as the thrust piled the water up in front of it.

But he had used his brute strength recklessly and he didn't gain on us any more.

The fog thinned out as night fell until it was no more than a tattered veil through which we caught glimpses of the stars. The young moon gave it a queer luminosity so that we could still see Higgins following us, little drops of phosphoresence marking the oar blades as they lifted clear of the water.

We stopped once and Patch managed to jerk my shoulder back into its socket, and a little later I moved over to the centre thwart and took the left oar, rowing one-handed. Though I was in considerable pain, we were fairly well balanced, for by then he was very tired.

We continued like that all night, holding our course by the hand-bearing compass that stood at our feet, its card glowing faintly. The moon set and the luminosity faded. We lost sight of Higgins. A wind sprang up and waves broke on the swell, slopping water over the gunn'ls. But it died away again about four and at last the stars paled in the first glimmer of returning daylight. It was one of those cold, cloud-streaked dawns that come reluctantly. It showed a lumpy sea, full of tidal swirls, and a blanket of fog lay ahead of us, clamped down between us and the coast of France.

We breakfasted on three squares of chocolate. It was half of all we had left. The woodwork of the dinghy was beaded with dew, our clothes sodden with it. Water slopped about over the floor-boards as we pitched in the sea, and in our exhaustion it was becoming more and more difficult to row a course. 'How much further?' I gasped.

Patch looked at me, his face grey, the eyes deep-sunk. 'I don't know,' he breathed. His lips were all cracked and rimed with salt. He frowned, trying to concentrate his mind. 'Tide's west-going. Be with us in two hours.' He dipped his hand in the sea and wiped salt water over his face. 'Shouldn't be long.'

Not long! I gritted my teeth. The salt was behind my eyeballs, in my mouth; it pricked my skin. The dawn's chill gripped me. I wished to God I'd never met this gaunt stranger who rowed like death at my shoulder. My mind blurred to a vision of Mike and our plans. And now the future was dead, *Sea Witch* gone and nothing in the world to think about but the Minkies, with each stroke an agony.

The sea at dawn had been empty. I could have sworn it had been empty. I had searched it carefully – every trough, every swirl, every sudden humped-up heap of water. There had been nothing – absolutely nothing. And now, suddenly, I was looking at a speck away over Patch's shoulder. The sun was coming up in a great ball of fire and the clouds that streaked the east were glowing orange and blazing to red at their edges – and all this vivid surge of colour, imprinted in the sea, seemed designed solely to show me that speck etched black in silhouette. It was a boat with two oars and a man rowing.

Ten minutes later the fog folded its clammy blanket round us again. The speck blurred and vanished. And at that moment I thought I heard a bell, very faint to the east of us. But when we stopped rowing it was gone. There wasn't a sound, except the sea. It was all round us in our grey, boxed-in world – the wet slop of water. But a little later there was a murmuring and a sucking in the veil through which our eyes couldn't see, and almost immediately the fog darkened, became black, and a shape slid past us like the towering superstructure of a battleship. It was there for an instant, blurred and indistinct, a great mass of black rock with the swell frothing gently at its base, and then it was gone as the tide hurried us on. 'My God! We're there,' I gasped.

We had stopped rowing and all around us was the murmur of the sea. Another rock appeared out of the grey curtain of the fog, a sinister pillar of rock like a crooked finger that slid stealthily by with a froth of white water at its foot as though it were sailing past us. For a moment that damnable fog almost convinced me that I was in a geological nightmare in which the rocks steamed through the water under their own power. And then a swell came up, grew big and broke suddenly. Water surged over the gunn'l and we were thrown backwards as the dinghy hit a submerged rock. The tide swung us round and dragged us clear before the next swell broke. We were soaked, the dinghy half-full of water. It was hopeless to go on with the tide swirling us through a maze of dangerous rocks. We had reached the Minkies, but in an area of reefs almost twenty miles by ten we had no hope of getting our bearings. 'We'll have to wait till the fog clears,' Patch said. 'It's too dangerous – almost dead low water.'

In the lee of an ugly island of rock we found a little inlet where the water was still, like glass, tied the dinghy to an up-ended slab and clambered stiffly out. We stamped and moved about, but the sweat still clung to us in an icy film and we shivered under our sodden duffle coats. We ate the last of our chocolate and talked a little, grateful for the sound of our voices in that cold, dismal place.

I suppose it was inevitable that Patch should have talked about the *Mary Deare*. We were so close to her, frustrated by the fog. He talked about Rice for a bit and then he was telling me about Taggart's death. He seemed to want to talk about it. 'Poor devil!' he whispered. 'For the sake of that girl of his he'd sold his soul in every port in the Far East. He'd ruined his health and drunk himself stupid, engaging in every shady deal that would pay him more than a captain's wage. That's why they got him up from Singapore.'

'Did Gundersen engage him then?' I asked.

'Probably. I don't know.' He shrugged his shoulders. 'Whoever it was, they picked the wrong moment. The old vulture was going back home to his daughter, and he wasn't going to sink a ship on his last voyage.'

'And so Dellimare got rid of him – is that what you're suggesting?' I asked.

He shook his head. 'No, I don't think he intended to kill him. I think he just got hold of his liquor and was waiting until the old man was sufficiently softened up to do what he wanted. He couldn't have known he'd die that night.' He smiled at me out of the corner of his mouth. 'But it amounts to the same thing, doesn't it?' He had sat with Taggart for several hours that night, listening to a life story told in scraps of delirium – the risks and the crookery and the shady deals . . . and then two men had been drowned. That was what had started Taggart drinking. 'Like most of us, he just wanted to forget.' And he went on, conjuring up the ghost of that dreadful old man, completely absorbed in the tragedy of it, standing there on that rock like a Trappist monk, his body shivering under the limp brown folds of his duffle coat.

He switched suddenly to the daughter . . . that photograph, what it had meant to him. Her image had been his confidante, his inspiration, a symbol of all his desperate hopes. And then the meeting in St Malo – the shock of realizing that there were things he couldn't tell her, that she knew he was hiding something from her.

'You're in love with her, aren't you?' I said. We were strangely close, alone together in the eerie stillness of the fog with the sea all round us.

'Yes.' His voice had a sudden lift to it, as though even here the thought of her could raise his spirits.

'Despite what she did to you in Court?'

'Oh, that!' He dismissed it. That last night in Southampton – she had come to apologize. And after that he had told her every-thing – all the things he had confided to her picture. 'I had to tell somebody,' he murmured.

He lifted his head suddenly and sniffed at a breath of wind that came to us out of the dripping void. 'Still westerly,' he said, and we talked about how soon the fog would clear. He hadn't liked the look of the dawn. 'That depression,' he muttered. 'We've got to reach the salvage ship before it starts to blow up dirty.' The words were ominous.

And shortly after that we had to go back to the dinghy. The tide had risen, covering the rocks of our inlet, and it kept us con-stantly on the move then. We were in a strange submarine world where everything dripped water and the floor of the sea rose steadily until the towering bastion of the rock had dwindled to a miserable little island barely two feet above the level of the sea. It was two o'clock then and the swell had increased and was showering us with spray as we sat huddled together in the dinghy.

I was barely conscious of time. The fog hung round us, very thick, so that it seemed as though nothing could exist in the whole world except that miserable strip of rock and the ugly, surging water.

We didn't talk much. We were too desperately cold. We took it in turns to sit and drift into a sort of coma. The tide went down again and the rock re-emerged like some monster lifting its dripping body out of the sea.

It was just after five that the fog began to clear. A wind sprang up and gradually the greyness lightened until it was an iridescent dazzle that hurt the eyes. Shapes began to emerge, forming themselves into rocks, and the sea stretched further and further away from us. Above our heads a patch of sky appeared, startlingly blue, and suddenly the fog was gone and the sun shone. We were in a sparkling world of blue-green water littered with rock outcrops.

We made the dinghy fast and scrambled up the barnacle-covered, weed-grown fortress of the rock. It was suddenly very warm, and from the top, which only a few hours before had been a bare, wave-worn little island, a fantastic sight met our eyes. All round us the sea was islanded with rock – mile upon mile of sinister reefs and outcrops – the Minkies at one hour before low water. Beyond the rock islands, we had glimpses of open sea – except to the south-west; to the south-west the islands became so numerous that they merged to form a solid barrier.

The beacon on Maîtresse Île, which stands 31 feet at high water, was easily identified, and from it Patch was able to get our bearings. The rock on which we stood was on the northern side of the Minkies, about a mile inside the outer bastion of the Pipette Rocks, and he reckoned that the *Mary Deare* must lie almost due south of us. I have checked since with the large-scale chart and find that he was just about right. But the three miles that separated us from our objective constituted the main body of the reefs. We didn't appreciate this at the time, nor did we fully understand the extraordinary change in configuration of the above-water reefs that could occur in the last stages of the falling tide.

The wind was blowing quite fresh and an ugly little chop was forming on the long swell that marched steadily eastwards through the reefs. Already there was a good deal of white water about, particularly in the vicinity of submerged rocks, and I think we should have been more cautious if we hadn't suddenly caught sight of Higgins. He was standing on a big rock mass not half a mile to the east of us. It was probably the Grand Vascelin, for there was a black and white beacon on it, and even as Patch pointed him out to me, I saw Higgins move and begin to scramble down to his dinghy, which we could see bobbing about at the base of the rock, its blue paint looking bright and cheerful in the sunshine.

We moved fast then, slithering and tumbling down to our own dinghy, scrambling into it and pushing off with no time to plan our route across the reefs, knowing only that the tide, which was west-going at that time, favoured Higgins and that we had to cover those three miles and reach the safety of the salvage company's vessel before he caught up with us.

Of course, we should never have shown ourselves against the skyline at the top of that rock. If we had thought about it at all, we must have known that, the instant the fog cleared, he would be standing on some vantage point watching for us. It wasn't that we had forgotten about him. You can't forget about a man when he has followed you all night through a treacherous, abandoned stretch of sea with murder in his heart. But I think the fog had so isolated us mentally that the moment it cleared we rushed to the highest point to get a sight of the world that had been hidden from us for so long. It was an instinctive reaction, and in any case we were dull-witted with cold and exhaustion.

The one sensible thing we did was to put on our life-jackets and then we pushed off from the rock that had been our perch for almost twelve hours and Patch began to row, heading south-west across the tide. Away from the lee of the rock we were conscious immediately of the weight of the wind and the way the sea was kicking up; it was a west wind, blowing over the tide, and already the waves were beginning to break. It crossed my mind that this might be the beginning of the depression. The sunshine had a brittle quality and long tongues of pale cloud, wind-blown like mares'-tails, were licking out across the sky.

The tide wasn't strong, but it carried us inexorably towards the greatest mass of the dried-out reefs. This mass is actually split by two channels, but we couldn't see that and for a time Patch attempted to make up against the tide to pass to the east of it, where we could see there was open water. But then, suddenly, he altered course. I was baling at the time, using a sou'wester, and I looked up at him enquiringly. I thought perhaps the tide had become too strong or that he felt we were shipping too much water. But he nodded across the stern. 'Higgins,' he said, and I turned to see the big blue dinghy emerging from behind a jagged huddle of rocks. It wasn't more than two cables behind us.

We were in open water then, in the broad channel that separates the outer wall of reefs from the main fortress mass. There were no rocks to shelter us and the breaking wave-tops constantly slopped over the gunn'ls so that, though I never stopped baling, the water in the bottom of the dinghy steadily increased. I could hear Patch's breath escaping between his teeth and every time I glanced aft, it seemed that Higgins was nearer, the big metal dinghy riding higher and easier than ours. He was keeping a little to the east of us, heading us off from the open water, and all the time the outer rocks of the main reef were slowly closing in on us, the swell breaking all along their edge, the white water piling in over the black teeth of the outer fringe.

'You'll have to turn into the wind,' I shouted.

Patch glanced over his shoulder, still rowing steadily, and then nodded. The twenty-foot wall of rocks were very close now. But each time he turned, the starboard bow of the dinghy caught the full force of the breaking waves and water poured in, threatening to sink us. There was nothing for it but to hold our course, head for the rocks and hope for the best.

The tide helped us here, sliding us westwards, along the face of the rampart, into a bay where the swell built up to 4 or 5 feet and broke on outlying ledges in a cataract of foam. Every stroke of the oars carried us deeper into the bay, making escape from it more impossible. 'We'll never get out of this,' I shouted to Patch.

He said nothing. He had no breath left to talk. I glanced over the stern and saw that Higgins had closed the distance to less than two hundred yards. Patch had to go on rowing. And then, over his shoulder, I saw the rocks at the inner end of the bay draw apart and, unbelievably, there was open water between them. 'Look!' I pointed.

Patch glanced quickly over his right shoulder, saw the gap and turned the dinghy towards it. We were in the first of the two channels with the wind behind us. The dinghy rose and fell to the steep swell. We shipped hardly any water now and I was able to bale her right out so that we rode light and easy. 'We'll make it now!' Patch's voice came to me through the wind and the noise of the sea breaking along both sides of channel and it was full of confidence. He was grinning through his bared teeth, recklessly squandering his energy as he rowed with quick, straining tugs at the oars.

As soon as I had finished baling I took my place on the thwart beside him and we rowed in unison, not saying anything, just pulling and watching Higgins as he fell into the troughs of the endless waves and was borne aloft again on the next crest. The world smiled with the brittle glitter of white water. Only the rocks were ugly and their menace was oddly enhanced because the sun shone.

We reached the narrowest point of the channel, guarded by a single rock outcrop, and then it suddenly opened out into a broad area of water with a reef mass ahead, but plenty of water round it. It was protected somewhat from the wind so that, though the swells still surged across it, there were few whitecaps – just patches of broken water here and there.

But as we moved out into that broad patch of open water, a strange and terrifying change began to come over it. The first indication of something wrong was a swell that suddenly reared up behind the dinghy's stern and broke, slewing us broadside in the surf and very nearly turning us over. Patch shouted to me that we were on a reef and we pulled the dinghy clear of the danger spot. The swell was building up and breaking continuously at that point. And now, looking round, I noticed it was breaking at many other points – places where it hadn't been breaking only a few minutes before.

'The tide!' Patch yelled in my ear. 'Pull, man! Pull! It's the tide!'

I needed no urging. I would have pulled both arms out of their sockets to get out of that fearful place. All around us now were patches of white water, patches that joined up with other patches till there were irregular lines of surf breaking. What had been, only a few minutes ago, open water, was now, suddenly, transformed into a seething, roaring cauldron of broken water as the tide dropped like a lift to expose the rocks and gravel of the sea bed contained within the ramparts of the central reef mass.

I had only just grasped what was happening when a sudden wave lifted us up and crashed us down on to a rock. The jolt of it ran right up my spine like a blow to the base of the head. Water boiled all round us, white in the sunshine, glittering like soapsuds; rocks and boulders showed for an instant and then vanished as another wave of green water swept in, lifted us up and crashed us down again. And in the instant of being uplifted I have a sort of panoramic recollection of the scene: black reefs piled round that arena and the water all brittle white and boiling mad and little sections of sea bed showing – all passing before my eyes as the dinghy was swung violently round and then finally smashed down upon a little exposed hillock of grey gravel. It was a tiny oasis in the middle of chaos that came and went as the surf rolled across it.

We stumbled out, knee-deep in the spill of a wave, and, as it receded, we tipped the dinghy up, emptying it of water. But one glance told us that it was damaged beyond any repair we could effect on the spot – two planks were stove in for practically the whole length of the boat. 'Doesn't matter,' Patch shouted. 'We'd have to abandon it, anyway. Come on!' He bent down and removed the hand-bearing compass from its case. It was all he took. 'Come on!' he repeated. 'We walk and swim the rest.'

I stood and stared at him. I thought for a moment that he'd gone mad and imagined he was Christ, capable of walking the surface of that surging carpet of broken water. But he wasn't mad. He was a seaman and his mind worked quicker than mine. Already a change had come over the scene – there was less white water, and rocks and boulders and patches of gravel were appearing as the tide receded. And two hundred yards away Higgins was ploughing through water up to his knees, dragging his dinghy after him.

I bent to pick up the painter of our own dinghy and then realized it was useless. 'Come on!' Patch said again. 'We've got to be out of here before the tide comes back.' He had started to walk south and I followed, stumbling over hidden boulders, floundering into pot-holes, wet and dazed and exhausted.

The noise of the surf rolled back till it dwindled to a distant murmur, and in a moment, it seemed, all those acres that had been a roaring holocaust of tumbled water were suddenly still and quiet. No waves broke. Little raised beaches of boulder-strewn gravel shone wet in the sun and about them lay pools of water ruffled by the wind, and all round were the black rocks of the reef.

The sense of isolation, of loneliness and remoteness, was appalling. And it was enhanced by something that Higgins did, following on behind us. He came to our dinghy and, glancing back, I saw him pick it up in his two hands and smash it down against an outcrop of rock. The splintering crash of the wood breaking up was a sharp, savage sound. All the bows were stove in and my last contact with *Sea Witch* was wantonly destroyed.

And then Higgins started after us again, still dragging his dinghy. The tinny sound of it striking against the boulders was with us for a long time as we stumbled across stretches of exposed beach or waded through water that was sometimes so deep we had to swim. And at the back of my mind was the thought that we were twenty miles from the French coast, in an area that only a few local fishermen ever dared to visit. And in six short hours all this area of rock-strewn debris would be thirty feet below the sea, compressed, imprisoned, flattened by countless million tons of

347

water. The only thing that kept me going was the thought of that salvage ship, so close now. It couldn't be more than two miles away, three at the most . . . and there'd be a bunk and dry clothes and hot soup.

I saw Patch stumble and fall. He got up and staggered on. We were halfway to the black southern bastion of the reefs, floundering over a stretch of jagged, up-ended rocks. He fell several times after that. We both did. There was no strength left in us and when a foot slipped, the muscles gave. Our sodden clothing weighed us down, tripped us up.

The sun gradually died amongst the mares'-tails. Thicker clouds came up. I didn't see them come. The sweat was in my eyes. I saw nothing but what was immediately at my feet. But rock and gravel became drab and sombre. And later, much later, there was a light drizzle on my face. The sound of the sea began to come back, but by then we were crawling amongst the great up-ended slabs of rock that lay strewn about the main outcrop.

I hadn't looked back for a long time then. I didn't know where Higgins was. I couldn't hear the sound of his dinghy any more. It was lost in the noise of the sea and the drumming of the blood in my ears. And then we were clawing our way up the final slope of weed-grown rock. I paused to see Patch up at the top, leaning against a shoulder of rock and staring southwards. 'Can you see her?' I gasped.

'No.' He shook his head.

I came out on to the top beside him and stared south. It was still the Minkies. But different. More sea. There were still rock outcrops. But they were fewer, more isolated. All ahead of us was open water, dimmed and blurred by the drizzle of rain. 'I don't see her,' I gasped.

'She's there somewhere.' His voice was flat and weary. His black hair hung wet over his eyes and his hands and face were streaked with blood where he had fallen – blood and dirt and sodden, shapeless clothing. He took my arm. 'You all right?' he asked.

'Yes,' I said. 'Yes, I'm all right.'

He stared at me and for the first time I saw an expression of concern in his eyes. He opened his mouth to say something and then thought better of it and turned his head away. 'I'm sorry,' he said, and that was all.

'How much further do you reckon?' I asked.

'About a mile.'

A mile to swim. I wondered whether we should ever make it.

He took my arm again and pointed across the litter of outcrops to a compact mass that stood higher than any of the others. 'I think that's Grune à Croc.' It stood on the edge of visibility, half hidden by the drizzle, and at the mention of its name it abruptly vanished as the rain thickened and drove across it. Somewhere beyond that rock lay the *Mary Deare*.

Behind us, the tide came licking hungrily back across the beaches, coming in from the north-west, driven by the wind and the south-going set of the stream. But Higgins was clear of it by then, rowing slowly, easily, to a nearby rock, where he moored his dinghy and sat watching us like an animal that has treed its quarry. He could afford to wait, for with each foot the tide rose the size of our rock perch was halved.

We found an over-hanging slab of rock that gave us some shelter from the wind and the rain and still enabled us to watch him, and there we crouched, huddled close together for warmth whilst the tide rose and night closed in. If only the visibility had been better; if we could have seen the *Mary Deare*, perhaps attracted the attention of the salvage people. But we could see nothing; we couldn't even hear them. All we could hear was the waves pounding on the other side of the reef mass and I wondered what it would be like at the top of the tide. Would the waves break right over these rocks? But by then we should be gone. Our plan was to slip into the water an hour before high tide and make for Grune à Croc. We were relying on a southward thrust from the tide coming through the main reef body to spill us out towards the rock, and though Patch had lost the hand-bearing compass, we thought the rock would be reasonably conspicuous, since it was the only one in the whole area to the south of us that would be exposed at high water.

Once we had decided what to do, we had nothing to occupy our minds. It was then that I became conscious of hunger pains for the first time. It wasn't only the pains that worried me, but the feeling that I had no warmth left in me, as though the rain and the bitter cold had reached the central fires on which my body depended and put them out. I fell into a sort of coma of misery and through bleared eyes I watched the rock to which Higgins had moored slowly submerge. And then he was rowing again, and gradually the tide beat him. Oddly enough it gave me no sense of pleasure. I was too tired. As the tide ran faster so he had to row harder to keep abreast of our position. And then gradually his strokes became weaker until he was forced to steer to another rock and cling to it. But the tide rose and covered that, too, and, though he started to row again, the tide carried him slowly further and further from us. Night was closing in by then and I lost him in the gathering darkness.

It meant, of course, that we shouldn't have to worry about where Higgins was when we abandoned our rock and took to the water, but when you are faced with a long swim and are afraid you may be too weak to do it, then the question of whether there may or may not be a dinghy in the way doesn't seem very important. In any case, I was slipping into unconsciousness. I was so cold, so utterly drained of warmth – I had no sense of feeling left.

It was the water that woke me. It was warmer than I was and it lapped round my legs like a tepid bath. And then it slopped into my face. That was when consciousness returned and I felt Patch stir. 'Good God!' he murmured. 'It must be just about high water.'

We stood up, stiff to the joints, forcing our bodies to unbend. Was it high water? Had the tide turned already? My numbed brain groped for the answer, knowing it was important, but not knowing why. The rain had stopped. There were stars and low-scudding clouds. A glimmer of moonlight made pale reflections on the ink-black water. 'Well, do we go? What's the time?' Patch's voice was no more than a croak. 'What's the time, for God's sake? My watch has stopped.'

Mine had stopped, too. There was no means of knowing the time, no means of knowing which way the tide was flowing. Jolted by sudden fear, the sleep cleared from my brain and I saw clearly that we had no alternative. If we stayed on that rock we should die of exposure – tomorrow perhaps or the next day, but we should die. After tonight we should never have the strength to swim that mile. And the water was warm – warmer than the sodden, icy clothes draped round our bodies, warmer than the wind and the ice-cold driving rain that would come again. Besides, we had life-jackets and, if the tide was wrong, there were other rocks to cling to and die on. 'Ready?' I said.

Patch hesitated and I suddenly realized that he wasn't sure of himself any more. He was a seaman. He was used to boats, not to the sea itself as an element in which to exist, body buoyed up by water. 'Come on,' I said. 'We're going now. Keep close to me and don't talk.'

We inflated our life-jackets fully and then together we stepped off the ledge of rock on which we had huddled. When we had first come to that ledge it had been a thirty-foot drop to the rocks below. Now we stepped off into water, warm, buoyant water, and, lying on our backs, swam slowly south, our feet to the Pole Star, glimpsed every now and then through rents in the tattered cloud-base.

We kept abreast of each other, just two arms' lengths away, moving steadily and unhurriedly. Soon we were clear of the rocks, rising and falling gently to a big swell that was rolling in across the reefs. We could hear it pounding against distant rocks – the rocks to the west of us that got the full brunt of it. 'Storm coming up,' Patch whispered.

The wind had dropped. The swell was big, but gentle-sloped with no broken water. The sea slept, heaving as it slumbered. Yet I was sure Patch was right. Though the wind was light, the clouds were hurried and torn to shreds and the pounding of that surf was ominous, like gunfire to the west. A wave suddenly reared up out of nowhere and broke, pouring surf over us, spilling us away from it. My feet touched rock for an instant. And then everything was quiet as before and we rose and fell, rose and fell to the swell. We had crossed one of those sentinel-like pillars of rock that we had seen at low water.

The rock on which we had spent half the night was disappearing now – disappearing astern of us so that I knew we were all right. We hadn't missed the tide. Patch stopped swimming, treading water. 'I can't see Grune à Croc,' he said, and his teeth chattered. 'I think we should strike more to the west.'

So we swam on with the Pole Star and the Plough to our left and I wondered how long we could last. My teeth were chattering, too, and the sea, which had felt so warm at first, was now a cold compress chilling all my stomach. We had no food inside us to generate warmth. Soon one of us would get cramp, and that would be the end.

Our sodden clothing weighed us down. The inflated life-jackets made us clumsy. Each stroke had to be powerful to drive our bodies through the water; and power meant energy – our vital, last reserves of energy. God knows how long we swam that night. We seemed to go on and on for ever. And each stroke was imperceptibly weaker than the last. And all the time I was thinking if only I were wearing a foam rubber suit or at least had my fins on my feet. It was years since I had swum in this clumsy fashion. My mind sank into a coma, a slough of pain and deep exhaustion, in which I saw myself again ploughing down to the old tanker through clear bright Mediterranean waters that glimmered with colour – the white of the sand and the silver gleam of fish; and myself, buoyant and carefree, exactly balanced, warm and breathing comfortably through my mouthpiece.

'John! John!' I opened my eyes. Black night surrounded me. I thought for an instant I was deep down, on the verge of going into a rapture of the depths. And then I saw a star and heard the surge of a wave breaking. 'John!' The voice called again out of the darkness.

'Yes. What is it?'

'There's a rock. I can just see it.' It was Patch's voice. Funny, I thought. He'd never called me John before. And then he said, 'You gave me a scare just now. I couldn't make you hear. I thought I'd lost you.'

The concern in his voice filled me with a sudden warmth for the man. 'Sorry,' I said. 'Just dreaming. That's all. Where's this rock of yours?' I turned, treading water, and there, not more than a hundred yards to my right, the dark shape of a rock stood out for an instant against the white gleam of a breaking wave. I searched the blackness beyond it. More waves were breaking out there and I thought I saw the solid mass of something.

And then it came to me that there would be lights on the *Mary Deare*. With a salvage company working on her there would have to be lights. I searched the blackness all round, each time I was lifted to the top of a swell, but there was nothing, not the faintest flicker of a light. Perhaps they were being so secret about their salvage operation that they didn't show lights. And then the thought came to me that perhaps they had lifted her already and towed her away. The cold came back into my body, more intense now, more destructive, and I felt the muscles of my left leg begin to screw themselves together in a knot.

'There's something beyond this rock' Patch croaked. 'Shall we make for that?'

'All right,' I said. It didn't seem to matter. To die in the water was better than to die of exposure on one of those God-forsaken rocks. I lay back, kicking out feebly with my legs, thrusting at water that was no longer warm, but icy cold, swimming automatically whilst my mind tangled itself up with the matter of those lights. There should have been lights. Unless we'd been swept back into the central mass of the reefs we should have seen lights right from the start. 'There should be lights,' I mumbled.

'Lights. That's it. There should be lights.' His voice sounded weak, a little scared. And then, after a bit – 'Tell them to put the lights on.' He was back on a ship, his mind wandering. 'Put those lights on, do you hear?' And then suddenly he called 'John!' His voice was very faint.

'Yes?'

'I'm sorry I landed you into this.' He muttered something about my boat. And then I heard him say, 'I should have slit my useless throat.' Silence for a moment and then: 'They booed me, that first time. Outside the Court.' Broken water slapped my face and the next thing I heard was – '. . . kick against the pricks. I should have chucked it then.' A wave broke and silenced him. He didn't speak again after that. His arms didn't move. I could just see the outline of his head, motionless.

'Are you all right?' I called out.

He didn't answer and I swam over to him. 'Are you all right?' I shouted again.

'Look! Do you see it?'

I thought his mind had gone. 'Wake up!' I shouted at him. 'We're going to swim to that rock – do you hear?'

He caught hold of my arm with the iron grip of a drowning man and, as I wrenched myself free of him, he screamed at me. 'Look, man. Look at it, damn you! Tell me I'm not dreaming!'

He had raised his arm and was pointing. I turned my head and there, against the stars, I saw the tall finger of a mast and, below it, all the black bulk of her superstructure caught for an instant in the white phosphorescent glitter of a breaking wave.

We swam then, cold and exhaustion forgotten, tugging our weary, unwieldy bodies through the water. We were coming up on her bows and they were like a reef awash: the waves rolled over them, but in the troughs their shape emerged as the sea cascaded from them. And then, beyond the bows, beyond the tall finger of the mast, the bridge deck emerged and the funnel and all the line of the decks sloping upwards to her cocked-up stern.

In the trough of a wave a hard line sprang suddenly taut, catching at my left arm so that I screamed with pain, gulping in salt water; and then it flipped me over and the top of a wave engulfed me. I swam clear of the bows then, moving painfully down the ship, just clear of the streaming bulwarks, and then swam in on her where the fo'c'stle dropped to the well-deck and Number One hatch. I came in on the top of a wave that broke as it surged over the bulwarks and then I was flung down on to the hatch coaming with a force that jarred all the torn muscles of my side and my feet scrabbled on weed-grown, slippery plating whilst the wave receded in a swirl of white water.

I fetched up in the scuppers with my hand gripped round the capping of the bulwarks, and as the next wave piled in, I fought my way aft until I was clear of the water and could reach the mast, and there I clung, shouting for Patch in a high, cracked voice, for I was scared I'd lost him. That moment of panic seemed endless. I was the better swimmer. I was trained to the sea. I should have stayed with him, seen him safe on board, and I knew I hadn't the guts to go back and search for him in the darkness; I was tired, desperately tired, with all the muscles of my body curling up with the threat of cramp. And, even more, I didn't want to be alone on that ship. It was a dead ship – dead as the rocks of the Minkies. I knew it, instinctively. I could sense that it was dead through all my body and I needed him desperately. And so I clung to the mast and screamed his name and the seas came thundering in across the bows with wicked gleams of white as the water surged and swirled and poured off them in the troughs.

I didn't see him come aboard. I was still screaming his name and he was suddenly there beside me, staggering drunkenly, an ungainly, top-heavy shape in his life-jacket caught in silhouette against the break of a wave. 'It's all right,' he gasped. 'I'm here.' He reached out and caught hold of my hand, and we clung there, gasping for breath, grateful for the sudden comfort of that touch. 'There should be lights,' he said at length. There was a sort of childish disappointment in his voice, as though the salvage company had robbed him of a pleasure to which he had been looking forward.

'They've probably closed down for the night,' I said, but without conviction. I knew the ship was dead.

'But there should be lights,' he said again. And then we staggered aft, past Number Two hatch, up the ladder to the upper-deck. The door to the deck-house stood drunkenly open, crumpled and torn from its hinges. We felt our way along the alley, past his old cabin and Dellimare's and out through the empty gap of the door beyond, out on to the upper-deck, where the twisted shapes of the empty davits stood like crooked fingers against starlit patches of the sky, and on, past the dim-seen shape of the funnel, crumpled and lying away from us at a precarious angle.

Squelching soggily on the steel of the deck, our bodies thin as paper in the cold night air, we traipsed the length of the *Mary Deare*, aft to the little deck-house on the poop and back again up the starboard side, and every now and then we shouted – 'Ahoy! Anybody there? Ahoy!' Not even an echo came back to us. The frail sound of our voices was lost in the cold, black night, buried in the noise of the waves surging over the bows.

No salvage boat lay alongside. No light suddenly flickered to guide us to the warmth of a cabin. We called and called, but nobody answered. The ship was dead, devoid of life – as dead as she had been the day we'd left her there.

'My God!' Patch breathed. 'We're the first. Nobody has been here.' There was a note of relief, almost exultation in his voice, and I knew he was thinking of the thing that lay buried amidst the coal of the port bunker. But all I cared about at that moment was that I was cold and wet and hurt and that, instead of the bunk and dry clothes, the warmth of food and drink and the companionship of human beings I had expected, there was nothing – nothing but the slime-covered, barnacle-encrusted shell of a wreck that had been battered by the seas for six long weeks.

'We'll get some dry clothes and have a sleep,' he said. 'We'll feel better then.' He had sensed my mood. But when we had staggered back to the bridge-housing and felt our way down the black iron tunnel of the alley-way to what had been his cabin, we found that the sea had been there. The door grated on sand as we forced it open and a freezing wind drove at us through portholes that stared like two luminous eyes, empty of glass. The desk had been ripped from its fastenings and lay on its side in a corner, the drawers of the bunk that contained his and Taggart's clothes were full of water and the big wall cupboard contained nothing but a sodden, gritty heap of blankets, coats and old papers.

We tried the main deck then, where the saloon and the galley were. But that was worse. The sea had swept the whole length of the alley-ways, into the officers' cabins and right aft to the crew's quarters. Everything we touched in the pitch-black darkness was sodden, filmed with slime; there wasn't a place the sea hadn't reached.

'Maybe the poop is still dry.' Patch said it wearily, without hope, and we began to move back down the port alley-way, feeling our way, bodies dead and numbed with cold, shivering uncontrollably. God, let the poop be dry! And then I staggered and hit my shoulder against the wet steel plate of the wall, thrown there by a sudden movement of the ship. I felt it through my whole body, a quiver like the first faint tremor of an earthquake. And then the ship moved again. 'Listen!' Patch's voice was urgent in the darkness. But I could hear nothing except the noise of the sea lapping at the hull. 'She's afloat,' he whispered. 'Just afloat on top of the tide.'

'How can she be?' I said.

'I don't know, but she is. Feel her!'

I felt her quiver and lift, and then she thudded back into her gravel bed. But she still went on quivering and from deep down in the bowels of her came a slow grating sound; and all the time she was trembling as though she were stirring in her sleep, struggling to free herself from the deadly reef bed on which she lay. 'It's not possible,' I murmured. The ship couldn't be afloat when her bows were submerged like a reef and the waves were rolling over them. This must be a dream. And I thought then that perhaps we had drowned out there. Did drowned men go back to their ships and dream that they shook off the reef shackles and voyaged like ghosts through dark, unnatural seas? My mind was beyond coherent thought. The ship was dead. That I knew, and beyond that, all I wanted was to lose consciousness of cold and pain, to lie down and sleep.

A hand reached out and gripped me, holding me up, and my feet trod the iron of the passage-way and climbed, without volition, up into the cold of the night air, to glimpses of stars and a drunken funnel and the unending noise of the sea. Down aft we stumbled over a steel hawser laid taut across the well-deck. It thrummed and sang to the sea's roll, and the ship moved like a drunkard, tottering its masts against the sky, as we climbed the ladder to the poop's platform and vanished into the black abyss of the little deck-house. There was clothing there in the bos'n's cabin. As I remember, it was neither wet nor dry, but it had more warmth than my own sodden clothes, and there was a dank bunk, with blankets smelling of wet like a dog's fur, and sleep – the utter oblivion of sleep, more perfect than any heaven ever dreamed of by a well-fed man seated by his own fireside.

A long time after, it seemed – many years, perhaps – the tread of a man's feet entered into that heavenly oblivion. I can't say that it woke me or even that I struggled back to consciousness. Not immediately. It was just that the tread of his feet was there; a solid, metallic sound – the ring of boots on steel plates. It was a penetrating, insistent sound. It was above my head, beside my bed, first one side, then the other, and then further away – a slow, unhurried, purposeful tread . . . the march of a dead man across the sleep of oblivion. And when it was no longer there I woke.

Daylight stabbed at my bleared eyes and a huddle of sodden blankets in the corner of the dank steel prison in which I lay, stirred and rose. It was Patch, his face ashen with fatigue. 'I thought I heard footsteps,' he said. His eyes looked wild, black marbles sunk deep in ivory sockets. 'I swear I heard somebody.'

I crawled out of the bunk, sweaty with the salt-heat of a soggy mass of blankets, but cold and stiff with a gnawing pain in my belly and my shoulder aching like hell. It all came back to me then, hitting me like a physical blow, and I stumbled to the door and looked out. It was true then – not a dream. I was back on the *Mary Deare*, and . . . God, she was a wreck! She was a rust-red nightmare of a ship, smeared with a film of green slime, with a stubble-growth of grey that was the barnacles. Her funnel lay over at a crazy angle and all the bridge-deck was twisted and gnarled and battered. The tide was low and, beyond the wreck of her, the Minkies gnashed their black teeth, foam-flecked where the stumps of rock stuck up out of the sea. No salvage ship lay anchored off, no tug, not even a fishing boat. There was nothing – just the ugly, familiar shape of Grune à Croc and the mass of the reefs beyond . . . not a single sign of life, and the sky savagely grey, with an ugly pallor that made the cloud shapes black and cold-looking.

'My God!' I croaked. Instinctively, perhaps, I knew what we had to face – what the pallor of the dawn meant and the savage grey of the sky.

And Patch, sniffing the air over my shoulder, muttered, 'There's a heap of dirt coming up.'

The sky to the west of us was sombre, a black wedge of cloud that left the horizon sharp as a line ruled between air and sea. There wasn't much wind, but the thunder of the waves on the exposed reefs had an ominous sound, and, even here, in the shelter of the rocks, the swell that slopped against the *Mary Deare*'s side was big and solid.

'Those footsteps,' I said. 'What were they?'

He shook his head, not answering, and his eyes avoided mine. God knows what he was thinking, but a shudder ran through him, and it crossed my mind that a lot of men had died because of this ship. And then a strange thing happened: a little cloud of rust rose like red steam from the well-deck bulwark as a steel hawser ran out over the side. The bight appeared, checked on the rail, and then fell over into the sea with a faint splash. When it was gone, the ship was still again – no movement anywhere, and I was conscious that Patch was gripping my arm. 'Queer,' he said, and his voice had a hollow sound.

We stood rooted to the spot for a long time, staring along the length of the ship. But everything was still and motionless – nothing moved except the sea.

'There's somebody on board,' he said. His tone was uneasy and his face was as drawn and haggard as it had been on the day I had first met him. 'Listen!' But I could hear nothing – only the slap of the waves against the ship's side and the pounding of the swell on the reefs. The wreck was as still and as quiet as the grave. A lone sea-bird drifted by, soundless on the wind and white like a piece of paper against the clouds.

Patch descended then to the well-deck and stopped to gaze at the cover of Number Four hatch. And when I joined him I saw that it wasn't the usual tarpaulin cover fixed with wooden wedges, but steel plates fresh-welded to the coaming. He had a look at the derrick winches and then we went past Number Three hatch, which was also plated over, and up the ladder to the boat deck. Here all the ventilators had been removed and lay about the deck like truncated limbs, the ventilation holes covered by rusty plating. The funnel had been cut through at the base by a blow-torch, shifted to one side and the vent plated over. The engine-room skylight was screwed down tight and the water-tight doors to the port and starboard main-deck alley-ways had been removed and the holes plated over.

There was no doubt whatever that the report of the St Helier fisherman had been correct. A salvage company had been working on the wreck. They had sealed off the whole hull of the *Mary Deare* and probably they had also repaired the leak in the for'ard holds. It explained the way she had lifted at the top of the tide and the rake of the decks to the cocked-up stern. The ship was water-tight, almost ready to float off. I found Patch standing by the port bunkering chute, his eyes riveted on the hatch cover, which had been torn from its hinges and lay abandoned on the deck. In its place a steel plate had been welded over the chute, effectively sealing the bunker off. It meant that Dellimare's body would remain there in its steel coffin until the hulk was towed into port and officials came on board with equipment to open up the ship. It meant days, possibly weeks of suspense for him, and there was despair in his face as he said, 'Well, that's that.' And he turned away, to stare aft along the length of the ship. 'They should have had a stern line out,' he said.

I wasn't following his trend of thought. I was thinking that there was all this work completed and no salvage ship. 'Why do you think they left?' I asked him.

He glanced at the sky, sniffing the breeze from the west, which was coming now in irregular puffs. 'The forecast was probably bad,' he said. 'Maybe they had a gale warning.'

I stared at the jagged reefs, remembering what it had been like before. Surely to God . . .

'What's that?' His voice came sharp and clear, and through

it, beyond the barrier of the bridge-deck, the cough of a diesel engine settled to a steady roar. I could feel the deck vibrating under my feet, and for a moment we stood, quite still, listening to the music of it. Then we were running for the bridge-deck alley-way. We came out at the head of the ladder that led down to the for'ard well-deck and there, just aft of Number Two hatch, stood a big suction pump, lashed to the deck. The engine was going full bat and the thick suction pipe was pulsating with the flow of water where it disappeared through a hole cut in an inspection hatch. Water was sluicing out of the far side of the pump, flooding across the deck and disappearing through the scuppers. And yet there was nobody there. The well-deck was empty and in all the fore part of the ship there wasn't a living soul.

It was uncanny.

'Try the bridge,' Patch said. 'Somebody started that pump.'

We dived back into the alley-way and up the ladder to the bridge. It was all so familiar, but horribly changed. The glass was gone, the doors smashed and the wind was whistling through it, pushing little rivulets of water across the sand-smeared plat-form. There was nobody there – nobody in the chartroom. And then, out on the bridge again, Patch gripped my arm and pointed. Beyond the bows a pillar-like rock stood like a bollard with the bite of a thick steel hawser round it. The hawser ran taut from rock to ship, an anchor against the pull of the tides. It was the hawser that had fouled me during the night as I swam in over the bows.

But Patch was pointing to something else – a small blue dinghy pulling out from under the *Mary Deare*'s bows. It was Higgins, and he was rowing out to the rock. The peaked cap on the bull head, the massive shoulders and the blue seaman's jersey – it was all so clear in the cold grey light. It was clear, too, what he in-tended to do. I shouted to him, but he couldn't hear me from the bridge. I dived back down the ladder, down to the well-deck and up on to the fo'c'sle. 'Higgins!' I screamed at him. 'Higgins!'

But it was blowing quite strong in the gusts now and Higgins didn't hear me. He had reached the rock and was tying the dinghy to a snag, and then he began to climb. He reached the bight of the hawser and, with an iron bar he had brought with him for the purpose, began to lever it up the rock, whilst I shouted to him, standing up in the wind, balanced right on the slippery point of the *Mary Deare*'s bows.

He had his back to me all the time and when he'd freed the loop, he pushed it up over the jagged point of the rock and the whole line of the wire that anchored the ship, right from where it ran out through the hawse-hole, went slack as it fell with a splash into the sea. Then he clambered back down the rock and got into his dinghy.

He saw me just as he'd unhitched the painter and he sat looking at me for a moment. His face was without expression and his big shoulders sagged with the effort he had made. And all the time I was shouting to him, telling him to fix the hawser back on to the rock. 'There's a gale coming,' I shouted. 'A gale!' I kept on repeating that one word, trying to din it into his thick head.

Maybe I succeeded, for Higgins suddenly let go of the rock, pivoted the dinghy on one oar and began to row back towards the *Mary Deare*. Whether he panicked and was making a desperate attempt to get back on board, or whether he was moved to un-expected pity by the desolate character of the place and was trying to take us off, I shall never know, for the tide was north-going, about three knots, and though he worked like a man possessed to drag that heavy dinghy through the water faster than the tide ran, he made not more than twenty yards' headway. He tired quickly and, after the first burst of energy, he made no further progress; and then, gradually, the tide took control and he drifted further and further away from the ship, still desperately rowing.

In the end he gave it up and steered the dinghy across the tide into the lee of Grune à Croc, and there he sat, clutching the rock, staring at the ship, his head bowed to his knees, his whole body slack with exhaustion.

The noise of the suction pump died and ceased abruptly so that I was suddenly conscious of the wind whining through the broken superstructure. Patch had switched the engine off and as I climbed down off the fore-peak he came to meet me. 'We've got to flood the ship,' he called out, his voice loud and clear. 'It's our only hope.'

But there was no way of flooding her now. Every vent and hole was sealed off and we couldn't get at the sea cocks. Even the doors of the engine-room had been welded to keep the water out. The salvage company had sealed that hull up as tight as a submarine. 'We'll just have to hope for the best,' I said.

Patch laughed. The sound had a hollow ring down there in the steel vault of the alley-way. 'A westerly gale will bring a big tide. She'll float off at high water. Bound to, with nothing to hold her. She's pumped dry, all but the two for'ard holds.' His voice sounded hoarse and cracked. 'I wouldn't mind for myself.' He was staring at me. 'But it's tough on you.' And then he shrugged his shoulders and added, 'Better see if we can find some food.'

I was appalled by his acceptance of it, and as I followed him back down the alley-way to the galley, I was thinking that if only I had woken in time. The French salvage men had had her securely moored with hawsers fore and aft, and Higgins had let them go. I couldn't hate the man. I hadn't the strength to hate. But if only I'd got up the instant I'd heard those footsteps . . . And as though he knew what was in my mind, Patch said, 'One thing – Higgins is going to have a bad time of it out there in that dinghy.'

The galley was dark and it stank. The sea had been there before us, and so had the French. There wasn't a tin of any sort in the place. There was a cupboard full of bread that was a pulped, mildewed mass and there was meat that heaved with maggots and butter thick with slime and sand. All we found was some cheese that was good in the centre, a jar of half-dried mustard, some pickles and a broken pot of marmalade. We broke our fast on that, wolfing it down, and then we searched the saloon and all through the officers' cabins and the crews' quarters. We found a sticky mass of boiled sweets and a jar of ginger and, best of all, some stoker had gone to earth with two tins of bully beef. We took our miserable haul back to the little deck-house on the poop and ate it, sitting there, shivering and listening to the rising note of the wind.

The gale came up fast with the turn of the tide and soon the waves, breaking against the side of the wreck, were reaching up to the bridge-deck and we could feel the stern beginning to move under us. Once, when I went to look out of the door, I saw the blue dinghy still bobbing in the lee of Grune à Croc.

By midday it was blowing full gale. All the forepart of the *Mary Deare* was being pounded and battered by huge seas, her bridge-deck hidden every now and then in sheets of white water, the whole hull quivering to the onslaught. Water swirled across the well-deck below us and the boom of the waves striking against the plates of her side was so shattering that I found myself holding my breath, waiting for them, as though the blows were being struck against my own body. The noise went on and on. It filled my head and left no room for any thought beyond the terrible, ever-lasting consciousness of the sea. And out beyond the sea-swept wreck of the *Mary Deare*, the stumps of the reefs dwindled as the Minkies gradually vanished in a welter of foaming surf.

I saw Higgins once more. It was about two hours before high water. The *Mary Deare* was beginning to lift and shift her bottom on the gravel bed and Grune à Croc was a grey molar stuck up out of a sea of foam with water streaming white from its sides and spray sweeping across in a low-flung cloud, driven by the wind. Higgins was moving on the back of the rock, climbing down towards the dinghy. I saw him get into it and pick up the oars. And then a squall came, blurring the shape of the rock, and I suddenly lost sight of him in a curtain of rain.

That was the last I saw of Higgins. It was the last anybody saw of him. I suppose he was trying to reach the *Mary Deare*. Or perhaps he thought he could reach the mainland in the dinghy. He had no choice, anyway; Grune à Croc would have been untenable at high water.

I stood in the doorway of our deck-house for a long time, my eyes slitted against the rain and the driving spray, watching for a glimpse of him through the squall. In the end the seas drove me in and when I told Patch how Higgins had gone, he shrugged his shoulders and said, 'Lucky bastard! He's probably dead by now.' There was no anger in his voice, only weariness.

The cabin in that deck-house was about ten feet by six, steel-walled, with a bunk, some broken furniture, a window that had no glass in it and sand on the floor. It was damp and cold, the air smoking with wind-driven spray, and it resounded like a tin box to every sound throughout the ship. We had chosen it for our refuge because it was perched high up on the stern, and it was the stern part of the ship that was afloat.

For a long time we had been conscious of movement, a rising and falling of the steel walls that coincided with the gun-fire bursts of the waves crashing against the hull below us. But now there was a shifting and a grating of the keel. It was a sound felt rather than heard, for nothing was really audible except the incredible, over-whelming noise of the sea. And then gradually it lessened. Spray ceased to come in through the window. The door blew open with a crash. The *Mary Deare* had struggled free of the sea bed and was turning head to wind.

I looked out and saw that Grune à Croc was no longer on the port bow, but away to starboard. The *Mary Deare* was afloat. The movement was easier now, the noise of the sea less terrifying. The high stern was acting as a steadying sail and she was bows-on to the breaking waves. I could hear them thundering against the bridge-deck, see them burst in a great cloud of spray, forcing water through every opening of the bridge-housing as the broken tops swept by on either side. And all the time Grune à Croc was fading away.

I shouted to Patch that we were clear and he came out from the cabin and stood looking at the incredible sight – a wreck floating with her decks streaming rivers of water and sloped down so that all the fore part of her was below the waves. 'We're clear,' I cried. 'If we clear Les Sauvages we're all right.'

He looked at me. I think he was considering leaving me in ignorance. But then he said, 'It must be very near high water.'

I nodded. 'Just about,' I said. And then it came to me: for six solid hours after high water the tide would be north and west-going – driving us back on to the Minkies, back on to the Minkies at low water with all the reefs exposed. 'God Almighty!' I breathed, and I went back into the cabin and lay down on the bunk.

The hell of it was, there was nothing we could do – not a single damn' thing we could do to help ourselves.

We struck towards dusk in a maelstrom of white water where there wasn't a single rock showing. I don't know whether I was asleep or merely lying there on the bunk in a sort of daze, but the shock of our hitting threw me to the floor. It came like the blow of a mailed fist, a fearful crash up for'ard and then a slow crunching as the plates gave and the rocks disembowelled her; and the thunder of the seas became suddenly louder, more overwhelming.

I lay quite still where I had fallen, feeling the probing teeth of the rocks through my whole body, expecting every moment that the waves would engulf us as she slid under. But nothing happened, except that a thin mist of spray touched my face as it drifted over the ship and the grinding, gut-tearing sound went on so continuously that it became a part of the general uproar of the sea.

The cabin floor was canted over and, as I got to my feet, a sudden shifting of the ship flung me through the door and I fetched up against the bulkhead with a sickening thud that wrenched at my arm and drove the breath out of my body. I saw the ship then, and the pain didn't seem to matter any more. She was lying heeled over, all the length of her clear against a boiling background of surf. Her bridge-deck was a twisted, broken mass of wreckage, the funnel gone, the fore-mast snapped off halfway up and hanging loose in a tangle of derrick wires. And over all the for'ard half of her the seas broke and rolled and tumbled incessantly.

Patch was lying, half-reclined against the steel plates of the deck-house entrance and I shouted to him: 'How long . . .' The words seemed to get caught up in my throat.

'Before she goes?'

'Yes. How long?'

'God knows.'

We didn't talk after that, but stayed there, too cold and tired and fascinated to move, watching as the first jagged points of the reef showed through the foam. The weary half-light faded very slowly into darkness. We heard the bows break off; a protracted agony of tortured metal, tearing and rending up there beyond the wreck of the bridge-deck. And then the remainder of the ship lifted slightly as it was freed of their weight, shifting across the saw-edged rocks with a terrible trembling and groaning. We could see the bows then, a black wedge out in the break of the waves to port, with cargo spilling out of a cavern of a hole where the plates had been torn open. Bales of cotton bobbed about in the white water and the waves played with the great square cases that were supposed to contain the aero engines, smashing them to match-wood on the reef.

Patch gripped my arm. 'Look!' he shouted. A case had been flung towards us and it was splitting open. The contents cascaded into the sea. God knows what it was. The light by then was very dim. But it certainly wasn't the solid lump of an aero engine.

'Did you see?' He had hold of my arm and was pointing. And then the sudden excitement left him as the wreck on which we stood split across at the after end of the upper-deck. A great crack was opening up across the whole width of the ship. It tore the port ladder leading down to the well-deck from its fastenings, twisting it slowly as though an invisible hand were squeezing it. Rivet fastenings were torn out in machine-gun bursts and steel plates were ripped like calico. The gap widened – a yard, two yards; and then it was dark and night clamped down on the *Mary Deare*. By then the falling tide had exposed the reef, the seas had receded and the wreck was still.

We went back into the cabin and lay down under our sodden blankets. We didn't talk. Maybe we slept. I don't remember. I have no recollection of that night. It is like a blank in my mind. The sea's incessant roar, the wind piping a weird note through twisted metal and the sporadic clanging of a loose plate – that is all my recollection. I didn't feel any sense of fear. I don't think I even felt cold any more. I had reached that stage of physical and mental exhaustion that is beyond feeling.

But I remembered the dawn. It filtered into the dim recesses of my mind with the sense of something strange. I was conscious of movement – a long, precipitous roll, first one way, then the other. I could hear the sea, but there was no weight in the sound. The crash and roar of mountains of water smashing down on to rocks was gone, and someone was calling me. Bright sunlight stabbed my eyeballs and a face bent over me – a face that was sweaty and flushed under the greying stubble of a beard with eyes sunk deep in hollow sockets and skin stretched taut across forehead and cheekbone. 'We're afloat!' Patch said. His cracked lips were drawn back from his teeth in a sort of grin. 'Come and look.'

I staggered weakly to the entrance and looked out on a strange scene. The reefs had disappeared. The sun shone on a heaving sea, but there wasn't a sign of a rock anywhere. And all the *Mary Deare* for'ard of the well-deck had gone, vanished. The well-deck itself was under water, but it was as Patch had said – we were afloat; just the stern section and nothing else. And the sun was shining and the gale was diminishing. I could feel Patch trembling where he stood against me. I thought it was excitement. But it wasn't. It was fever.

By midday he was too weak to move, his eyes staring, his face flushed with unnatural colour and the sweat pouring out of him. He had been too long in the East to stand up to nights of exposure in sodden clothing without food. Towards nightfall he became delirious. Much of his raving was unintelligible, but now and then the words came clear and I realized he was back on that voyage up through the Bay, giving orders, talking to Rice . . . disjointed scraps that were an appalling revelation of the strain to which he had been subjected.

Towards evening a small aircraft flew over. I watched it circling low down to the north-west, its wings glinting in the setting sun. They were searching for us on the Minkies. And then night closed in and we still floated, very low in the water. There was a young moon hanging in a clear sky full of stars and the wind had gone so that the moon carved a small silver path across a placid, kindly sea that still heaved gently like a giant resting.

That night I was almost too weak to move and Patch lay like a corpse, shivering occasionally, his face still hot and his eyes wide in the faint moon-glow. Once he started up and seized my hand, trembling all over, words tumbling from his lips, words that had no meaning. But this sudden outburst – this raving – lasted only a short while. He hadn't the strength to keep it up and he suddenly fell back exhausted. I lay close against him all the rest of the night, but I had no warmth to give and in the morning he looked like a ghost, small under the stinking blankets.

I saw the Minkies again just after the sun had risen. They were on the horizon, small, jagged points of black etched sharp against the western sky. And then, much later, I heard the sound of an aircraft's engines. I had dragged Patch out on deck to get the warmth of the sun, but he was unconscious then. The aircraft went past us. I saw the shadow of it cross the water and I pulled myself up, searching the sky for it through bleared and gritty eyes. Then I saw it turning, banking out of the sun and coming back, very low over the water. I clutched the rail for support and waved a blanket at it as it zoomed over just above my head with its engines snarling. It flew off towards the Minkies and a long time afterwards, as I lay on the warmth of the deck in a semi-coma, I heard the putter of an engine and the sound of voices.

It was the Peter Port lifeboat. They came alongside and life stirred again at the sound of friendly voices . . . strong hands helping me over the rail, a lit cigarette thrust into my mouth. They stripped us of our salt-stiff, sodden clothing, wrapped us in blankets, and then sleep came to me, the wonderful relaxed warmth of sleep. But I remember, just before I lost consciousness, a voice saying, 'Want to take a last look at your ship?' And a hand lifted me up. I shall always remember that last glimpse of what was left of her. She was stern-on to us, very low in the water so that the deck-house, in which we had lived for two nights, looked like a chicken coop floating on the surface of the water. And then, in the trough of a swell, I saw the rust-streaked lettering of her stern – *MARY DEARE* – *Southampton*.

As far as I was concerned the story of the wreck of the *Mary Deare* ended there on the edge of the Minkies. But for Patch it was different. He was more directly involved and I was reminded of this as soon as I woke in the hospital at Peter Port. I didn't know it at the time, but I had slept for more than twenty hours. I was immensely hungry, but all the nurse brought me was a small plate of steamed fish, and she told me there was somebody urgently waiting to see me. I thought perhaps it was Mike, but when the door opened it was a girl standing there.

'Who is it?' I asked. The blinds were drawn and the room all darkened.

'It's Janet Taggart.' She came to the side of my bed and I recognized her then, though she looked very tired and there were dark hollows under her eyes. 'I had to see you – as soon as you woke.'

I asked her how she'd got here and she said, 'It was in the

papers. I came at once.' And then she leaned down over me. 'Listen, Mr Sands. Please listen to me. I'm only allowed to stay a moment.' Her voice trembled with urgency. 'I had to see you before you talked to anybody.'

She hesitated then, and I said, 'Well, what is it?' I found it difficult to concentrate. There were so many things I wanted to know and my mind was still blurred.

'The police will be coming to take a statement from you soon.' She paused again. She seemed to have difficulty in putting whatever it was she wanted to say into words. 'Didn't Gideon once save your life?'

'Gideon?' She meant Patch, of course. 'Yes,' I said. 'Yes, I suppose he did.' And then I asked her how he was. 'Didn't somebody tell me he had pneumonia?' I had a vague memory of the doctor telling me that when he was examining my shoulder.

'Yes,' she said. 'He's very ill. But he passed the crisis last night. He'll be all right now, I hope.'

'Have you been with him all the time?'

'Yes, I insisted. I had to – in case he talked.' And then she went on quickly: 'Mr Sands – that man Dellimare . . . You know what happened, don't you?'

I nodded. So he'd told her that, too. 'Nobody need ever know now,' I murmured. I felt tired and very weak. 'All the for'ard part of the ship broke up on that reef.'

'Yes, I know. That's why I had to see you before you made any statement. Don't tell anybody about it, will you. Please. He's suffered enough.'

I nodded. 'No. I won't tell anybody,' I said. And then I added, 'But there's Mike. He knows.'

'Mike Duncan? I've seen him. He hasn't said anything yet – either to the Press or to the police. He said he'd do nothing about it until he'd seen you. He'll do whatever you do.'

'You've seen Mike?' I pulled myself up in the bed. 'How is he? Is he all right?'

'Yes, he's here in Peter Port.' She was leaning down over me again. 'Can I tell him you're going to forget what Gideon told you? Can I tell him you want him to keep quiet about it, too?'

'Yes,' I said. 'Yes, of course – there's no point in saying anything about it now. It's over – finished.' And then I asked her how Mike had been picked up.

'It was a fisherman from St Helier. He found the motor boat just before the storm broke. There was a man called Burrows on board, too. He was badly injured, but he made a statement to the police – about Higgins.' And then she said, 'I must leave you now. I want to see Mr Duncan and then I must be with Gideon when he wakes – to see that he doesn't talk. It's the sort of silly thing he might do.' She smiled wanly. 'I'm so grateful to you.'

'Tell Mike to come and see me,' I said. And as she reached the door, I added, 'And tell – Gideon – when he wakes that he's nothing to worry about any more . . . nothing at all.'

She smiled then – a sudden warmth that lit her whole face up; for an instant she was the girl in the photograph again. And then the door closed and I lay back and went to sleep. When I woke again it was morning and the curtains were drawn back so that the sun streamed in. The police were there and I made a statement. One of them was a plain-clothes man from Southampton, but he was uncommunicative. All he would say about Patch was that he'd no instructions at the moment to make any arrest. After that there were reporters, and then Mike arrived. The police had refused to let him see me until I had made my statement.

He was full of news. The stern section of the *Mary Deare* had gone ashore on Chausey Island. He showed me a newspaper picture of it lying on its side in a litter of rocks at low water. And yesterday Snetterton had been through Peter Port. He'd had a salvage team with him and they had left for Chausey Island in a local fishing boat. 'And I've been on to our own insurance people,' he said. 'They're meeting our claim in full. We'll have enough to build to our own design, if we want to.'

'That means losing a whole season,' I said.

He nodded, grinning. 'As it happens there's a boat for sale right here in Peter Port would suit us nicely. I had a look at her last night. Not as pretty as *Sea Witch*, of course . . .' He was full of plans – one of those irrepressible people who bounce back up as soon as they're knocked down. He was as good a tonic as I could have wished and, though he still had a piece of adhesive tape stuck across the side of his jaw where the skin was split, he seemed none the worse for his thirty hours on the water-logged wreck of that motor boat.

I was discharged from hospital next day and when Mike came up to collect me, he brought a whole pile of London papers with him. 'Altogether you've had a pretty good Press,' he said, dumping them on my bed. 'And there's a newspaper fellow flew in this morning offering you a tidy little sum for a first-hand account of what happened. He's down at the hotel now.'

Later we went and looked at the boat Mike had discovered. She was cheap and sound and we bought her on the spot. And that night Snetterton turned up at our hotel, still neat, still dapper in his pin-stripe suit, though he'd spent two days on Chausey Island. They had cut into Number Four hold at low water and opened up three of the aero engine cases. The contents consisted of concrete blocks. 'A satisfactory result, Mr Sands. Most satisfactory. I have sent a full report to Scotland Yard.'

'But your San Francisco people will still have to pay the insurance, won't they?' I asked him.

'Oh, yes. Yes, of course. But we shall recover it from the Dellimare Company. Very fortunately they have a big sum standing to their credit in a Singapore bank – the proceeds of the sale of the *Torre Annunziata* and her cargo. We were able to get it frozen pending investigation. I think,' he added thoughtfully, 'that Mr Gundersen would have been better advised to have organized the resale of the aero engines through another company. But there – the best laid schemes . . .' He smiled as he sipped his sherry. 'It was a clever idea, though. Very clever indeed. That it failed is due entirely to Mr Patch – and to you, sir,' he added, looking at me over his glass. 'I have requested the H.B. & K.M. . . . well, we shall see.'

I wasn't able to see Patch before I left Peter Port. But I saw him three weeks later when we gave evidence before the resumed Court of Enquiry. He was still very weak. The charges against him had already been dropped; Gundersen had slipped out of the country and Burrows and other members of the crew were only too willing to tell the truth now, pleading that they had supported Higgins's story because they were frightened of him. The Court found that the loss of the *Mary Deare* was due to conspiracy to defraud on the part of the owners, Patch was absolved from all blame and the whole matter was referred to the police for action.

A good deal of publicity was given to the affair at the time and, as a result of it, Patch was given command of the *Wacomo*, a 10,000-ton freighter. He and Janet were married by then, but our diving programme had prevented us from attending the wedding and I didn't see him again until September of the following year. Mike and I were in Avonmouth then, getting ready to dive for a wreck in the Bristol Channel, and the *Wacomo* came in from Singapore and moored across the dock from us. That night we dined on board with Patch.

I barely recognized him. The lines were gone from his face and, though the stoop was still there and his hair was greying at the temples, he looked young and full of confidence in his uniform with the gold stripes. On his desk stood the same photograph in its silver frame, but across the bottom Janet had written: *For my husband now – bons voyages.* And framed on the wall was a letter from the H.B. & K.M. Corporation of San Francisco.

That letter had been handed to Janet by Snetterton at their wedding reception, and with it a cheque for £5000 for her husband's part in exposing the fraud – a strangely apt figure! At the time Mike and I had been working on a wreck off the Hook of Holland, and when we got back I found a similar letter waiting for me, together with a cheque for £2500 – *as some compensation for the loss of your vessel.*

The body of Alfred Higgins was never recovered, but in August of that year a metal dinghy, with patches of blue paint still adhering to it, was found wedged in a crevice of the rocks on the south side of Alderney. It had been battered almost flat by the seas.

One final thing – an entry in the log of *Sea Witch II* made on 8 September, just after we had located and buoyed the wreck in the Bristol Channel. It reads: *11.48 – Freighter WACOMO passed us outward-bound for Singapore and Hong Kong. Signalled us: 'Captain Patch's compliments and he is not, repeat not, trying to run you down this time! Good wrecking!' She then gave us three blasts on her siren, to which we responded on the fog-horn.* A month later, with *Sea Witch II* laid up for the winter, I began this account of the loss of the *Mary Deare.*